Other titles by Patrick Summers

A Collection of Brevities

The Prison of Time: Poems from 2023

The Spirit of This Place:
How Music Illuminates the Human Spirit

KEY CHANGE

An Alternative History of Mozart

A Novel by

Patrick Summers

Contenti Press

ISBN 979-8-9876023-1-7

This is a work of fiction incorporating some historical events from Mozart's life.

With grateful acknowledgment to Carolyn Haley and
Sadie Dill for their editorial assistance.

Designed by Pattima Singhalaka.

{ *This book is dedicated to Jim Luigs,*
in whose home it began, and who has
supported and encouraged the writing. }

Dear Reader,

What follows is a testament of my long life,
as I do my best to recall it.

—Wolfgang Amadé Mozart

CHAPTER 1

On the night when death first came closest to me, I was dreaming about the dragon. So many years have fled that my memory is fogged, but it must have been December 4, 1791. *Dio in eterna*, that is thirty-two years ago, a distance of nearly half of my long life now. I may have already lived more days than my dearest papa, more than Haydn or my dear sister Nannerl, more than my adored kings and emperors who were so generous to me. More days, even, than Konstanze...and I must come to terms with Ludwig upon these sheaths if I possibly can. I may have lived longer, even, than Jefferson, though I have heard nothing of him in these early months of 1823. How is it possible that I have lived so long? As I write, Sarah and John go on, but be patient, dear reader. Cherubini lingers, a dragon of a different kind. I am approaching seventy years on this enormous earth, and I retain memories as though they were yesterday. Others of my age lose the images of their life, whereas I seem to have the opposite problem. I cannot forget anything. Dates, even, linger in my mind like little groups of notes. I beg your help, dear one, as my mind wanders around my life as bees seeking their daily sustenance. Here, there, then over there, then back here. What a lovely shibboleth.

Do we always know ourselves so well? On that distant December night in 1791, the dragon came roaring down the mountainside near my naked body. I had not noticed him before because I was too busy paying attention to the light as it played on the water, which had a sound that was not itself. I had always noticed sounds in light and light in sounds, but this was definitely music. All these years later, I can hear it still. I noticed things others did not, as I've said, but this water was not a place of knowing. Phrases and fragments came into my hearing, almost all of it my own music. I knew it must have been a dream because I was swimming, and the last real thing I remembered was telling Emanuel backstage at *The Magic Flute* that I was going to fall over. The rest was like a hot fog. The dragon was a giant many times my size, breathing fire, and it was searching the valley for me. The dream had a salty smell of home, of Salzburg, that turned to musty moldiness as I got nearer waking.

I am a world away from that night now, a world I never imagined inhabiting. I did not mind an occasional swim in a shallow pond or river, but I did not believe I could ever survive an ocean crossing, though I knew so many who did. Even as a child, when Papa took me to London, I felt on the edge of survival, though the shores of both Gaul and England were visible for the entire journey, separated only by *La Manche* and the intricate desires of their complicated verbs. This place where John has moved us reminds me not of Salzburg but of England, and it makes me miss those distant days. The long candle of my life seems to finally be burning out, and it is John and Sarah's wish that I write down my memories of the time since I met them both. Because I owe them everything God has seen fit to bestow on me, I must do their bidding, and I must tell you about them for they were, are, among the great. There is so much in life for which I have not expressed proper gratitude, so this testament must make amends.

I have taken to a nightly whiskey rather too easily, but I must say that it succeeds in arresting the wrong kinds of ghosts. The dragon has returned, it is true, but not every night and not at all with the violence of that long-distant night in Vienna, a night that demands reappearance in my memory no matter how often I refuse. The dragon now seems almost benign or comic, something out of *The Magic Flute*, with none of the terrors of *Don Giovanni* or *Richard III* or…well, that most important one that I will try to write about later.

CHAPTER 2

I always knew things others did not, from as early as I can remember. My first memories are of Salzburg, even as early as 1759. As I am now on the summit of my last journey, so my body tells me, I cannot escape death as I have before. It is a relief in many ways, as few people live so long as I, and each body must eventually return to infancy. John moved us here to this beautiful house where we can be happy and safe until my time comes. My son Franz is near with his own wife and they visit often. They will all be here when my final measure arrives, I am sure. Their little boy is named Amadé Leopold, after me and my dear father. It was Franz and John together, with encouragement from Sarah, who decided I should dip my quill for these thoughts instead of writing more music, as the exertion of composition was, they felt, too much for me now. We are all but one breath away from being forgotten, no?

Oh, you who are kind enough to be reading this: your quest to know me is unfair, for I will never know you. Tamu knows nothing of this testament, but Sarah and John, and my dear Franz, even in recent days my sweetest Alice, have continued their encouragement for this endeavor. You, dear patient reader, do not yet know Tamu or Alice, though Sarah and John carry their own fame separate from mine so you may well have deduced everything about them already. I will, as they have asked, tell what I can recall about them all, but I am an old man so please hold steadily with me as my mind wanders my memory's unpredictable corridors.

CHAPTER 3

There was a carriage ride home from the theater on that cold night in 1791, and I recall moving through the darkness of familiar streets. Something felt momentous. Konstanze and the boys were home, and tiny Franz was screaming. Konstanze sent Karl to her sister Aloysia, I believe. I was put to bed by someone but I have no memory of getting there, and I recollect freezing under an avalanche of blankets despite the fireplace raging in my room. A pungent stench had its origin in me, partially from dried perspiration, but mostly from an effluvium from deep within, as though death had entered my bowels and was seeking escape. Bathing could not eliminate my fetid odor.

As I went in and out of sleep, the dragon appeared. Upon one of my wakings, I noticed a woman I did not know. Konstanze had brought her to help care for me. The woman spoke German with a strong Romaní dialect that I had heard in the countryside around Praha each time I had visited there, including just the summer before. They call it Prague here, strangely, with hard *G*. Why do they do that? I had often heard her type of speaking not only in Praha but right in Vienna in the Naschmarkt. I still miss that beautiful place in Bohemia, Praha, a place I always felt most like myself. That was the place of clemency, both my own and *Tito*'s. I refuse to remember all of those malicious singers complaining about their ranges and the demands I placed on them. Not all singers are such beasts, but sometimes they crowd into combinations that bring out their worst.

No matter what happened in Praha, I always found a way to forgive all hurts there. It was, you see, that kind of place. I wonder if it remains so.

At first I wondered if the dragon might be some kind of message from those I had offended. I am afraid I was quite demanding in dealing with the *La clemenza de Tito* singers, though my illness had softened whatever I could have said to those in *The Magic Flute* company. In Praha, one of them asked me, "Why write a *corona* followed by a *corona*? What is the purpose of such superfluity?" I told them I wanted a silence followed by a silence, which makes such perfect sense that only an idiot could misunderstand. If their musical abilities had matched their silly opinions, they would have had no difficulties. I remember feeling so cold that night that I was sure I would never be warm again.

The dragon spotted me and jumped from the mountain in my direction, its enormous claws knocking over pines and sending great boulders scattering. A force was at work that I could not overpower, and I knew the dragon was going to consume me. I remember waking to find the Romaní woman so close to me that I could smell the tobacco from her stomach. She fed me cheese or something as revolting as cheese. I hated cheese, which I tried to tell her, but she was busy muttering an incantation in her language that I could not understand. I wondered how Konstanze had found her. It was strange to see the glow of candles without being able to see their flames, for the large smelly woman was in the way. I crossed into the other side at the very moment the dragon approached, heaving fire toward me. I was falling into an abyss. Shadows danced behind the woman.

I remember it now as the night of December 4, but it was for me one long nighttime that lasted many days. Dawn and dusk merged several times. I always knew things others did not, and I was able to remember everything told or taught to me, but that night was different. On the opposite side of everything I had known to be me, I was definitely swimming and the sun was high. The dragon disappeared behind a mountain and suddenly I was at Untersberg trying to kill the beast. As a boy I knew all of those mountains so well that when Papa took me and Nannerl traveling I was surprised that the rest of the world was not so beautiful.

The dream did not feel like a dream. Yes, I was definitely swimming in an eddy of calm water in the Salz where I used to go on summer afternoons. One phrase of music kept trying to ring through, as though it was under the water to protect itself from the dragon. The music was distant but it had desire inside it. It was *my* music, just eight battutas from the end of the horn concerto I had finished ten years earlier for Leutgeb, the old goose. I miss him. I have lived such a long time that he could surely not still be among the living. I will never know what came over me, but it was the most beautiful single phrase of music I ever composed, if for no other reason that it has no ending. I gave it not a single thought until it emerged from my quill. Yet that night as I was about to die, there it was under the water trying to make itself whole. My fever kept refusing it, pushing insistently to replace the music with itself.

Over and over, the noise of the dragon overwhelmed the gentleness of my phrase. The Romaní woman was both terror and comfort. Everything she did to save my life was something that should have killed me. The line between life and death had never felt so thin, not even when I was almost carried off as a child. There was haze in my thoughts as I tried to remember anything about *The Magic Flute*, where there was also a dragon, but one not nearly so terrifying as the one invading my dreams. In moments, I could recall writing each note of the opera, and I knew what it all meant, but on that night I had only memories of memories. The dragon neared the Hohensalzburg and found me for a final time. It braced to devour me and everything I had ever known. A moment came, probably on December 5 or 6, I cannot recall, when I was going to die.

CHAPTER 4

The memory still fills me with terror, dear reader. The dragon lunged toward me but something grabbed it and tossed it in the direction of the Kitzbüheler Horn, where it hit with an unimaginable force, like the earthquakes one heard about in the south.

I knew I was alive because some minutes later, I do not know how long, I suddenly heard phrases of my own music return to me, as though I had written them twice. Small pulses of light darted between me and the ceiling, and they were pieces of light similar to light on water. This light stood alone, floating not on water but upward with the air. I heard sound within the light, as I always could, but this was something I had never heard before. It was not as I had heard Emanuel say so often in the theater in the magnificent *Hamlet*: the rest was not silence at all. This light was *all* sound.

I remember Papa saying that a life will unfold in the moments before death, but as I knew things that others did not, I knew this unfolding represented the moments *after* death. I had not been taken. I was alive. I heard fragments of my own music: the beginning of *Così*, the A-major duet from *Clemenza*, the piano fantasy, the D-minor concerto. I was hearing music within my own memory, but there was another sound. It was a bird, my dear starling Pamina. She reminded me of life, and she rekindled the memory of my first bird, Star, who used to sing parts of my music to me, though she could only sing in something close to G major.

I knew every sound of which Pamina was capable and this was definitely a new song for my new life. A new day was beginning outside as well, as the morning sky was streaked with a soft blue, the color of a new egg. I felt a small pang of hunger and I remember asking for water. The great bell of St. Stephen's sounded, that marvelous low D natural that I loved so much, even as its after-sound was always slightly out of tune. At certain times of day, depending on the wind, the bell would activate other notes above itself, and I loved seeing what I could hear of those extra notes. I was alive, and I had not expected to greet another dawn.

Somewhere nearby, a rooster crowed. For some reason I had memories of suckling, though in all of my travels I have never met another person who could remember so far back into their infancy. Though I struggled to remember anything that had occurred during my heaviest fevers only hours before, anything other than the dragon, I swear to you that from that night forward I could remember suckling.

And I remember hearing Konstanze's voice calling for me. I loved the way she said my name, the name everyone in Vienna called me: Amadé. As she awaited that dawn, also awaiting my death, she had drifted into a light sleep with little Franz in the nursery. She raced into the room to embrace me and cry, "We did not think you would live to see another day, my darling!" I agreed with her. I asked for water. My mouth felt sandy.

The Romaní woman was sitting in the only chair in the room. As Konstanze tried to wake her, I had a vision of what happened: the Romaní woman had killed my dragon, and had given her life for mine. Konstanze tried to wake her but said her arm was like marble. Was it possible, Konstanze asked, that this woman had saved my life? I told her she had, but Konstanze wondered what force could have taken this strong woman. Konstanze asked me what had happened, what had made me cry out so terribly before going quiet for several hours. I was too weak to tell her, and in truth I could not fully remember. After I recovered we would never find time to speak of it again.

Konstanze gave me a weak tisane of orange and lemon, and within a few hours a bit of bread. I asked her for a quill to write down some of the music that had come to me during the fever and found there were many ideas lurking in the darkness of that time. An old priest arrived not long after dawn and, learning of the Romaní woman, returned with four helpers who removed her to a common grave outside the city reserved for non-Christians. I inquired about her family and where she'd come from, but Konstanze asked the priest to say nothing of the Romaní woman in front of me. There were secrets. I disliked secrets then. Now that the secrets are mine, I have a more charitable view.

The priest assured me and Konstanze that the woman's soul would be prayed for, and it comforted me to know that the Creator, God of us all, would be merciful to her whether or not she lived within belief, and would hopefully look kindly upon her for saving my life. It was sad that we did not know her name, that she would always just be a Romaní woman.

The priest reminded us both, particularly me, that because my life had been spared I had a duty to commit myself to the service of the church for the remainder of the time with which I had been blessed. I was to do constant penance through music for the clemency and mercy I had been shown and, if I did, my health would undoubtedly continue to improve.

Konstanze offered that I could often be stubborn about work.

"*Sturheit* is not a recommended indulgence for those spared the ravages of death," the priest declared. I can still hear his ominous voice. I promised to curb my stubbornness.

CHAPTER 5

They carried the Romaní woman's body away as the priest carried incense behind her, intoning something symbolizing comfort. Franz was blessedly asleep and Karl Thomas was with Aloysia. It was the first time Konstanze and I had been alone since Franz had been born only five months before. Konstanze came to my side, weeping with happiness that my life, and thus our life together, was to continue. She said it was nearly Christmas, which was impossible for me to believe, as December had only begun for me and I was accustomed to knowing things that others did not. The sun was in its usual midmorning position for December, and normally I knew precisely how many steps were between our home and the Prater, or our home and the Theater an der Wien, and thus how much light would be left in the day, but on that day I could not know such things.

I took a stronger tea. I am sensitive to the gradations of tea, as they always seemed to me harbingers of future happenings. I told Konstanze how grateful I was to her for persisting in finding someone to save my life. I was making water every few minutes, and I passed vast amounts of bile for many of the following days, but my strength slowly returned. I farted without cease, and I knew my soul was returning when every fart made me laugh. We should never reach a point in life when farting is not hilarious. Belching is not nearly so funny as farting. Konstanze always tried to hide her farting from me, but she could not. I cannot control my laughing as I write this, dear reader!

The Magic Flute had not been hampered by my illness, and it had continued performances through that entire winter in Vienna and was a big success, I am happy to say. By February I was excited to accept a visit from Schikaneder, my dear Emanuel, with whom I had written it. It had been his idea, and he fired my imagination. I chided him for not always singing in time or in tune, and he scolded me profoundly for writing a role that was so difficult for him to sing in tune or in time! Emanuel was my best friend in those years, especially after Lorenzo disappeared, and I tried my best always to honor him, which I believe I did by writing *Richard III*, an opera of which I am most proud. It was Emanuel's fiery performances as the demented king that inspired me to create my opera, our opera, as he helped me develop the libretto. Little did I imagine in those early *Magic Flute* days, though, that Richard's madness would eventually overtake Emanuel, too; and as I remember that distant part of my life, I realize that shards of his malaise were already visible and audible in those days following my almost-death. What could I have done to help him?

By March I was able to walk the short distance to St. Stephen's and visit cafés within its great piazza. The birds that circled Stephansdom in those years, and I assume they still do, were the dearest birds to me because within their vast numbers I could often hear vestiges of elaborate choral works. I knew on that single March day, sitting outside enjoying a coffee with the most delicious *Millirahmstrudel* of my entire life, that to pay my debt to the Romaní woman and to the force that brought me back from death, I would write a mass of thanks.

For months after my illness, I still felt chills through my body, even when sitting by a fire or wearing a coat. I knew at those moments that my savior, the nameless woman from Bohemia, was paying me a visit. Over my long life, I have learned that the dead linger in the passageways of the soul and in the essences of the spirit. I know it, dear reader, as surely as I know that I am sitting at my desk at this moment looking at the leaves depart the trees, which have been the only home they have known, leaving the trees lonely and bare as they find their way back to the earth. I know this feeling of inexorable time, for when I feel the throbbing presence within me that I know is my heart, it cannot be possible to imagine that this force exists without a power greater than whatever struggles for life within my frail body.

The shivers arrived for months afterward but quickly departed, and they helped me to write my mass of thanks, *Dankenmesse*, which we performed that April of 1792 within the very cathedral where Konstanze and I had married ten years before, the glory of Vienna that is St. Stephen's. Did Konstanze know—she must have—that all of those repetitions of "Mein liebevolles Herz" were all about her? That *Abduction from the Seraglio* aria settles into an embracing love at the moment one hears the last *Herz*, just as Konstanze and I always tried to do. Love, until I met Alice, was always more of a special poetic *idea* than something I actually lived. Konstanze and I were different people with each other than we were when alone. We teased each other and often had tremendous fun, but then everything turned to an eternity of longing that would not allow either of us to fulfill the other completely. Only God can understand the mysteries of the heart.

At the premiere of the *Dankenmesse*, little Franz was almost a year old, too young to attend or even to be known outside our home. Our little Karl, only eight years old that day of the first performance of the mass, was alone with Franz and our nurse as Konstanze and I left for St. Stephen's. In the minutes before leading the *Dankenmesse*, I reflected that of all our issue, only Franz and Karl had managed to make it beyond infancy. Where had the other four souls gone in their journey to try to reach us? Little Theresia, whom I loved long before I ever saw her, was not allowed to breathe the air for even a few hours, and I felt the coldness of death enter her body as I held her in my hands. In my moments of thanks for the sparing of my own life, how was I to reckon with a God who would deny us four of the six blossoms of our love? I shut the feelings away, thankful for that which was before me on that day. But even now, these many years later, I can still see their infant eyes looking into the eyes of their loving parents, only to have their lives snuffed out, their little eyes seeing nothing of the world but our tears.

The final movement of the *Dankenmesse*, the Benedictus, was in two parts, and it ended with an extremely complex fugue. I based it on the plainchant theme on which I had built my C-major symphony, the one

Johann Peter Salomon insisted be called *Jupiter* because of the thunder-bolts of the opening chords. In those years I never liked the naming of works that only needed or deserved numbers, but there was never any arguing with someone like Johann. I came to know him well in London, in circumstances I shall later endeavor to describe.

The fugue, complicated as it was, came as easily to me as anything I wrote in my old life, and it fell out of the quill quickly, with Süssmayer making the orchestral parts at lightning speed. He commented to me that something in me seemed to have sped up and gained clarity after my illness, leaving me with an impression that everything that preceded that fateful December had been filled with indecision. What was Süssmayer trying to tell me? I notice now that I never called him Franz, but "Süssmayer" or "Süssie." Why did I not simply call him by his name?

The mass was a success because I copied and expounded on what I knew of Handel. I dislike admitting this, even to these pages which will be read long after I am in the ground, but it is true. In the latter years of the 1780s, I had the privilege of getting to know many of Handel's works, as they were published around that time in Vienna. I played through some portion of them each day, struggling with my terrible English through the half of his vocal works that were not in Italian. Through his sparse scribblings, he showed me page after page of truth. Even his keyboard compositions, which rated almost no merit at all in Vienna, were far beyond anything known to me at the time. Johann Christian Bach, so dear to my young life, had told me much about his own father, Johann Sebastian, and even played some of his music for me, but I had not had the honor of seeing his music nor the time for its study until much later, long after J.C. himself had shuffled off. For me, Bach was inferior to Handel, not that it mattered, for almost every musician to whom I would bow respect has said the opposite. They are both in Heaven now, I have no doubt, and though it pains me to say it, Handel was better at music than anyone has ever been at anything. His operas differ from mine in that they have almost no ensembles, which were my favorite aspect of opera, but his arias are beyond comparison with anything before or since.

CHAPTER 6

The *Dankenmesse* was such a success that a post I had long sought, Kapellmeister of St. Stephen's, became assured to me, making my life in Vienna comfortable for the first time in at least ten years. I was generously given a small composition studio within the cathedral, a room vacated by the Archbishop, who decided to depart its confines for a more palatial palace nearby in the Prater, guarded and protected from the increasing needs of the growing diocese.

Upon gaining the post, which was the summer following my brush with death, I moved all of my composing materials to the cathedral, which liberated a great deal of space within our home for Konstanze, Karl, and Franz. I took so many ideas that had been baking within me and set to work with a vigor I had not known in years, composing a major mass each month for each of the next five years. I wonder how many masses there are in my catalogue now? It must be over fifty. Joseph Haydn, dear man, told me he found the writing of masses to be toil and penance, whereas I loved writing them. For me, they were a way to pray that I could never summon by any other means. I expressed a wish to write a mass in the memory of my beloved Kaiser Joseph II, as I owed everything to him. Though he had died in 1790, I had never found the spirit to write a memorial mass to him. The Archbishop readily agreed that we should take the opportunity to commemorate the beloved Kaiser. Also, it must be said, he was eager to have anything that intimated that the monarchy looked favorably upon the church, even as he acknowledged that the world should be structured in the opposite way: with the church approving, or not, of the monarchy. I was always aware of these cultures of power, and they shifted slightly from month to month, or from day to day in wartime. I was aware but not interested, for politics bored me beyond anything.

There will never be another man alive as great nor as humble as Joseph II. He was entombed with an inscription that listed his political failures. What other great man can admit such defeats in the face of life's ultimate battle? I always knew that the dear Kaiser ordered the inscription himself, as no one would have dared place it there without his permission, in death or in life. In my 1792 *Mass in Memory of Joseph II*, I included a movement that referenced this inscription, something that approached blasphemy to my employers. I was brought before them, but there was no argument they could support. The wishes of my Kaiser had to be respected.

I thought it was easy to count a man a failure simply because he tried to move the world forward, only to cause unexpected chaos. Naturally, this would appear as failure to all of the people who had never attempted to advance anything. Was it not better to have tried and failed than to sit on the sidelines and complain? I knew this well from the opera house. I was the one putting everything out into the world; all of the *liebevolles Herz* was mine, after all, before it was Belmonte's. The notes that the characters sang, the feelings they felt, the dramatic tempo of the drama itself, were ultimately mine. I could hear the whispers meant to be just outside of my hearing, complaints about the demands I was placing on them, on the ranges I demanded, and all manner of other difficulties. They complained about the speed of the faster arias even as they complained about the breath required for the slower ones. Did they know how to do anything but complain about what was *not* there? Where was their appreciation for what *was* there, the very thing they took as due to them? I placed not a single yoke upon a singer they could not bear, yet they complained anyway.

I have come to learn that only the very greatest artists are without complaint, for if an artist can fulfill any demand, why parse the details? Over time I placed more and more demands on singers, but I have been allowed to let my imagination soar, and whatever musical challenges arose would eventually sort the grain from the chaff, and thanks be to God for that. As my time in Vienna came to an end, I increasingly sought situations of performance that would not cause me agita. I wanted only to be with performers of like mind and standard, and Providence somehow brought that miracle to me. I fear, though, that my own musings on these pages will only serve to reveal that which I most fear. Does it surprise you, dear person reading these words in great quietude, that I lived in fear?

Within a short time, we brought the orchestra and chorus of St. Stephen's to prominence within Vienna, and their performances began to draw congregants. My employers noted that my music brought believers to the church, but they also offered that this was not wholly desirable, as faith alone should bring the faithful. "They should want to be here for the salvation of their eternal souls, not for a memorable tune," the Archbishop said to me. To be fair, the Archbishop had long held the opinion that our temptation with venial arousals, and our constant search for momentary entertainments through something so ephemeral as music, seemed to him a new type of sin against which he must warn. I could offer no defense that would suit him, but for those few years, the crowds flocking to St. Stephen's and filling the collection coffers answered whatever questions I may have raised.

For me, music was a way for people to worship. Indeed, it was the only way I knew to do so, since the people coming to the cathedral could not understand a word of the mass, nor could they hear properly in the vast cold expanse of the church even if they understood. I tried always to fill the empty air as though music had been there all along, for if one listens to silence it tells you what it wants to become. As I reflect on those years that followed my return to life, I hear a great deal of desire built into my music, desire that was within the realm of what was acceptable. I tried always to create an earthly image of heavenly desire, for we must have desires in the next world. The dragon who sought me as I swam naked in the Salz felt *only* desire, and how could a creature of the underworld possess something we do not?

Though St. Stephen's paid me generously, I was beginning to get yearnings and offers from beyond the church, and as much as I tried to keep them secret from the Archbishop, it was only a matter of time before they spilled beyond Stephansplatz. I might have been able to convince the Archbishop of the need for symphonies and concertos, that these were also God's work. But opera was another unimaginable desire entirely. Opera, for the Archbishop, was the highest and most absurd of possible decadences that lead only to the most depraved of emotions. Any intention I had to write an opera in those years had to be burned and eaten, like a hungry dragon on a mountain.

CHAPTER 7

I am unsure of a few things, my sweet reader, such as how I will possibly remember all of what is being asked of me. My memory has always been one of the most perfect things about me, and it remains so. But I can no longer recall exactly *when* things happened. I know generally, of course, but not in the very clear way I should. The publishing house Artaria, for example, knew nothing of my church music even after I obtained the important post at St. Stephen's, because they could have no ownership of the works I composed for the cathedral, even though they were obliged to print them. It must have been around then that Konstanze become so interested in publication, because once she was freed from my constant presence in the home, when my days were occupied at St. Stephen's, she began to receive inquiries from other churches about performing my organ sonatas and the many masses I had composed. Since Artaria did not then have a habit of scouring the churches for money, Konstanze would arrange for Artaria to have materials and charge a small amount for them. She never made them pay a very high price, but with the number of churches in the area, my income accumulated. I became nervous about what might happen if this small indulgence was discovered, for St. Stephen's kept a tight rein on my income, with many within the diocese considering me grossly overpaid in the service of the Lord. I was not among the indulgences the Archbishop could sell at year's end.

As our financial position improved through the 1790s, Konstanze began to dream of publishing my music herself, bypassing Artaria or any of the other Viennese publishers altogether. This had never been done before and was a hefty risk. She reckoned, correctly in my view, that if we could manage an annual concert series that featured a new concerto or symphony, our annual income could double. I knew that if we additionally produced some very popular operas, we could double our income again. It infuriated Konstanze that *The Magic Flute* was already being performed in other cities yet neither Emanuel nor I had been paid for it. Our work was making money for theaters but they were paying nothing to us. This had been true for so long that indignation did not occur to me, but indignity overtook Konstanze's entire way of living.

Konstanze kept all the necessary materials for performance, which lined every bit of my old billiard table room, and she would not only charge for their use but require that they be returned to her. If a single bassoon part was not returned after a performance of one of my symphonies, she tracked down the player and retrieved it. It had infuriated her that Artaria would not be so vigilant, and yet the publishing house continued to make money from performances of my older works. I knew my works only by their keys, so each of the symphonies in D major, for example, were grouped together in my mind, but Konstanze knew them all by the date of their publication, and she numbered them in ways that always confused me: "Number 36," etc. How was I to remember which was my thirty-sixth and which my thirty-fifth? Particularly as I approached a time of life when I would soon write three times that many symphonies, it seemed perverse to me to remember them by chronology. I knew them by key, something Konstanze could not understand.

I received a lovely letter from Paris in 1795 about successful performances there of three of my previous symphonies, the E flat, G minor, and the grand C major that so many were stupidly calling *Jupiter*. I relayed to Konstanze how wonderful it felt that my music had sounded through the grand city of Paris, the place that meant so much to me because of dear Mama, whose body was in eternal rest within its walls. Konstanze went into a rage at me for failing to notice that no payment had been arranged. "How did they obtain the materials to play those symphonies? Artaria shipped them, did they not? How else would they have played them?

Where is the payment for that?" I thought she might hit me. "Something born from the genius God gave to you is being used for someone else's profit, Amadé!"

She was right to admire Emanuel for sharing with us the profits he made on *The Magic Flute* at his theater, even after I had been fully paid to compose it. But outside of the theater where initial performances are given, there seemed to be no limit on what could be made from the Mozart name. *Clemenza* had made me no money at all, as fashions had moved beyond political dramas about kings, no matter how benevolent. I wondered if that was true, or if *Clemenza* simply was not to the public's taste. For me, it is a score that haunts me to this day, absolutely one of the greatest of my life. I was so longing to hear it again, and so sure that I never would, that my little Franz arriving with a score and materials for it sent me into sobs of joy. But my road diverges, dear reader, for which I apologize. I must try to stay on the path.

I suspect but do not know that what Konstanze found beautiful about my music was my handwriting. She was an artist herself, and always attuned to how something looked on the page, whereas for me my notes were the simplest of symbols. She would have thought this a mundane observation about her, but I think it was one of the most beautiful things about her, and perfectly symbolic of Konstanze: to value the symbol over the symbolized. She could always tell at sight whether I had written something quickly or with labor, or if I had altered my mind midway through a passage. Konstanze had a fine ear, and she could look at the page and nearly hear it. She once noticed that my writing was all fast strokes of the quill, as though I was in a struggle to get it out before it disappeared. I loved it when she observed these things so beautifully in me. If only that could have lasted.

As my quill scratches across these sheets, I am so inundated with memories that I wonder if I have ever had the gift of forgetting anything. Konstanze's memory was always tidy but only relatively accurate. She could clear her mind of meaningless details as I often could not. I recall works from my youth with great accuracy, and even pieces I heard as I walked through Vienna or Paris half a century ago. I never forget music, but I forget everything else. I can remember what time of day I composed phrases of music, and when I hear them now in my mind I can hear night and morning or candlelight or a breeze. Sometimes, when the memories stack upon one another, it is difficult to feel it was actually me composing, as it felt some force like the breeze was simply moving through me. I had no power over it.

Artaria would take my manuscripts and meticulously place them onto ink blot plates that would turn my music inside out, backward to my eye, yet when they printed it would look correct on the page. I found this miraculous, though sometimes the setter would make an error and the notes would appear backward, which confused the eye of many a player. I rarely looked too closely at the plated prints because it could consume an entire morning I would prefer to spend another way, and I always got distracted by the inevitable errors that appeared. Trained musicians could just as easily note these errors as could I, just from their own instincts. Fixing errors was tedious, and required a type of looking back that was a bore to me though interesting to Konstanze, because she loved the perfection of how music looked on the page. For this reason, I knew she would be good at publishing, and the details that held no interest for me.

CHAPTER 8

Konstanze sensed with incredible accuracy how I had labored over *Così fan tutte* and I am sure she knew why. The second act of *Così* was the most emotional music of my life up to that point, music of such deep longing and pain that both Konstanze and I often found it too much to bear. Konstanze always said she felt my music for *Così* to be too complex, though what I knew she meant was that it was too upsetting for her. I remember her crying at the soft repeated triplets near the end of "Per pietá," and looking at me during the outbursts of cascading scales and trills that hurtle the aria toward its end, because she knew what I was trying to express to her about our love. I knew during all of the months of writing *Così* that Süssmayer had taken my place in Konstanze's bed and body, that he had entered where I alone had ever been. I struggled to express this pain to her, but I could say in music whatever words my heart refused to utter.

In truth, I needed to confess to Konstanze that I had many times exceeded the bonds of our marriage, which meant I often accused her of sins I had myself committed. She knew of none of my many infidelities, but she had only strayed one time, and I allowed that to hurt me beyond measure. When I imagined Süssmayer inside her, and thought of the sounds she would make when she was being pleasured, my sobs would erupt like Vesuvius, uncontrollable and violent. And Konstanze was much more honest than I: she confessed to me that she had allowed Franz access to her body and soul, that he had brought her great physical pleasure. She told me she had sinned, that she had stopped it before it went further, words that hurt me like knives. This was much more honesty than I had ever given to her. What if the central premise of *Così*, the thing most of the hypocrites denounced within it, is actually true? What if we can love more than one person intimately? This is every possible level of heresy, even blasphemy, and everyone was afraid to utter it, yet there it is in our opera. Particularly in the years when I was working at St. Stephen's, those were words that could not be spoken. I sensed that Konstanze's affection for Süssmayer remained unaltered even after she insisted she had ended the affair.

Our lives in those years largely returned to what they had been ten years before, as our income had increased and we were able to indulge again in a maid and a wig master. Wigs were an enormous expense because they required two things that should always be expensive: expertise and time. It was unthinkable to move in and out of the Viennese salons that Konstanze so loved without them. "Only the poor go wigless," she said, and I could still hear those words when we had to dismiss our wigmaker because we could no longer afford him. One could tell a great deal from a person's dress, naturally, but many people possessed an ability to build a fine dress or cloak, one that might even be thought aristocratic, but a proper wig could only be achieved by someone trained and paid for the service. No one possessed this ability as their own instinct; it required intricate training. If one's wig was full of bugs or tangles, this was a sure sign of someone from poverty trying to pose as well-off. Our wig master in those years of the 1790s was an effete young man who had apprenticed at the royal court and was thus a virtuoso at his craft. He and Konstanze spent hours laughing with each other, and to me he seemed nearly a woman in his sensibilities. I had known men like that all my life, as they were forever working in courts or backstage at theaters, and I found it curious as to why women always loved them so. I suppose that liberation from sexual interest affords a female comforts. I understood the desires of these men, and I knew that what they did was a terrible sin, but they also carried an honesty within them that often eluded me. I could only be honest with my quill, both then and now. In life, with Konstanze, I kept many secrets. Too many secrets. I keep them still.

CHAPTER 9

Konstanze had longed for us to purchase a carriage again and to have a mews keeper like our Viennese neighbors. This was an extravagance that I had resisted because we were able to go anywhere we needed by foot, but I finally relented. Our mews became a center of daily activity, and our horses were beautiful. We could again picnic in the forests on beautiful spring days as we had when we were first married, and safely return home in time for darkness. We could attend concerts and the theater whenever we desired, and not have to worry about returning home under the blanket of night, when it was so easy to fall on the cobblestones. On moonless nights walking was extremely *pericoloso*.

I often wonder what happened to the paintings that were made of me during my time at St. Stephen's, even one by the court painter. Konstanze and I were able in those years to afford other works of art to place on our walls. She found me a lovely painting of my beloved Salzburg, which we placed over the lavish new billiard table she purchased from Budapest. I had worn out the table I owned during the early years of our marriage in Vienna. The combination of chance and skill at the heart of billiards is something profound to me even now, though the table is a luxury not afforded me here in the woods, nor do I desire its comforts any longer. I realize that I was drawn to anything that had within its nature the essence of something that it was not, an essence of something *else*. I always wanted something other than music at which I could excel, but there was nothing. Even billiards, which I adored, was something I could never master. For me, billiards were a science that helped my art. On the days when I could discipline myself enough in billiards to place all of the balls in pockets in the order I'd placed them on the table, all by ricochet, then entirely reverse the process, I knew I would have a good day of composition. I could often create a fugue out of the order the balls entered the pockets, turning each into a tone. The game of billiards, then, was entirely of my own devising. I did not enjoy playing billiards with friends, as these became long distractions from working. All of my greatest fugues were written with billiards.

In the world of nighttime, through the whole of my long life, I have had a repeating image that has carried great meaning to me. It is just an image, a dream one might say, though it always felt more real than a dream. I was always on a bridge. It often felt like Salzburg, but it might have been any of the places I knew well that were filled with bridges: Vienna, Paris, Praha, or Linz. From my earliest childhood, there were times when I would compose and perform almost without sleeping, and those periods could last months. They would be followed, though, by great patches of time when I found it difficult to even arise from my bed. Always, I came to notice, these times were accompanied in my nighttime hours with images of the bridge, my bridge. The beginning of the dream had little variance throughout my life. I always entered the bridge from the morning sky, from the east, and I proceeded across it with great fear. I saw frightful images on the far side of the bridge, things I found so terrifying that I never wanted to know what or who they were. Sometimes, though, a force compelled me to keep advancing across the bridge, and when it did, I lost my hearing. Everything on the far side of the bridge was terrifyingly silent.

There are so many maladies that afflict us all, but surely the cruelest is deafness. To have known the sounds of birds only to have them taken away seems the act of a devil, not God. What transgression could possibly warrant such a punishment? Whenever the bridge appeared, I would try with all of my own power to stay off it, but I could never stop myself. For weeks after dreaming of the bridge I was unable to work, sometimes being unable to remember how to play a simple chord, and I lacked the energy or willingness to even move across the room to try. The appearance of the bridge during my sleeping hours was the warning that I was entering a period of inactivity. All my life, though, I have been able to keep from fully crossing the bridge.

CHAPTER 10

At the premiere of *Tito* back in 1791, I was invited for an audience with Emperor Leopold II when he became King of Bohemia. He was the reason we were all there, for it was in his honor the opera was commissioned. He was the brother of my treasured Joseph II, whose death the year before had broken all hearts, most especially mine. I felt more lost at the death of Joseph II than when my own father departed. But as *Tito* approached, the dream of the bridge came. It was the first time, though, that my progress across the bridge had gone so far, nearly reaching the other side. As I crossed the halfway point of the bridge and all of my hearing was gone, I could see the silent chaos on the far side, the point at which terror held me in uncontrollable stillness. A force was trying to move me all the way across the bridge, but I resisted. The memory pulled me back to the side of my origin, where my hearing returned. When I woke from the dream, I knew I would not be able to leave my bed. I was barely able to eat or drink water. I missed an audience with the emperor, a man I revered and the brother of my greatest patron. Even as my quill scratches across this page years later, I am humiliated by my insult to the great man, but I had no choice. My body simply would not allow me to move. I thank capricious God that I had finished *Tito* by then, for I could not write music. Emanuel was patiently awaiting *The Magic Flute*, and whenever I could I assured him that I was working, but in truth I could not compose in those terrible days. I finished *The Magic Flute* in my imagination, but the spell of the dream had to pass for me to write it all down, and I had no power over the length of my malaise.

This testament must also include what was weighing heavily on me during that time, on Konstanze and many others: Da Ponte's banishment from Vienna by Joseph II's successor, the very patron of my *Tito* who well should have banished me for my insubordination. Lorenzo Da Ponte, my brother in art and friend in life, was accused of court intrigues of which he was doubtlessly guilty. He could behave so recklessly. But once he was banished, I never heard from him, not even a single letter. It is possible that he thought me dead for a time, as no one expected me to live after *The Magic Flute*. But he would have read of my recovery in the broadsheets, I feel certain. We had so many operas awaiting us together, and there were no other poets with whom I wished to write an opera, even if the Archbishop at St. Stephen's could have managed to find a magnanimity that always eluded him.

I adored writing every mass, but there is nothing like the thrill of opera, so it was not long into my tenure at St. Stephen's that my desires veered. Opera is everything, the highest form of praise to God who gives all gifts. Konstanze and I were finally relieved of years of crippling debt, thanks to my generous salary from St. Stephen's. By 1795 we were even in a position of lending money ourselves to our friends in need, which is a wonderful feeling that Konstanze sadly did not share. Konstanze and money rarely parted happily. Many times I wondered if my soul had perhaps been mistakenly placed into the body of a poor and musical servant, when it was in the giving of money, as a philanthrope, that my spirit soared.

I heard that Lorenzo had fled home to Venice, but I knew that whatever problems he faced in Vienna would eventually find him in the Veneto. Lorenzo could never resist the advances of women, particularly young women, and the most religious of Vienna's courtiers did everything they could to do away with Lorenzo, who unfailingly asked the wrong questions of the right people, and vice versa, which was often worse. I never convinced him to be more circumspect; he only needed to be quiet about what he had heard or done. But lying in front of all of Lorenzo's weaknesses were the incredible rafts of poetry he could craft. He amazed me. The entirety of *Figaro* was in rhyming couplets that begged for music. I could hear the whole opera on first reading of his texts, which came to me piecemeal but each fragment in order from beginning to end, in a leather packet from a sentry he used. I didn't see him until I was nearly finished with the opera's composition. We managed to complete *Figaro* through Act Three before anyone at the court found out we were even at work. It is a wonder to me now that we were not both arrested, for the play had been banned by the man whose support for me had never before wavered.

The intrigues of Vienna fluttered around St. Stephen's, the court, and the city's theaters. Lorenzo found it all irresistible, and the rumors became Lorenzo's work, whereas I simply found them distractions to laugh at over a nightly port. I was furious that Lorenzo had been banished, but even more so that he had been stupid enough to be noticed. For years I inquired with every possible friend as to Lorenzo's whereabouts, but no one knew anything. As the years progressed, my repertoire of church music increased to match the number of symphonies and piano concertos I'd written earlier. I was longing to write more operas. I was thrilled to receive invitations for new symphonies from Berlin, Mannheim, Dresden, Milan, Amsterdam, Paris, and London and I fulfilled them all, though I did not travel in those years.

By 1796 I had written fifty-eight symphonies, the most popular of which was Dresden's, my first symphony in E major, a key I had not thought suitable for a symphony or piano concerto. How wrong I was. The newly made clarinets and horns found the key so sympathetic that I wrote two additional piano concertos in the key, premiering them myself in Vienna. I had to wonder why in my young life I had written so little in E major, at least for keyboard music, when it was the key in which the fingers most naturally fell upon black keys without any manipulation of the hand. How I loved to think in keys, then as now, for they are the lodestar of music, the place from where we can see all of the possibilities for straying and, most importantly, what it sounds like to be home.

CHAPTER 11

I did not find out until after she had done it, but Konstanze had for some time been corresponding with the music publisher Johann Breitkopf in Leipzig about moving the plating of my musical works from Artaria to Breitkopf. Konstanze had no way of knowing that Breitkopf was close to the end of his life as he was writing to her, but she seemed to have a gift for such circumstances. She wrote to Johann that he should consider printing in several capitals and not just Leipzig, as it would increase the possibilities of royalties for him. Konstanze convinced Breitkopf to open a Viennese printing house, which he did, not far from Stephansplatz, and when Breitkopf died shortly thereafter, Konstanze was perfectly positioned to buy it. Well, I bought it, since women were not allowed to purchase businesses, but it was entirely Konstanze's work that got it started and kept it going. She managed the plating and publishing of all of my works, and she concentrated on fine editions and getting multiple copies of my pieces around to the musical capitals. She was relentless in those years about getting people to pay us properly.

Around that time I began to be known simply as Mozart, even by those who never met me, and accompanying my name there began to be stories of me as a child, stories that were passed along in cafés and aristocratic circles. There was a new energy surrounding my name, and people multiplied the lore around my childhood. The stories always puzzled me, because I liked that the stories helped to sell my music, but

I was ready to leave tales of my childhood behind, to stop being thought the boy genius.

Six years after I neared death, on the very same December night, I led a concert that featured my sixth concerto for clarinet, one of the instruments that most fascinated me. The same concert featured a beautiful concerto for glass harmonica, an instrument that was becoming popular across all lands, the first sign of musical civilization from the wild world in America. Also around that time I first read in broadsheets about several fascinating men emerging in that new country: Thomas Jefferson and Benjamin Franklin. George Washington seemed a bore by comparison, and his story too simple to be true; he was nothing more than English gentry replanted on new soil. But Jefferson and Franklin came off the page as did *Figaro*, ripe for revolution and newness. Both Jefferson and Franklin shared a love of Paris and had both been successful foreign ministers in Gaul, though sadly my time there did not coincide with theirs, at least that I could recall. I believed I would never have opportunity to be in the presence of their greatness, for they lived on the other side of the world.

They would have taken from Paris a primacy of music, something they surely would want to bring to their great experimental idea of a country across the sea. I was told that Franklin had actually invented the glass harmonica. As I wrote my complicated concerto, learning all about the swirling glass and water, I had Jefferson in mind, hoping that many months hence he would read about the concerto in a broadsheet in America and be pleased by it. Franklin, though, died a few months after Joseph II, and I recall hearing of his demise with great sadness while we were still in mourning clothes for our Kaiser.

I sat in my favorite café near Stephansplatz reading a long broadsheet about America, which was then celebrating twenty years of life—"barely the life of a horse," as Jefferson put it—and there was a feeling of so much possibility. I knew Benjamin Franklin had spoken of me in his travels, as this was often relayed to me. By the time Franklin was his country's emissary to Gaul I was as well known as he, if far less deserving to be so. I struggled with jealousy through my life, but never of figures like Jefferson or Franklin, only of my fellow artists. I hated petty intrigues then and I hate them more now, as far too much of my younger life was consumed with them. Now that I am old, I have earned the ability to say to the young Amadé: indulge in no rumor, and neither worry for those you will offend, for there is no avoiding their offense. Music is a religion in disguise, so worship it as though it was itself a creation of God. It has taken me a lifetime to come to those revelations, if indeed they reveal anything.

In thinking of my modest talents, I realize that I had a gift for languages, something many of my fellow musicians did not possess. I do not simply mean the language of music, though getting to know the possibilities of the glass harmonica was a new language I had to learn. There is no artifice to glass, as the craftsmanship required for it has to be precise and honest. By its nature, glass can be seen through even as it reflects light, yet I found that it has profound tones within. The harmonica made of glass is for me the perfect symbolic instrument of God's music: it creates music through which you can see.

Besides my native German, I learned French and Italian when I was still a boy, greatly helped by the Latin we learned in school. French was infinitely easier and more useful than any other outside my native tongue, for it was the *lingua* used by the learned classes in those years. I always struggled in Italian, having to constantly think of the equivalent word in German, which I never had to do in French. The language of Amsterdam was at first perplexing, but I was able to manage reasonably well in Dutch and Flemish. English was the last for me to master, and it came later in my life, but master it I did. Indeed, years would later pass when I spoke only English. I do not fully understand how language came so easily to me. I was not afraid of making errors, and I could laugh at the stupidest of my mistakes. I spoke always with an accent, and I admired those who could speak a language free of any clues to their birth. In each language I sounded like a boy from Salzburg. What I did not know until these final years of my life, probably even these final months, is that each language changes you. I was not the same Amadé speaking French as I was speaking German. There is a deep change from within when one is speaking a different tongue, and it is a change as clear as the ones that come in sleep.

I was able to speak and think in each of my mastered languages without having to think back to German, and my dreams are often in French.

There were few people who could play my concerto for glass harmonica, but as with the clarinet, if one wants more players, just write concertos for them. My first clarinet concerto was a big success, but it feels rather forgotten now compared to my newer ones, each of which is greater. I loved the trumpet concertos of Johann Hummel and Haydn, and I added four to their number, the most popular of which is the fourth, in C major. One of my closest friends, Anton Weidiger, showed me a new trumpet with five keys, which allowed the player many more notes between notes than had been possible before. Anton and I tried many ideas together, and I am proud that my C-major concerto for trumpet contains every possible note that a trumpet could then play. It all seems so very long ago.

There was much praise for my trumpet concerto, so when I read in a broadsheet a vicious criticism of it, I felt uniquely attacked. There were many young musicians in the new generation of Viennese who looked on the rest of us as passé. I was happily passing an hour in a café when I came across a young writer accusing me of an overuse of chromatic notes in the trumpet concerto, when all I had done was exploit all of the new things the instrument could do so beautifully. The new valves and keys had been intricately explained and demonstrated to me. The finale of the concerto did indeed contain chromatic scales, great cascades of them, and this had not been heard before. They were a delight to the ear, I must say, but not to this writer, who was a young composer I had heard of in whispers around Vienna for several years. Joseph Haydn had told me years before about the amazing gifts of a youth from Bonn, and a member of the noble Esterházy family joked with me around that time that I finally had a competitor. I did not realize until reading his bile about my trumpet concerto that Esterházy and Papa Haydn had been talking about the same young man. I had been due to meet the youth shortly after he started his studies with Haydn, but then I became ill during those months of *The Magic Flute*. I had forgotten about the boy and assumed him to have disappeared from Vienna as did so many other composers, their wishes either fulfilled or dashed before returning to their homes.

As I think back on the years after my illness, I recall that this boy occasionally attended services at St. Stephen's to hear my masses or to hear me play the organ. The intensity of the work at the cathedral left me little time to meet young musicians other than my private students. It was sometimes a days-long task to keep up with my thematic catalogue, and near the end of 1796 I pored through stacks of music lining my shelves and was astonished to realize I had marked down twelve new piano sonatas, seventeen piano trios, and eight new serenades for various combinations of instruments. The church music, though, was the bulk of my output: fifty masses and one hundred fifty organ sonatas or concertos. I was very industrious in those years!

The young man criticizing my trumpet concerto with such intemperance was no longer a young man. Not only was he still in Vienna, but also he could not be ignored any longer. I discovered that he had even approached Konstanze in a marketplace about trying to meet me. But then he wrote this about me in 1797, when he was but a lad of twenty-seven, the impertinent ass:

> Herr Mozart's C-major concerto for the trumpet demands complete vulgarity from its players, and it is monstrous. It contains endless roulades and unachievable ranges, not to mention the rotundity of its melodies, which come across like a corpulent matron. How could a composer capable of such sublime works as his first and fifth clarinet concertos, or any of his magnificent symphonies of late, foist upon the world such a degrading work as this? Many passages put one in mind of the worst excesses of his immoral and overlong Così fan tutte. When will our greatest composer return to honoring the immortal within him instead of indulging his worst impulses?

I had, of course, endured many opinions about my work for my whole life, but this was something else entirely. It was not a random and meaningless opinion from a non-musician trying to make a name for himself. It was a purposeful attempt by a competitor to place himself above me. This would not stand. I had to read it repeatedly, trying to fully absorb what this upstart was attempting. I wrote to Haydn about it, asking to see him, and as always he was gentle and helpful. He said only that the young man was "volatile," but he said it in such a way that made me feel even the untouchable old Haydn was afraid of this renegade. Until that afternoon with Haydn, I had even forgotten the name of the boy who had become a man, and even his name was formidable: Ludwig van Beethoven.

CHAPTER 12

The words Joseph Haydn had uttered to my father right in front of me years before echoed in my ear for the rest of my life, and I have heard they have even made their way into books. Haydn told Papa that I would grow into the greatest composer in history. Because these words came from the man universally considered to be the greatest himself, his words grew more mountainous than if they had been uttered by anyone else. My papa remembered those words almost daily to me, using them as a selling point whenever he could, and Haydn's kind observation remained the highest compliment of my life. But it was not true. I was not the greatest composer in history, and Haydn knew it. I knew it. Papa knew it. There were many who were greater, then and now.

I knew my dear papa would neither have countenanced nor enjoyed the symphonies I wrote in the years after his death, because he would have found them too explosive, too energetic. I felt shame then and I feel it again now that there was relief in my father's passing. Pleasure and pain live within the same vessel of our hearts, and I felt music must always express this. But suddenly that terrible upstart, talented though he might have been, was openly criticizing *me* in front of the entire Viennese public. The pathways I had meticulously carved from those begun by Haydn and Gluck were being used for a gentle stroll by this arrogant child from Bonn, yet he somehow thought the privilege belonged to him. All of my Masonic brethren saw his diatribe, and what ever could I say to them about it?

What worried me most, though, was not the idle talk of my fellow Masons. They were men of the highest personal mettle. I worried about Joseph Haydn, who had settled into his grandfatherly role for several years by that point. He continued to compose with his usual inventive sweetness, but he was from another era, calmly directing all of us with a patriarchal kindness that came naturally to him. Haydn's words about any composer carried great weight in Vienna, much more than any writer in a broadsheet. Around that year, Haydn started using words about Ludwig that had formerly been reserved only for me. I found myself saying his name aloud—"Ludwig van Beethoven"—unable to believe that he existed at all.

The memory is distant, but I believe I might have met Ludwig's father when Nannerl and I toured Bonn. I might even have met young Ludwig, but I have no memory of that. What I had also tried to forget was hearing Ludwig's first piano trio at an event at Prince Lichnowsky's palace, perhaps because I did not want the obvious truth to be so obvious. The trio had moved me deeply. It began with an obvious homage to me, as Haydn had instructed Ludwig well, but the piece showed extraordinary imagination. This was clearly a major composer filled with all kinds of new ideas that were going to be the future of music. Ludwig was not just another talented Viennese composer among so many. He was already a major figure, and he had made the choice to attack me in the cruelest way he could dream up.

Court intrigue and many circumstances conspired to make Salieri my nemesis for many years. But this was only for show. In truth, I liked Antonio very much, and we spent many hours laughing together. Salieri was by nature a dour and serious person, so one had to ply him with a lot of wine to get him to laugh, but then he had a wicked sense of humor, and he seemed to enjoy the jovial breaks from his own gravity. Behind my back, though, Salieri could be biting, but it didn't bother me much. He was never my rival as a composer, no matter what others tried to invent. There was no comparison between us and we both knew it, however much fashion put him occasionally at the forefront. Since *The Magic Flute*, which Antonio adored, with my papa gone, and with Haydn praising Ludwig,

I had actually grown closer to Salieri as a father to me. In those years following *The Magic Flute*, he liked that I had finally devoted myself to church music, removing myself from opera for a few years at least, and Salieri could often be seen at St. Stephen's for each new mass or work for organ that I wrote. We lost a need for rivalry within our friendship, which was not so interesting for those who loved rumors, but was much more pleasurable for us.

That night at Lichnowsky's never left me, and Ludwig's single E-flat piano trio rang through my sinews for months. The intense energy he created in the trio's final movement was thrilling even as it held terror within it, and it was more passionate and inventive than anything Haydn or I had ever created. I wrote trios all my life, as it was a form to which I was constantly moved to return, because trios move music back to its most basic element of three opposing and complementary sides, a pyramid. Anyone who listens to trios is a true music lover, not interested only in show, power, or size, but in the actual matter of music. Like Haydn I wrote many string quartets, and they were extremely easy, sometimes taking barely longer to write than to play. But for me it was the trios that held the musical matter. That is one of my favorite words, *matter*, for it comes from the Latin word for *mother*. Matter is all. How I miss dearest Mama.

At that moment I had long considered myself the master of the piano trio, or at least second only to Haydn, then this young man turned up with one trio, his Opus 1, No. 1, and eclipsed all we had done. Haydn had been tutoring him, so he must have blessed Ludwig's ideas. In December of 1796, nearly a year after I'd heard the trio I was working hard to forget, Artaria delivered a plated copy to me. This was one of the moments of ultimate truth in my life. Could I, considered by every musician of the time the best pianist in the world, play Ludwig's first trio at sight? I refused to be heard playing it at St. Stephen's, so I used the fortepiano at home, but I made sure the house was empty and Konstanze away with the boys.

I began the first movement, which I well recall was an affectionate nod to some idealized version of me. The beginning of the trio was gracious indeed, and the following passagework was simple. I could have written it, but I had not. My trios prior to then were fonts of pride, but they were not as good as this one. I kept playing. There were some challengingly unpredictable triplets, but I caught them all. Upon repeat, I sang as much of the first violin part as I could manage, where I could more plainly see that Ludwig was copying me but also taking my ideas into terrain I had never traveled. He copied Haydn, Cimarosa, even Salieri, but he also did not directly shape any single phrase as any of them might.

Then came the shift to A flat, which made me laugh out loud with joy. Ravishing. More triplets. My fingers had to crackle like a fire and define many unique shapes, but I did not find it challenging. The voicing was pure Haydn, but thicker and more satisfying, I am ashamed to write. After the layering of the main theme, Ludwig followed with a terribly difficult chromatic scale, upon which I said to the empty room, "You little shit fart!" and made myself laugh. This man had criticized *me* for writing chromatics!

The slow movement was perhaps the most beautiful music written up to that time, a noble rising melody that I loved, and little romantic fragments of it passed among the three instruments in ways Haydn and I had both done, but it went a step beyond. A shift to minor made me exclaim, "*Unglaublich!*" I had to wonder why Ludwig felt it necessary to have such massive C-major chords to follow, with four notes in each hand. Vulgar. And yet this parvenu got praised for the very thing for which he criticized us! Oh, dear reader, I sound to myself like my father.

The scherzo movement was real music, too. The final movement made me angry because the fast leap which began it was an effort for my small hand, as though he had fashioned it to be particularly agonizing for my fingers. The top note of the leap was a black key that was easy to slip from, and this dragon of a composer had the gall to slur the figure just to torment me! This was a movement that could only be played by an accomplished pianist, and I coped. I had composed some equally challenging works for the keyboard, like the final movement of my favorite A-major sonata for violin and piano, then already many years old, but even it could be played by many people, and the struggle was part of the fun, but not with this trio. This was all struggle and nothing else.

Vienna was too small a place to live in with genuine rivals. I knew I was going to have to befriend Ludwig and follow Papa Haydn's example of embracing all Viennese musicians with generosity, with never a twinge of jealousy. I asked him once how he did it, and he offered that the gestures were easy for him, since he always claimed that statements made about musicians are always forgotten unless they are true. I was never sure I agreed with him on that, but he was the master.

I discussed with Konstanze having Ludwig to dinner, even proposing a concert together wherein we could play together my D-major sonata for two pianos, which I had written when I was Ludwig's age. What a sweet memory to have played with Josepha, whom I nearly married. Our concert together in Passauerhof had led to invitations for many others, but Josepha hated Konstanze for reasons I never wanted to know. After that, I occasionally saw Josepha at musical events around Vienna, but she never forgave me for not returning her affections. What might my life have been like had I married her? A lady pianist remains such a rarity, and there is no doubt it caused a lot of scandal in Viennese households then, but that never was a great bother for me. I admired her enormously but I did not love her, and I was never talented at pretending I loved someone.

CHAPTER 13

Josepha brings on the memory of Aloysia. That name! Aloysia. Konstanze's sister who was, it must be said aloud at least one time, the woman I most loved in my life until Alice. Might my life had been very different had I married her? I always knew things that others did not, but the might-have-beens nearly drove me mad as the years went on. What if this? What if that? Music, the music that I wrote down, was my only definite. I could fulfill the dreams of what I had time to write down, but with everything else I had doubts. People naturally assumed that I was an expert on the performance of my own works, but I doubt I was. Musicians will take chances on musical works that they have not created, risks they would not endeavor if the music has come from their own heart. Decisions were fine, but doubts made up the bulk of my life, and I spent so much time thinking of how my life might have gone if I had married Aloysia, or if I had stayed with Konstanze instead of leaving her, or did she leave me? I no longer know. I have wondered every day of my long life what would have happened had I not been saved by the beautiful Romaní woman, if I had passed into the next world that night. I knew I needed a new stage of life, where I would not have to know of Ludwig, but I did not have that kind of power over my life. In this imaginary other life, would I worry about money? Would it bother me that my little son was likely from the seed of Franz Süssmayer? Would any of that matter? That word again: matter. Would it?

Parallel worlds emerged in those years, and hours of my waking life were spent in the dreaming of them.

The problem of my life has been that I've had no one with whom I could speak of my fears. Most people have such a person, but I was the famous Mozart, or the famous Amadé in those years, and I could not be allowed the indulgence of fear. And I did not know what I feared, at least not with any precision. I never feared being unable to compose, for the ideas poured from me without cease, and so rapidly that on many days I had to struggle to get them all written down. I harbored no fears about playing the fortepiano, and even in recent years, so late in my life, I could improvise for hours and still create fugues and retrograde them, surprising myself. I still possess every musical power I have always had, except my string-playing has noticeably declined; but I am now on a promontory of life from where I can see many years distant, and the pain of almost dying is within me always, coursing through my veins as surely as blood. Our elder selves are present in us as children, and I know this because I can still feel a part of myself that is a child.

Fear remained my great constant. Fear is the only thing which has made me tired in life. Fear came not in a public display of animosity toward Ludwig, but hidden within the small comments from piano students that made me suspect that Ludwig was quietly working to steal my finest pupils. Ultimately, what would have been wrong if he had? Yes, my piano students were my regular income outside of St. Stephen's, and I learned more from teaching piano than from composing—a surprising revelation. Piano students had more individual challenges than composers, and learning to solve problems of the hand was infinitely easier than problems of attempting to find in music the longings of one's own heart, a place that lacks easy access.

Writing down music I had composed did not teach me anything, as much as I loved doing it. Teaching piano or violin, though, required a quarrying into my own musical gifts as nothing else did. Each student arrives with a challenge that cannot be found without a teacher's help. Too many teachers search for a hidden child within the student, yet most of the students are far beyond adulthood in their playing and thus far beyond the teacher. So many teachers find the musical needs of their students to be cries for affection that they may not necessarily be, and they try to correct the sins of the parents. Anyone who teaches becomes a parent, but it can be terribly confusing.

Since my papa, Leopold, died, I have often reflected on him. I was able to keep his violin book alive for the public, and over time I added many ideas to his as to how to teach violin, plus I created a book on teaching piano. Ludwig had the audacity to be critical of "that brute Leopold" and his teaching methods, and of taking me all over the world on tour as a child. This was nothing but jealousy, as Ludwig would have sold his own mother to have toured the world. And I have the feeling that Ludwig's own father was indeed a terrible brute, whereas my dear Leopold was gentle and loving at all times. He did not approve of Konstanze, but I cannot imagine now or then any woman of whom he would have approved. Ludwig apparently said to Haydn, "Expecting so much from a tiny boy is a sin against God," but look at what happened. Life will always get the best of people who say such abominations.

I have been to parts of the world that few ever see: virtually no one besides those who lived there went to Napoli. Roma, of course, was a destination for many, but how many pilgrims took the time to notice the great flow of the Tiber, or the myriad other things that Papa and I were able to enjoy while there. I recall the great murmurations of blackbirds which would soar above the city. They must have been starlings; oh, my wonderful starlings! The birds seemed to be seeking favorable air, and they were aware of the changing light—or perhaps they were feeding on swarming creatures too small to see from the Quirinale Hill, where we loved to picnic at the end of the day. We watched God's great sun drop behind the unfathomable dome of St. Peter's Basilica. Roma had a unique golden light in those years, which I tried constantly to re-create in sound. God came to me in those moments, in those combinations of light and sound.

I have spent my life teaching Leopold's methods to my violin, piano, and voice students. My piano students are all taught the great preludes and fugues by Johann Sebastian Bach, J.C.'s father, a man I so wish I had met. The Bach preludes and fugues are marvelous: complementary works in the major and minor of each key, yet there is nothing academic about them. They inspired me to write my own set of keyboard preludes and fugues in Bach's memory, and I am very proud of them. Just before we moved here, among the last lessons I taught was of the D-major fugue from Bach's second book, the most beautiful fugue I have ever known, and I taught my own D-major fugue along with it. They complement each other nicely. How I wish I could have known J.C.'s father, as his spirit haunted Leipzig as profoundly as few spirits haunt any place, and his fugal melodies seemed to emerge from crevices of every building, as though more were still there awaiting extraction.

Bach, for me, was not Johann Sebastian but his son Johann Christian, one of the dearest of all musicians I met. To my father's horrified embarrassment, I always called Johann by the name of Jesus Christ, and we would both cackle with laughter. I was only eight when I met J.C. in London, by which time J.C. must have been nearly thirty. He was the first person to speak to me as though we were the same age. He did not reprimand me for harmless nicknames that I made up about everyone, and he laughed when I said things as a child that only adults were allowed to say. J.C. listened to me improvise and, unlike Leopold, he did not try to moderate my musical character within improvisation or to calm any hint of intemperance. J.C. also taught me one of the best lessons of my life: how to turn the tumult of my ideas into music, just as water is launched into the air when heated. I had always to honor my father, but quietly I know that whatever success I achieved was due to J.C.'s encouragement. How extraordinary that often those we encounter briefly teach us the most. Johann's own operas found their way into mine, sometimes note for note, but I borrowed well.

There was only one art that eluded me. I always wished I could sing. To be a great singer is to be among the greatest artists. Though I sounded like a sick chicken, I taught many singers, and I had an ability to help them even without singing myself. There was no forgetting Adamonti and the way he rendered "Mein liebevolles Herz" at the end of my love song to Konstanze. Adamonti was one of my favorite singers, and I wonder if he is still alive. We altered the name of *Seraglio*'s leading character to Belmonte simply to delight him. Despite Adamonti's southern name, he was actually from the beautiful valley of the Rohr river, where I visited as a child. I listened to him over and over in my memory for the whole of my long life.

CHAPTER 14

It seems impossible to me now but it must true, for this memory has lived through these many years with a stone's persistence. We likely thought of little but each other in those years, in the late 1790s. Though Ludwig's music and criticisms of me weighed heavily on me, and though he had met Konstanze on numerous occasions, at the time of *Richard III* Ludwig and I had not yet met. Years flew then, and they fly faster now. He was to play some of his music for me around the time of *The Magic Flute*, but then I became ill. After he so brutally criticized my trumpet concerto, I had no desire to meet him. I heard him play his trio, it is true, but we avoided each other at Prince Lichnowsky's villa and spoke no words to each other, both fearful that we would choose poorly. Haydn had, as usual, tried to put us in the same room, but to no success. How is it possible that we made it to 1798 before confronting each other? Peter Winter and dozens of other Viennese composers could go years without seeing me and their lives would have been no different. But Ludwig and I? We were destined to be linked together, and each of our spirits pulled on the other. There was no escaping it.

Our first meeting in 1798 was terrible, an unexpected eruption that left us no choice but a feud. Emanuel and I were playing through *Richard III* in the salon of the Theater an der Wien. Ludwig burst through the door and pointed at me.

"This man has been plotting for months to steal my opera!" he yelled.

I said quietly to myself, "Months?" not understanding what he meant. I remember Emanuel's words as though he was speaking them just now.

"Months! Ludwig, there is no need for anyone to steal anything."

"I demand to know at this moment if my opera, *Vestas Feuer*, is or is not to open the season of Theater an der Wien as you promised me it would." Ludwig's voice was in a tight rage and his face looked like a langoustine.

Emanuel looked to me but I said nothing. I knew Emanuel had already decided to open with *Richard III*, and he knew I knew that he had never mentioned *Vestas Feuer* to me, so no words were necessary.

"Would you be willing, Ludwig, as the younger composer, to be our second opera? It would give you a little more time to finish your work," Emanuel said, with soft fear.

"I am finished. The score is complete. Are you going to be about the future or the past?" Ludwig asked.

The future or the past. This creature actually thought that only *he* was the future. My chest was crushing in on itself, as it always did in confrontations, but again I said nothing.

Emanuel looked ashen, an unarmed man at a war. I knew him well enough to know that he had no interest in the future or the past; he simply wanted a great opera season. *Vestas Feuer* was Emanuel's libretto, but for all any of us knew Ludwig had set it to music without being asked to do so. Emanuel probably had crafted lovely poetry for it, but he knew himself to be no Shakespeare. I toyed with offering for *Richard III* to become the second opera of the season, just to maintain peace, but this was Emanuel's cross to bear, and I was not the man who had burst uninvited into a room. There commenced a long silence.

"This is not the way for two such great men to meet for the first time. Let us take ourselves to a café, break bread, and have some wine together," Emanuel said.

I indicated with my eyes that I would be willing to sit down with Ludwig, who betrayed no emotion at all. After more silence, Ludwig spoke.

"I am humbled before Herr Mozart. But styles change. Music changes. It is time for Vienna to welcome a new generation and, with respect, I am that new generation."

Emanuel offered, "*Vestas Feuer* is an opera of ancient Rome, vestal virgins, things we have seen in opera for years. I crafted the poetry in a very old style. *Richard III* really is something new, Ludwig. I promise to you both that I will do both of your operas."

Ludwig pointed at me again. "For months, this man has worked to steal my place and I cannot believe you are going to allow it. What kind of man are you, Emanuel?"

CHAPTER 15

I saw something die within my dear friend Emanuel in that moment. He knew my own epiphanies and the places to which my music would never return, but he also knew that Ludwig was radical, new, and more destined for immortality than I. More than anyone I have known, Emanuel was the sort of person to know this about an artist. If Emanuel made Ludwig angry enough, he knew Ludwig would take *Vestas Feuer* to the court theater, though there he would find controversy over a vestal virgin within a love story. *Richard III* could only play at the Theater an der Wien, for the court would never allow the portrayal of an evil king, no matter how brilliant the music. Emanuel further knew that Ludwig had made it impossible for either of us to happily accept second position to the other. Had Ludwig not burst into the room with his accusations, and not trodden all over my trumpet concerto, I would have done anything Emanuel asked, but Ludwig removed all choices.

Finally Emanuel spoke. "My decision is to open our season with *Richard III* and to follow with *Vestas Feuer* the following month. Please, my dear friends, accept this difficult compromise."

Ludwig asked me how I could possibly remain silent at such a moment. I told him I had nothing to say except that I hoped we could do a concert together to show Vienna that art can unite. And I said that all anyone would remember of that season would be operas by Beethoven and Mozart; no one would remember the order in which they appeared.

"I am honored by the suggestion, Herr Mozart, but I cannot accept."

Ludwig turned to Emanuel.

"There will be no performance of *Vestas Feuer*, not here, not ever. I am throwing it in the Donau."

Ludwig left the room, and I have no doubt he walked directly to the river and did as he decreed.

Ludwig's bearing had the timbre and cadence of my sainted father. Emanuel and I sat in silence. The memory of that day has confused itself with a much older time, for reasons I cannot understand. I remember returning to Salzburg as a boy from a successful trip to Paris and many other places with Papa. We greeted Mama and unpacked, telling her about so many things Nannerl and I had done. The first thing I always did when we returned from a trip was to climb the Festungsberg so that I could see the great vista from there. There were much higher mountains all around, with snow lasting even into the warm months, but from the Festungsberg I imagined I could see all the way to Vienna. I knew I could not *really* see Vienna, since it was three days' riding, first to Linz then to Sankt Pölten. (Once we had done it in two days, which was arduous.) That spot up on the Berg was my favorite place in Salzburg, and from there I would dream about all the happenings in Vienna, all the music going on, the lessons being taught, the publishers hard at work. In Vienna, I thought in those youthful days, I would be liberated from archbishops and men who spit and pissed in the street or women who shit right into the river, hiking up their skirts with no shame at all. I never imagined that such a confrontation such as I had with Ludwig would be possible in such a cultivated place as Vienna. He shut out the world after that, and I barely saw him again. Few people did. My mind kept returning to the Festungsberg, the place of my childhood dreams, and I know the vista from there will look exactly the same in a thousand years, by which time all of us will be long forgotten.

I told Emanuel not to worry, that Ludwig would undoubtedly write him another opera. I had seen Ludwig watching me in cafés, always trying not to be seen, and he appeared at St. Stephen's from time to time. Haydn continually tried to call a truce between us in the months after this encounter, but Ludwig never responded to any of his pleas. We avoided each other as best we could, but Vienna was not large enough to allow this for long.

Around that time I finished *Richard III,* and I knew I had a dozen more operas within me waiting to emerge. Emanuel was supportive and helpful, but he was never fully himself after that day with Ludwig. Somehow it changed him, and I remain amazed that one terrible encounter could so alter a person's soul.

As we prepared to rehearse *Richard III,* one of the most stressful times of all my years in Vienna, Haydn invited me to dine with him. He always had such beautiful remembrances of my cherished parents. Haydn set out the purpose of this dinner immediately, telling me that he had suggested to the court of King George III of England that I become the Master of the King's Musick, the most prestigious musical post in the world. Haydn had spent years in London to great success, and refused the post himself when offered to him. He explained the terms, even presenting me with a letter from the Lord Chamberlain expressing the King's intent. I could read little English in those years, but I could see very clearly, written with the most expensive ink I had ever seen, my own name spelled in the way of the English: Wolfgang Amadeus Mohzart.

Haydn described what would be expected of me: regular concerts, operas, church music, and music for the court. I would be given a house not distant from the Palace of St. James, and the salary was beyond anything I had ever earned. My memories of London were from my boyhood, but it was a blessed place for me, the place of Johann Christian Bach and so much else. I had actually met George III in the early years of his reign, when I was a child, and it remains miraculous to me that he sat on the throne of England for so long.

CHAPTER 16

I owe more to Franz Joseph Haydn than could ever be repaid, gentle reader, and I left his home that night with a heart so full that I thought I might become one of Papageno's birds and soar high above the Viennese homes. I could not wait to tell Konstanze. Our little Franz was old enough to understand my words, as well. On that happy night, our wonderful little boy was the age I had been when our carriage rollicked out of Salzburg for my first journey to Paris, the age I was when I wrote down my first works for clavichord. I remember our coach driver, Heinrich, and how he taught me to flick the whip onto the horses. I loved those horses, particularly when they grew to understand the needs of the carriage, but I could not bear the sound of tired horses. I could hear it in their breath, their fear that they may not be able to fulfill *our* desires. Horses are such beautiful and generous creatures. They were born to the burden of getting people from one place to the other, but they do this with such deep love. Horses opened the world to itself, liberating man from having to walk everywhere. Papa and I could never have seen the world without horses, and horses would carry me across the world again to Paris, then to a port where I would endure the horror of crossing the channel. Man is not meant for the sea. So many memories, dear and patient reader!

I thought it best to first tell Konstanze some good news about *Richard III*, that Schiki and I had progressed to a point where he could schedule a premiere to open the season at Theater an der Wien in the autumn of 1798. Konstanze was excited about attending a new opera of mine again, and excited because she knew opera could be lucrative compared to even a fine position like what I had at St. Stephen's. *The Labyrinth*, to speak in a vulgar way, made more money than *The Magic Flute*, and the Archbishop had allowed me to write it because its Masonic content kept it free of religious controversy. *Richard III* would be another matter, so on that night I had to tell her how deeply our lives were to change: I was leaving St. Stephen's and we were moving to London where I was to be Master of the King's Musick.

Konstanze never took well to change. She seemed fixated for a long time on the folly of leaving the security of a post like St. Stephen's, yet I assured her that the position in London was much more prestigious and my wages would mean security for the rest of our lives, and real security for the first time. She liked that George III's consort, Queen Charlotte Mecklenburg-Strelitz, had personally asked for me, and I could see in her eyes excitement about having a role in the royal court that would never be open for us in Vienna. She asked what was to become of her music publishing and how I could be so thoughtless as to not think of it. She cried several times as we spoke, especially when observing that we could not take all of my music with me. She asked how I could possibly expect her to arrange such an enormous trip at the same time I was rehearsing *Richard III*. She asked if we were ever returning to Vienna, and I had to be honest and say it was unlikely, for I had experienced whatever satiety was available to me there. Konstanze raged as if against death for several hours, crying out at what I had not had the simplest courtesy to discuss with her. I did not like little Franz seeing her cry so desperately, as he was excited simply to ride in a carriage, just as I had been at his age. I told Konstanze that we would leave for Paris and London after the premiere of *Richard III*, and thus within two months. She wept long into the night. She did not want to leave with winter lingering, but spring would be too wet. I could not wait for summer to make the journey, as my contract was to begin. One thing was certain: 1799 was going to be a year of enormous change for us both.

CHAPTER 17

Rehearsals for *Richard III* began, and immediately the singers found my score the most demanding they had ever encountered, several of them calling their roles "impossible." There were endless complaints to Emanuel as well as to me. The first scene alone, between the roles of Richard and Anne, took over three days to rehearse—much more time than I had experienced in early rehearsals of anything since *Don Giovanni*, when the many ensembles brought every rehearsal to a halt from their difficulty. Usually in the early days of rehearsing an opera, singers learned their music quickly and only the memorization took much more time. Not so with *Richard III*. It became clear that the planned weeks before the premiere would not be enough. At the end of each day I met with Schiki to keep him abreast, but after the first week I sadly had to inform him that we had to delay the first performances by at least a fortnight.

To my horror, Emanuel refused. "It is impossible, and you know it is impossible. We have announced. The public will kill us both if we delay. We would be telling everyone that it is already a disaster!"

I tried to explain that Richard was, and is, like no other character in opera. "He has been made evil by his lust for power, but lusts are learned, Schiki! You know this," I said. "God takes a strong hand against anyone who lusts too much, and it makes Richard so angry that he has no control. I believe it is the wounds that Richard saw and learned that deformed him. He could be deformed by some strange accident of birth, but any deformity would have been loved had he not fallen so deeply in love with lust. He drank it like a poison. Richard lusted for women, then lusted to kill just for the feeling of having done so." I had never understood a character so profoundly as Shakespeare's great Richard.

Emanuel was not moved by my own lusts to make the singers go deeply into the world of *Richard III*, at least not enough to give me more time to do so. I was consumed with this opera as I never had been consumed by anything. I was, I suppose, feeling some of Richard's lust, but mine was for the glories of Shakespeare's play. I asked Emanuel how he portrayed Richard or Hamlet with such passion and realism, and I begged him to help me get that from our singers, and I begged him for more time. He continued to refuse, protecting his business over our art, and I was certain he was not quite himself in his mind by that point. Something had crossed a bridge inside him. He was behaving as though all operas were equal, but they are not! The same scalding water that softens the potato will harden the egg: everything depends on what you are made of.

I had to begin the orchestral rehearsals, and the violinists complained bitterly about the F-sharp minor, C-sharp minor, and other related keys. They said those keys were uncomfortable, but I would take my instrument and play it with ease, and they were all much better violinists than I! Everything about *Richard III* was a struggle, and difficulty is not all that interesting. What obsessed me about *Richard III* was how lifelike it is: life, the terrible harshness of life, is only to be truly found within a wound, but we must also keep the wound hidden. Richard's wound is unimportant, but he had within him no power to hide—that is our fascination. But everything I tried to convey about Shakespeare's drama was being lost in the difficulty of what I demanded of the singers and orchestra—and it was too late to compose anything differently or to try to simplify, and I had no way of achieving that. My music had to reflect the complexity of the man and the chaos created by his rage. I had no choice.

As the premiere approached, I was reminded of the announcements of criminals to be executed in Salzburg. Extravagant pleas were often made for mercy, but the criminals all were marched to the scaffolding anyway. My father once watched the executions, but I could never bring myself to set my eyes upon them. However, while waiting on the premiere of

Richard III, I gained an idea of how those criminals must have felt in the days, hours, then minutes before whatever gruesome end had been concocted for them, usually hanging. I watched people arrive at the Theater an der Wien. Librettos were handed out. I heard that Ludwig was in the theater and, sure enough, his distinctive wig was visible from the angle of my perch with the violins. Many times I had to stop playing in order to use my hands to keep the singers in the correct portion of the measures of music.

The rehearsals had been so consuming that I had forgotten that singers need an audience. Though someone is always watching them in rehearsal, they need strangers. So I was astounded by the difference between the opening performance and what they had shown me in the final days of our preparation. The opera's opening scene and duet drew long applause, and as each ensemble progressed, and the web of fugues grew ever more complex and dizzying, the applause grew. The singers met the audience's approval with more of which to approve. Even now, many years later, I can still feel the explosive energy of that afternoon. The cool weather bestowed on us was an added blessing.

CHAPTER 18

Konstanze was the first to visit me backstage, just a few moments after the extended battle scene, the largest orchestra I had ever summoned. The final scene alternated between F-sharp major and minor, then A major and E minor, and back again to F-sharp. Then my coup de théâtre arrived, never before seen or heard anywhere: seven onstage trumpets in A major announcing the defeat of Richard, a full five minutes after his cries of "A horse! A horse! My kingdom for a horse!" (which in Schiki's version was, "*Ein Pferd! Ein Pferd! Mein Königreich für ein Pferd!*").

Konstanze was polite but I could tell something was bothering her. I knew she was still angry about my decision to move us London, and I had so rarely been home in the final preparations for the opera that all of the work preparing the trip fell to her. When Konstanze got angry, she generally stayed that way for many days and sometimes weeks. I had to ask her if she liked the opera, as she would not offer me her opinion. She confessed that she had, and she cried, saying she knew this opera would separate us. I did not know at the moment what she meant. She then turned to a subject that held more safety and asked how complicated it would be to take all of the materials for *Richard III* with us to London. I had not thought about my orchestral materials, assuming I would leave everything in safekeeping with Süssmayer, but my heart bristled at the thought of him. How would we know if we were receiving royalties from performances of my music? He had stolen from me already; not money, but something much more valuable.

Others arrived backstage, each of them polite. I had heard those kinds of compliments before, the sort uttered from a false kindness meant only to move the moment along, and one knows they change completely once they are outside. Only in the privacy of my own imagination could I hear and feel my music as it actually was, liberated from the perceptions over which I had no control, nor from the observations I had no desire to hear. What did they imagine I was to do with their opinions? They surely did not believe that I would alter a note of my music simply because they disapproved of it. I knew Ludwig would not come backstage and I was glad he did not, but I was sure I could hear his opinions without him there.

Konstanze took our carriage home, as I had promised Emanuel dinner after the performance and I was to meet him at the café nearby. It felt strange to leave the theater alone after so many people had so recently filled it, though I do love empty theaters, sitting quietly inside them when I arrive early or stay late, as I did that night. There was a woman mopping the floor who reminded me of the Romaní woman to whom I owe everything but whose name I will never know. I sat for many minutes catching my breath, absorbing the beautiful silent darkness that not long before had been full of sound.

I entered the small and dim café near the Naschmarkt, unsure of Emanuel's mood. Upon sitting down, I noticed Emanuel was crying. I asked him if I had failed him.

"Ami, my dearest friend, I tell you from my heart that *Richard III* is not only your greatest work, it is the greatest opera yet written."

I reminded him that Joseph II had said the same of *Figaro.*

"It was true of *Figaro.* But *Figaro* might well be forgotten after tonight. You will have to take care to be sure it is not. How one man could have written both is more than I can comprehend."

We talked late into the night about the performance and other projects that we both wanted to bring to life. I felt so fully alive again, ready to commence work on anything, and to have Emanuel, dear Schiki, so fully approve was all I needed. He reminded me that I was shortly to leave Vienna, probably forever, and he wondered how we could realize any future opera together.

I told him he could send me text ready for music and I would send him back a completed opera. We found so much laughter that night, even knowing that several more successful performances of *Richard III* remained our responsibility in the coming weeks, weeks in which I had to prepare to leave Vienna. I made my way home slowly through the darkness of the streets, lit by a brilliant moon that night that was a portend of large changes to come. I knew things others did not.

CHAPTER 19

It was time to turn my attention to the daunting journey that awaited us. Music was circling me strongly in those days, for *Richard III* had awakened more ideas. In the peaks and valleys of my ability to work, this was a peak, and I had to seize those moments. I lit a candle when I arrived home, as the entire household was asleep, and I sketched some ideas that had come to me on the walk home. There was, I thought, a string serenade coming to form. I was preoccupied with how much music to take in trunks on the trip. I knew I should take *Flute, Labyrinth, Richard III*, possibly *Clemenza di Tito, Figaro* of course, and many symphonies. The Londoners loved concertos and I had many by that point. The masses might also be of use.

Konstanze asked me without cease how much room we would have in the house, as though I was in possession of the knowledge to answer her. I told her I was going to be writing new music constantly, including new operas, so I was not sure how much of my older music would be necessary. Perhaps we should leave it with Franz Süssmayer, I said, the feel of his name burning my tongue.

Her rage continued. "Opera! You are being asked to work for the greatest throne in the world for a monarch who loves symphonies and choral anthems. You told me so yourself. So why insist on opera?" Her words stung, so close as they were to the success of *Richard III*.

I told her I was reading the works of an Englishman at that very moment, and that I had been promised by the Lord Chamberlain a great deal of artistic freedom. Emanuel had given me the writings of this man, published just recently in German. He is an Englishman now living in the New World, a man named Thomas Paine. Fascinating reading, though much of it made me angry.

"How can you possibly have time for reading when we are moving out of our home with a little boy while you traipse us off to London for God knows how long?" Konstanze demanded.

I asked her if she did not want to go, or if she wanted me to refuse. She said nothing. I told her this was an opportunity that Ludwig would murder for. And I reminded her that once you say no to royalty, all roads to patronage are cut off. There is a Ministry of Culture in London who would immediately share with every royal house that Wolfgang Amadé Mozart had accepted an appointment from George III and then changed his mind and left him with no one. I could feel the bones in my chest tightening and I had to force myself to breathe as Konstanze and I discussed such a terrible outcome.

And with unpredictable swiftness, Konstanze changed course and assured me that she was ready and eager to leave Vienna, having been so angry at me moments before for the very same. Her voice became gentle and loving, and she offered that little Franz would get to share some of the experiences I'd had when I was his age. She eased my mind about the household and the trip, as she had already arranged our carriage to Paris, and the horseman and carriage master has assured her they could be in France within three weeks depending on the state of roads.

She assumed I wanted to stop in Salzburg but I did not. "Straight on to Paris," I told her, stressing that we would not stay more than a few weeks in Paris, as I was seeking the fastest route across *La Manche* to England as could be found. Passage across *La Manche*, which I sometimes hear called "the channel" now—not nearly so musical a word—could only be arranged through a company in Paris. Konstanze and I would purchase passage from Paris to Calais to await the ship at a fine inn, then take another carriage from Dover to London, all within no more than a week. I remember waiting with Papa in Calais for many days, practicing on the piano of an establishment selling alcohol that lacked even wood for a floor. Our inn was very nice, though. I loved telling Franz about the huge white cliffs that would welcome us to England, and how thrilled I had been when I saw them first from the shores of Gaul. Watching them come closer as we approached Shakespeare's island, and keeping our eyes on the distant cliffs, would help calm the fears of the water that were already weighing upon me.

CHAPTER 20

In those last months in Vienna, many of our friends began to call our little Franz "Wolfgang," something encouraged by Konstanze so she could lessen the rumors that Franz was the son of Süssmayer. I would not indulge in this *subterfugium*. I called our beautiful son by his name. Franz is near me even now, by the grace of the most gracious God. I never missed an opportunity, especially in front of Konstanze, to use his name. Franz has the bearing of Konstanze and her family, which gave much fuel to the rumors that he was not of my seed. It is of no matter to me, for he is my son, and his birthright is to be called by his name. Konstanze was forever chipping away at those kinds of hurts, which I found increasingly tiresome and distracting.

My now long-suffering reader, I have found it nearly impossible to truly notice something at the moment it is happening. One needs memory and then a quiet moment that allows one to fall in love with the memory. We cannot remember what we do not love. Memory is the opposite of music, but they are both the children of time. In my later years, as time came to mean everything to me, I kept a set of hourglasses, and many people have been kind enough to give them to me as gifts. I have a small number of my favorites here with me even now, as their sand must be in movement for me to find the energy to move my quill across the paper. One of my favorite hourglasses is a small one gilded in gold that is said to be five minutes in total, but I do not know how one is to truly know. I know only that when I turn it over and my memory turns to my final rondo of *Eine kleine Nachtmusik,* if the tempo of the music is exactly what I imagined, the sand will finish at precisely the sounding of the final note. I would test this delightful hourglass several times a week, and if my memory was even a moment too slow, the sand would run out before the music finished. In those days when my heartbeat made me think of my own music too quickly, which was rare, there would always be a small bit of sand eagerly awaiting the bottom of the glass. I found I could do this with several of my short compositions, but the jaunty little movement of *Nachtmusik* was a favorite of my later years, since it is a work now so distant in my life. It seemed to play with the sand itself, and I always giggled when its joy was contained within the boundaries of the hourglass.

My larger hourglass was of unknowable duration, but easily took at least an hour to exhaust itself. I used it each day. It altered something about the time in the room whenever I was composing, and it gave me a goal. If I did not turn the glass over, I would not achieve the same amount or quality of composition. Now I find it difficult to achieve the same precision of memory as I gaze back on my life unless the hourglass is in motion. The midday bells of St. Stephen's, all of those years ago, that great low D, would arrive sooner if I had used my hourglass. It always bothered me in Vienna, but it was true in all of the large cities I knew well, that the midday chimes did not usually happen simultaneously, as though the midday arrived at slightly different times. How could they lack such important precision?

We were allowed many performances of *Richard III,* delaying our journey but allowing us more time for preparations. *Richard III* could be said to have brought with it a new era of music and theater, unlike anything that had been seen or heard before. I knew that I could not write an old-fashioned opera like *Figaro* or *Don Giovanni* again, as there was no turning back, though I must confess as I would to a priest that there is little in life that gives me as much as joy as my *Figaro,* and it has brought me overflowing delight for the whole of its long life, for by the grace of God it has lived as long as I.

I am ashamed that I thought so constantly of Ludwig, and that one of my darker thoughts upon *Richard III*'s success was the realization that anything Ludwig were to produce at that time would seem old-fashioned. This pleased me in a way that it should have not, but because he had been the one to accuse me of miring myself in the past, it seemed just. I was at that moment finding new emerging energy for traveling to Paris and London, places I had not been since I was a child. A whole new set of operas was beginning to take shape in my imagination.

I lived in a small world of theater and music, but the larger world outside of us was also transforming, a world that I had never much heeded beyond my own whereabouts and destinations. Ludwig kept making grand political announcements and attending meetings with political agitators and disruptors, and I thought this particularly vulgar for someone dependent on the patronage of those against whom he was agitating. I loathed politics, then and now, but I could never avoid them. The political revolutionaries of Beaumarchais's amazing plays had not interested me; only the love that the revolution thwarted or inspired was worthy of music. Political machinations do not have music within them. Even in *Richard III*, an opera that lives in a highly political world, it was not the stratagems and intrigues that interested me. Love is the only revolution, as it is the only thing that has ever truly changed a life.

Ludwig, having learned of our departure, began to send me letters of effusive praise, proving to me that all along there were at least two Ludwigs, the man who screamed in Emanuel's office and the man who could construct sonnets of esteem with my name upon them. Ludwig's ambition, I thought, was a third Ludwig, one who knew not the other two, and each had his own mind and heart. I had seen many petty fights in the theater, mostly between singers and impresarios over minutiae that held no interest for anyone for long. But something new entered my life with Ludwig. Through students, many of whom were coming to see me in those final Viennese days, and most especially through Haydn, Ludwig was revealing himself to me. This man was vindictive, jealous, volatile, humorless, indecisive, and so desperately unhappy that he was a nuisance to anyone he encountered. His talent was undeniable, but I felt that if he found no temperance of his passions, God would not allow him a long enough life to bring his gifts to full blossom. As much as I attempted to ignore the man, everywhere I went in Vienna involved questions about Ludwig. Had I heard his latest work? Did I know Ludwig was writing a new opera? Did I realize Ludwig had conceived a symphony in C major that would rival my seven symphonic triumphs in the key? Did I know that he had been sketching on this symphony for at least four years? I did not know these things, but neither was I in possession of wanting to know anything about this disturbed person.

Haydn, in his endless kindness, always told more than he probably should. He said that Ludwig had taken to calling me his "brother in Apollo," which I found odd. I knew things that others did not, and I felt in those final months in Vienna that I was getting to know Ludwig. He must have uttered the words in sincerity. Without his knowledge, I attended a rehearsal of his new ballet, the strangely titled *Die Geschöpfe des Prometheus*—the "creatures" of Prometheus—and in it he composed something that has haunted my life. This was music of extraordinary progress and—what would be the word?—*vision*. It was a vision like those had by the most holy of the Bible. As much as I reveled in the success of *Richard III*, and no matter how many people considered it the finest of its time, to me it felt old-fashioned compared to *Prometheus*. Ludwig had the arrogance to see himself as a Prometheus, and with this ballet I was forced to see him in the same manner. Prometheus had ambition that made him into a God, because he used all of his power to create progress beyond description, a man filled with all kinds of fires. It was an enormous relief for me when Ludwig decided after rehearsing it that his Prometheus was not yet finished, and he revised it several more times before it premiered long after I had fled, in 1801, by which time I was far enough away for it not to affect me. Ludwig was, for me, an uncontrollable fire. For all I knew, that is who he was to everyone, even himself. In my final days in Vienna, I was consumed with fear that Ludwig might follow his ballet with a full-length opera on the subject, and follow it with all of kinds of Promethean themes: Zeus, Hercules, Atlas, or others, and I would be thought ever more old style by comparison, and comparison is what fed the Viennese public.

In my quietest moments, I felt I could hear a world of new operas by Ludwig, each of them better than mine. Besides Haydn I had never met another rival composer, and even with Haydn, were I to utter the truest truth of the confessional chamber, that as much as I loved him I was his musical superior. I had met musicians with gifts that felt unbelievable to me, as though they had been kissed by God himself, like Düssek. He was the great musician of my life. He could play absolutely anything he had ever seen written down or even just something he had heard once. He could improvise far beyond my own abilities, which were once considered fine enough to be heard by kings and emperors. Düssek had gifts at the keyboard far beyond the greatest of mine, and his compositions were wondrous. Düssek was born into a family with greater means than mine. I looked forward to seeing him in London, though I did not know then if he was still among the living. But even as great Düssek was, I did not fear him, perhaps because he was not present for the constantly gossiping Viennese. The world could easily house us both.

One truth had to be faced: Queen Charlotte wanted me in London by the summer of 1799 and found the way to get me there through Haydn. But I did not want to cross a sea, not even a small sea like *La Manche*, not even for the most prestigious post in the world. I did not want to leave Vienna and did not ever want to be so far from Salzburg, which I knew I could not live without seeing again even if I never wanted to live there again. The deepest desire of my heart was to stay in Vienna, for there was always a presence of Salzburg there; you could always sense it. I left for one reason only, a reason that by now you know: Ludwig. I am overflowing with shame even to admit it, most especially for reasons you do not yet know. Please have tolerance and mercy for me whenever I find the courage to tell you.

CHAPTER 21

At my farewell to my Vienna Masonic Lodge in February of 1799, some of my brothers told me that Ludwig had composed a *Konstanzetanz* to say farewell to *her*, not to me. I was shown a score. Ludwig had the courage to take notes directly from my old *Seraglio* in which I set to music her name, and he had turned the tune into some kind of beerhall ländler. He believed he was paying some manner of tribute to her when actually he was making fun of me in trying to woo her. *Woo* was a word I learned in London as a child, and I find it the best word of its kind. Konstanze was always susceptible to wooing, I knew, because I worked so often and she was constantly at home or tending to the publishing with Süssmayer. That shit butt, Süssie.

The first time I knew Süssmayer was with Konstanze was when I away in Praha the year before Franz was born. She was lonely and yearning for me, so for her to welcome the attentions of a man could be understood, even though the pain of my heart was the same as if I could not understand it at all. But now Ludwig was directly threatening to make advances on my own wife right under my own gaze. How many more humiliations could I have endured from this man? As if I needed further cause, I had to take Konstanze away from Vienna forever. I could not find words to explain that it was my boundless love for her that was pushing me to take her away to safety, for any words I found sounded like the simplest of professional jealousies and intrigues that happen in all theaters. This was something so much stronger than petty rivalry. Ludwig was a danger impossible to ignore, and it was impossible for me to remain where he could harm me.

These complex simplicities took root as they gnarled at everything I knew to be me, Amadé. Ludwig was throwing his unexplainable force in the direction of Konstanze, who in those days before we left Vienna had taken to crying after we took the pleasures of the flesh with each other. Little Franz had begun to experiment with tunes on the clavichord or the fortepiano, just days before they were to be locked away for unknown length of time. He played well, with the kind of talent I had hoped and expected to come from my son. But only two or three sunsets before we were to leave Vienna forever, the unbearable happened: without the benefit of a score, he improvised a tune of Ludwig's. How was he hearing these melodies long enough to remember them? I wondered if they were emanating from the streets or wafting out of open Viennese windows, as my melodies had once done. I had to wonder to God why my own son did not play music of mine, or of Düssek or Haydn or, better still, someone recently departed like Handel or one of the many Bachs. Why, of all music, did it have to be *his*?

Because I always knew things, I believe I knew what was looming inside of Ludwig before he did, as though an oracle had whispered it to me and asked me to protect it. There was some distant kind of image, similar to what I saw on the bridge in my sleeping hours, of Ludwig hearing sounds within his own ears that were not meant to be there, a music that only he heard, just as I knew things that others did not. There was a sound like a bee flying close to his ear, for in the image I could see the creature buzzing near him, irritating him, causing him to commit all manner of outbursts that he might have avoided without the nuisance. I wonder still if I was hearing what Ludwig was hearing, as though we shared some unearthly muse. It felt far too earthly for my own ease.

CHAPTER 22

I owe to a Masonic brother the respite from the pain and fear I felt in those years, for after hovering around the madness of Richard for so long I knew I needed a comedy, but one unlike any other I had written. A particular play, unknown to German speakers, had lingered in my memory for many years, as the laughter it had inspired in my youth when I was fortunate enough to attend it several times in Paris had continued through the many years since. Molière's magnificent *Tartuffe* would, I was sure, make a marvelous opera and I would surprise many with my first opera in the language of Gaul. I had acquired a copy of the play in my youth from a seller along the Seine, and I decided that since I was absent a French poet I could try my hand at arranging the text myself. I knew that much of *Tartuffe* must be ensembles, and that is always a difficulty for the poet, because characters rarely all think the same thing at once, but that problem was one I wanted to conquer with *Tartuffe*: to give each character a unique character but in ensemble. I intended no arias for my opera, as I thought it best for the great hypocrite Orgon to not be gifted with an aria, but eventually I surrendered and wrote for him perhaps the greatest aria I had written up to that time: "Oui, mon frère, je suis un méchant…" It eventually, in the long life and difficult birth of *Tartuffe*, garnered much applause, but it was not that of which I was most proud. Rather, I was proudest of my extended intricate ensembles. French operas of my experience, though there were many I was never allowed to know, did not at all relish that single most glorious thing about opera: many things can happen at once.

I had read *Tartuffe* dozens of times before I decided to write my opera, but I could not possibly have chosen a more inopportune time for this labor. I had longed for Emanuel to adapt the poetry, but not only was his French unequal to mine, but also by the time I was ready to write *Tartuffe* it was becoming clear to those who loved him that Emanuel was losing himself. In the days before our departure, Emanuel, dear Schiki, was irritable and morose in ways that he never had been before. By then I had known him for twenty years, and he was one of my closest and most treasured friends. We had all seen similar decline before with the older people, those who are allowed to live into their old age, and their later life is nothing like the simple pain allowed to most people. It is, rather, a slow death, a steady regression to infancy. I began to think it imperative to remove myself from Vienna, the city of afflictions: Ludwig's ears and Emanuel's everything. To have stayed in Vienna and watched Emanuel's hilarious, brilliant, and pure mind disintegrate into foolishness would be an unbearable grief. My sweet Papageno caged forever in a madhouse was but another reason to escape. It didn't occur to me until recently, when I reached my own old age, that Schiki might have needed me to help him.

Lorenzo, my endless Da Ponte, was forever on the run from the order of the world. He simply could not accept life as it was given to him. He had to fight. Lorenzo never once gave me a verse for an opera that did not immediately generate music in my mind. He was devoted to rhyming Italian couplets, for which I was always grateful, for his rhymes practically wrote their own notes. He was unique among all poets in knowing the direction of music without being able to match a pitch himself. Lorenzo resisted every law, every monarch, and every attempt to monitor the morality of people's actions, if not their words. He never accepted the aristocracy that made his deepest passions even possible. Joseph II understood us both, for he had an artist's soul. But with Joseph gone, Lorenzo lost his own way, and I had to be sure his path was not mine.

I do not know what force took possession of me, but I set to work on *Tartuffe* with incredible fury and inner fire, both of which infuriated

Konstanze, who needed my help in getting our household ready to leave Vienna. I decided that I wanted to arrive in Paris with a completed opera in their native language, and Konstanze knew as well as I that once a decision like that is made, there is no returning from it. In our younger life together, Konstanze had greeted each of my ideas with smiles and admiration. In those final Viennese days, though, not a single idea I ever confided in her elicited anything but exasperated sighs. The very secrets that I portrayed to her in our earlier years she now dismissed as nonsense. For Konstanze, I had stretched my music and thus myself too far. She said I was obviously trying to "keep up with Ludwig," and that the people who loved my music when I was young were left with little choice but to move their loyalties to one or the other of us. These words hurt me much as they emerged from her. They still do.

And when she said, "Would Haydn, Beethoven, Salieri, or even Düssek, not to mention Simone Mayr…would any of them waste their time on such an unworthy project as Molière's *Tartuffe?*" I realized that all of our years together had been considered a folly by own wife. Konstanze, my most constant supporter, thought one of the passions of my life to be completely absurd.

Despite her feelings, I marked my copy of *Tartuffe* and began fashioning the poem for the opera. Konstanze had paid for the carriage ride to Paris from the most noted *fiaker* in Vienna, and the journey would last at least four weeks, depending on weather. Our four coaches were to join the regular caravans that traveled westward from Vienna on any morning. The two children would stay with me and Konstanze in the most comfortable coach, though it was the smallest. The large coaches were laden with our trunks, as Konstanze seemed determined that anything we enjoyed in Vienna had to accompany us to London, as though the luxury that would be greeting us in London was a fairy tale. Konstanze was meticulous about all my of my music, and she spent days packing it away, a tedium I could never have endured. She knew I desired many of my operas, symphonies, concertos, and chamber music in London, and she knew which of them had already been printed in London and so would not be necessary to bring with us. She worked for weeks to get the materials collected and packed and wrapped in boxes that limited their danger from rain or whatever else we might encounter. Although I desired to help her, my spirit would not allow me to do anything except compose *Tartuffe*, night and day. It had to be mined from me at that moment, to Konstanze's justifiable frustration. She needed my help, but I was incapable of giving it.

Konstanze was never shy about expressing her fear and frustration that the journey could take longer if I insisted on writing an opera. Many times a day she would ask, "Why can you not wait for us to get to Paris?" I had no answer. Whatever were my passions, Konstanze found a way to make them into demanding distractions, particularly as the date of our departure neared. She knew me well enough to expect that if I insisted on composing an opera during our journey, we would be unpredictably delayed while I rid myself of ideas at the end of each day's travel. How, my treasured reader, could I ever forgive myself for the way I treated Konstanze? She tried always to find the most gracious accommodations and quiet places for me to work whenever we were traveling, and she took care of everything.

CHAPTER 23

Weather, of course, was the great unpredictable element of travel, and wet weather could easily delay any journey by weeks, but Konstanze took all possibilities into consideration. She hired the best coachmen, and the best coachmen could predict the following day's weather, and often take the best alternate route, but much about travel cannot be known until undertaking it.

Konstanze was always interested in my works, but not *Tartuffe*, to which she paid no attention. I kept my feelings in for many days, but finally I could not hold back.

"You were so excited about *Richard III*. What has happened?" I asked her.

She looked to be considering her words, but then they poured forth. "You take too many chances, Wolfie!" She only used *Wolfgang* or *Wolfie* when angry, for otherwise I was her *Ami*. "You are gambling everything every time! What if *Richard III* had not been successful? We would be ruined. You are giving up so much security for this frivolous journey."

Frivolous. Konstanze thought the most honored musical post in the most powerful court in the known world was frivolous. I reminded her that we would be living in a palace, that London would be a place of freedom and ideas and great energy. I tried to joke with her that London was not stuck in its old ways like Vienna. I said that if people gossiped about us in London, our English would not be good enough to notice, trying to get her to join in my laughter. She held silent. I told her I wanted to see London again, to relive my childhood, and to share it with her and little Franz.

As our departure approached, Karl Thomas, nearly fifteen in those months, refused to join us, wanting instead to stay with his Aunt Aloysia to help her keep our publishing enterprise alive. Konstanze thought him far too young to stay without us, but he was a mature boy and by the time I was his age I was writing operas and about to take my first trip to the Italian peninsula. I wanted him to have the life he wanted. He was a talented musician, but by his nature he was going to be a businessman. If, after a year or so, he was unhappy in any way, I assured Konstanze he could join us in London if he wanted.

Konstanze said that if I wanted to return to my childhood, we should return to Salzburg. We had the same conversation a thousand times. Salzburg held nothing for me, and my finest memories of childhood were from my family's travels outside of it. Moving back to Salzburg would have meant a forced return to the cathedral to beg for mercy for my earlier actions. She said again that I did not understand her.

This was the truth; I did not understand her. She also did not understand me. But none of this felt strange, for I did not understand myself in those years, either. For those frenzied weeks I knew only *Tartuffe*. My every waking moment was *Tartuffe,* which at first reminded me very much of *Figaro*, but it gave me opportunity to have fun with church music. I could even finally make humor from my own mass of thanks, and the third and most popular mass in C minor that I had finally been able to finish at St. Stephen's. Whenever Tartuffe put on his fake religious piety to fool Orgon and his family, I could reference a different one of my own masses.

I understood Tartuffe and his hypocrisy. I was in the employ of a great cathedral where I saw much hypocrisy. I lived it, too, in expecting so much of Konstanze while not holding the same responsibility for myself. I had many occasions to visit the special confessional reserved for servants of the church. It had no grill of anonymity. One walked into the small room at almost any time of day and there he was, the confessor, lit only by candlelight, nothing visible in the room but a crucifix.

I grew to love my confessor as well as his promised liberation. But though I know it is a blasphemy, I detested the crucifix. The constant reminder of such pain and cruelty was not, for me, a call to piety. It is naturally our duty to remember the agony of the suffering Christ, but I did this with each waking and sleeping prayer. Must this anguish of *one* life be emblazoned everywhere, as though the worlds' suffering did not continue? What of the countless who have suffered just as grievously but who are never known? I must wonder now at the end of my long life who has been saved by this savior? I believe profoundly in God and pray to him twice daily just as I was taught as a boy, and we raised Karl Thomas and Franz to do the same. But each time I endured the confessional, there was the torment of man's cruelty to greet me, dwarfing any trouble in my own heart, touching me equally each time, drawing me ever toward it, and despoiling my desire for forgiveness. This is a grave sin to face as I near my Creator, but there it is. I have never understood the intemperance of these feelings.

In spite of this grievous fault, I would confess my transgressions, nearly all of which were thoughts of lust or their indulgence. I had been told I should write down my sins, but I was certain such a book might someday be found, either by Konstanze or others, and I could not have the entirety of my own depravities laid bare. Would people not then find in me the very hypocrisy they sought? What would my enemies make of a list of lusts from the man who conceived *Ave verum corpus* and masses that symbolized the most devout thoughts of the whole world? Instead, I dutifully confessed every fornication, every fantasy, every kiss, every flirtation, to the confessor I loved, all in the presence of that horrible invigilating cross. I had been saved from dying, and I still pray each day for the woman who mysteriously exchanged her life for mine.

For *Tartuffe* I wrote some of the liveliest music I had conceived in years, and the fleetest. Some of my music was a labor, but many works, and certainly *Tartuffe*, began with me singing a few lines aloud and within moments the vibrations would come. I can only describe this as a vibration, one less violent than the shaking of the ground I'd felt in Napoli as a child but kindred to that. There was a never-ending oscillation going on somewhere, I have never learned where, and when I composed I simply joined it. A quiet room was best, but in truth I did not require silence or inspiration. I only needed time. Composing takes vast amounts of time, but once inside the pulsation there is no stopping it.

Tartuffe demanded all of my time, but I did manage to move my personal papers from St. Stephen's, and there was even a small mass of thanksgiving for my departure, during which the chorus and orchestra, each of them closely chosen by me over those years, sang a movement of my *Dankenmesse*. The Archbishop, in his only words of German in the service, said that "Herr Mozart had been given great gifts that he has shared in his own thanks to the Lord, and may he continue to thank and praise his Creator as he embarks on this new journey."

Following the mass, the organists and other choir masters took me to a café where we all shared in beer. I was very moved that that someone had taken advance notice and had me served nockerl, which I had not tasted since I was a boy in Salzburg. I had never known it to be made in Vienna, and I thought Konstanze had perhaps provided this idea for the party but she said she had not. Oh, to taste that sweet and airy soufflé again! Father used to only allow us to have it once a year.

CHAPTER 24

My years at St. Stephen's were a manifold and now a convoluted time to remember. I had greatly needed the structure and security of the position at the time I accepted it. My finances were in shambles in the months leading up to *The Magic Flute*, and after my illness I was in even more danger. The cathedral brought my life back to stability, something that would have been impossible without the organized anatomy of St. Stephen's.

But I never fully felt a part of it, either. Just as I had felt in Salzburg, whatever bonds were imposed by the needs of the cathedral weighed on me and constantly interrupted what I felt to be the work of my life. I loved to work all day, from shortly after waking until the quill dropped from my exhausted hand. But the interruptions at the cathedral were constant. I resented eating and shitting, for each was necessary but they took so much time. Shitting required me to be alone and naked in the water closet, itself dark and small, and cleaning up took many minutes: washing and drying my whole behind, disposing of the chamber pot, trying not to let Konstanze see or smell its contents, and placing outside the rags we used to clean after our evacuations, where they could be cleaned by our only remaining employee, a chambermaid who mainly helped Konstanze with little Franz. It was always so mortifying.

It caused me horrible embarrassment that our chambermaid knew what my insides smelled of. Shit was an enormous distraction during my whole life, and also a great fear, for I suffered from a terrible stomach for all of my days until I reached old age. I always tried to make jokes of my fears, especially shit and piss, but really, I resented bodily functions because they frightened me. Dear reader, that night with the gypsy woman, that distant December night I'd felt like my very soul was coming out of my bung hole, and ever since that night I have had terrible daily fears of my own functions.

But the other distractions, though not scary, were just as irritating and disruptive. There were constant meetings at St. Stephen's, constant pressures as to the nature of their daily services, what kind of music should be played and who should play it. There was canonical law that needed monitoring and adherence, and the musical selections had to support and reflect it. Rounding up the musicians was a constant job, as they were scattered around Vienna, so any irregularity in the schedule caused pandemonium. There were illnesses and substitutions, and a set of rivalries among my fellow organists that made opera houses look stable by comparison. How was it that organists were uniquely interested and immersed in intrigue and gossip? Was there something inherent in the art, in a single musician holding within his own power such a vast amount of sound, that made him ambitious and vicious? Even my dealings with jealous sopranos were petty compared to the warfare of the organists, and this, too, was a distraction to which I was ready and happy to say farewell. I long ago conceived but never composed my own *Abschied Symphonie*, a comic one, in which the organ is prominently featured.

The overture to *Tartuffe* was a broad inversion of *Figaro*, beginning with grand announcing chords in D major, followed by page after page of scampering music. Perhaps only Ludwig would ever notice that I was taking the *Figaro* overture and playing most of it backward and upside down, just as *Tartuffe* himself was duplicitous and scheming. I changed many things in this inversion process, but I did want the overture to wind down to something quiet, and to segue directly into an opening scene on the organ, played offstage by a character named Orgon! This was most innovative for the time, though now everyone seems to invert everything.

CHAPTER 25

Excited about London, I was also eager to see Paris again, and to visit the royal palaces I'd known so well as a child. I read in several books that I played with the future Queen of France, Marie Antoinette, at an age when we were both happily unaware of class and royalty. She was a child like me, in Vienna, though she lived at the Hapsburg Court while Papa and I were in a dark and small *pensione*. I slipped and fell right into her lap, declaring that I would someday marry her. I had never uttered a word I did not feel to be completely true, so I must confess that I harbored affection for her for all those many years, sure that my own fame would one day lead me back to her. I had a clear image of myself as the royal consort of Austria, and thus a member of the royal house hiring my own court composer. I'd known that Marie was destined to a luxury I would never know, though at the age we met I could not fully comprehend how utterly different our lives would be. A monarch has so distant an idea of how their subjects live that I am sure the opposite must also be true.

Many years later, hearing of Marie's vehement opposition to Beaumarchais's *Figaro*, which she thought dangerous and subversive, I wondered how she could possibly be the same little girl with whom I played as a child in Vienna. What happened to that girl? How had *she* traveled to Paris? In what luxurious set of coaches was she ensconced in the royal entourage, traveling from castle to castle with great ease, and arriving in Paris to a parade, celebratory masses, and fireworks, consuming every imaginable type of delicacy at day after day of feast to commemorate her arrival? I often wondered if she recalled me at all, particularly after I had the audacity to turn *Figaro* into an opera. Would she ever have considered receiving me again, so that I might sing parts of *Figaro* to her, so that I might explain to her in person why I found the play so compelling, and why those characters so appealed to me? What had happened to the little girl to make her the object of so much hatred? What forces had gathered around her that she could not control? I read about how deeply the people of France hated her, as though she had infiltrated from Austria and infested France with a pestilence. I wondered how different Paris might seem.

Marie surely could not have turned so far from her mother, Marie Therese, one of the kindest women I ever encountered. The French, apparently, thought Marie uneducated and gauche, and from what I read in the Viennese pamphlets, Marie had reacted badly against the high courtly manners of the French ruling classes, yet I knew Marie to be a champion of the poor because I was poor myself. It seemed she had been condemned before she'd been tried, and well before the Bastille had been stormed and her head removed. She had, I felt sure, been the subject of such jealousy and calumny that it wouldn't have mattered what she did. I longed to ask Lorenzo if it was somehow possible that Marie was a puppet, that she had been placed within France to set it into decline and make it vulnerable to Austrian expansion. She was blamed for debt, but she was not responsible for so much spending. How could she? A jury had found her guilty of treason, and I always struggled with the memory of knowing her and the reality of what she'd seemed as a child. In those frightening days, as we were leaving Vienna for the last time, could the same kind of trickery be foisted upon me?

Lorenzo had a way of talking about these complicated political situations that helped me understand intrigues and politics. Lorenzo seemed able to view life all at once as it was happening, as if from a mountaintop. Though I knew things others didn't, I could never see the happenings of courts accurately until years later, upon reflection. It always surprised me when someone within the court spread some lie about me, and this problem was also terrible within the two cathedrals where I had long employments. It was painful to be defined, and because I lived long enough to hear what others thought of me, I can say that few people knew me well. Ludwig constantly spread a vista of me that wasn't true, but truth made no matter in the Vienna of those years, which seemed all too ready to believe the most outlandish rumors.

All of those irritants could be laughed at in *Tartuffe*, and as I was composing there were moments when I had to stop and roar with laughter, not at my own creation, but at Molière's brilliant depictions of hypocrisy. I assumed that the Paris we were going to enter within a few weeks would welcome this new comic opera.

For days our belongings were loaded into the four carriages, all while saving room for our three bodies to travel in as much comfort as possible for the many days ahead of us. There was no way to know in advance where we would arrive at the end of each day. The driver had to weigh the sunset with finding an inn for us to spend for at least a night, sometimes more if the horses needed more rest or if the carriage needed repair. Konstanze was highly involved in the selection of inns. At each stop I worked more on *Tartuffe*, and Konstanze generally took Franz for a walk around whatever little town the coachman chose for us. There were no large cities on our journey between Vienna and Paris, as the coachman preferred routes that kept us on rural paths, thinking it more efficient. In earlier travels with Papa, we nearly always stayed in cities, for in the cities we had a chance for audiences at spontaneous concerts and often our income from those concerts was considerable.

My father twice organized concert tours during my childhood, concerts that revolved around palaces within courts, or at the magnificent homes of relatives of the monarch. This meant we had to arrive in precise places at precise times, making much of our travel arduous, leaving me often tired and vulnerable to fevers. Many times we did not have opportunity to eat properly. I was determined that my own wife and son would not travel in a way that exhausted them. If we made only a few kilometers a day but were able to stay in nice inns, as long as I had a desk on which to write, I would be satisfied. If the journey took a month or more, so be it. Konstanze, ever frugal, wanted to get to Paris as soon as possible, hoping that our expenses would be accepted by the royal court. Little did we know what awaited us.

I had never seen or felt a revolution, except through the eyes and ears of others, so how I might have my music played in Paris was then a mystery, as I was certain that Paris was much changed from my youth. I hoped to convince some of the great Paris churches and cathedrals to play my masses, but I was unsure how we might make money from such performances. Everything would depend on my visit with the palace upon arrival.

The day of departure finally arrived, and the coachman brought the horses. We said farewell to Aloysia and our dear boy Karl, who both wept when the horses came. My tears were uncontrollable, as I had to face that I might never see my little Karl again. Franz was still too young to fully realize what the journey was going to mean for him. We all knew, though no one said it aloud, that none of us would ever return to Vienna.

My mind was already in Paris, where my first errand would be to the office near the Tuileries, arranging our passage to England. I would take Franz with me to give him some sense of the scope of our journey. If I could get the boy to realize the distances we had traveled, he would most likely not want to return. In Franz I saw myself as though no time had passed, as though I were still a child of his age. He was the same size I had been when we first visited the royal courts of Vienna, where I had played my own compositions and had improvised for great lengths of time, making everyone laugh and keeping everyone aghast. The time had come to say farewell to that, and I held my boy as I watched another. We were ready to depart as I apparently fell into a small trance.

CHAPTER 26

Music should always present a balance, for there is such a thing as music being too expressive. Departing Vienna caused us all to pour tears. So much music appeared in my mind that day, music that tempered my sadness, and music that was never an invitation to excess. Though Konstanze had dealt with almost all of the packing herself, one of the notebooks I discovered had sat unopened since the mid-1760s at least, a set of sketches I'd made in London as a child, and I thought it would be nice to take them back to where they started. I'd often recalled them, those little fragments of ideas, some of which I had used in other pieces, but much of which I'd forgotten. I vowed not to look at them again until I slept a night in London. They were my assurance that I would return, a set of gifts to myself from a distant past.

My dream was to return to one of London's beautiful gardens that are spread across the city, and on a lovely summer day open my long-closed folio and hear the blusterings of my seven-year-old self. I imagined I would be ashamed of my simplicities. I wanted to play them for Franz, perhaps translating them in some way that allowed them to become his. I longed for Franz to take his musical studies more seriously, as he had a compositional mind. I had heard him improvise when he didn't know I was listening. Franz had a gift for trills between second and third fingers on the clavichord, and often he would do them in sequences that impressed me enormously, as I had been several years his senior before I could accomplish the same. He could do second- and third-finger trills in many keys on both hands moving in opposite directions at great speeds. But then Franz could do something even more impressive: parallel motion with the third finger in the right hand imitating the second in the right, and he could keep these perfectly coordinated trills going for sometimes three octaves, something I had never been able to do, though many of my concertos demand the skill. I had once achieved it in improvisation during the C-minor concerto. I tried it again after hearing little Franz do it, and I realized anew just how challenging it is. I decided to write a short piece, an opening of a new piano sonata that would feature Franz's unique abilities, and hope that a new work just for him would inspire him to continue his musical studies. It worked.

Early memories of London were melded into memories of Johann Christian Bach, the Music Master to Queen Charlotte years before, nearly forty of them, in London, when we played clavichords together at Hanover Square. J.C. was a second father who showed me many ideas in London and divulged many shortcuts. So much could be learned just from noticing the light in a room, especially a room with someone like J.C. within it. The light is never the same, moment to moment, as it is always shifting the mood, playing with the air itself, revealing something while concealing something else. Light is everything.

I had never been able to hear Ludwig improvise, and I was always frustrated by that, but I could not bring myself to be seen in the salons where he played. I wanted to hear Ludwig improvise because of what Haydn had said about the effect of it, that you could "tell the weather from it, as from the slightest shift in light." I love ingenious improvisation at the keyboard precisely because it could never be written down. Like those images that come in our sleeping moments, one most often remembers the mood more than the dream itself.

J.C. taught me to take music and toy with it, turn it over, play it backward. Groups of notes delighted in doing certain things with one another, events predetermined by the music's science but which can only be found by an artist, by a composer. The real composers, as Haydn taught, would never exhaust their ideas because their ideas existed already somewhere just beyond us, and composers alone had the ability to pull those thoughts back into a human realm. No one is precisely sure how this happens, but compositions are proof that it does. I always assumed that the church had some answer for this unexplainable phenomenon, and I was happy to trust in them for as long as my powers held. As a young man, I thought perhaps God had gifted me and a few others with this rare skill, but I knew that was the extent of the gift, and the rest was left to hard work and diligence.

It has always troubled me that I did not turn to God on that December night when I neared death. At that time I was fulfilling a commission for a requiem, and was linked to its devotion; but when I actually felt the life flowing out of me, I did not ask for God's help and would always wonder why. The guilt followed me and multiplied.

Impatience was my greatest flaw, according to my father, yet both Emanuel and J.C. Bach had told me the opposite, that impatience was the greatest part of my gift. J.C. said impatience is what helps us fully develop a theme and fill out a sonata movement, or to create tension in a symphony that must be released. Emanuel added that a patient person can never be a musician, because nothing of worth is created calmly. He always pointed to great storms, or the shaking of the earth, or the huge eruptions from volcanoes, as proof of the Earth's volatile creative energies. I privately thought it must be some type of blasphemy to credit the Earth with having created itself, as Emanuel claimed. Surely God placed the volcanoes where they were, and it was God who summoned the storms; that was what I had always believed, but I knew that belief was divergent from knowing. In those early years, I believed God had created everything in the world, that He had created both the world and its own need for itself. I believed that God was responsible for those fragments of creation that were always just out of reach for me, like the air at the highest places I have ever been around Salzburg. There seemed to be less air on the mountaintop but the hand of God was more visible up there. I believed these things, even as I also knew them not to be true, which created no end of struggle within me as I lived longer and longer. Men did not emulate God; they emulated other men. And men did not create; they were given access to a place of purity, a seemingly calm place in the mind that sits on the edge of a giant and dangerous cauldron, a place I hoped never to see.

In the weeks, often months, of my joyous times, I existed within a calm and peaceful place, safe from everything, and it was a place of nearly unbearable beauty. But in my opposing weeks, when no joy was to be found anywhere, I glimpsed a cauldron. It seemed to be just out of sight, just over the bridge, but I could sometimes smell it, and I would turn corners with fear in Vienna, terrified that it might have opened up near me, waiting to swallow me whole. I was ready to leave the crowds of Vienna, and the endless buildings inside its walls, because of my fear of the far side of the bridge. Joy was my natural state, the place from where *Tartuffe* would finish itself; but as we left Vienna, I felt a potentiality for a joyless time arriving, and it frightened me that the carriage was about to leave without my knowing which side I might be on.

CHAPTER 27

K onstanze shook me, telling me I had been in a kind of trance and she had been trying to wake me for many minutes.

"The carriage is ready and we must go!"

I thought we had already departed, so I had indeed gone into a type of spell. I boarded the carriage and Franz moved immediately to my lap, just as I had imagined in my trance. The day was beautiful and the weather perfect. It was February 28, 1799. I shall never forget it.

"We might be able to get near Linz on a day like this," the coachman said, with an accent like the Romaní woman. I thought it impossible to reach Linz in the span of a day, but my heart quickened hearing the name, bringing to mind my two symphonies, in C major and the more recent one in A major, which I believe counted as my fifty-fifth, which both owed their vital lives to Linz. I quickly toured through the themes of all eight movements.

Aloysia and Karl had gone inside, sobbing. With no ceremony at all, the coach pulled away. This was no trance. We were leaving Vienna. I turned to see our house for the last time. I expected a flood of emotions but all I felt was relief. To finally place the burden of Vienna behind me, to never see Ludwig again, to see so many of my childhood cities again, all authored new joy. Franz and Konstanze both bobbed with sleep despite the uneven road before we even reached the outer boundary of Vienna.

The fair portion of an hour had passed when the coachman slowed the horses and quietly told us to be cautious. A single rider was chasing us. I had traveled enough to know this was most unusual. Horses did not chase carriages unless we were to be robbed, or unless someone had been promised a great deal of money to find a specific person within a coach to deliver something vital.

"Herr Mozart! Herr Mozart!" the horseman shouted, riding alongside our carriage. I instructed the coachman to stop for the man. We were still so close to Vienna that I saw no cause to fear robbery. Konstanze took Franz and made her disapproval known, though thankfully the coachman only paid attention to me. I stepped out of the carriage to ask the man why he had pursued us.

"I have a letter for you, Herr Mozart."

I think now that I already knew the answer, but I still asked him, "From whom?"

"From Herr Beethoven. He'd hoped to get it to you before you left, but when he was unable, he made me ride as fast as possible to find you. Herr Beethoven guessed your route."

I found this very suspicious, and it occurred to me that Konstanze had told him our route. And if it was so important, why had not Ludwig made his way to our home in time?

I gave the man a few coins for his tenacity, then took the letter, sealed with wax, and placed it into one of my trunks. I did not want to read it at that moment, nor did I want Ludwig anywhere near my memories of leaving Vienna. The carriage resumed. Konstanze begged me to open it, as she thought it must contain information of import. She said it might contain news of a position in Vienna, or Ludwig might need help, or Haydn might be dead. Emanuel was in precarious condition, too, and the letter might contain news of him. How, she nearly shouted, could I not even look at it?

I was not quick to anger, but it infuriated me that Ludwig had taken this absurd step to contact me and steal my farewell to Vienna. He had long known we were leaving and on what precise date. Haydn must have told him all, and they lived in proximity to each other, rather far from us. There was no reason I could not have been contacted earlier without the wild theatrics. It was Ludwig overdoing everything again. I decided to keep the letter unopened for a few days at least, and find the right moment to turn my attention to whatever Ludwig considered so important. Perhaps in Paris, I thought.

Several hours later, while watering the horses, the coachman confessed that he had been too optimistic about making it all the way to Linz in a single day, which would have put us halfway to Salzburg, but I had firmly put the coachman onto a more northerly route that would avoid my hometown altogether. There were far too many memories there, things that I did not want resurrected. I did not want to get sight of the mountains, nor did I want to get stuck for too many days on a journey that was going to require many weeks even in good weather. The letter from Ludwig had set my mind spiraling toward my natural opposite, and I developed a genuine fear of a slump in my spirits as we pulled into Sankt Pölten for what I assumed would be a single night. The horses needed rest. The local inn was lovely, and after a short settling, Konstanze took Franz for a walk. I took out my folio to concentrate on *Tartuffe*, picking up precisely where I had stopped the day before. The endless distractions during the journey meant my mental writing, the "time in the noodle," had been less and so I had frustratingly little I could actually write down.

Konstanze, always quick to accustom herself to routines, allowed us only one night in Sankt Pölten, insisting we move on immediately, "especially when the weather is so generous," and so the following day took us fully through Linz to an inn just beyond it, and our travel pattern was established. Only at Speyer, near Mannheim, would Konstanze countenance a long rest, and in the three nights at the inn there, I finished the fair copy of *Tartuffe*, which I thought I might be able to have plated in a new process I had heard was being innovated in Paris. Haydn had mentioned this new type of copying, and I hoped all of my French words had been copied down correctly, but a French copyist would catch any errors. It was so consumptive of time to pore over scores I had long finished to see if there were errors. I hated that kind of work, so I hoped to find someone in Paris or London who was happy with such tedium.

Having completed *Tartuffe* and while our journey was under way out of Mannheim, I tried to create a jumble of ideas, but travel disrupted many of them. Most of the burgs where we stopped seemed so quiet on their surfaces, but I could feel vast stirrings coming from them, could feel the grandeur of so many emotions and dreams. I remembered the feeling from childhood, that it was not only Vienna and London which needed music, it was everyone, but only the large cities with monarchs could afford it. What did they all do in Neuberg, Hohenfels, Rosstal, or Wolpertshausen? They, too, felt the great arousals of the characters in *Tartuffe*, the great need to expose a hypocrite and hand him a comeuppance. They, too, felt the great call of peace at the end of *Figaro*, the transformative power of any level of forgiveness. My ideas stayed stubbornly within me as we left Speyer, as well as during our nights in Kaiserlautern, Waldmohr, Sulzbach, and Saarbrücken. I cannot remember all of the little towns, though as a child I could always remember every name, marking them down in my copybook. In this trip to Paris as a man, with my own young son in tow, I could not remember.

After *Tartuffe* was completed, I did not write another note on the journey. I felt a dark spell coming upon me. From Speyer to Paris I was silent, my inner voices mute. It seemed the journey would never end. I remember asking the coachman, "Is Paris still out there somewhere? Have they finally dispensed with it?" and I laughed, even though my voice was despairing. Our last stop overnight was in Meaux, after days of trekking endlessly through the forest of Montceaux, and we made it into Paris the following afternoon. I could not bear to think of how many days we had been in our carriage, but the journey took the month the coachman had warned it would. We arrived on the first day of April, 1799.

The accommodations arranged for us by Haydn were near the beautiful old church of St. Sulpice, and they were considerably smaller and less comfortable than promised. I felt a valley approaching, the precipice that sometimes visited me in dreams, and I smelled the cauldron. I wanted to make my way to the palace and arrange our journey to England, but I was so weary from travel that I had to lie down. From the moment I set my head to the pillow, a tide of grief cracked open in me. I had feared it, but I had hoped *Tartuffe* could keep it at bay. By that point *Tartuffe* was obviously gone, finished, tucked away in a folio. However much I told myself I could keep it away, Paris was full of grief. Konstanze could not, would not, understand why I was lying on a bed crying like a child, and in front of our own son. She admonished me, then she expressed concern, wondering if perhaps I was actually in pain. She had a complex gentleness.

Indeed I was in pain, I told her, but it was not a pain she could understand and it was all the more profound because it caught me by surprise. Suddenly seeing Paris again made me feel that no time had passed since Mama had died there, yet it had been well over ten years. She was lying in a Paris cemetery, far from everyone she had ever known, but was at that moment very close to me. How could I not have realized that this terrible grief had been within me all the while, and the smell of Paris had revived it, like All Soul's Day? Unlike *Allerseelen*, though, this felt like something that might never pass, a heavy stone I had been handed with no choice but to carry it. Grief for my wonderful and sainted mother brought grief about my dear sister Maria Anna, always known to me as Nannerl, to whom I had not spoken since Leopold died. Nannerl was alive in Salzburg but I had avoided visiting her, for to me she had chosen to be as dead as our own mother, Anna Maria, after whom my dear sister had been named. Twin griefs appeared at once and gripped me, leaving me helplessly unaware of anything else. Having been so alive to returning to Paris, I quickly felt dead, and I wanted more than anything to get out of there.

CHAPTER 28

S o many years before, Mama had traveled with me to Augsburg both
to visit Papa's family and to seek a job. After many happy weeks in
Mannheim together, we finally entered Paris. In Mannheim, we had
enjoyed many meals and concerts together, more than at any other time
we had shared. Anna Maria, my dear Mama, as I always called her, seemed
to put herself away in a drawer in Papa's presence, rarely raising her voice
and even more rarely raising an objection. Of course she doted on us,
because she had so often known the unbelievable pain of watching life
leave an infant, a type of grief greatly multiplied by the silence of everyone
about it, and forever after. But the lashes of grief for Mama never lost
their force. Few days passed when she did not intone the names of each
of her children, not only her Amadé and Nannerl, but also the five souls
not allowed to arrive.

My eldest brother was Johann Leopold, who had lived just over five
sickly months while Mama was with child with the first of three Maria
Annas, only the third of whom would live, the first expiring within days
and the second allowed only two months before Nannerl was blessed
with life. They tried the name of Johann on their fifth child, Johann Karl
Amadeus, only to have him quickly taken; and it seemed all life was going
to leave both mother and child during the birth of their last Johann, me,
Mama's most adored Johann Chrysostomas Wolfgang Amadeus, but we
both survived. Mama always called me Wolfgang, though everyone else
called me my preferred name, the less formal Amadé. To be called Johann

would have brought Mama too much pain, and my other names were simply too long. Mama said she could tell from her confinement which of the children would live, but that never lessened her pain. She thought as though they had all grown to adulthood, and she imagined full lives for all of them, complete with spouses and grandchildren on whom she could lavish attention and gifts.

She loved to tell about the midwife on the night I was born, who severed my cord from Mama, but the egg in which I had lived within her had not come into life with me. The midwife explained that it would have to be removed from her or she could die. The midwife summoned a doctor. I had sprung into life and my cries were already filling the house. But Mama was floating between life and death, and the pain was so extraordinary on her life side that she felt she should cross over, but my crying kept calling her back. She said it sounded like I was calling her name. The doctor arrived to remove the egg barrier from her, which required him to enter her womb with his own hand only hours after giving birth, itself only occurring after many days of effort and labor by the midwife. Mama's body had convulsed for days as I tried to move from her into life. When I think of my life almost taking hers, I feel grateful to not have borne the pain of that through my long life.

Mama told me that on that night she had prayed to the image of the crucified Christ as I was being born, sure that she felt a similar kind of tortured pain, and she then prayed for the forgiveness of her blasphemy. She said the midwife tried to prepare her for the doctor with a strong brandy wine, hoping she might drink enough to forestall the pain to which the malady had consigned her. It is horrible to think of my own mother in such pain simply to bring me into the world. The affliction must have been beyond what a person could bear, yet she often told me her only worry was that I should have a peaceful passage into the world. Only on the night of her death did my dear mother tell me of the gentle Romaní woman who was her midwife at my birth, the woman to whom she owed all. She had often mentioned a midwife, but never this extremely important detail, not even while we traveled together to Mannheim in that golden year of 1778 when we told each other so much. Had I known of the Romaní woman, I might have faced my own encounter with death with less fear.

How could I not have noticed until the moment of laying this quill to paper that both my mother and I had been saved by gypsies? The Romaní people were everywhere in Vienna and Praha, doing the work that others were too proud for. Is there a large collection of people anywhere who could survive without them? I grew up being taught they were thieving and dark people who were never to be trusted, especially with children. I have not only to wonder of the origins of these legends, I also must turn that wonder to myself and why I believed such foolishness for so long. I have multiple gratitudes, for had a Romaní woman not intervened in my mother's life, it would be apparent to the gravest fool that *my* life would have been impossible. I owe everything to the Romaní, yet they are reviled and treated with the worst kinds of indignity.

My mother spoke often of the hardship of my journey into the world, yet how deeply did I hear more than just her words? Do sons simply never view their mothers as fully real? She was confessing to me the great tender secrets of her heart, thoughts secluded deep within her that she probably did not even share with Papa. She told me these things not to engender guilt, but to give me an understanding of the nature of her love, and how joyous she always was that I survived the most difficult moment of life: its beginning. She wanted me to understand how miraculous my birth was, and thus how miraculous all birth is. I have learned this myself over great lengths of time, yet my dear mother tried to allow me to understand it sooner, to increase life's joy and the cherishing of a miracle, yet I did not hear her. I know there is no greater moment of love between two people than the moment of conception, and I have unquestionably tried to have as many of those moments as would be allowed me. But the profoundest love of all is between our Creator and a baby entering the world, for never is life more vulnerable.

CHAPTER 29

A man's burst of life, for it has no name that I have ever learned, is surely one of life's fullest feelings. My father, dear Papa, used to claim that I lacked the golden mean, that ability to balance the intellect and the emotions. I have become comfortable with my quill, you see, and perhaps I have had a second whiskey, or perhaps there is just a liberation that arrives with the crown of age, but I must say a word about that which is never spoken, for if art is ever to advance, these things must be said by someone. Every man of a certain kind of feeling, you see, believes that if such things are spoken aloud they might become endangered. These feelings exist on many levels, the most surface of which is the physical. There arrives a moment of breaking, when a man accustomed to control can no longer govern the spasms of his body. The sensations at that moment seem to be arriving from elsewhere, outside the body, and touch us with tendrils we cannot name or see. When the moment arrives, the moment over which we have no control, I feel an instinctive, possibly primal, need to bury myself within a woman so that I can feel as much of her body as possible wrapped around the symbol of all that is me. I love more than any sensation seeing her eyes at this cherished and sacred moment, feeling that I am claiming her as mine alone. That she has allowed me inside of her at all is miraculous, and that we can also pretend for a few private moments that I have dominated her is perhaps the greatest wonder of all.

But the sensations beyond the body are the most profound. Our souls float in clouds of infinity that briefly touch in the moment of our highest emotion, as our bodies are reaching a peak of pleasure that authorities ask us to pretend is not pleasurable. History tells the story of our work, but our lives are utterly absorbed in searching for the moments of transcendent physical pleasure that we hope will continue their pathway into our creations. Mama described my birth to me as though she had not been there at all. All over the world that I have seen, I have tried to walk through the permanence of cemeteries, and many of them are beautiful indeed. I notice that cemeteries are filled with infants, and in many years they overflow with little souls who were never allowed entrance into the work of life. Until we visited Mannheim together, Anna Maria Mozart had only been my mother, she was not also a woman who had lived a life before I existed. Everyone is one mother's child, but everyone is also a singular being. These are, I suppose, the revelations of old age.

We had a beautiful time together in Mannheim, and our arrival in Paris was unique for its ease. I was by that time able to speak what I surmised was passable French, at least by comparison of my childlike Gallic of earlier years. I had lived twenty-two years at the point, and I had the singular pride of bringing my mother to enjoy the wonders of Paris. I took delight in how her face greeted our apartments at the Tuileries Palace as guests of Louis XVI, who admired my music initially because his father had, but he grew to learn his own affections.

Mama and I were allowed an unlimited stay in Paris as the guests of the court, and she so enjoyed our gentle and spacious apartment that she further allowed herself a rare moment of want: she wanted me to assume a position within the French court so that she might be able to stay forever. With the sincerity only available to a mother, she told me she was satisfied not to return to Salzburg or Vienna. The luxury and ease appealed to Mama, as she had spent her life in which both were forever being dangled in front of her and promptly removed. We had so often moved as a family that it is impossible to imagine that Anna Maria felt fully at home anywhere.

The luxury at the Tuileries was not to last, sadly. For reasons never explained to me, we were relocated to a far less grand hotel on the Rue du Sentier. We were allowed no more than a few days' enjoyment at the

Tuileries, and were forced to leave it before I had the opportunity to fully arrange the number of concerts I had hoped for. That was when my dear mother became ill, vomiting blood and struggling for breath. I was due to leave for the distant Palace of Versailles the very day Mama took ill. I ran from our hotel and gratefully found a nearby doctor. Earlier trips had been miserable attempts to put verbs into their right configuration, leaving many wondering what I meant, but I was proud I could by then use my French to help Mama. The kindly doctor understood me perfectly, though he offered no reassurance as to her condition.

The doctor bled and poulticed her, but my mother's fever never broke. It was a hot July day. My mother passed into Heaven holding my hand, and I felt it the greatest privilege I had ever known to be with her, the woman to whom I owed my life, as hers was ending. I stared blankly at her lifeless form as her hand quickly turned cold in mine. Life departs as swiftly as it is created in those frenzied moments of explosion. The hours that followed remain foggy to me, just a set of indistinct images. I wrote Papa. A casket arrived and I said farewell to her without tears. I remember a churchyard and a small gathering, and little else from those days.

So it was surprising to me all of those years later when I turned suddenly to Konstanze and cried, "My mama is dead. I cannot believe it!" Konstanze must have wondered if I was losing my mind, for Mama had been gone from my life for many years by that time, and Konstanze did not know her at all.

Of course I had known it all along, but in the terrible year in which she died I had one of my most debilitating bouts of melancholia, unable to rise from my bed for weeks, and my recovery was slower than usual. When I returned to myself, though, I worked day and night for months to try to ease my pain, and though I may well have succeeded, the grief arrived those years later with a force I could not have conceived. On that day with Konstanze, it felt to me that the disease that killed Mama was still in the room with us. I asked Konstanze to forgive my terrible weakness, for I could not control my tears as memory lumped upon memory. I sobbed without cease for many hours, longing to hear Mama's voice again, and a sudden inability to accept that I never would.

Konstanze asked if there was a marking stone, and I told her I had purchased one for the churchyard at Saint-Eustache. Konstanze suggested we pay a visit to the churchyard, which was not far, and as usual she knew the right thing to do even without knowing the right way to do it. Seeing Mama's marking stone and imagining her in eternal sleep cooled my tears. But all of my excitement about London and Paris vanished. I missed Vienna terribly then, and I even missed Salzburg. I longed for Nannerl, and for Konstanze's sister Aloysia and our wonderful boy Karl. I had traveled through the whole of my life, and I assumed my life to be over at that point, yet this, too, felt strange and different. Being a person who knows things, it was odd not to know what I was feeling, but I knew something was very wrong.

CHAPTER 30

I had tried to get Nannerl to marry the man she truly loved, Franz d'Ippold, a fine gentleman Papa had rejected for the silliest of reasons. He would have felt no one suitable for his daughter, just as every father in the history of the world has probably felt. But Franz was more than suitable for her, and they adored each other. The air was different around them because one knew they were profoundly in love. And I knew, because I know these things, that Franz had entered her with great tender force. Papa would not think of such things, and he would strap me even now for uttering it. But I knew d'Ippold was the first to deflower the purity of my sister, something a brother should abjure, but I thought it was delightful because I could sense what it meant to her. Nannerl gave in to Papa's controlling demands too willingly, feeling she had no choice but to follow his wishes. I told her that if she fought Papa with half the vehemence she used with me fighting her love for d'Ippold, she could be happily married within the month. Franz was a great man, thoughtful and aware enough of himself to be aware of my sister.

When she sent Franz d'Ippold away, creating everlasting sadness for herself, I tried to get her interested in my friend Emil, my dear Gottfried, as he was quite enamored of her. But Nannerl found him too cold, which was a natural response from a woman who had run away from a man she loved, something of which I never failed to remind her. Emil wanted Nannerl to continue her musical studies despite Papa finding the idea absurd. Nannerl's playing as a child was far superior to mine, and she was the major draw for royal courts, as they had never seen a girl perform so astoundingly. Papa never allowed her to do much composing, though I heard many of her improvisations and they were like poems. She was marvelous. Papa kept telling her there would be no future for a woman to write music, and even performing as an adult would be almost impossible for a female. This has always seemed grossly unfair to me.

Papa was interested in Nannerl's musical gifts only when she was a child, and he expressed hope that she would grow to be a music teacher. But her talent was superior to that of a music teacher. Her needs to write operas and symphonies were as strong as mine, and her gifts undeniable. But Nannerl would never confront Papa, so a year later she married a man named Sonnenburg, and they lived in a village near Salzburg. He was a nice enough man—Sonnenblurp, as I called him—but I did not see them enough to know if my dear sister was happy with him. The truth is that Nannerl and I drifted apart in the years after her marriage. It would feel easier in my memory had we some kind of decisive battle that could be recalled. My battles *for* her became in the memory of us both battles *with* her, but in truth we did not fight about anything. She naturally felt protective of the decision she had the courage to make over defending any reminder of her own weakness. As usual, I only noticed our estrangement years after they occurred, and this was the constant of my life: I could not notice happenings as they occurred. Only with a lover does one notice letters which do not arrive, whereas with family and friends it comes upon one more slowly. As old as I am now, with the sand in my glass mostly run through, I most especially feel the wounds that cannot be repaired.

Just as it had when I was child, Paris brought with it an ability to illuminate my darkness. I was often unable to leave my bed to enjoy the great city. Somehow the two images combined into one: my mother's death and my full realization and acceptance that I was unlikely to see my sister again. I was suddenly no longer a man, but an orphan with no father, mother, or sister.

I descended. I knew in those dark moments that I was in Paris, and I knew I was a man in my fourth decade of life, but not much more. In those endless Parisian days, I felt that I was stepping back a few paces from the edge of a foggy and terrifying place that I knew existed only in my imagination. Yet many times, half asleep, it felt so real that it was of no matter to my fear whether it was false or true. My grief for my mother and sister sat back while some other force arose and walked toward me. I often wondered if I was sleeping or waking. This was something new and unstoppable.

If one is aware of a force, is it still a dream? I remember lighting a candle and telling Konstanze that we should visit Mama's gravesite again and move my grief to where it should have been all along. I realized, too, that I needed to write to dear Nannerl to tell her of our plans to live in London, as in the haste to leave Vienna I had neglected her. I wanted to write to ask her to visit me in London, knowing she never would. I had so many tasks to accomplish in Paris, like arranging concerts and delivering *Tartuffe* to the best engraver I could find. I was so eager to read my own score in engraving, which always gave me the feeling of hearing a work for the first time as though I had not written it. After what must have been several weeks in Paris, a veil lifted. I hoped it could be for many days, but I was never able to know how long it would be until my melancholia returned.

I needed to escape the suffocating heartache with which Paris had greeted me, so as soon as I felt able I set out to find the company near the Tuileries that could sell us passage to England.

I remembered, too, the letter from Ludwig, and I knew precisely which piece of baggage it inhabited. I knew that it would be easier to post a reply from Paris, and knew I should, but I felt that whatever the letter contained could remain unread, for I knew without question that whatever words it contained would hurt. I wondered what other letters might be tucked into our Vienna doorway, which by then the elements would have eaten away or been carried off by the wind. What words from our dearest friends had been scattered back to the earth? Had I heard from Lorenzo? How could I ever know now? Might he be in Paris? I suspected he was in Italy, but he might have found his way to London.

Konstanze, as my dear mother before her, would have been happy to stay in Paris for months, even in the *pensione* to which we were confined.

For her, anything was preferable to the suffocating carriage. But my long melancholia had altered something within her, even though she had experienced it with me many times before. Our time in Paris tipped a balance that until that moment I had not known was precarious.

Once I was able to take long walks, Paris felt different to me than it had when I was boy. Politics became very real, far from the empty theatrics I always felt them to be. I could not stay in a country that so blithely removed the heads of its monarchs or, indeed, removed the head of anyone. I thought for years that I admired Robespierre, as had many of my friends, but that sand began to shift as my age progressed. I disliked the idea of politics, but in Paris there was no denying that politics were the only sphere of life in which freedoms once withheld were returned.

As child I was welcomed to France and covered in adulation. A single announcement of a concert by Nannerl and Amadé, as we were known, would brim a hall with the aristocracy. My church music, scant in those days but richer later, filled the huge cathedrals of what was then the most beautiful city in the world. Paris was capricious, welcoming me one minute and discarding me the next. I struggled to realize that it was Paris that had changed in the years between my childhood and my final journey there with Konstanze. For all of the time I was away from Vienna, it was always the same for me when I returned. This is, of course, the life of a city not the city of life, for upon return from a long journey one would also hear shocking news of lives cut short by unexpected death, or the scandalous behavior of some surprising person.

During that final Parisian sojourn, attempts to arrange concerts, even with groups sympathetic to me just a few years before, turned to nothing. I could not attract the aristocracy to my concerts not because of lack of enthusiasm for my music, but because the aristocracy was gone. I called on several noble families of long acquaintance only to find their town estates deserted and little news of them to be found. The director of the Paris Opera found *Tartuffe* an interesting idea, but he would not commit to performing it, and did not even ask me to leave him a copy of the score. I was accustomed to opera houses welcoming my works, so it was particularly searing to be rejected in the city where I had received a lifetime of acceptance. All of that work on a French opera was for naught in the capital of music, and I was forced to take the unperformed opera with me to London.

Someone had cleared away what I knew to be Paris. It looked the same, but it had been altered into a new city that held no life for me within it. The only remaining positions in France were in churches, which was a life I had finished living. I could not possibly delay my original intent to arrive in London for a royal appointment, in pursuit of whatever measly opportunities Paris might have offered. My hopes to make extra money were dashed. To be finished with both Vienna and Paris in only the fourth decade of life was to be in a terrifying place, because the very reasons Paris felt so empty could just as easily spread to London like a mysterious invisible pestilence. All of my life was lived on the edge of rejection, as I was eternally at risk from one person's decision, after which I could be destitute.

I understood then what I understand more fully now: the overwhelming human thirst for freedom. Yet at that moment in Paris I was uneasy with the overthrow of monarchs who provided that freedom. It was Joseph II to whom I owed everything, and he would have allowed me much more had he not been called to Heaven on the battlefield. The workings of the world required monarchs, for the lack of them left people to create their own false idols. Inventing a king or queen was too large a disruption for the world, ensuring chaos. There was a hierarchy of monarchs for a reason intended by God. I was raised on it and still believe it. Where dear Joseph II went wrong, perhaps, was in making me feel like a king in the world of music, for that is false royalty. Having tasted that feeling, though, it is difficult to return to being a subject. Paris was in chaos, and it was from chaos that I had to flee.

Within a few days my Parisian tasks were achieved and we were ready to pack for London. There were to be no concerts, no *Tartuffe*. Even an attempt to play both of my Paris symphonies along with Haydn's could not be arranged. Konstanze and I visited the cemetery almost daily, for it was but a short walk, and I placed many flowers at my mother's marking stone. By the end of our journey, I was able to visit the memory of my mother, her scent still hanging in the air, without dissolving into tears. I secured our passage to England from the company near the Tuileries, a transaction much easier than I had thought it might be, though very much more expensive than anticipated. Everything in those weeks in Paris was toil, and there was no play at all, none of the great elegance and beauty of earlier Parisian memories. I was happy to pay for the privilege of moving us out of there. It was late April.

CHAPTER 31

I enjoyed telling little Franz of our upcoming adventure: a two-day journey by coach to a coastal town called Boulogne, where neither I nor Franz's grandfather had ever been, for my childhood passage had been from Calais to Dover. No, I told Franz, we would be crossing *La Manche* from Boulogne to Hastings, a city on the southern coast of England, and the passage would be beautiful, probably the most exciting thing he had yet to do. Once we were on the other side, we would have another two-day journey to London and then our arrival at the court and our new home. I told him about the excitement of sending a letter to the Lord Chamberlain explaining the approximate time of our arrival, a letter that would leave Paris and travel in a bag hanging off the ass of a horse all the way to London, in a way far faster than coaches. Franz was happy and excited. Konstanze, though, was ill at ease and I could not discern why. Usually her moods were easily revealed to me, but not in Paris. Nothing was easy for me in Paris, not even my need to read Ludwig's letter. I decided to let it travel with me to London where I would hopefully find the courage to open it.

She seemed oddly furious that we faced more travel, though she had known this all along. I had spoken often of Calais, so I was unhappy with the change to Boulogne, yet still she berated me for trying to save money instead of ensuring our comfort. She said I had ignored Franz for days, and no elucidation of the arrangements I had been making would appease her, nor did she show any sympathy for my total rejection from every Parisian institution, leaving us with no income from our long stay there. The Parisian streets were crowded and filthy, she said, and I had allowed some of my best clothes to be soiled in ways that would never have happened in Vienna. The departure for London could not come soon enough to please me, as I hoped that our new life would dissipate her fears.

We packed the few trunks we had unpacked for our weeks in Paris, and two days later the horses arrived. Three of our coaches, so the bulk of our belongings, had gone on to London without us and would be awaiting us. Our party now comprised just two coaches, one with our belongings and another with the three of us. What I had not understood, though, and which ignited even more perturbations in Konstanze, was that we were to be but two of fifty coaches, something I discovered only when our coachmen took us to a field near the Butte Montmartre, quite a distance from Paris. There we waited for several hours for the entire caravan headed north and then westward through the beautifully verdant fields that I recalled with such clarity from my first Grand Tour with Papa and Nannerl. As Paris receded so did my grief, but the journey did not lift Konstanze's spirits.

I recall asking Konstanze who would care for the marking stone of my mother now that we were leaving.

"You will achieve such fame in London that your admirers will care for her, darling," she said, in words that comforted me to my depth.

I joked in reply, "My fame will never matter in Paris. They were only interested in me as a child."

There was something in Konstanze's countenance that made me harbor the idea that she thought we might someday return to Paris or Vienna. I had assumed all along a permanent move to England, but perhaps I had never said anything to her about it. Could she really have thought that amid the months of planning and packing that we would return? I reminded her that we would be living in a palace, or at least near a palace. I refreshed in her what she had also forgotten, that we would be sitting for a painting, something she always loved. My likeness had certainly changed since my last portrait, and Konstanze had not been painted since we were married. I longed to do a sitting with Franz as well. With my new position in London, I finally felt worthy again of a portrait. All of my earlier likenesses had been distractions from more interesting work. It took days to sit for a portrait, which can be boring indeed, though I must admit to having written many concertos while sitting. I can easily finish them in the span of an hour, and the writing takes a small amount of time after they have been completed in the noggin. In a portrait I could have a full head of hair again, and the pockmarks all over my face could be smoothed. I loved paintings, as they give men the chance to be gods, to make the world more beautiful than it is.

Just as I had not expected heartache to overtake me in Paris, I was surprised by the number of people occupying my thoughts on the journey from Paris to Boulogne, which required an overnight stay at Amiens, which looked just as it had when I was there as a child. We arrived shortly after nightfall, and with such a large group of coaches there was only one place prepared to serve us dinner of bouillabaisse and bread, both of which I remember with enormous sadness at this moment of quill to paper, because both were totally and perfectly of the earth that it brought tears. I had not had bouillabaisse anywhere except in the south, so to have it in Amiens was itself a great treat, for if regional dishes were traveling it meant the taste and openness of the world was growing, and that gave me hope.

On those short days leading to Boulogne, I tried to move toward several compositions that were occupying me but I could not concentrate. Every village through which we passed, though strangely not Amiens, had torn down their statues of monarchs and replaced them with rough and temporary monuments of extravagantly robed women holding torches. Many of the statues were battered by weather, with worn signs of "La liberté" dangling from them. I hoped that my memories of Amiens were not confusing themselves with Strasbourg, for I was certain I recalled walking with Papa along the Somme. Both Strasbourg and Amiens invited memories, so on that particular night the two were equal to me, and it made no matter which one I was occupying.

In Amiens I realized beyond all doubt that I would never again see Vienna. I would also never see France again and so would never see any more places in the world where I had been known before. My expectations were all focused on London, but where was my own elder son, still just a boy? Was he with Aloysia or was he already roaming the Italian countryside? Nannerl. Or had he managed to find my dear Tomaschek, one of my fellow composers, too good to be near, so I might have been able to live without him, but I hoped my dear little son could find a teacher worthy of his musical gifts.

I suddenly ached to see Joseph Gelinek, though I thought I might see him in London. I missed Joseph's irreverent laughter and the afternoons of playing fortepiano with him, not to mention talking endlessly about women. I wrote so few variations on themes because Joseph had so completely mastered the form. I can never forget the night I heard him improvise two dozen variations on my flute melody in *The Magic Flute*, "wie stark ist nicht ein Zauberton." His work was endlessly inventive, much more than any of my variations, and he made me laugh with pure exhilaration. Some themes are naturally more suited to variations than others, and it always helped if a theme was relatively easy so that a listener could hold on to it in memory. As the number of variations progress, a listener should become more and more aware of the theme. Variations transform one idea into another, and that was for me the great joy of travel. Variations were musical travel.

In Amiens I smelled the sea for the first time in years. Gelinek was all over my thoughts, and I knew I would write him once I was in London. Part of his appeal to my memory must have been his longtime criticisms of Ludwig, with which I could agree without responsibility. I had been the subject of so much criticism that I was sensitive to how it can sting. Ultimately, though, one learns not to worry much about it, as it makes no difference to a person's life. Did any of the criticisms leveled against me by Ludwig or others have any validity? Some of them must. But why should it matter to anyone? Everything for which I was so harshly judged had to do with how those jealous of me perceived my character. They were making moral and not musical judgments, and only God should do that. They always seemed to think they were describing or analyzing or even openly defaming my music, but they were not. They were only capable of denigrating a person and not their creations, and they needed to stay always in the vicinity of ridicule. I had heard every kind of charge leveled against me, particularly in the service of cathedrals; but were any of them truly able to describe and criticize even a single note of my distant *Idomeneo* had they never heard about it from others? Of the operas of my youth, *Idomeneo* was the single one I thought I might revise, and I still feel that way, though there are things about it that I could bring more up to date if only I could find the new energy it would require.

Though we had brought so much with us, and so much was already ahead of us on the way to London, I suddenly grew panicked at the amount of music we had left behind in Vienna, music I would never see again. Konstanze had packed it all away so perfectly that it would be organized and ready for anyone who discovered it, but who would that be? And looking back from my old age, why did these fears overtake me at that very moment? Our minds are so very strange sometimes.

Amiens to Boulogne was a fast journey. We arrived in time to see the sunset over the water, one of God's glories that I had not seen in years. The scent of the sea was invigorating and I felt like a child again, watching the sun sink into mist. I had to wonder what was out there beyond England. And how could anyone possibly cross such a vast thing as an ocean? I knew that people did, and I had heard about the American colonies and their amazing story of liberating their territories from the King of England, my new employer. I did love the stories of the wild and beautiful country across the seas, of the two Americas which spanned the entirety of that part of globe, and both were to be found across the unimaginable vastness. I had little fear of anything physical, but I harbored an incurable terror of the sea, an anguish that I knew would keep me bound to England for what I hoped would be the remainder of my life.

The thought of looking out from a ship and seeing no land slowed my blood within its natural alleyways. We watched the sun descend behind England somewhere, and not fully over the water, for the distant outline of the country across *La Manche* could clearly be seen. Our new home is out there, I said to Konstanze, and the life that I dreamed for her and Franz was only days away. Konstanze said she was tired and returned to our quarters with Franz to prepare for sleep. I was not ready to return. I was energized, and I decided to walk around Boulogne, to get to know a place I would never see again. After a while, I read a posting on a building at the Port de Plaisance that we would have passage to Hastings within three days and to keep watch for the presence of a ship called *Reine de la Manche*. All passengers to Hastings would need to have their belongings loaded onto her at sundown the night before crossing at the following daybreak.

CHAPTER 32

I rushed back to inform Konstanze that she had no reason to fear, that we would soon be leaving for England. I decided to move us to the Grand Hotel for our final nights in France, an indulgence to celebrate the near end of our journey. Three months had passed since we had departed Vienna, the summer nights were lengthening, and I could perceive the slightest change of light at the close of each day.

Konstanze was not at the inn. I thought perhaps she had decided against retiring and taken Franz for supper. The light of the day faded to blackness and still there no Konstanze, no Franz. I had heard terrible stories of pirates kidnapping women and children in port cities. The docklands of most cities drew the dregs of the world, bringing the devils in close proximity to more upstanding citizens, so I immediately imagined the worst, even though I had walked all around and sensed no danger. I was known just enough in the world to draw pirates to kidnap my wife and child. Had it become known via the coach company that I was in Boulogne? If so, it was conceivable that someone had hatched an idea to abduct Franz and Konstanze to extort money from me. I saw the picture in my mind's eye: Konstanze was trying to rescue Franz and the abductor murdered her and was then in sole possession of my little boy. I fell into a panic and ran to the innkeeper to see if he had any knowledge, any news. But the innkeeper was old and enfeebled, and had clearly seen nothing beyond the inside of his brandy bottle.

Near hysteria, I went out into the moonless night with a lantern, calling Franz's name continually, then Konstanze's, my cries punctuated by tears from knowing I would not be able to find them. It was the darkest night I could remember. Had little Franz called out for his papa? And had I simply not been able to hear him? Boulogne was not large, and I traversed it several times in a short span of time, my memory of a few hours before preventing me from being lost. I searched the immediate area of the port countless times. My desperation grew as I realized there was no hope until morning. I arrived back at the inn exhausted and hoarse, just as morning was streaking the eastern sky. Morning would bring the gift of light to find my wife and son. I retrieved my key behind the sleeping innkeeper and even the creaking stairway could not stir the man.

I entered our rooms, weeping from panic, and fell onto the bed. I continually asked the empty air where they were. I prayed to God with a promise of any sacrifice for their return. I had never prayed so fervently. The thought consumed me that they must be on a ship, so perhaps someone at the dock could help me. They could not simply have vanished. I fell into a half sleep of grief, always aware of the sounds of the awakening day.

Those lonesome and exhausted hours brought a vivid dream. I was lost in the forests around Salzburg, and a Romaní woman was there wanting her life back. I was asleep but not entirely. I was floating near the same bridge of which I had dreamed repeatedly since I was a child. I was swimming near the bridge. Men on the bridge were close. Sometimes they became women. They were pissing, all of them, off the bridge, peeing all over me. The smells of the dream were foul. I was outside myself in the dream, crying, then laughing, then crying again. I was flying high above Salzburg, just barely above the peaks and ridges where no man had ever been. There was the sound of wind. I had climbed to certain high vistas as a child, but there were always higher unapproachable summits. There were voices and words.

I heard my name.

I was still asleep, but there was a voice.

"Wolfgang!" the voice said, sternly.

I startled myself awake. It was Konstanze. I sobbed. I told her of my thought that she had been kidnapped or killed and that Franz had been taken by pirates. I could not cease crying.

"We are safe," she said, and then she went on. "I took Franz to a hotel and we were both fully asleep. I left you a note."

I told her I had found no note.

"You really are so hopeless, Ami. I left you a note that it took me ages to write, and even longer to gather courage for, and you do not even bother to read it."

I saw the note across the room on the desk, on top of my folio. I asked her to tell me what it said, though I already knew.

"I'm taking Franz and returning to Vienna. I've decided it is best this way."

I asked where he was.

"He's in our room, where we stayed last night, just across the street."

I thought of the ordeal I had passed in the previous hours.

"All this traveling is hard on him. I wanted to come with you to London, initially, truly I did. But these months, these endless hot months, all the difficulties and uncertainties in Paris and not knowing what is beyond that sea, I just cannot follow you any longer."

I was silent for many seconds, incredulous that my wife was going to leave me with a letter.

I told her I would return with them to Vienna, that I would not go to London. I knew I was lying.

"I am going home without you, Ami," she said with quiet finality.

I asked if I could say good-bye to Franz.

"Perhaps when he is older he can visit you in London. I do not think a terrible scene here at the dock would be good for him. Who knows what destiny may bring?"

It was destiny that brought us together, I thought. I began to sing phrases from the aria I wrote for her, one of many, the one that begins with her name. "Mein liebevolles Herz!" I kept repeating. My voice could not hide my exhaustion, and I creaked as I reached for the notes. I told her we had always been able to find a way through our difficulties, and I knew we could again. I asked her to talk with me about all of her fears. I appeared calm but inside, my breathing was trying to crush me.

"This is not an opera, Ami. Destiny did not bring us together. Our sister brought us together. You wanted to marry her and you got me instead. We have both carried the weight of this for our whole lives," Konstanze said.

"All these years, our children, the love I have continually expressed to you, and you can leave?" I cried.

"It has always lingered, Ami. I love you deeply and always have, but love alters itself outside of our control. We have forgiven each other too many times. We need to face that our lives are now going on two different paths. These things happen."

I was a "thing" that happened. I begged her to come to London and try it for a few months. There was no time for indecision, as our boat was to leave within days.

"I cannot learn another language," she said. I reminded her, yet again, that everyone at the court speaks German or French, as did she.

"I do not want to live in a court. I want to go home to Vienna. I will manage the publishing, which is what I love."

She was happy to still have money from my name, but not to be married to me. I felt my face turn cold.

"Surely you would not leave your wife with nothing," she said.

I reminded her that I was the one being left alone on this vast journey. She was taking our son, yet she thought I was leaving her with nothing. "It is I being left with nothing," I repeated.

"You can earn an income, Ami. I cannot. I must depend on you." Her voice sounded cold, separated from her body as though a stranger had entered the room with us.

I felt the day's new light darkening. Something was caving in. Konstanze went through her litany about our marriage, the ever-longer list of reasons I was such an unsuitable husband for her or anyone. She was speaking truths we had both long known and ignored, and I knew real truths did not ever become untrue: where the finger alighted on the G string of the violin was true every day in every country. What was true in Vienna would be true in London. I could hear her words and mine, but we were already separated. The thread was broken. She said she had become a terrible burden to me and then delivered the deepest cut of all, that I had placed her where my affection for Mama used to be. I listened to her words, each of which cut into what formerly was me. I thought of our four children who were lying in gravesites, their little souls unable to find us.

CHAPTER 33

"If I go to London with you I will be a prisoner," she said. I did not understand this at all. I remembered that Konstanze had berated me and Lorenzo for the Countess so readily forgiving the Count in *Figaro*. "He deserves more of a comeuppance!" she kept saying. We had actually fought about it. At that moment I wondered if she might be right. I did not know how I could ever forgive Konstanze. She had never forgiven me for my infidelities, at least the ones she knew about, and I do not think she had forgiven me or herself for our little children who did not live. I had seen this in Mama, this immovable guilt.

This was not merely a farewell. It was a tirade of past hurts. I wondered if any two people who knew each other as Konstanze and I did would not eventually come to a hurtful ending. Death brought difficulties into focus, and the unfinished becomes an inheritance. Even when I recall it now, I can only think of the place in Praha that I happened across where spiders had been left to create their world without disturbance for the passing of many seasons, sheltered from the elements. I had endless fascination with the place, where the sunlight on the webs made them newly beautiful, each a world in miniature. I once met a professor from Heidelberg who had so much knowledge about spiders, creatures feared by so many but who were actually benevolent. The man said there were lands across many seas where spiders were an extraordinary danger, but I knew that I would never see those places. Still, I loved that at least one person cared so much about learning that they studied what others would find a nuisance. I was one web and Konstanze was another. We were entwined.

These revelations brought no solace. If Konstanze and I separated in Boulogne, we would never again see each other, and little Franz would grow up with little memory of me other than the distant foggy image of a man who once took him to Paris. If I ignored Konstanze's wishes and returned with her to Vienna, it would mean I would not appear at the appointed hour in London. This would result in full banishment from every royal court in Europe. I would be unable to work anywhere except perhaps to return to St. Stephen's or even Salzburg and beg for a position. How would the publishing of my music possibly work from two such disparate and distant cities as London and Vienna? I was not so much worried about my old music, but more about the music I had yet to write, as it was only my new works that held any interest. I could not imagine anyone preferring *Così* or *Figaro* to my new *Tartuffe* or *Richard III*, which were both far superior by comparison. I had so much waiting inside of me, but Konstanze's unexpected departure threatened to crush any future works, as the pain of her words might replace whatever music was within me.

I feared being in London alone until I thought of what Vienna might be like if I returned vilified for a failed marriage. No one in Vienna would blame Konstanze for anything, and it would be impossible for us to divorce, as no royal appointment could be accompanied by such a scandal. At least if Konstanze and I lived in two places, we could remain married in the minds of those for whom it was important. A separation of so many miles would be a liberation, I knew, but I did not want to admit it.

Something loosened within me. "You are going home to be with Süssmayer!" The words shot out of me before I could fully consider them.

"Perhaps I am going home to be with Ludwig, or Süssmayer, or any number of other men you have accused of taking pieces of my virtue."

"Accused...because it is true. Süssmayer is the father of our little Franz, is he not? Admit it."

Konstanze resisted all of my attempts to have the truth be spoken about Franz Süssmayer. He had helped me so much on *Tito* and *Magic*

Flute that both Konstanze and I felt we owed him a debt. By the time of *Richard III*, Süssie had established himself as a major composer of his own reputation, and one even Ludwig regarded with suspicion. Having been my pupil of fortepiano and composition, and having then assisted me for so many years, Franz had some of my personality within him. Little cadences, phrases, a certain way of noticing the world, traveled from me to Süssmayer, and often I would hear my own voice come from his. Mimicry is how we learn, indeed how everyone learns everything. Konstanze had noticed how I had copied a few turns of phrase from Haydn, and a great many from J.C. Bach. Every time one of J.C.'s letters arrived, there were suddenly new words around the household; and even after the writers had passed on, I would often pull out their letters and read them anew. Those were my favorite letters, and the only ones I brought on the great journey, which became one of the ways Konstanze knew I had no intention of returning.

I noticed that Konstanze often had mimicked her sister Aloysia, and in the dark of night no one could tell them apart. I knew Franz had all of my zest for life with none of my hardships, the very qualities that drew Konstanze to me. She, too, would have seen a lot of me in him. Süssie spent a great deal of time in our home during the long summer of 1791 when I had taken on far too much work, and he had taken a number of lessons from me before that. He was present when I was not. Süssie took an interest in Karl, interest in everything about our lives.

Konstanze would never utter the words that burned within her, that she preferred Süssie's music to mine, because I represented pain and frustration, whereas he could be associated with things carefree and full of laughter, things I had once been. His music was solidly constructed, but nothing more, which I recognize as faint praise indeed. Süssie's compositions offered few challenges for a competent musician, while I often demanded dozens of arpeggios and endless scales, moving Konstanze to once say to me that I was constantly "showing my cleverness," instead of simply loving the obvious: that I was more clever than he. She heard my music and saw and heard all of the flaws within her husband that no one but a wife would ever see. I know this because Konstanze admired women who were able to overlook the deficiencies of their husbands, and she was not the sort to admire in others what she could do herself.

CHAPTER 34

The complaining made us both weary, and in truth not only Konstanze was complaining. When my spirits would swing, it wore down both of us, and over the years it must be true that my bouts of inactivity increased. When I was in one of the happy times, I could laugh about her complaints, and she would then complain about that. But in my downward moods, when I would dream of the bridge, her diatribes sent me into darker despair, and into an increasing depth that always made me fear for her stability. There had been moments when I thought I might try to step out of life itself, as I had heard of people doing. Konstanze spoke of distant relatives who had opened their own wrists and been found days later in forests, for it was always seemed to happen in forests, or others who had put great stones within their clothes and walked into the Danube and were sometimes found great distances from where they committed their sin, swept out to wherever the Danube ended. Frightful images plagued me of where rivers end, and I assumed all rivers end in seas, where the bodies must eventually be eaten by the great monsters of the deep that no man has yet seen. How horrifying to be consumed by a creature who swims in inky darkness, never seeing its prey.

When Konstanze was within a moment of intemperance, she had no control over what she said to me, and then her guilt would follow. Those final hours in Boulogne were no different from the episodes between us that had increased in frequency in recent years. Konstanze always emerged from these times with a certainty that she had destroyed what love we still had, and that my affection was being slowly drained away by her actions.

In Boulogne, she continued packing her things, not missing an opportunity to bring into our fight the embarrassment I had tried to conceal, though she had noticed it back in Paris. Red bumps that would open and itch appeared all over my prick and its environs. It was another source of despair, to be sure, but I had to tell Konstanze why we'd had no physical relations since arriving in France, and why we could not copulate until the pestilence departed. A doctor told me that Konstanze was possibly already infected, for the infection likely existed within me before my awareness of it. These things, the doctor said, can often lie silently within the body before being pushed to the surface by some inner force.

I had not wanted to tell her about this embarrassment at all, as I always loved our time in bed together and, though she considered it unseemly to admit, she craved me entering her body. Konstanze was desolate to hear my news, but not so desolate as to be unable to summon hours of admonishment for my having obtained this pestilence at all. She knew I had acquired it by entering a woman, but still she demanded to know who had brought this into our world, and demanded the precise circumstances that brought the assignation to reality. She repeatedly said she needed to know. I was embarrassed to confess all the details, for I had enjoyed relations with several singers, all sopranos, and this always compounded Konstanze's hurt, because the infidelity somehow spoke upon her artistry as well as her wifely status. Most recent to my infection, I had a most satisfying time with a chamber maid in Paris, a way of distracting myself from my grief, and there had been a woman at St. Stephen's just before we left Vienna. I could not find a way to confess that I had copulated in my chambers within the cathedral. I was so ashamed, unable to take this particular detail even to my confessors. Konstanze loved hearing my confessions, though, even when they caused her pain. There was something titillating for her within them.

It made her angry when I honestly could not remember all of the details. Copulation had a significance for her that it lacked for me. I was perpetually confused about this, as the release of tension during the act was followed by profound guilt as to why I had placed myself in the pathway of such temptations, but then the desire I had quelled just as quickly returned. Indeed, it returned ever quicker as I aged, the opposite of what priests said would happen. They fulminated for years that the forces within me that called so furiously for satisfaction would diminish with the years. I kept waiting. I still am.

Konstanze held herself responsible for the decision she was making. She said she was not forced to leave, yet she also felt I had left her with no remaining choices. I was despondent, crying at her endless words. Only after the long trip from Vienna to Paris to Boulogne had she chosen to confess that the incision in our marriage had started with her, and that it could no longer be repaired.

She told me something in Boulogne that surprised me: she missed singing, proclaiming a great love for her own voice and feeling herself considerably more accomplished than had been acknowledged. She said that when I extended compliments to other sopranos, she lacked the courage to say to me that she was jealous or hurt or scared, so she poured everything into helping me with my life. My life became hers, and for a time, this felt something like love to her. I had confessed to this woman standing before me every image of my waking and sleeping dreamtime, and she was the only person in the world to hear those intimacies.

I hated hurting her, but she was inflicting pain on me as well. I tried, again and again, to assure her that I had never shared my dreams with another woman, and that only she, only my Konstanze, knew me so intimately. I told her we had traveled too far only to travel this far. I needed her more than I had ever needed anyone, despite knowing she was about to walk out the door forever.

But at that moment, to my humiliation, the very cock in question was covered in little red pustules and I could not screw at all. I could not even bring myself to eruption, though I would try, and often in my sleeping hours of those weeks my prick would erupt on its own. In my youth I had written down each explosion I experienced, either alone or with a woman. I lived in terror of Mama or Papa finding that salacious journal. Each name was recorded in my own hand, rather like my thematic catalogue, and though there were not so many names of women, I counted *every* eruption for many years, and not only those that occurred inside a woman. There were thousands that happened alone, and I would record many of the thoughts of their duration. Often I had only to look at the list to pleasure myself anew. There were many delightful memories in my book of shame, though it went into the fire at some point when my embarrassment ascended the throne of control.

Papa Leopold assumed Konstanze to be my first copulation, and he dutifully and dryly explained to me the sacred nature of the prick, and that each eruption of seed could bring a child to life and was thus itself sacred. Papa said repeatedly that I should never spill my seed without the intention of bringing a soul into the world. Even as a very young man I wondered how this might be so, though I always listened with great interest to anything involving copulation.

I had probably erupted thousands of times in my sleep, and many more times waking, so how could it be that each time was meant for a child? It felt wonderful, beautiful even, so why was I taught to believe otherwise? I refuse to allow my two boys to be ashamed of their cocks, though in Boulogne I had to face that I would never see either boy grow to manhood. I was not a handsome man then or now, but I had the advantage of knowing certain things that others did not, and these things were not beliefs. I actually knew them. One thing I knew was how to bring a woman's body toward bliss, and to closely touch what could only be God, and I knew how to sustain the pleasure simply by listening to the woman, by feeling her breath, and allowing her to feel safe with me so that she would convey to me her deeper needs. Awakening that feeling in a woman is a miracle, and I had brought Konstanze to that prolonged cliff's edge many times, seeing her very soul open and close like a firmament. I knew I had done this solely with my touch, my words, and with the masterful listening force of my thrusts. I had tried always to compose the *feeling* created from that journey of two bodies, and perhaps I succeeded a few times, not enough for my desires, but more than many people. I took especial pleasure from women who had never experienced the act before. Not virgins, but women who knew certain pleasures but not others. I could tell, just by talking to a woman and looking into her eyes, if she had ever experienced the edge of pleasure that I was uniquely able to achieve. It was never my intention to hurt Konstanze in sharing this bliss with others, for she alone had it always.

Konstanze asked me to help get her baggage to the waiting coach. We both knew we had reached an ending. The moment I dreaded the most arrived with awful swiftness.

I helped her get her trunks to the coach. Franz was there, playing with a small toy I had given him in Paris. He was too young to realize what was happening, but he knew I had come to tell him farewell. Konstanze begged me not to cry in front of our son. I had to give him something to remember his father by when years from now there would be nothing to recall except this farewell on a windy morning by the sea. I told Franz I loved him, told him to be a good boy and to listen to his mother, and I told him I would see him very soon. Franz hugged me and cried. I somehow managed to hold in my own tears then peeled away and closed the carriage door and walked to the other side where Konstanze was waiting.

She said coldly, "I will write you once we return to Vienna, but I would appreciate if you would send me a letter in a few days so that I know you are in London safely."

I agreed. I tried one final time to get her to stay with me, to go to London with me and delay this decision for a few months. Even if our parting was inevitable, I said, surely I deserved a chance to improve. We could return to Paris for a time and delay my trip to London. She refused every possibility except the one on which she had already decided. She was leaving and all other choices were removed.

"I have to tell you that I, too, have been infected with a pestilence. All of my nether regions are covered with the same rash you have."

I was about to tell her I was sorry that I had given it to her when she said, "I confess to you my humiliation that Süssie gave me the infection, I am sure, and I am the one who passed it to you. I am sorry."

I had been holding something within me for hours, demanding of myself to stay silent. At the moment of farewell, as Konstanze's body leaned into mine for a final short embrace, something liberated itself from me. I could scarcely believe it as it was happening, and I was powerless to control myself. I was both mortified and delighted in equal measure that at this most important moment of my life I surrendered to the most powerful, extended, and mellifluous fart that I had ever dreamed. It went on and on for what felt like an hour, yet just when I thought it had finished it returned, and by then it had taken on a vivid and growing life of its own, ending with a small cadence in what instantly I knew was G minor. My anguish fell into a laughter I expected Konstanze to share, but she turned to incredible rage, entered the carriage, and instructed the coachman to leave for Paris.

CHAPTER 35

I watched the coach leave the street, reappearing briefly along the far side of the quay, and then it was gone. The world I had known for more than half of my life, and everything I thought I could ever know, drove away that day. Part of my soul would always laugh at the great fart, but everything that was my blood and heart and body was in pain. I was aware of every bone, each of which felt weighted, and I felt hot, even as the morning air off the sea was damp and cool. I had been awake all night, and my final hour with Konstanze had been a resurrection of every anguish of my life. I wondered if I had ever written a note of music. Would there ever be another moment of happiness?

I noticed the sun's rays stretching out in the eastern sky. I already knew that before it reached midday this would be the saddest day of my life, but the sun would rise tomorrow, and after one more rise I would be crossing the water to England. I realized how full and rich my life had always been because at that moment I faced a chasm of overwhelming emptiness. Death had taken people from me many times before, so I knew the pain of parting, but no one had ever left me with such cold surprise. I knew I would see my parents and my lost children in our next life in paradise, and I was always comforted by that hope. But I felt Konstanze and Franz would never be seen again, as somehow I believed that a breaking of bonds in this world remained in the heavenly realm. I was not sure *how* I knew this but it definitely was among the things I knew. My body ached so terribly that I could scarcely lift myself up the stairs.

As I reached my room, the innkeeper yelled to me that my passage to England was to be at the very next dawn, and so my trunks would need to be at the ship by sundown.

I pondered returning to Paris in the hope of reconciling with Konstanze, but I knew she would deliberately stay where she could not be found. I wondered how much Franz Süssmayer was behind this decision. Had he somehow managed to woo her, or gotten a letter to her in Paris, promising her this or that? Franz could be very persuasive, and he probably offered Konstanze everything I lacked. And his prick was probably in working order, since he passed his rash onto me through her and was probably free of it, the little shit fart. I could not imagine life without a working prick, and prior to that horrible rash it was not among my contemplations. It was a horrible sight, swollen and red as a ripe tomato, covered in bumps that were even redder, and a few of them bursting and leaking puss. The pain was just tolerable if I could be distracted from it, but if I made water it was like pissing out fire and there was not even a slight possibility of it getting engorged and erect, as that was agony. How could I go to a doctor and show him such an ugly appendage? But what if this condition worsened and the entire apparatus fell off? I had heard tales of such things, and it was possible that at Hastings they might ask me some question about it, and I would be terrible at lying in a language I could only speak like a child. I asked the innkeeper if I could find a doctor who would not report me to the church, or who would not make any sort of statement that could get to my employers. I knew that the admission of a disease of this kind, bestowed only on the promiscuous, was not the way I should arrive at the court.

The innkeeper said a doctor would be obliged to report any pestilence to the ships bound for England, so seeing any doctor at that moment could endanger my passage the following day. My growing agony was visible to the innkeeper, so he suggested I drink an extremely strong whiskey or gin, as that would have medicinal qualities as well as ease the surface pain. I had too much to accomplish in the day to risk drunkenness, but I had to find help. The heartache, the hammer blow delivered by Konstanze, had undoubtedly forced more sickness to the surface of my body, and if I didn't find help, the infectious agent could spread.

I fell into a light, brief sleep before waking and putting my trunks together to take to the ship. Every movement was agony by the time I hauled the trunks downstairs. I caught the eye of a black man in front of the inn, and I asked if he could help me transport the bags to the ship. The man agreed, speaking to me in perfect French, which I thought unusual for a black man. He said his name was Tamu, a name I had never heard before. I thought it sounded tuneful. It took us only a few minutes to walk the short distance, and Tamu noticed that I was in terrible pain. He loaded my bags onto the ship, bless him, after which I offered him money in gratitude. A dock worker, a white French man, laughed, and Tamu told me quietly to put my money away for now. I did not understand but did as I was told.

When we were a short distance from the quay, and I was planning to return to the inn for a bath and some rest, Tamu asked me if I was experiencing some malady, as it was obvious to him that I was in a great deal of discomfort.

I thought I had successfully hidden the affliction, but Tamu was also one of those people who, like me, knew things. Something in his eyes made it possible to trust him. I explained to him all of the embarrassing details. Tamu's face never moved. Tamu said he knew a doctor, but that I would have to do exactly as he said. I was in such physical agony that I agreed. I had to do something.

Tamu told me we would have to walk, as Tamu would not be allowed in a carriage. I was confused. "Slaves are not allowed to take carriages," he explained.

"You are a slave?" I could not believe it, as I had never met a slave before, and did not know they existed in France.

"I am unowned at present, but I will be sent to a chateaux, or so I'm told, and I'm to wait here until I am bought and taken away," Tamu said, with complete calm. "But enough of that. Let's get you better." His French was cultivated, far more than mine.

We walked slowly toward a portion of the shoreline where a stream entered the ocean, creating small pools along its way. Tamu instructed me to remove my clothes and sit in one of the pools, one in which the water from the stream and water from the ocean mixed.

"I will return in a moment. I'm going to collect some leaves for you," Tamu said.

I asked when we were to visit the doctor.

"I am the doctor," Tamu said.

CHAPTER 36

I was ashamed of my own surprise. Of course Tamu was a doctor, considering the cultivated way he spoke and the healing gentleness of his eyes. My body ached as I sat in the pool. The water initially felt cold, but quickly became soothing. I had bathed in the sea before but not in many years. I wondered if this would really make any difference to my red and swollen prick. Tamu returned with two handful of leaves, small and green, and one larger one. I had to ask three times to be sure I heard clearly what he was saying, even though it had been pronounced clearly in perfect French that I immediately understood.

"Yes, you heard me correctly. Take these small leaves, tear them into smaller pieces, mix them with a little sand from the pool, and rub them all over your man-self." Tamu gestured in such a way as to make it clear, using his hand as the boys did in school when they were joking about causing their own plumes. "I do not need to watch you, but you must scrub hard so that the salt water can help you."

I was embarrassed, even though I was not erect and knew the pain would keep me from being so, but I had never touched my prick in front of a man, and it felt odd. Tamu did not watch me but he lingered nearby. I did as I was told, meekly at first when the pain forced me to cry out. It was a profound pain, one I could not control, but Tamu said I must take the pain to its limits. "Your healing later will only be as great as your pain now." So I scrubbed harder with the leaves and the sand, crying out as I did. After a few minutes, Tamu instructed me to sit in the pool and do nothing. He prepared the other set of leaves, wringing them into a leather pouch that I had not noticed him carrying. He told me to begin a second round of treatment with the small leaves and sand. It hurt just as much as the first time, but I trusted Tamu. I noticed that though he paid attention to me, he did not leer like some of the priests used to do when the boys bathed in front of them.

I did not know what Tamu was concocting, but he was mixing whatever he had drained from the leaves with some salt water. I became momentarily frightened that someone might happen upon us. How would it look with me naked in a pool of saltwater, and Tamu preparing some kind of ointment? I thought of Konstanze speeding toward Paris, and how furious she must be and would likely stay.

I completed three rounds of treatment, after which my member was nearly raw to the touch, but the salt water, though it stung initially, did bring ease. Tamu then brought me a small leather pouch and instructed me to remove myself from the pool, go to a private place in the bracken, and apply the contents of the bag to my member and all around the area. Let it dry for several minutes, as long as possible, and then put my clothes back on. If I applied the ointment in the leather pouch each of the next three days, the pestilence should disappear within a few weeks, and my functioning should return within only a few days. But he also said there should be no relations with women for at least a year. I could not imagine holding off for an entire year, but I vowed to do exactly as Tamu said.

When I was dressed again, though miserably sore, I was ready to return to my inn for a last sleep. The sun was setting. I told Tamu that it would be the last sunset I experienced in France, my last before sailing into a new world.

Tamu confessed how good it felt to help someone feel better. He had been a doctor before he was tricked into getting on a ship, having been told there were sick passengers who needed immediate help. It was especially cruel to have his healing profession used for evil. I queried Tamu at length about his origins. He was from a place I was ashamed to admit I had never known existed, from Senegambia, on the west African coast, and Tamu was certain he would never see it again. He had traveled to the area of Lagos where there was a large settlement, because he had learned French from missionaries and that made him useful to the traders who came into port. He had learned all of the traditional medicines from his father, who was also a practitioner. Tamu told me the grisly details of getting tricked onto the ship to treat a set of sick officers. He was offered money to entice him, but he told them he would happily go on board to help them without being paid at all.

"For being a doctor, I was very stupid. It didn't occur to me that there might be bad people there, that there might be no sick officers at all. I never once considered it," Tamu said.

"You trusted them. How could you ever trust anyone else? And why should you?" I said.

Tamu went on. I loved hearing his voice because he intoned words with such beauty and art, though his words cracked the heart. "I thought I would be taken to the New World. I had heard of so many being stolen, so many families destroyed, separated, and killed in place if they refused to go. Like me, many of them went along at first, trusting in human kindness."

"I'm so sorry, Tamu. What will happen?"

"I will be found. I did not completely tell you the truth. I am not awaiting an appointment into a noble family. I was taken to England from Lagos on a ship that was going back to Africa for slaves, and on to America. They did not realize that I could understand most of what they were saying. My choices were to be slavery in England or slavery in a different world across the wider sea. I heard some men speaking French in the British port, and I hid myself away on their ship, not knowing to where it was bound. We docked not far from here, in Calais, and I escaped into the night. I have been living just fine, helping people in the port, sleeping around the water. No one yet has questioned me. It is very cold, but otherwise the sea and the reeds and plants feel familiar. But my free days are numbered."

CHAPTER 37

The sun had completely gone by then, and I had to return to my inn. I wanted to hear everything about Tamu, and to share a meal with him, but he said that would raise too many suspicions.

I had heard about slavery, of course, but I had imagined it to be something that would never make its way near me. But here was slavery, sitting on the other side of a small beach fire of driftwood that Tamu had made before sunset. For a day that had begun in such pain and turmoil, as close to total despair as I had ever felt, it was ending with this generous and accomplished man who, I hoped, had healed my body. That it was time to say farewell to him so soon after our meeting seemed impossible, for there had been quite enough loss between a single revolution of the sun. I had not yet had time to hear Tamu's thoughts about the sun or the stars. I knew many people, and quite a number of learned ones, who insisted that it was the sun revolving around us that caused the days and nights; but I, who knew things, was certain that it was not the sun that was setting, but us here in this world, who were on a constantly rotating globe that was itself traversing a wide arc around the great sun. I had happened upon the idea many times, and I loved trying to express it, beginning *Figaro* and *Flute* in keys that rotated the spectrum and arrived back home. I had loved the study of Copernicus as a child, even though my own father thought it heresy to learn such things. Rotations were beautiful, I thought, the cause of the seasons, and the author of absolutely everything. I wanted to talk to Tamu about Copernicus, and I wondered if he even knew of him, but we were out of time.

I surprised both of us by saying, "Tamu, come with me in the morning. You can go with me to the royal court where I will be employed. It will be safe for you there. And from there perhaps I can find a way to get you home."

The fire reflected itself in Tamu's wet eyes.

"No, my kind sir. I will be safer here. Anywhere near nobility, I will be enslaved."

"How can I ever reach you? How can I know that you are safe?" I asked him.

"I am afraid you cannot. I am going to wander this coast for as long as I can, as I am very good at hiding. One day, perhaps, I will figure out a way home. Thank you for letting me help you with your problem." Tamu's voice was beautiful, like a well-played bassoon.

I tried one more time, explaining to Tamu that I needed help, and that I was frightened of the sea. Having Tamu by my side would make the journey less frightful. I realized he was the only person I had ever met who knew me but knew nothing of Konstanze, nothing of my musical life. My heart pounded at the thought of her.

She was at that moment, I assumed, settling into her inn on the outskirts of Paris, a respectable place for women with children, probably next to a church. They probably had a basket of breads for her, most of which Franz would gobble up before falling asleep from the day's exertions. Was Konstanze in the same agony of the heart that night as I? As I uttered a melancholy farewell to Tamu, a sad little melody in a minor key came to me. I sang it to him, and he smiled as he walked back into the reeds. I missed my new friend already.

I returned to the inn for a last short sleep before leaving for England. My mind that night preferred the more recent new memories of Tamu over the painful recollections of Konstanze, Franz, and the more distant feelings about Salzburg and Vienna. How many, I wondered, had passed through Boulogne on the same journey? I thought of all of the numbers I knew: how many steps existed from home to St. Stephen's, or how many paces from home all the way to the Prater. I knew how many windows there were in San Pietro, or how many people could sit in Salzburg Cathedral. I knew the number of measures in almost all of my works, and I knew I could play any one of the thousands of phrases I had written without ever consulting a score. I knew how many times I had seen Ludwig, and how many years since my father's death, and how many days had passed since I last saw Joseph II, and how long since Lorenzo. But meeting Tamu on that eve of a great journey, I was confronted with a new host of things I could not know. I snuffed out my candle and drifted into sleep while staring out the open window. Somewhere out there in the dark was England. And somewhere nearby, nestled among reeds or plants, was Tamu. Next to my bed, I felt the moist leather pouch Tamu had given me, a reminder to apply the ointment the next morning. I realized that my nether regions felt better for the first time in weeks. Tamu's treatment was working. Just before sleep overtook me, a small fart emerged that made me giggle.

CHAPTER 38

Within what felt like a few minutes, I heard the innkeeper pounding on my door, warning me to get to the ship lest my luggage leave for England without me. I sprang to alertness and left, quickly paying the inn for the eventful few days. The ship looked like some kind of hulking sea monster. I walked across the heaving plank, gave my name to a man who asked for it, and something was mentioned about passage for three, forcing me to explain that I was now committing to the passage alone.

The ship tossed in its berth, too heavily for my stomach, and I felt queasy before we even set sail. I remembered a relative calm when I crossed as a child, but I had turned many memories into serenity, or perhaps I had simply forgotten. The channel was heaving strongly and all of the passengers were warned that the crossing was likely to take many hours, as they had to find the right crosswinds to sail to Hastings. It was announced that the winds were not looking favorably on the day, but they had loaded too many goods to wait for another. We set sail, and the huge ship dizzily rocked from side to side, sending me into an anguish of nausea and fear. I knew, though, that I could not turn back. There was an indoor area to the ship where I might go to apply Tamu's treatment, but I could not find the courage to set myself loose from the railing on the back of the vessel. It seemed to move very slowly, but the land was already a distance from us within just a few minutes. Within an hour, I felt I would never see land again. France was a hazy shadow but still in sight. The ship calmed for a bit when the sun was directly overhead. I made my way inside long enough to apply the ointment in an area reserved for men, and I took advantage of there being no one present, as everyone was on deck.

England came into view off to the right, and we seemed to be following the coast in the direction of the sun. The ship began heaving again as we neared Hastings, and overshot to the west, then the east, like the curved paths over the Salzburg mountains. I managed to stave off vomiting until we were nearly at our destination. There was no way for me to stop it; the contents of my stomach had to be emptied, for the stench of the ship in the late-day wind was overwhelming. I saw a man empty himself into a chamber pot only to miss it because of the rolling of the ship, and the sight and smell of his load of shit sent me across a boundary I had managed all day to contain. I hurled my vomit off the back of the ship, the wind carrying it far, and I could not understand the laughter of much of the ship's crew, as though they had placed bets on whether or not I might make it across without the eruption of Vesuvius.

The ship slowly made its way to a jetty in Hastings Harbour, by which time I felt considerably better than when we had left France. I had vomited, yes, but that had passed, and with it any feeling of what had come before. I stepped onto English soil for the first time since my boyhood, and I shall always remember that it was the first day of June, 1799. The carriage was there, exactly as promised, though I was surprised to learn that I was not to stay in Hastings and would instead be driven partway to London that very night, to a small town the name of which I did not clearly hear at first. My luggage was loaded and within only a few minutes, the harbor and the ship were behind me. The roads in England were clearer and less bumpy than in France, though I noticed that carriages veered to the left instead of right when faced with those coming in the opposite direction. I wondered why this would be so and vowed to find out. It was known to the coachman that I was to be driven into London for royal appointment, and I was informed that our journey might take up to three days, as the weather had been unusually foul in the capital, which would require a few days' stay in the south of the country. I was proud that my English was good enough to discern what the coachman was saying at all. He said he would receive a report on the roads once we arrived at my inn in Lewes, as I was finally able to understand the name of the little town of our destination, which I had seen written down in Boulogne, but had pronounced it as "Leves." The English pronounced it as "Louis," clearly sounding the "s" at the end, unlike the French. There was so much I needed to learn.

I had carried some English with me since childhood, and it was a language I loved. German, naturally, was the language of my deepest thoughts. Italian was always the most musical, and French the most useful for travel. But there was something uniquely beautiful about English, at least the formal English that I learned. I felt infinitely closer to the language since composing *Richard III*, because the German translation I used to create Emanuel's scenario also had the English on the opposing page. I thought it was such an ingenious language, so pliable and of infinite expression. It was thought an unmusical language by learned musicians of the day, but I had played for hours through a small set of Henry Purcell's songs and found them to be exceptional, perfectly pitched and set, with words landing on precisely the right note.

I loved particularly "I attempt from Love's sickness to fly in vain," and thought it Purcell's most perfect song, along with his "An Evening Hymn." I often thought of both, because for me they were perfection, an immediate wedding of words and music. I sang both songs repeatedly, with or without a keyboard, delighting sometimes in the way the word *fly* would so naturally take flight, or how the painful emotions were set on descending phrases, and I loved to exaggerate *fever* and *pain*. I remembered just where I was—in Praha—when I realized I understood each word of the song, even the line "with pride no more swell." And I loved discovering that the song was about the singer and not about a silent other, as I felt so many songs to be.

I thought through my own catalogue and realized I had written very few songs, just intimate works for one singer and one keyboard. I hoped I would be allowed to create many songs as part of my new duties. Song-writing would, after all, be one of the fastest ways to improve my English. The court had no official tongue, but there was an unspoken expectation that business be conducted in the Gallic, in French, but informally nearly every courtier was German. I knew, then, that I would hear the comforts of my native language but still would need a command of English. I wanted to create music that could be enjoyed by everyone, even the lowlier speakers of English who had never had benefit of education. My own dialect of German was thought more lowly than the German spoken closer to the sea in the north. Even at the Viennese court, my German had been criticized and noticed, singled out for its lack of cultivation. I always took on languages easily, and I knew I could mimic the sound of any speaker. Lorenzo used to laugh at how perfectly I could imitate the nasal Italian of Antonio Salieri, always followed by a vow never to tell the senior composer of my mimicry. I could sound precisely like Joseph II as well, and anyone else. My ability to truly hear someone was so unique that as I got older, I had to take care about who I was around, because within a few minutes I would sound like them, assuming their cadence and tone. It made me quick to learn, but also vulnerable to whoever I was hearing. Konstanze used to complain that after long journeys she could sometimes not recognize my voice, as it had been so altered by those I had met.

CHAPTER 39

The carriage was very fast, and though I was unsure of the distance we traversed, it seemed very little time before we arrived at a steep and high street in the small burg of Lewes, where I was to stay at an inn until news came about the roads to London. There were several possible routes, and each might require an additional overnight stay somewhere, depending on the reports. I loved the wet and cool breeze that filled the place, and my room at the White Hart Inn was the nicest place I had stayed since leaving Vienna. It contained a small desk by a window out of which I could see grassy hills and a small river. The kindly innkeeper showed me around, in notable contrast to the old drunk in Boulogne. He directed me toward various points of interest, and he called the hills "downs," a word I did not fully understand at that time, as it felt that hills went up and not down, but I was too embarrassed to form such a juvenile observation into a question. The man spoke very fast. I wanted him to speak for as long as he could, because his voice was melodic and so that I could remember individual words he uttered.

The day was windy but beautiful, so I took a walk, as several hours of light remained. It had been so long since I had felt like walking for leisure. It made me realize again that Tamu's treatment was working. I was far from Boulogne now, but not so far as to feel completely different from it. Indeed, it felt that at one time they may have been closer together, which I thought impossible. It was not like the change from Salzburg to

Vienna, for example, neither of which felt close to the other, yet elements of each were ever present.

My first walk in England was wet, and I had to find dry places on which to tread. The pathway down to the River Ooze or Ouse, as I had been told it was called, was perilous indeed, but the gentle river, much smaller than the Salz, was comforting. It seemed more a creek than a river, as one might easily cross it even on foot if necessary, whereas the Salz could never be crossed without a transport or a bridge. There was a small bridge in Lewes, red and slightly arched, and I thought it the prettiest bridge I had encountered in a long time. I walked over and around it several times, delighting in its ingenuity. There were steps all around it, allowing people to arrive by boat if they lived some distance away, and they could leave their boats and return to them after their shopping. There were even horses on pathways to help a boat begin its journey upstream, and I wondered if this brilliant convergence existed elsewhere, along the Donau, perhaps. I assumed it must, but I had never before seen it or had not noticed it.

I recalled a truth about travel from my youth: you notice things in new places that may be all around your home, but they are only revealed for the first time in a place that feels foreign. I had seen many bridges before, but there was something about the simple and practical elegance of this one that I enjoyed. I thought that long contemplation of this lovely small bridge might alter the huge terrifying bridge that appeared in my dreams. I sat for some time by the river in Lewes. It seemed not to move at all, more like a lake than a river. I tossed a handful of leaves onto the surface and they spun a few times while they slowly made their way in the direction of Hastings. The river made no sound at all. I heard only the wind and the birds, and those sounds were of remarkable beauty in those first English hours. I could sit and listen to those sounds for days on end. Music drifted in and out of my mind, competing with nature. I was grateful for the arrival of musical ideas, as they were a presentiment of a productive time in London. I trusted they would return when I next sat down to write. On that first day in England, I recalled Praha, where I also sat by a river and just listened to it. I was free. Every moment by a river seemed to teem with freedom, as though music sat in the wind itself. Nature was so strong everywhere, but there was a special feeling to the gracious air and water in that little English place. My appointment would keep me rooted in London, but I wondered if I might be allowed some magical place like this where I could sometimes listen to nature with no distractions at all.

As the sun rapidly descended, I panted my way back up the hill to the White Hart. Horses filled the street, all of them being readied for journeys to London. The innkeeper told me I would likely have to stay for at least three days, possibly two, because of the condition of the roads to London and the availability of horses. My coach, to be shared with three other gentlemen, would leave at the third dawn unless I was otherwise informed. The innkeeper assured me there would be plenty to do and see in the area. I thanked him as I relished two days at my desk sketching a backlog of ideas that were accumulating. I had hardly had time to even open my folio in Paris, and there had been so much turmoil with Konstanze, and my own body had been a constant distraction.

New opera ideas were arriving, but so were many things. I desperately wanted to learn English, and this was a deep desire, as I wanted to write reams of songs in Shakespeare's language. I wanted to surprise the King and his employers with a set of variations that I could easily compose within a day. An air of freedom had come upon me since the boat arrived in Hastings, and the themes were flowing.

The innkeeper offered me an ale, which I happily took.

"You look like that Paine fellow. Are you related to him?"

The question confused me. Did he mean "pain," as in Purcell's "I am myself my own fever and pain"? Was Pain a man's name?

At my expression, the innkeeper explained, "Thomas Paine, from up north, but was around here for years before he left for America. You must have heard of him. He was quite the most famous person we've ever had at the White Hart. Of course, that was years ago. No one will remember it now."

I did recall the name, but I had never heard an English person say it. I remembered Lorenzo giving me a copy of *Common Sense*, in German, and as much as I'd tried to forget the provocateur, I had to admit that his writing had stuck with me. Interesting fellow, but the right of a people to overthrow their own government did not seem to me any kind of right at all. What Paine advocated was violent anarchy, and I wanted no association with that.

I remembered hearing of Paine in stories about the French Revolution, but I had not paid him a great deal of attention because it is useless to listen to a man who disavowed God completely. I wondered why those revolutionaries always had to bring God into their own machinations. The world had been formed around God's design and surely that also meant a design for man to learn how to govern himself. Politics and politicians were epic bores, and so Thomas Paine must be doubly that, as he was trying to argue that it was commonsensible to have a nation free of God. I often longed for the certainties of youth, because as I grew older more doubt crept into my spiritual soul. I despise doubt.

The innkeeper said Thomas Paine had been around many years before, but had resurfaced in Lewes more recently on the run from authorities trying to lock him up for inciting revolutions. The French would love to find him, the innkeeper said, his countenance turning sinister. He relayed a story about Paine at the White Hart, where they had a signal that would send Paine out through the kitchen and down the hill until a specific candle was placed in a certain window, signaling the all clear, whenever authorities came looking for him. I struggled to understand the appeal of Thomas Paine, but my English could not yet keep up with the innkeeper's speed. Nonetheless I could feel Paine had stirred something deep within these people, and understood I needed to learn more of him lest my judgment be formed too hastily.

It was soon time for my first full sleep in England since my boyhood. The air was cool and I drifted quickly into slumber under a down blanket as the scent of the ocean and the downs caressed me. I thought of my little Franz, and hoped I might have a dream about him.

But there were no dreams that night, as I slept so soundly that I wondered upon waking where I was and why. For more than an instant I could not recall even who I was; a strange sensation I had never felt before. I was in a frozen purgatory just before waking, locked in my body and paralyzed with fright. I struggled against the sensation, struggling to wrest my body from forces immobilizing it, becoming aware of sensations in my arms and legs. I tried to sing out loud but that, too, was locked. Presently I startled myself awake, to find the sun already midway up its morning journey. I had been asleep for many hours. The air and the liberty had guarded me, right up through my locked-in sensation. The liberation was a wonderful feeling.

I went immediately to my folio after the chamber pot, and ideas poured out just as swiftly as my morning water. Two themes for piano sonatas, two potential symphonies for my new employer. I wondered if a second Shakespeare opera might serve me well in the court as a complement to *Richard III*. Perhaps *Hamlet*, which I had loved when I saw Emanuel play it so many times. I hoped I could find a poet to help me convert *Richard III* from German back to its native English. Italian opera was popular in London, so perhaps I could put on *Figaro* or *Don Giovanni* and make some money. What to do with *Tartuffe* in London? A French opera would surely be accepted, and it was difficult to imagine the story in anything but French, but again I needed a poet. I had with me in one of my trunks all of the materials for *Flute* and *Tito* as well, and I was sure we could develop a fine *Magic Flute* for the court theater, as it had to be done in the vernacular, unlike *Tito*, which should and could remain in Italian, as it was such simplistic Italian oft repeated in each portion that anyone could understand it. I noted down two cello sonata themes and loved them instantly, working through them both in my head and vowing to finish them soon.

I was eager to hear my new court orchestra that Haydn had said was so very expert. I had packed several serenades, and vowed to compose more, as it was a form that was easy for me and I had done too few. Depending on what I found at the court orchestra, there would undoubtedly be many more concertos to bring to life. I thought of composing variations to a theme of Purcell, but my mind kept returning instead to a tune Haydn had played for me that he said the King loved, and it had a feeling of Purcell or Handel. I had heard Haydn play it only once but it was easily committed to memory. I liked that it was about God's protection, and I hoped the court would not consider it disrespectful if I composed variations on Haydn's tune, which naturally would not have any words. The tune did not make for easy variations, because it did not vary much, but I spent some time staring at the fourteen measures of triple meter, contemplating what I might be able to do with it. On a clavichord that existed only in my imagination in those days, I played a variation of arpeggiated semiquavers in the right hand over a walking bass. I wondered if it might be too flowery for a first variation, so I left it unnumbered on a folio sheet and began doing more. Changing the triple meter to common time brought a new range of ideas, including an elaborate scale passage of more than two octaves that surprised me even as it appeared in mind. Several minor variations came up, and many with complex finger work for the left hand.

I noticed the sun tipping low in the sky behind the hotel and realized I had been working on the short tune, "God Save the King," for many hours. I sorted through my folio and was surprised and delighted to find sketches for fifty variations, so I placed them in a desirable order, numbered them, and placed them in my folio, as happy with a day's work as I had been in months. Each variation had a unique character that I hoped would delight my new court. I could shorten the work if it might be thought too long, but I knew it would hold the interest of the appreciative.

CHAPTER 40

Downstairs, the innkeeper had a surprise for his guests. A deer had been stalked and successfully killed on the downs, and it would feed the entire inn and many others that evening. I loved venison, and as my stomach had been quite alone through the day, the poor deer was welcome news. I ate in the dining room of the inn for the first time, a lively and large room filled with men taking tobacco in a range of forms, speaking mostly in English but in enough French to make conversation intelligible. All they seemed to want to discuss was Thomas Paine, as if Paine was there in the room, or still roaming the high street talking about his revolutionary ideas. Several men in the room knew Paine, and one man in particular, nobly dressed, said to the entire room, in both French and English, that I looked like Thomas Paine. Having heard the accusation twice since arriving in Lewes, I thought it must be taken seriously. I could do nothing about how I looked, I said, to laughter, and should not a man be judged by his character instead of his resemblance? This, too, brought laughter, and it was a delight to be thought humorous.

"Paine is the most famous man ever to be in this inn," a man said, repeating the innkeeper's refrain.

"What about Mozart?" I said, testing the gentlemen, as the wine slightly soaked my mind. I doubted anyone had heard my name before.

"The boy wonder!" a man said.

"Mozart would never be in Lewes. He plays for kings and queens," someone said.

"He is for them, not for us," another said.

"The likes of Lewes will never see or hear Mozart," the innkeeper offered.

I found it all delightful. The innkeeper did not know who I was, nor did anyone. These men had heard of Mozart, and I was a name they could say, but they had actually *known* Thomas Paine. I enjoyed being known while simultaneously not known. I knew that when I arrived at court within a few days, everyone would know me, so I decided to remain a secret to the White Hart, and to enjoy what these men knew of me. One mentioned *Magic Flute*, and another sang the simple C-major sonata. It amazed me that anyone this far away would know anything I had written. One playfully chortled through the "Turkish March." One said he had read that Mozart had died. When one of them mentioned Haydn, I felt homesick.

When Ludwig's name came up, I decided it was time to go to sleep. The venison was delicious, and I had eaten several portions of it. I went outside to relieve myself before bed, where the huge animal was still hanging on a spit behind the White Hart, with dogs lurking in the shadows waiting their turn. I was known, and my music was known, but they had no way of knowing me by sight. To the dining room at the White Hart, I was just another traveler heading for London. Tamu hadn't known me at all, and I had spent hours with him just days before and never mentioned that I was a composer, never sang him a tune. Tamu, like the men in Lewes, looked at me and saw only a man, not a man who had accomplished something. I was worth to them exactly what they were to me.

They had all known Thomas Paine. What had Paine found that so magnetized them? I thought of my favorite part of *Così* with the magnets. I searched back into my memory of reading Paine and talking about him with Lorenzo and others in our favorite café a world away. I had largely dismissed Paine because of religion, and I owed so much to monarchs that I found it unseemly of a man like Paine to suggest the abolition of an institution that had done so much good. Lorenzo had thought Paine a genius. There were copies of Paine's writings in French and German, so I thought to try to read them now in my new life, where perhaps they might mean something new. I knew I should try to read him in English, but that would take many months. I could not possibly take a copy of any writings by Thomas Paine into the court, so I began to think of ways I could safely read him.

Something else one of the men said stayed with me, and repeated itself. He had asked me about coming through France and traveling to England "while there's a war on," and implying that I must have achieved some special kind of status in order to arrive on British shores from France when I was a citizen of the Holy Roman Empire. I had understood every word he said, and there was something in him that was frightening. I knew nothing of a war, though I had seen its ravages all around Paris. But war itself? Seeing actual combat? I had seen none of that. Our carriage had gone through France without sight of a gun or a battle, and no one at the dock in either France or England had asked about my Austrian nationality. I heard stories of war but were there still, in fact, battles raging? Could such conflicts exist and no one know about them? Wouldn't they occur over huge tracts of land? Would not so many people be displaced and forever uprooted?

War. So much of my life had been affected by war, but I had never seen war with my own eyes; I had seen only its aftermath. These men in the White Hart, the men who knew Paine, had actually been in combat, had looked into the eyes of a man and run him through with a sword or pulled a latch and watched the man's face as he fell like a tree. These men must have seen arms and legs blown off by cannons and muskets. Was that the type of war actually happening somewhere in France or England at that moment? The world must be enormous for such happenings to achieve such secrecy. There must be conflicts everywhere, yet there were monarchs as well, sitting in luxury and being served by a huge class of servants. And Tamu was hiding among the reeds when he should be healing others as he had healed me. It all felt confusing because of the wealth of things the men had talked about in the White Hart, and they all agreed with Thomas Paine that monarchs should be no different from those at war. I had never thought of this.

CHAPTER 41

I loved order and balance. Despite Papa's complaints about my intemperance, I knew I could write with a combination of light and dark, and I knew the world to be the same. There must be lightness and darkness all at once, but it was difficult to imagine war going on anywhere at that moment. The night was extremely dark with no moon, and the air cool and coming through my window with a slight aggression. I fell into sleep, wondering what my next day in Lewes might bring, and I realized how many months had passed since I had prayed.

I used to pray each day upon waking and unfailingly before retiring to sleep, yet my daily discipline had been lost. Prayer was communion with the infinite, the only possible way of knowing God—that was what I had always been taught. But the travels and upsets with Konstanze had set the habit aside, and so before falling into sleep in Lewes, I sent up a prayer, right from my bed. I prayed for the safety of Konstanze and Franz, and I prayed to see my sons again. I prayed that my new position in London would be fulfilling and fruitful, and I prayed for the intercession of the souls of my parents and my children. Just before drifting off, I sent a small prayer, too, for Tamu, that he might be safe on the coast of France, and that he might someday get to see his homeland again.

The next morning, the innkeeper told me of a man just up the road in Lewes, walking away from the river, who would take me on a coach ride through the countryside, even stopping at some noble homes for a small meal. The innkeeper said this would be the perfect way to pass some of the day before my passage to London the following morning. I did not want to be away from my desk for so many hours with so many ideas to write down, but I knew that a pleasant carriage ride in the country could be a way to fill my imagination with even further ideas, as I worked best when I placed some restrictions on my own time. It was a paradox that I could write more when faced with the sand descending in the glass than on a day completely unfettered by time.

I woke early the following morning, startled into the day by a dream, more of a vivid recollection, of *Don Giovanni's* unsuccessful reception in Vienna years before, after having been such a triumph in Prague. I never could understand it. There were a few musical changes between the cities, but in my view the Vienna version was slightly more interesting. Perhaps there had been some cabal organized against me—always a possibility with operatic connoisseurs—who could not resist chopping off the heads of beautiful flowers. Ludwig had not experienced it yet, at least that I knew, but it would come. It came for everyone. *Holy Roman Empire* kept repeating in my dream, as if to correct in sleep what I continually uttered in waking, calling my homeland Austria, even as I knew that was not its proper name. Would the court in London be so obsessed with official names?

As I woke, I felt renewed gratitude for the distance I had placed between myself and Ludwig, sure that some other competition or showdown was likely. The public, even the new court, would be unable to resist a Piccini-Gluck type of competition between us. On that day in Lewes, I hoped that I would never hear of Ludwig again, though his letter tucked away in my baggage called out to me. I had, then as always, an ability to ignore any possible unpleasantries. I felt I knew what his letter said, but as long as I did not look at it I could pretend. My life was terribly afflicted by the things I ignored.

Before finding breakfast, I jotted down a few ideas. Having thought of Christoph Gluck, I pondered a new modern orchestration of his *Orpheus*, possibly *Alceste*, as I thought them beautiful operas that needed modernizing if they were ever to be heard again. I thought *Orpheus* one of the finest operas I had heard besides my own. That left some time before my carriage ride, so I walked again down to banks of the Ouse, finding it the most peaceful of places. I had seen many rivers through my life, and many were mightier than this gently coursing stream. Still, there was something infinitely compelling about it. It was a stream with its own calm, peaceful, and healing life. I hoped many such places could be found in my new life. I would provide a set of new works to celebrate my appointment, at least six, including a new mass of thanks for my new employer. So much to put into my sketchbook! I left the riverside to meet the coachman who would drive me through the countryside. I wondered if I had packed the materials for my version of Handel's *Messiah*. I must have, but could not at that moment recall.

The coach departed the White Hart uphill, which excited me because I had not yet been in that direction, and had not yet seen what was around the corner. The castle, naturally, dominated the view. I had little interest in castles, even as I knew their function and their value. They always felt like painful places to me, where horrible punishments had been meted out. The cold, permanence of castles frightened me. Palaces were usually more interesting.

Almost ignored, though, opposite the road from the castle, was a very old structure with thick windows covered in mud. Great beams sagged, making the building lopsided. I inquired to the coachman, who told me it was a shop that sold books, and one of the only such places outside of London. It had even been said that patrons came from Hastings and Brighton to find purchases, which the coachman relayed with fascination and disbelief. I made the coachman stop so I could enter the establishment. I had left so many cherished books behind in Vienna, and nearly all of those had been purchased ten years before, during our most lucrative time. The beautiful German edition of *Richard III* had been a sadness to leave at home, but it was large and cumbersome. The shop had no name, but I thrilled at the sight of the place, and the smell of so many books was like stepping into paradise. I'm sure it was a sign that the title of *Tartuffe* appeared so soon inside the door. And what wonders there were inside! Shakespeare, Edward Gibbon, Goethe, and in English! Such famous minds! The bookseller inquired of my interests, something I could not recall ever being asked. In Vienna, books were brought to me by friends who knew my interests.

I apologized for my poor English but managed to ask if he had a copy of anything by Thomas Paine, the local hero. The man lit up and handed me a bundle of pamphlets by Paine, and to my astonishment they were in French as well as their native English. Paine kept appearing in my life, uninvited, which I decided was an auspicious sign that I must own his books. I offered a sum to the man, but to even more astonishment he refused it. "I heard you were at the White Hart," he said.

I was perplexed. Did the man know me? Suddenly, there was sound. Whistling. The man was whistling. Papageno's song, "Der Vogelfänger."

"How did you learn that?" I asked.

"I am a bookseller. I received the very first parcel of your scores that ever came to this country. I sold almost all of them to shops in London, but I kept a few for myself. I was able to play a few parts of *The Magic Flute*. I must have played that Papageno song a thousand times. It fit so perfectly in my hand. Being where we are, so many people are here only for a short time on their way to London. I heard many tales of your playing, of your father, and of your operas. A bookseller hears everything, you know? I have heard the name Mozart for a least thirty years, so imagine my excitement in hearing that you, too, were in Lewes. This would happen only one time in my life, and only for a few brief days, and you will never be here again. I longed for you to wander in here and for one of my books to go to London with you. And now, even more than I imagined, writings by my dear friend Tom will be in your hands."

I was overwhelmed. Just the night before I had gone unnoticed at the White Hart. I tried to express my gratitude, but everything came out as gibberish. I somehow managed to say, "I am muted with thanks," trying to convey that my gratitude had exceeded my abilities in English at that moment, but I hoped the man understood me.

"What will you see today, Herr Mozart?"

I understood him, and I was impressed by his musical pronunciation of "Herr." I explained that I was only biding time until the next sunrise, and the innkeeper at the White Hart had suggested I have a ride through the downs.

"Could I be so presumptuous, Herr Mozart, as to accompany you? I have lived here throughout my long life, and it would be the greatest of all honors to show you our beautiful village and the downs," the man asked.

I had never expected such kindness, and I had encountered it now with strangers, both Tamu and this man, who said his name was Trevor. Tamu and Trevor, the kindest men I had ever met, and Trevor actually played my music, which I thought amazing. He locked his bookshop with a large key, and accompanied me to the waiting carriage. We departed up the high street, farther up this time, away from the castle. Trevor waving greetings to the equerry at another inn, the Shelleys, which Trevor explained was the inn for the nobler patrons making their way to London, though any actual nobility would stay as a guest of one of the manor houses in the surrounding area, as no noble person would ever pay for accommodation. This practice was new for me, something I had not before considered.

I told him about Tamu, and Trevor told me of many slaves who, he had heard, were similarly living in the downs and around the coast. It was increasingly challenging for escaped slaves to hide in England simply because they were getting so crowded. There was hardly a place in the downs from which you could not see some other place, which had not been the England of Trevor's youth. I found myself telling Trevor all sorts of things, including works I had not thought about in years. Trevor mentioned *Ave verum corpus* and so I sang it for him. He knew *Figaro* but only the famous tunes that had come through the shop in an edition from Paris. Trevor had heard stories about *Richard III* from several visitors, and he delighted in hearing me describe it. He asked about Beethoven, and for once I did not bristle at the thought of him. A safe distance had been achieved.

CHAPTER 42

Our open carriage moved swiftly through gracious countryside, the hills undulating in tall grasses, and cows and sheep dotted every vista. The views were beautiful and spacious, and the groves of trees seemed to organize themselves so as to maximize the distant downs. It felt like I could see all the way across England or, if we situated ourselves on just the right spot, even see back to France. But Trevor explained that, as far as he knew, France was invisible from this part of the world; yet, he was quick to point out, many things were continually surprising him about the place. Not too many years before, a great fire could be seen in the far distance, and days later it was revealed that a bonfire had been lit at Portsmouth, and Trevor and others were in disbelief that such a distance could be seen from Lewes.

We traversed country roads and lovely farms, and Trevor greeted the owners of each by name. Small rolling hills brought us into the lovely little village of Glynde, a name that sounded to me like "glide," and the small hillock seemed as though it was gliding. The breeze was constant, a hint of the sea, and the church and another small building, all built from the surrounding rock, seemed to be talking back to the land. Trevor knew of a pub in the little village, and he directed the coach to it.

After lunch, I asked if it might be possible to take a leisurely walk through the countryside, even walking back to Lewes. The coachman thought this a poor idea, placing me in danger of being lost, but Trevor thought it splendid, offering to join me. The coachman was despondent, but agreed to let us go. "If you end up at the sea, you've gone the wrong direction," he joked.

We were alone for at least a few hours in the quiet of this new country. The first presence I noted were the birds, and I loved birdsong so very much. The wind created a slight music, more at a distance than close, and the most precious gift of the earth, silence, overtook us. Silence had been as rare in my life as it was in all lives. Vienna was a constant whirl of noise, as I was sure London would be. Carriage rides were noisy but at least rhythmic, and inns and pubs were often deafening to me.

In the blissful peace of silence, my mind could race for a few minutes before giving over to its strong force. Trevor and I walked, and I understood the silence, feeling no need to fill it with chatter. The churchyard at Glynde receded behind us, and hedgerows divulged efforts to tame nature. The hedgerows had their own beauty, and butterflies seemed to enjoy them. Great old trees hovered in the high breezes. We came upon a beautiful brick manor house, ungated, protected only by a few bushes. There were no gardeners or servants lingering, though this was obviously a very grand home of a noble and wealthy family. It was nothing approaching what royalty would own, but it far surpassed any home I could imagine. We still had a long distance back to Lewes, but there was a spot canopied by huge trees that was too inviting to pass. Trevor pointed to a pathway and said it was the way back to Lewes, and he thought it best to head back himself and let me have some time.

"This has been the greatest day of my life, Herr Mozart. Hopefully I will see you again before you depart."

"How did you know I was at the White Hart?"

"I see the manifestos of the inn, you see, for I am its owner."

I thanked him for his kindness and we parted.

I stretched out on the manicured lawn to take a short nap before the long walk back to Lewes. I had not been this alone in nature in so long. I removed my shoes, because other than my painful adventure with Tamu, I had not been outside my shoes, and not since long afternoons at the Esterházy estate had my toes delighted in touching grass that had been cultivated with such care.

To my surprise, I quickly fell asleep, the world and birds a lull, and the sound of distant sheep amusing. I awoke after what seemed like not very long, but felt as refreshed. Something out of the ground beneath, perhaps, was energizing to me, and I returned my shoes to their rightful place and resumed my journey back. How fortunate to have enjoyed the luxurious grounds of this home without the burden of maintaining it. I left having never seen a person on the estate. It was a congenial place.

CHAPTER 43

I climbed a sizable hill beyond which I assumed I would find Lewes. By late afternoon the village came into view, nestled on the hillside, a white chalk cliff to my left that reminded me of those on the coast, and sunlight was reflecting off the meandering River Ouse. The battlements of the castle assured me I was in the right place. It was to be my last night in Lewes, possibly my last night before my new life in London fully opened.

I arrived back at the White Hart to find my volumes of Thomas Paine awaiting me, wrapped in a package clever enough to conceal them from the court. Trevor had been kind enough to bring them, along with a copy of *The Magic Flute* in an edition I did not even know existed, along with a note asking me to sign it for him. I had not before been asked to autograph a score, as the idea had never occurred to my friends and colleagues in Vienna or Prague. I had signed many documents in my life, but this was a signature I was particularly delighted to provide, because the request came from someone who knew my work without expecting we would meet. I signed, "To my new friend, Trevor, who showed me his beautiful country."

The innkeeper reminded me that my transport to London would be at dawn the following morning, so I had a small dinner and retired to my room to do a few more sketches for the London piano concertos. I fell asleep with excitement mounting.

The dawn came quickly, and soon I and three others were on our way to London, our luggage filling a coach behind us. The roads were clear and the journey remarkably fast. There was never a question of us having to overnight at another an inn. The coachman took a route into the city quite different from what I could recall from my youth, when we had crossed a beautiful bridge across the Thames and made our way to the west of Buckingham House, surrounded by beautiful fields. On that morning journey from Lewes, the coach took us along several curves of the Thames until a final turn northward revealed Westminster Hall and the great Abbey behind it, towering over everything in immediate view. Only a few moments later, behind us, the tallest structure imaginable came into view, St. Paul's Cathedral. I remembered it from my youth, but it looked so much bigger this time. I wondered how anyone could conceive of something so enormous. Surely there would never be anything higher built by man, nor should there be. Even with my convulsing excitement at finally arriving in London, the sight of the Abbey and St. Paul's was a reassuring reminder of stability, for I had seen them both before, while everything else felt new, but also they were reminders of ideals. They held within their vastness the profoundest possibilities of achievement and honor, and they kept watch. St. Stephen's had kept watch over Vienna, too, and I often prayed for the direct intercession of the patron saint himself. My saint would now be Paul.

The carriage was going so fast that the months of expectation turned to memory. Within a few minutes, I was delivered to an equerry at St. James's Palace as instructed in my letter of royal appointment. I was embarrassed to make my fellow passengers wait, but they were impressed by my employment, not a word of which I had mentioned in the journey from Lewes. They were all to be delivered to points more easterly, in the far less royal and green parts of the city of London. The equerry, having disappeared for a short time, told the coachman to deliver me to an address near Grosvenor Square, instructing him on the best route to the house that was only a short distance away. I was handed a key to my new home, and the carriage took off, arriving at Grosvenor Square after some struggle to get through the incredible crowds and bustle, something I had not remembered from my earlier journey. I would have to contend with these crowds each day as I made my way from home to palace.

A small package of instructions accompanying my keys said that I had been given by the King the privilege of mail delivery, a dispensation given to few, as a way of easing the pain of homesickness. Mail delivery would allow me to stay closely in touch with those I left behind, the letter said. My address was to be Upper Brook Street, number 50, Grosvenor Square. The carriage arrived, my possessions carried to the small house, farewells said, and I was suddenly alone in the silence of my new home. All of my trunks from Paris were awaiting me. There was a drawing room and music room, almost connected, and a bedroom upstairs, facing a garden shared by many other houses. The basement kitchen and larder were more luxurious than any I had envisioned. My instructions indicated I would be welcomed for meals at the servants' quarters of St. James's Palace if I liked, or I could use my own kitchen. A chambermaid would be provided twice a week to assist me with household matters. As a court composer I was a royal servant, and so was not allowed my own equerry, as he would be a fellow servant, but I could apply for carriage transport around London in order to carry out any court-related duties. I was advised that carriage service was best applied for many days in advance of any anticipated need.

I liked the house. I played a few phrases on the clavichord, which needed tuning, a task I would be obliged to carry out myself. The notes reverberated through the empty dwellings. The feelings I had been expecting to accompany this moment did not arrive. Melancholy was present but distant. Grief, for there had been so much loss, was also hovering, but it, too, seemed to be remaining outside the home, awaiting entrance. I searched myself, and I felt a new and specific kind of joy. I was free. I knew I was only free of Vienna and of Konstanze, but there was liberation in that. I would not be free in the sense that nobility understood the word, and I would be bound by the strictures of the court and subject to the whims of George III, but that did not in that moment feel a hardship. After all, George III had extended the invitation on Haydn's recommendation; it was not something I had sought. And besides, I knew His Majesty from years before. I had played for him as a child. I had to compose official works now, but beyond that I had enormous freedom to compose what I liked, and I was promised I could compose operas and even promised that they be produced, subject to royal approval. The possibilities were inspiring, and they were all ringing through the silence of those rooms so new to me. I began to unpack my belongings and get to work.

CHAPTER 44

I reported the next morning as requested to St. James's Palace, where I was taken to meet the Lord Chamberlain, my direct boss. I was also told by this gruff and serious Lord, to my enormous surprise, that as court composer I would report directly to the Master of the King's Musick, William Parsons, who would approve all of my compositions. The Lord Chamberlain would be my guidance for anything nonmusical. I had been led to believe, from my invitation and from Haydn's description, that Sir William would be retired upon my arrival. I searched my memory. Had not Haydn said this? Yes. Certainly so. He had. Sir William was to retire. My papers had said so as well. I had left my papers at the house. My heart fibrillated in panic. The Lord Chamberlain continued to speak. Like Konstanze, talking, talking. I wondered what to do, as I did not want to appear difficult on my first day.

"I was told that Sir William, eminent musician, was to be retired upon my arrival and that I am now Master of the King's Musick. Are there now two men sharing the post?"

The Lord Chamberlain, unaccustomed to inquiry, corrected me. "You are the new court composer, Herr Mozart."

"But Herr Haydn, and my own papers, say I am to be the Master of the King's Musick," I said.

"They said, and he said, exactly what I telling you now: that you are to be His Majesty's *court composer*."

I could feel a familiar dull pressure in my chest, and I knew I must leave that room. I asked what my first duties were to be, and the Lord Chamberlain deferred to Sir William, explaining to me again that all of my artistic duties would be outlined to me by the Master of the King's Musick, to whom I would be subject to regular report. I was to meet Sir William at the Chapel Royal at midday, and handed instructions as to how to find it, just a short distance away. Niceties were exchanged and I quickly found myself alone again, outside, along a treelined street of cobblestones I had heard people call the Mall. It was a beautiful morning. I walked, panicked, unable to fathom how this could have happened or what to do about it. Perhaps Haydn could send a letter to the King, but it would undoubtedly be intercepted. Could I possibly get to the King himself? I would have to go through the Lord Chamberlain. I had heard Haydn speak of Parsons. Perhaps I should meet with him and simply accept this unexpected way of my new life. I had little choice. I had to meet with him.

I kept interrupting my own scampering thoughts. I had been promised freedom. This was not freedom. This was servitude, just as surely as work for Joseph II had been, but he had been benevolent and supportive; I had been able to push past other royal appointments and write what I liked, however controversial. What would Parsons allow? I wished I could talk to Haydn. I could never know what the appointment would be like without meeting Parsons, and if I did not appear for my midday meeting at the Chapel Royal, there would be no other necessity, for my new appointment would be over before it began. Through my entire life, though I had been interested in so many things—endless ideas for operas, and symphonies, masses, and concertos for all kinds of instruments—I had never been able to be single-minded, but there had always been one prevailing urge: I simply wanted to compose. Whatever my other desires, the ambition to get to the blank page each day overrode them all.

Even as I paced St. James's Park wondering what to do, I wished I could be home in my music room writing down the strands of the fugue forming in my mind. Would Sir William allow me to adapt *The Magic Flute* for a London audience, or *Richard III*? Would my many Catholic masses be thought too opulent for English tastes? I had assumed an ability to write what I liked, and to provide George III with ceremonial music, but also an entire repertoire of operas and symphonies that might symbolize this era for the King. I planned a new set of Coronation Anthems now that those of Handel were seventy-five years old or more, and George's successor would want to inherit anthems commissioned by his father. No, I thought, I could not come into service and immediately mention my monarch's successor. *My* monarch? George III was my employer but not my monarch. What to do? I had still to wait several hours for my meeting, so perhaps I could go home. No, too risky that I might be late returning. I had no manuscript with me. Westminster Abbey was nearby. I had not been there since I was a boy. I could go there and pray for some time. I could hear Papa's voice: "Go sit in the church and pray. The answers will come."

I entered Westminster Abbey, stopped by rows of beggars who had been kept out by boys in altar service. I was dressed appropriately enough to be allowed entrance. I knew from St. Stephen's that churches wanted as many people as possible at services, and they wanted to be charitable toward the poor, but they did not want their cathedrals to be used for shelter. People were kept out most of the time, because otherwise the buildings would become overwhelmed, so great was the need. To help the many, they were forced to keep out the few. I ached at the sight of so many hungry and poor people, and I prayed in gratitude for my employment. I wished I could help each of them, and I could never understand Konstanze's revulsion at the sight of them. She always claimed to be worried about disease, and she was certain they carried all kinds of pestilences. Even handing them a few coins could transmit it, she believed. Papa held within him similar anger toward anyone who begged, a reaction I came to understand as merely Leopold's fear of never having enough money. Monarchs, if they wanted to have their reigns blessed by God, had to be as generous as possible to their people. I knew this to be the only way for the poor to be helped. I did not understand why this should be so, but I knew it was. There would always be the poor and always the rich, and I knew I had no choice in life but to live between the two.

The Abbey was empty. It was as cold as I remembered, and markedly larger. The huge floor stones made me feel small, which must have been the builders' intention. The chill felt old, as though the air was lifeless. There was a mustiness buried inside the smell of the devotional candles, an odor that immediately returned my memory to Salzburg. I walked the length of the Abbey, the vast windows casting their soft light over all. The Abbey was completely silent by the time I reached the Poets' Corner. Chaucer, Shakespeare, Samuel Butler...I surveyed them all. The whole of English history was remembered in this spot. They remembered their greatest. I realized then I was without a country. If I died at that moment, where might I lie in peace? Where would there ever be a statue of me? Salzburg? Vienna? Would Konstanze do something to memorialize me? How might Konstanze learn of my death? I assumed an equerry would deliver a letter to her from the Lord Chamberlain. "Herr Mozart died," and little more. I had nothing to identify myself, so what would happen if my life were suddenly taken? I would simply not appear for my meeting with Parsons, then would not appear at my new home, and eventually someone in London might notice I was gone.

I stood in front of Handel's monument, which I did not remember seeing as child, and it would not have meant so much to me then, as that was before I had reorchestrated *Messiah* and played so many of his works. I owned a volume of Handel's keyboard suites that I cherished and wished I had brought with me, though I knew I could find another in London. I had played them so often that I might be able to recall each from memory. Handel and Bach, two I wished I had been able to meet. Bach. Those organ preludes and fugues were some of the very greatest music ever written. Organ sonatas I had mastered, I think, but I would be happy to write more. But preludes and fugues for organ? Writing fugues conceived for hands and feet, and in voices that could really be heard in huge cathedrals and abbeys like Westminster—that was a real gift. I needed to write some of those. In the distance, an organist was starting a quiet warm-up. Was it Samuel Arnold, whom Haydn has mentioned with such reverence, and who had composed several works that even Lorenzo had said I should hear? I tried to see the organ console but could not locate it. I assumed it was hidden somewhere within the enclosed choir area. The air was still slightly heaving into the pipes, as the bellows seemed reluctant to get going that morning.

I could not believe what I was hearing. It was a choir rehearsal. I had heard this music before.

"From harmony, from heavenly harmony / This universal frame began…"

They were rehearsing Handel's *Ode for St. Cecilia's Day*. Was it perhaps the feast of St. Cecilia, a feast day my own father never missed? Out of the silence of sitting by Handel's own tomb, and monument, the very music carved into stone was coming to life. It was not the music that Handel was holding in the statue, but it was depicted elsewhere in the beautiful monument. I longed to see the singers, to experience not the disembodied music but to see the actual performers. I had not been among performers for so long. The ode continued into the various movements, a few, small things were rehearsed, and an aria appeared I had forgotten about completely until it began. "What passion cannot music raise and quell?" I could not remember the precise meaning of many of the words, but I remembered my favorite: "to worship that celestial sound!" Oh, this indescribably beautiful aria! I was so happy to hear it again. I remembered the unique scoring of the aria even after many years, and it was evoked beautifully by the organ that day. Celestial sound meant a music you might hear in Heaven, and in this aria I thought it was true. This was the only music I could imagine hearing in a blessed place, the music of God. To hear it in the Abbey was a magnificent joy, arising as it had from the Abbey's enlarged silence. Handel knew how to play silence. Musical sound passed through me in the Abbey as though it had always existed and would never end, having paused just for that instant to be heard. It took many seconds for the silence to reclaim the Abbey after the music decayed.

I wanted to meet the organist, as I loved his playing, and wanted to see the choir, see who they were, how they dressed. More than anything I longed to see fellow musicians and just be with them again. I had not been in the company of musicians since leaving Vienna, not even in Paris where everything approaching music had been swept away as if by wildfire. My awareness of so many things was changing in London. In other situations I would have no trepidation of acquainting myself with new people, because I was confident that they would already know me. I was once a known person. But that had all been years before, decades since I had played in London as a child. My operas were famous and perhaps my masses, but they likely would be considered too Catholic for English abbeys. I was suddenly nervous to introduce myself to anyone because I was no longer sure of being known.

Besides my childish fears, I could find neither the organ console nor the choir. The Abbey was in full silence. I walked around until the organ began again, a soft D major, though the sound was distant. I had managed to walk farther from the sound. I was astounded once I heard it, as the coincidence was entirely too miraculous that this small work had made its way to London. The choir in the distance was singing my *Ave verum corpus*. I recall now as I did then my dear friend Anton Stoll in Baden for whom I composed it in just a few minutes while I was visiting Konstanze. It made me wonder if I had brought my pestilence back to Vienna from Baden, because it was after that visit that my health began to decline. I never liked the baths because they smelled of a witch's brew, of sulfur. The baths were religious to the many people whose belief in their healing qualities went beyond reason. I thought them merely a purgative, and a virtuoso shit always helped one feel better.

The choir was singing my *Ave verum corpus* a bit too slowly, so I thought perhaps they might appreciate me telling them how I thought it should be rendered. Almost all of my slower movements are played too slowly. Each time I tried to begin a middle movement of a piano concerto or symphony, their natural way would be too slow, which always puzzled me. This organist was good, but I could not see who, if anyone, was leading the choir. It continued. I loved my chorus. It was too slow, yes, but this gave more time for contemplation of its beauties, so perhaps it was not too slow after all. I began to question my own wishes. I wrote it and conceived it but maybe sometimes it was best if others decide how it should be rendered. Maybe different speeds could reveal something I did not realize in conception.

I listened further. I was correct. *Ave verum corpus* was simply being sung too slowly. Should I tell them I had planned *Ave verum corpus* as the music for the priest's chorus in *The Magic Flute* before changing my mind once I saw Emanuel's words?

I never did find the choir, so perhaps the music really was a celestial sound.

CHAPTER 45

It became time to walk to my meeting with Sir William. I had to meet him without a protector, and in just a short time I would hear the fate of my new life in London. The entire reason I had made the trip, uprooted my family, lost my wife and son, and given up all I had in Vienna, was to be put before me. Upon leaving the beautiful silence of the Abbey, a fear arose that I had been horribly misled, or that I had misunderstood instructions or expectations. Whichever the case, I was finally walking to the Chapel Royal where Sir William Parsons would be awaiting me.

I knew from childhood how to greet and pay obeisance to noble men, most especially those who were to be my employers. I greeted Sir William with a bow and show of respect, both of which were customary etiquette. Sir William greeted me in kind, only briefly, and then warmly stepped out of the expected formalities.

"Herr Mozart, I'm so delighted you are here at last. The court is graced by you, and I am nothing but humbled," he said.

I thought he had peculiar eyes, in that they looked directly at me but they seemed to be speaking to an invisible third presence between us. Despite this strangeness, I was immediately put at ease. I thought Sir William to be kind and helpful, answering many questions before I had the opportunity to ask them. He also spoke slowly, in such a way that I could understand, and I loved when anyone made an effort at understanding.

"It must have surprised you to find that I was remaining with the court," he said. "It had not been my plan to do so. I heard from Herr Haydn that you were willing to accept a position, so I planned at that moment to retire to Oxford and live out my remaining days teaching. London has grown tiresome for me. It is crowded and noisy now, in ways it never was before. But His Majesty was not willing to accept my departure. He said I should remain and help you do your best in your role as court composer, so I intend to abide fully by his wishes."

I found his voice inviting and calm. I asked if he had heard any of my music.

"Oh, my boy. So much but not nearly enough. Haydn brought us a few of your masses of recent years, and of course the theaters have done *Figaro* and *Giovanni*. We have yet to see so many others: *Tito*, *Flute*, *Richard III*, and much else I am sure."

I asked how he knew of them.

"Travelers, of course, tell us much. Haydn is a fountain of information, always, and he loves you so."

"I've just written *Tartuffe*. It has not yet been performed."

Other than the few disinterested parties in Paris, I had not told anyone about *Tartuffe*. I had always been unable to accept rejection, and *Tartuffe* was merely one of the most grievous incidents of denial and the most recently available memory at that moment. Hearing Sir William praise my music, particularly when he did not need to, took me back to my distant days of childhood, when I had been praised by kings and nobles, and back to the greatest period fifteen to twenty years before, when everything I wrote or performed was hailed as a masterpiece. It had been years since I had heard that kind of praise. *The Magic Flute* had been Emanuel's success more than mine, and though many prelates and even parishioners had occasionally uttered kind words about my music at St. Stephen's; largely I was old news by the time I arrived in London. I was thought to be a reliable supplier of fine music, but one who had lost touch years before, living from the reputation of more inspired times. In my moments of weak darkness, and dark weakness, I would forget the praise heaped upon me for *Richard III* or the joy I experienced writing *Tartuffe*, when every moment was a new kind of joy.

CHAPTER 46

Nothing about the meeting was as I expected. Rather than being presented with a list of restrictions for my work, or with a clear set of assignments, Sir William calmly explained that I would be free to write as I liked, and that the King was most encouraging of whatever plans I might have for new operas. Just as Haydn had promised, an orchestra would be placed at my disposal for concerts of new symphonies and piano concertos, or any combination of chamber music I wanted. It was desired that I work with a poet to create an English *Magic Flute* as well as a version of *Richard III* that would play at the Theatre Royal, Drury Lane. I told Sir William of the English *Magic Flute* score I had seen in Lewes, but he declared the English too old-fashioned for modern tastes and strongly suggested that we have a new version. It was the first time I had experienced a "we" in London that included *me*.

It was "the King's wish," Sir William explained, that my two operas appear together for a season as soon as possible, and he recommended that I set to work on them immediately. I must have looked like a frightened child who had just been given everything he had ever wanted. Actually, I had been given so much more, and none of it felt real when standing with Sir William. It felt like more like my times on the bridge. I had left work in a spacious but dark room at St. Stephen's and, longer ago, the sparse accommodations of my small room in Salzburg; and now I had a house, my own house, in the center of London, and my supervising presence, whom I had feared would be a devil, was an angel.

I could only say, "Sir William, I am overwhelmed. How can I thank you, sir?"

"We can begin with your *Mass of Thanks*, the *Dankenmesse*, I thought it to be the most beautiful of your works."

I was so grateful for his words.

I am unsure why I asked, yet the words escaped me: "Are you familiar with Herr Beethoven's music?"

"Of course. Herr Haydn has mentioned him, but a special place has been carved for you here. It is not Herr Beethoven nor even Herr Haydn who has been offered a house, stipend, and total liberty."

"One like me who has never known freedom may not know what to create with it. With respect, sir, I would do better with a set of assignments." I was surprised at the swift accuracy of my response, for I knew I needed restrictions as much as freedoms.

"There are dreams being fulfilled here, young man. I have long wanted to provide a haven for an artist great enough to warrant such a summoning of His Majesty's generosity. For the reign of George III to be the greatest in the history of this nation, we must be able to move beyond our defeats. I cannot allow His Majesty to be defined solely by the loss of colonial possessions across the sea. It has been often said that each of us must do our part to ensure that the reign of George III be indisputably great. His other advisers can do as they see fit; what I can offer is music. I feel it my duty to ensure that I do what I can to associate him with music and art, despite his natural bent toward politics, which hold no interest for me at all. Haydn's presence in London was an attempt by me to accomplish this, but Herr Haydn, in addition to having no interest in living outside of Vienna, was not the musician I was seeking. One of the pieces he brought for performance here was not his own, as he is always so generous in the promotion of his fellow composers. The piece he brought was a great one, by a man you have mentioned, Herr Beethoven, his variations on your duet from *The Magic Flute*. It was played here to great success, and I was gratified to study it. Do you know of it?"

I nodded, but I was too embarrassed to admit to my new employer, who was at that moment on the cusp of complimenting Ludwig, that I had never found the courage to hear a performance of it. Ludwig had sent me a score but it remained unopened and packed away somewhere in Vienna. I thought then, this time with shame at my tardiness, of Ludwig's unopened letter tucked somewhere among my belongings in London that I had not yet had time to retrieve.

"Well, Herr Mozart, I studied that work very hard. Skillful it is, and most clever. But when I thought on the totality of what I knew of your music, and when I studied your original simple duet that gave birth to such complex variations, I knew I had to make a case to His Majesty that you and only you should be given the honor. I arranged for a performance of your works, including that charming duet for His Majesty one weekend at Windsor, and he agreed. It was because of that performance that a letter was sent to you via Herr Haydn upon his return."

"It was you who arranged it all?" I said.

"Yes. I wanted not only to meet Wolfgang Mozart, but also to do what I could to help him."

"I am forever in your debt, sir."

"You owe me nothing. I've heard your masses. The debt is mine to repay."

I realized how rarely in my life I had been at a loss for words.

"You see, Herr Mozart, I knew your father. I even slightly knew Joseph II."

"Have you any news of Lorenzo Da Ponte?" I asked, hoping to finally find my friend.

"I'm afraid not. I doubt he would show his face at this court again."

"Why?"

"It is not to be spoken of." Sir William paused, then continued: "I know the work of many composers. Signor Cimarosa, for example, writes delightful music, does he not? And Signor Salieri, your great champion? You must already know how well he speaks of you."

I was ashamed of my own thoughts about Salieri, as I had never been charitable toward him, nor had I been remotely as generous in my praise of Salieri's music as he had been of mine. I would never be able to atone for my sins against Salieri.

Sir William was a talker. "I've been so blessed to know all of these extraordinary men with their brilliant talents. I was so fortunate to be educated in music, to learn all of its rudiments and all of its science. And I was able to compose, though each time I sat down, I started writing the same thing. I reached the limits of my gifts, as I've seen with several. They reach the boundary and they do not know what to do. They cannot return, but they have also reached the end. Many of them hang on far too long. They fight with reaching an ending. Or they fight with everyone else. Or they are cruel to their wives and children. They drink to excess. Almost no one can face the end of their talent, the limits imposed by God himself. I'm not speaking of the end of life, but the end of the creative life, the death that precedes death. I decided that no matter what, I would face my decline better than I had seen in others. History could judge me harshly or well on the only thing that can eventually be known about me, the compositions I leave behind, but I will not allow history ever to say that I did not serve my King by making his court the greatest center for music in history. I was gifted with just enough knowledge to know what I can never be, and I was given the gifts to know the greatest talent in all of music when he is standing before me. Please, Herr Mozart, write the contents of your imagination. You will not find a boundary nor an end."

I had waited a lifetime to hear anyone utter the words to me that I heard at that moment from Sir William. Great bursts of C major erupted within me. My joy was so overwhelming that inevitably it brought thoughts of my bridge, the place in my almost-waking time, and I wondered if it led to a boundary. Terror lay in that thought. And I was embarrassed by the confessions of Sir William, so new to my life but so suddenly important. As a child, I would have embraced him and welcomed his courage in speaking so many truths, because I knew that the speaking aloud of a truth did something indefinably important for. But I was only able to speak truth in my music, never in my words. In those years, at least, I found truth in words to be inherently false by their very nature: they were designed to be heard, crafted individually by the speaker to soften the truth for whom they were being spoken. But music was written alone, and no one could know who might hear it and how it might be heard.

The truths it contained would remain no matter how it was heard. I did not at that time think this was true of words, at least not for me.

What Sir William had told me, if it was true, was the single most generous thing I had ever been given. But with no limits, I did not know if I could write anything. I proposed a few ideas based on my sketches, a few symphonies, as well as a new mass of thanks, a second *Dankenmesse*, and these would allow me to impose my own limits, particularly when combined with English versions of *The Magic Flute* and *Richard III*, depending on how much musical revision might be necessary to adapt them to English sensibilities. I had the forethought to ask for an English instructor, which Sir William said would be happily provided, and the Lord Chamberlain would provide me with the details.

Sir William and I parted. I bowed and placed his hand on my cheek, saying "Thank you." I could think of no other words. Sir William left the chapel from a door somewhere near the sanctuary, allowing me to depart alone through the front, where I soon found myself yet again on the Mall, where a major shifting of light had occurred. Shame accompanied me when I realized that I had doubted Sir William's sincerity. I examined myself as might a stranger. Why think ill of so gentle a soul as Sir William's? It cheapens a person to think such thoughts, and I had no reason to distrust Sir William, who would have held within him the power to impose any restrictions on me. So much more was offered than was ever promised, that Sir William would have no reason to be insincere.

CHAPTER 47

Where was Konstanze? I counted the days. She might have still been in Paris, but she and little Franz were more likely well across France and on their journey home. She had once mentioned a longer route through southern France and into Lombardy, even as far as Trieste and then up to Vienna from there. I remembered Trieste from boyhood. So many places blended in the memory, but Trieste was singular. Might she have taken that longer route home? If so, she might be at the seashore by now, somewhere near Marseilles. I remembered it, too, and cold nights in Arles and Carcassonne.

I wondered perpetually about Emanuel and so many Vienna friends. Praha. Munich. Mannheim. I had seen more places than most people even knew of. I knew there were far distant places I could never see, like Turkey and Egypt. I had seen extraordinary drawings of Alexandria, and I longed to go there. Spain sounded like such a beautiful place, and I had met Moroccan people in the South of France, but that was years ago. I often thought of going to Morocco. I had heard it could be seen from parts of Spain and so was but a boat ride away, like France to England, but another world completely. And always lingering in my memory was Tamu and the precious hours we spent together in France, my last moments on the old continent. I wondered, always, where he was, if he was safe, if he had somehow found passage back to his family.

All of those places coalesced on that beautiful midafternoon on the Mall. I had no reason to return to St. James's Park, so I decided to walk home and get to work. There was so much to be done and I would not appear back at the court until I was asked. Each day became consumed with my own industry.

In truth I feared the freedom I had been allowed, because I knew I had to have discipline imposed, as otherwise it was not to be found. What I admired about Joseph and Ludwig was that they seemed able to work at any time, and they could always use their freedom to produce. I had never been able to do that. I needed deadlines and structures and rules and…I had not often thought of it…shame. I needed to be shamed for being late with my work. And the shame worked. I was ashamed of my jealousy of Ludwig.

I was initially afraid to return to the silence of an empty house, but I loved my house on Brook Street. Within its silence, ideas flowed again. I wanted to go to the theater as often as possible, both to improve my English and to find ideas. But at the end of my long first day, as the light of the day lessened, I fell into a deep sleep from which I would not wake until the sun next appeared. After breakfast, I set to work writing down the keyboard variations on "God Save the King" in a way that could be deciphered by others, and I sketched my first set of London symphonies. I wanted to have at least two ready for my first meeting with the orchestra.

Vegetable and fruit carts came up and down Brook Street at regular intervals, so I could always find food nearby, sometimes even bread, right outside the door. Amazing. Vienna had street vendors as well, but they did not move around like this; you had to go to them. I wondered why such a small thing authored such joy. I had lived long enough by then to notice what got remembered and what was left forgotten. My melancholy about the passage of time, something on which I could not long dwell, was all centered on the small joys that went unnoticed. History would remember every battle, every political scandal, and it may even remember a few works of art, but it would forget the light in Vienna on a spring morning, or the dancing of a set of birds over Rome. Fruit sellers on Brook Street, of course, would long be forgotten, but the carts were so beautiful and their produce delicious.

In the following days, I was finally able to take walks and explore parts of London I had not seen since I was a boy or, more likely, things that had not existed at all until recently. Areas that I remembered as fields with sheep or cattle had filled with homes and churches and parks and squares. I remembered so many restaurants, though as a child I had eaten almost solely with Papa, who found restaurants an indulgent luxury. I was an instinctive tourist. I knew how to find the sights and the vista points from which to see them. I made use of the carriage put at my disposal. I went to the highest possible points, especially in good weather, to find a sense of my new city. St. Paul's could be seen from nearly everywhere. I even went to distant Windsor, where I had played a duo-piano recital with Nannerl forty years before, an inconceivable amount of time. Could that be possible?

Yes. I spent a night at an inn in Windsor, wanting to visit the next day a place I learned of from a song by Purcell, "On the brow of Richmond Hill." The Lord Chamberlain, or someone at the court, had filled my home shelves with song sheets by Purcell, Handel, Thomas Arne, John Blow, and many others writing English music. Purcell seemed the most interesting of them all because he was the most thoroughly English. His "Richmond Hill" evoked something I had never felt in music before: one could see the place by simply hearing the song, as though the song had been growing there along with the trees. I knew the feeling of home for the first time in England there on the brow of Richmond Hill.

Purcell's music often returned to me, even though I knew Handel to be the greatest composer to ever live in London. Greatness. Great. Those strange words I had heard my whole life. What did they mean? What could they ever mean? Was there really some quality that sneaked through the quills that rendered one greater than another? Is the measure of greatness simply something being remembered? Is it popularity? I knew that much of Haydn's music was more popular than my own, at least in Vienna, but how much of that was simply repetition? My time of greatest popularity had passed, but my powers had not diminished. Indeed, they had increased, as *Richard III* had proved to others and *Tartuffe* had proved to me. My masses had been of exemplary quality, yet they were unlikely to be remembered. I heard some of Sir William Parsons's music, his choral works, and I found them enjoyable, but then I wondered how my own emotions affected my assessments. Did Sir William's generosity alter my ability to render accurate judgment? I had never known Handel or Purcell, yet I felt able to see their work objectively. I had arranged new orchestrations of Handel's *Acis and Galatea, Cecilia,* and *Messiah* so was most intimately acquainted with them, and they were works of absolute greatness. Perhaps I simply evaluated others in terms of my own needs and wants at the moment. Did my need to feel at home in England lead me to hear "Richmond Hill" as something greater than it was?

I set to work quickly on my symphonies, completing six within a few weeks; and as promised, a poet—actually, a set of poets—set immediately to work on English versions of *The Magic Flute* and *Richard III.* Unsurprisingly, the *Flute* was easy to adapt into English and I thought it sounded delightful, though my own English was not yet strong enough to know how accurate it was to Emanuel's words. Many of the simpler phrases sounded perfect, so much so that it helped me with my English, which was improving rapidly. That my spoken English would always sound like Papageno filled me with more pride than embarrassment. *Richard III* proved considerably more difficult. The poets said to me that though I had set the German translation perfectly, there would likely need to be a number of alterations to revert it back to English and they would need time with me to outline exactly what they felt should occur. I agreed in principle, even while admitting to myself how much I despised going back into works I had already written, and I dreaded having to adapt *Tartuffe* or *Don Giovanni,* but it was necessary for their success. I felt many worlds and years away from Vienna now, but energized to work. I was capable, always, of forgetting about little Franz, Konstanze, Aloysia, Tamu, and so many others, whenever I set into a frenzy of work.

Aloysia. How often I had put her completely out of my mind, or at least placed her into a part of my memory where she could become something other than what she was. More than anything about her, though it slightly shamed me to think it, I missed her voice, which was greater than Konstanze's. I missed her effortless rise to a high E natural in the aria I wrote for her, the one I began with an oboe variant on the melody, and which Aloysia sang with such longing and beauty. I could always hear how she resonated through the hall with it, playing with the oboe, reacting to it, matching it sound for sound. I loved when singers could make themselves sound like instruments, but I also begged wind players to imitate singers, or at least the greatest of singers. It was one sound world, voice and instruments, and I longed for a time when they would not be separate, when I could simply write sounds, sounds that could create whole new places, just as the view from Richmond Hill forever lived within me. I wanted to write symphonies with chorus, naturally, but I also imagined music that didn't depend on words. I loved words, but I loved them in a way that I longed to express in their absence.

As the weeks of furious work turned into months, I knew something was circling me, something new that no one had yet conceived, yet there were no sketches, no clear way for me to grasp it. Normally I would have a clear picture of everything before I wasted a single stroke of the quill, but with this new idea I could not do that. Besides, the new London works were all-consuming, and I had not written such a volume of music in years. Miraculously, I was able to hear it all as soon as copyists could turn it around, and for once I did not have to compromise. It was not possible anywhere in the world to have players capable of doing anything but this newly formed court orchestra came close to it. At our first rehearsal, I brought materials for my old C-major symphony, *Linz*, to get a sense of their abilities. In other situations, I had to endlessly explain the opening measures, and could never get an orchestra at sight to fully understand my first allegro, much less to be able to play the final movement with the clarity and speed I wanted without dragging. Yet this orchestra, with just a nod from my keyboard, sailed through the *Linz* as though it was a work for beginners. I had known good orchestras in Vienna and Praha, and I had heard the limits of what orchestras could do in Mannheim, but this orchestra sent my imagination soaring.

It was a puzzle why and how they were so skilled. They were quite young, though all orchestras were in those days. But they viewed me as an elder, and that accounted for a certain respect, but it was more than that.

They were incredibly disciplined and skilled, and they seemed to enjoy playing in a way other orchestras did not. Part of me did not want to know why, I just wanted to enjoy it. I knew I could get no answers from a large group of people, so I decided to ask some players to read some chamber music so I could get to know them individually, and also to practice my English. To my surprise, the players were happy to play chamber music, and I was able to hear my own violin and piano sonatas, each written so long before. I had forgotten what a joy it was to play music conceived for only two or three people. They played my piano trios and quartets, and for weeks all I could think of was the composition of more chamber music for my new court orchestra.

Each day of those early months in London was joyously filled. In the early morning, I would try to finish composing whatever I had almost completed the evening before. The afternoons brought orchestral rehearsals and chamber music, a small tea in St. James's Palace, sometimes with the Lord Chamberlain, more usually with other players and courtiers. Evenings were for plays and the theater, whenever I could attend, and I liked to go to bed early.

CHAPTER 48

At least once a week, Sir William quietly slipped into the orchestra chamber, but when I would call a pause or announce the end of the rehearsal, Sir William would be gone. I realized it had been weeks and then months since I had seen him to speak with him. Without contact with an employer, I grew worried and anxious, sure that some kind of court subterfuge was nigh. It had happened before. Everyone thought it had been started by Salieri, because all Italians were suspect in Vienna, even though Salieri had lived his whole life in Vienna and spoke with no accent at all. To the Viennese, Salieri was one of them. The intrigue started instead, I was sure, with Caterina Cavalieri. She was one of the most beautiful women I had ever seen, and I often thought of her when I would pleasure myself early in the mornings. Even years later, her image would come to mind even when I tried to stop her arrival in my fantasy.

Salieri was enthralled by her, and he wrote her a number of roles, none of which could compare with the role I wrote for her: Konstanze in *Seraglio*. As the new saying went, I pulled out all of the stops for the role, and I always loved the reference to the pipe organ, perhaps my most beloved single instrument. For Konstanze, the role, I wrote every demand I could dream up, and Caterina learned it all quickly, delighted to show off all of her abilities to me within the first days of rehearsal, the minx. She used her voice to seduce me, brazenly, and right in front of everyone present. In private, Caterina exhibited none of this flirtation with me, which made me doubt her intentions. I had misread my own desires many times, assuming they were shared, but with Caterina I was sure she was trying to get me to make love to her. I could hear and see it in her, even in the saddest aria, "Traurigkeit," one of the lengthiest I ever wrote. Every phrase she sang went through my body like the lightning I had seen in the mountains. Just the sight of her would start a tingling deep within me. I wanted her so badly I was sure my member would erupt the moment I touched her. We never touched each other, much to my dismay, and from no lack of trying. She stayed always safely out of reach.

I wonder how much more I could have achieved in life had I been able to control my desires. I must have put more than a year of work behind schedule in my endless yearnings for her. I would sit down to write, playing billiards to relax, and I could feel myself writing and working, but my mind would never remove itself from Caterina: how she moved, how she sounded. And she knew how to tease me in ways that only I would notice, even if she did it in front of others. And she did it with her voice, the happy slut. She sent her attentions to Salieri just to drive me nearly mad. I imagined them together, hoping to curb some of my desire, but it only increased. I imagined her face convulsed in pleasure, welcoming my intrusion into her. I thought of her so often, reaching her sufficiency with Antonio, or even someday with me, and whenever I thought of her, the impurities would fill me and I had no choice but to remove them. I never felt love for Catarina. I knew that to have her once would satisfy me forever, but not being able to have even that satisfaction drove me to the brink for years.

I knew that Catarina was trying to harm my career and my reputation in the court, but I was never sure why. Was it because I had refused to indulge her? I would have happily done so if she had allowed it, but she seemed to both want and not want me. And she had a need to have vanquished me. The intrigue came unexpectedly to me at a most inopportune time, as little Franz was being born. Rumors circulated the palace that I had been found kissing a man, one of the musicians of the court who was known for his effeminacy. Being caught with the boy had expelled more than one man from the court, and landed others in jail, but because the boy had the favor of Salieri and was a fine violinist, he was never dismissed.

Rumors circled around the boy always, that he was planted by the court to capture men in their debauchery, and was not even of that ilk himself. I did not pay much attention to those kinds of silly intrigues.

I had known men to have female qualities, or I thought they might better be described as having remained very young in their precocity. I assumed that some men stayed a certain age in their mind no matter their years, while others had a talent for aging, just as I had a talent for the violin or the fortepiano. But it had never occurred to me within the myriad of my many desires to ever kiss or touch a man in the way I might touch a woman. So, when the rumors began that I had been seen kissing this violinist in the orchestra, my thoughts immediately turned to who might have benefited from such an intrigue. The court thought Salieri; I knew it was Catarina. She wanted to see me felled like a tree, to bring me low, as a way of exerting power over me or over Konstanze. I had always known Catarina hated Konstanze and Aloysia, initially as rival singers, but then as hindrances. I put up with the intrigue for several weeks, and was content to be the subject of laughter in the court, but it began to turn ugly. Church officials began to sneak around me and even hint at some kind of investigation. That there was nothing to investigate made it all the worse, because an invented crime required an invented defense. I became sure that at some point this intrigue would make its way to Joseph II, particularly if the Archbishop became involved. Catarina may have begun the entire episode as a kind of joke to arouse my attention, but within weeks it had turned dangerous.

I wondered why such an intrigue would have viability in the minds of anyone who knew me even slightly. My justifiable worry had always been being called out by the Archbishop as too profligate with women. I had confessed so many sins that I was certain some must have been reported. Always, I had been taught to confess my wrongdoings, and in my earlier life my father had made me rehearse my confessions so as to maximize their power in church. I grew to love confessing, cleansing myself of the venal and returning my body to its godliest state, from which it always insisted on seeking satiety in the conquest of another woman. I tried for years to understand these desires, because only a few moments after the brief explosion the need was gone. Then the awkwardness would begin with the woman. I hated the awkwardness, especially if it was accompanied by a confrontation. I was shocked when women expressed to me a desire similar in vulgarity to my own. It always felt brazen, more sinful, and that kind of desire successfully killed mine. If a woman pursued me, I had so little interest that her advance would inevitably retreat and disappear. But if she was aloof or if she ignored me, I was inflamed.

Catarina possessed a unique ability to pitch her actions to most infuriatingly increase my desires. So she likely began the intrigue in order to someday tease me about it in a Viennese bedroom. I dreamed of it, of punishing her little ass for causing such problems. But if she had been joking, it went badly. The intrigue stopped my life, filling me with terror. If courtiers thought me capable of kissing a man, or touching another man's member, or—God forgive me the thought—entering another man, that was more serious than the thought of actually doing all of those things. I assumed buggers did with men what I did with women, and they must enjoy it just as much; but as I felt none of those desires, I reckoned buggers just did not desire women. I could not imagine it, but neither was it necessary for me to imagine it. I knew things others did not, and one of those things was that people were all very different. I had learned this with women, and in the most absolutely intimate of ways: by the sounds they made when I made love to them. That was the only way to truly know a woman. More than any of the sensations of discharge or pulsation, what I most loved in lovemaking was sound. I had heard every sound a woman could make, and they were all so different, so endlessly and magnificently beautiful. Konstanze would slightly whimper, with her gasps getting closer together as I ascended toward surfeit. Once or twice I had made her cry out, which always embarrassed her and made her distant for days instead of bringing us closer. I loved the women who began with timidity and then begged me to force myself ever harder into them, begged me to try to reach a point just beyond possibility. If the woman screamed while ascending the summit, I inevitably released again even I had already done so.

But I could not understand these desires that were undeniably within me, so I held even less understanding of a campaign against me. What if such a thing happened in London? I would not have the depth of protection I had possessed in Vienna, and even after months in my new home, I had yet to meet the monarch. I had long expected consequences from the many women I had pursued or been unable to resist, so I was especially surprised, all those years ago, to be accused of harboring desires for a man. Women felt too perfect to even imagine such a scenario.

CHAPTER 49

Each day in London, when I walked to St. James to rehearse my extraordinary new orchestra, I relived the horror of Catarina's smear campaign. There were young men in the London orchestra, two in particular, who looked like the boy in Vienna. They shared a certain fastidiousness and manner of walking. I did not mind their manner, but I noticed it and singled them out. I imagined them both to be buggers, but I felt it none of my own concern. I had a job to do.

At the end of a rehearsal day, the Lord Chamberlain stopped me and asked to meet with him.

"His Majesty wishes to present a set of performances of the new masses and symphonies that you have written in his honor, and I am informing you to prepare them within a month."

"A month? Respectfully, sir, we are to open *The Magic Flute* within a month, according to Sir William, and your poet has completed a version the singers are now preparing. I am to hear the whole opera tomorrow."

"His Majesty is aware of *The Magic Flute* at the Theatre Royal. Nevertheless, he commands a set of concerts of your works, as well as masses either in the Chapel Royal or the Abbey, within the month. Sir William can prepare performances of the masses and you will prepare three concerts of your music with the court orchestra, which I hope you have found to your liking?"

"They are amazing."

"Of course they are. Sir William selected every musician and has trained them in the sciences of music over many months to prepare for your arrival," the Lord Chamberlain said.

Of course it was because of Sir William. I scolded myself for not thinking of it sooner, for wondering why and how the orchestra was so fine. I owed Sir William everything.

I thanked the Lord Chamberlain and assured him the concerts would be prepared as asked. The Lord Chamberlain told me I should present the programs written down on parchment within a few days so that the proper approvals could be granted, and because His Majesty wished to produce printed sheets for the audience, something I had never heard of before. I promised to turn them in as asked.

It had turned noticeably cold in London, and a thick fog made my brief walk home hazardous, as I suddenly found myself face to face with fellow walkers I could neither see nor hear until they were upon me. Horses and carriages could be heard but not seen, and though I could discern distance in their sounds, it was difficult to tell what direction they were going, as the London streets tended toward disorder. Several times I had to stop in safe places to wait for quiet. The cobblestones were precarious.

I found the fog frightening, reminiscent of many dreams over the years in which I wander a city unable to see what is in front of me. I had read about Handel's terrifying blindness, and I had often played his "Total eclipse" and thought of it. I would sing it with the old German scores that Papa had owned since he was a boy. Papa opened the world of Handel to all of us, to me but also Haydn and all of the Viennese. I found it so moving I could scarcely render the lines without crying. It was the same with other arias in *Samson*, "How willing my paternal love," which seemed the most beautiful of everything within *Samson*. A father willing to be the eyes for his blind son, willing to walk by his side and help him through all of life's hazards. I would sing the two short arias over and over, and the more I thought of them, the more my tears would flow. I knew that music was capable of engendering these emotions, that was no surprise; but I repeatedly wondered how Handel could say so much in so little time, and with so few notes.

I wanted more than anything on that day to do my own orchestration of *Samson*, as I had for *Messiah*, because that was the best way I knew to learn how Handel managed such extraordinary music. Instead I arrived home to Brook Street to make my lists for the Lord Chamberlain. I lit a lamp and set to work, resulting in these lists:

Concert One, for 14 August, 1799
- Symphony No. 41 in C major, *Jupiter*
- Piano Concerto No. 40 in C major, *London*
- 3 concert arias
- Symphony No. 60 in E major, *The King's Joy*

Concert Two, for 15 August, 1799
- Symphony No. 50 in E flat major
- Symphony No. 51 in D major
- Violin Concerto No. 12 in B flat major
- Trumpet Concerto in E flat major, dedicated to Haydn
- Symphony No. 62 in F major, *Vienna*

Concert Three, for 16 August, 1799
- *Samson*, Handel—in my new orchestration (if I can get it done in time)

I knew, naturally, that I would need approval for all of the ideas, but even without it I set to work on *Samson*, retrieving my Chrysander score from where I had left it. I knew I could get it done with diligent work, and I realized I had been doing it in the quiet of my mind for months. And I realized something else as I sang through my two most cherished arias from *Samson*: I now understood them in English for the first time, each word. "All dark amidst the blaze of noon" and "Whilst I have eyes he wants no light." I did not know exactly when it turned over for me, but I understood that *whilst* meant simply *while*, yet for singing and making the thought understood over a long distance, *whilst* was better. I suddenly understood it all, and it meant so much more. I wanted trombones and horns, a quiet and dignified choral warmth to accompany the father's great aria to his son, and I wanted to create a spare emptiness for Samson's aria, an orchestra that will sound sightless.

I wanted to create a homage to Handel, who I felt would have written for more instruments had he known of them. But he had to write for the instruments available to him when he was in London before I was born. Might there be anyone left in London who remembered Handel, who might be able to tell me what he had been like, where he had lived, how he might react to *Samson* being revived? I vowed to ask Sir William, who must know someone. Before I extinguished the candle, I had completed trombone, horn, and trumpet parts for the father's aria and added clarinets and horns to Samson's. I would be able to keep all of Handel's string materials, which would make the work go very quickly indeed, provided that a set of materials existed, which I would find out soon.

The following weeks were pandemonium, the longest stretch of chaos I could recall in my life. There were constant rehearsals with the orchestra, and the volume of music proved daunting even for such a skilled group of musicians. When we had only been rehearsing and experimenting, they had displayed no nerves. But now, knowing they would be playing at royal command, they became more difficult with me in rehearsal, challenging my ideas, and claiming some of the symphonies impossible to play. They openly stated that they didn't think they could successfully learn so much music so quickly. I, who had challenged them with so much, all of which they had reveled in and embraced, now had to encourage and convince where I formerly had only to present and expect.

Rehearsals became things I dreaded, and I began to feel sickness looming around me again. Nausea. I would awaken in pools of sweat. I had turned in the full orchestration of *Samson* to Sir William's office, and the copyists were hard at work on it, but they had endless questions. I had not thought my concertos to be terribly difficult, but in the rehearsals the same passages kept going wrong, slipping ahead or behind tempo, sometimes causing me to stand up from the keyboard and try to relax the tempo or feeling with my arms, causing endless consternation from the players who were accustomed to simply following what they heard from the keyboard, by watching my left hand, or from a simple nod. The gyrations of my arms looked angry to them, and thus I frightened them when I stood before them in such a way, as my whole aspect, especially my eyes, took on a kind of madness that they had never seen in me before, or so they said. The orchestra leader decided to speak to me privately, having been pressured by his fellow players.

"Maestro, we can see that we are causing you frustration, but we are trying our best."

"This orchestra is so fantastic! What has gone wrong?"

"We have loved getting to know all of this music, and hearing your ideas. The group adores you, Maestro. But learning so much music at one time for public performance is too much to ask."

"But it is the King's request, not mine!"

"We know that. But still, be a little patient. We are trying to play thousands of notes up to a level worthy of you. You seem to have an idea about every phrase, a new expression for each line. We want to give you what you want. It is the only thing in the world that we want. For all of us, this is the first and most important work we have ever had. This is work that is feeding our families and caring for our parents. The King's pleasure is our lifeline. If we do not play well for him, we could be destitute. I don't think you understand the pressure we are under."

I was silent, slowly absorbing his words. I tried to talk myself out of explaining. I thought of Sir William and how kind he had been. I thought of how disappointing it would be if I lost my temper. Each series of thoughts filled me with rage. How could anyone think I did not understand pressure? I almost let it burst from me, but I held it in. I thought of rehearsals of *The Magic Flute*, the three concerts I was trying to prepare, the choral rehearsals of *Samson* which I was almost never available for. I thought of my journey across many countries to accept this new post. I thought of Konstanze, my lost wife, and the terror of boarding a ship. And this violinist, who was not nearly at as much risk as I, had the gall to pull me aside and claim I knew none of their pressures? Had he ever written music? Had he ever spent months working out the details of a symphony only to have them dismissed in an instant? Anger boiled in me, but I kept it away, saying only, "Thank you for your concern. We will be fine, I am sure."

I emerged onto the Mall on what was a lovely late afternoon. The constant immersion in work was taking a private toll and I needed a walk. I loved walking in decent weather, and since I rarely walked to the Thames, I used the few hours I had before another rehearsal to cross St. James and past Horse Guards to the small park by the Thames. The river was busy, as always, with all manner of buckets, tubs, and pots having their contents emptied into it. Ash from fireplaces came in great carriagefuls, and women were laundering clothing in it. I had never seen so many boats, going in all directions. How did they keep from hitting one another? It was a frenzy of activity, yet I enjoyed the open feeling of the river. One could see for miles from the upper banks of the Thames, in the little neighborhood of Charing, which reminded me of where we had lived in Salzburg in its proximity to the river. And the grandeur of St. Paul's in the distance always reminded me of my beloved and feared Salzburg Cathedral.

The next few days would determine everything about the rest of my life. I feared what would happen if George III did not like my music, or if something in the performance did not come together. The Thames could never be crossed by swimming, as my friends and I used to do in the Salz, infuriating Mama. And even the little river down at Lewes that I loved so very much could be crossed with swimming if need be. I liked putting names to what I loved, and so I loved saying that I loved rivers. I realized the vast amount of time I had spent beside them, contemplating them, trying to cross them. More than anything, I simply enjoyed their beauty. Rivers were relentless, and I loved their predictability: even when it rained, it was known that the rivers would fill. How, though, could it ever be predicted that a river might rise if the rains came far away, unknown to areas in the close vicinity?

I did not know the origin of the Thames, but surely it came from mountains or some higher place. That was the only logical explanation for rivers. And what if it rained far away with those hills, while in London it remained beautiful and sunny? In many hours, it might take days, wouldn't all of the newly born water find its way to London and mysteriously flood the city? Might these floods be simply attributed by some as God's wrath? But I believed God would send rains if he saw a reason, so it was a constant puzzle and struggle to understand such things. My beliefs told me that God had a reason for everything, so I assumed—no, I knew—that I would soon find out what those reasons might be. I was only thoroughly peaceful with what I could experience alone, which is why composition was the only true solace. Only I could experience my music's initiation. However many would hear the music later, the moment of creation was mine. The river was witnessed and used by everything and everyone. Every soul who ever lived in London, or even just those who visited, must have seen it. Every monarch had sailed on it. Expectation accompanied every eddy of the Thames, and if anything happened in London, it affected the entire world. Vienna felt just the size of the city's old walls, whereas London felt incalculably large, and everything within it infectious.

After my walk, my body was still shaking, and I felt just as nervous and nauseous as before. The rehearsals did not improve over the following days, and my temper continued unraveling. The players got more nervous, and the leader continued his pleas in private to me. As the concerts approached, I was told how I would greet the King and his courtiers, and what complicated protocol would be expected. Everything centered on whatever pleasures the King might enjoy, and how best to utilize his time. A seemingly endless string of concerns were about His Majesty. I wondered if anyone in the court cared about the musical performances themselves, or about me. What if I got sick? Would the concert simply be postponed or would I be out of a job? Had anyone inquired about my health from the perilous journey I had ventured to be there at all? These were questions for the Lord Chamberlain or for Sir William, but I had no time to ask them. In the final day before the concerts began, time seemed to speed up. I had often experienced the diminution of time in the days before important performances, and then the seemingly endless hours before a concert is to begin after one has slept for the last time. There was to be no rehearsal on the day of the first concert, necessitating a rush to fit all of the details into the preceding day.

I fell immediately to sleep the night before, my fate outside the bounds of my own hands by then. I woke early and had only to wait until the late-afternoon beginning of the concert. Those hours were agonizing, as I had been told not to report to the palace until well after midday so as not to disturb the many preparations needed in the Great Hall to prepare for the King's arrival. Noting my own nervousness, I saw for the first time that others were nervous about the presence of the King. I had never worried about playing anything for Joseph II nor, indeed, had I been scared of any royalty before. But now, though every courtier was frightened of George III's volatile unpredictability, I was too frightened of the performances themselves to have any additional fears about my new monarch.

CHAPTER 50

The morning of the concert felt like a week, and I had a small lunch before a carriage arrived to take me to the palace. The day was bright and clear. The concert would begin "in a few hours," I was told upon arrival, and would be followed by a ceremonial dinner. I knew the subsequent several days would follow similar patterns, with the following day being a rehearsal for the next day's concert, and then a two-day period in which to assemble *Samson* for the third of the Royal Command Performances, after which I was granted two consecutive days free of responsibilities.

My memories of the three concerts would blur for the rest of my life, as they seemed to pass in silence, with the orchestra working furiously to please me. I could always remember the long rehearsal days of *Samson*, and how difficult the work was to perform, with so many diverse tempos and affects. I loved my new orchestrations of *Samson*, because they gave more body and audible rhythm to the work's many great choruses. I played my own harpsichord, and Sir William led the choruses from the organ, playing on registers that nearly inundated the poor choir members. It always amazed me that many people thought music just "came together," as if by magic. I knew there was nothing magic about it; it was pure work and discipline. I had worked diligently for weeks creating my new orchestrations that kept all of Handel's notes intact. I simply added clarinets, horns, trombones, and a few other instruments to fill it out. I thought *Samson* to be Handel's masterpiece, but it made me long to know more of his music, as there was much I had never heard and might never be able to hear.

By the end of *Samson*, with applause spreading across the Great Hall, I thought I might faint from the exhaustion. I had perspired through my formal clothes. I could not recall how the concerts had gone, not even at that moment when *Samson* ended and everything was finished, nor even as the musicians were applauding me. I was taken away into an audience room to wait for my monarch. I could hear the King's retinue moving him into place in the adjoining throne room where I would have audience. Sir William joined me in the waiting area, as did the Lord Chamberlain.

The King had displayed no emotion during the symphony concerts, though he did applaud each piece, most especially my playing of my own piano concerto. He seemed affable, but there had purposefully been no audience with him until after *Samson*, which made the moment especially anxious for me. It became clear the court was nervous to an extraordinary degree about how the King might react or behave toward me or anyone. Perhaps his mind had undergone some alteration since we had last been together so many years before.

Finally the door to the throne room opened and an equerry summoned "Herr Mozart." I was accompanied into the sumptuous room, at the far end of which King George III sat under a lush draping canopy. I approached him as directed. More than thirty years had passed since we had been so close together. I was, at last, in front of my employer King George III.

The King was quietly singing, and at first I could not hear him. He took my hand, still singing, and then I recognized *My Heart Is Inditing*, one of Handel's Coronation Anthems. The King continued singing, with great awkwardness for those courtiers present, as well as for me: "King's daughters were among thy honorable women," followed by unintelligible singing for some time, hanging on to certain notes, and returning to the text for "and the King shall have pleasure in thy duty." After that, the King held a long stretch of silence, then he resumed singing his own coronation anthem, *My Heart Is Inditing*. I was left to wonder if there was a message hidden within the anthem, if the King was trying to express his thanks to me in song. Courtiers tried to intervene but were stopped by the King himself, who would not relinquish my hands. Eventually the singing faded, and the King of England looked into my eyes, his own brimming with tears.

"So many years, dear Amadé. I was sure I would never see you again. And now, here you are in my very own court, and in paying homage to Handel you honor my father."

This King was not the person I had met as a child. I had never witnessed such an alteration. Yet he did still know me, and could sing notes of Handel's anthem. But he was unable to grasp what was immediately around him even as he recalled memories that had long receded. The river of time had flowed far from him, even though he was only a generation older than I. One heard about his madness, of course, but I knew that many people were talked about as if they were mad simply because they did not act as expected. What did madness feel like for the King? I wanted to cry for the pain my new monarch must have endured, and for the years of hiding and covering that his courtiers must have been forced to commit. How painful it must have been for everyone to have to pretend the King was the man he used to be.

I knew things, as always, and thus I knew that every man had within him the possibility of madness, as did I, who had glimpsed it in the small hours and in my visions of the bridge. Might madness be waiting on that side of the bridge I had never had the courage to cross? The monarch, in singing of his daughters, planted an idea into me, one so obvious that I was surprised I had not thought of it before. If I could somehow manage to meet one of King George's daughters, might that be a way into a new kind of life? I could see it all suddenly: I could marry one of the princesses and become a regent prince of the royal family. Yes. These things were possible in England in a way they were not in Austria. The thought occurred to me to take advantage of the King's audience and ask him about it, or might that be considered too formal and presumptuous? Surely, though, the thought had already alighted within the King's mind, or he wouldn't have remembered the portion of the anthem that held meaning about his own daughters.

"Majesty, were any of your daughters able to enjoy the concerts with you?" I asked, fearing that my boldness might mark me in the King's maddened mind. The air seemed to leave the room as the question was quietly pondered by the King, unaccustomed to inquiry. I noticed that both Sir William and the Lord Chamberlain had entered, and it was silently made clear to me that my time had come to an end with my query unanswered. The King began to sing again, unintelligibly. I asked the question again, prompting a quiet scolding from Sir William, "Herr Mozart, we must let His Majesty rest."

"I do not need rest!," King George said, as though coming out of a trance. "Herr Mozart, your concerts were miracles. I shall never forget them."

By the reaction of everyone present, I deduced that the King had not uttered such a sensible sentence in months. Even to me, in his presence for only a few minutes, the change was remarkable, and confusing. Should I pursue further?

"Herr Mozart, I remember you here with your dear sister. And the music of this past week, and next week's operas. You do me such honor."

I thought he sounded like Joseph II, and I had not heard such kind words from a monarch since. I thanked him.

He said, "Next week, I wish to attend *The Magic Flute*. I ask that you sit with Princess Amelia, my treasure."

The statement sent the court into some confusion because the King did not attend public performances, and *The Magic Flute* was scheduled for the Drury Lane Theatre Royal, the locale only ever visited by the King for command performances attended solely by him. If the court now had to arrange a performance of *The Magic Flute* for him, there was very little time for so many details. *Richard III* was to appear at the Haymarket Theatre Royal.

King George could sense the concern. "Not a command performance. I wish to attend with the public. I shall occupy the Royal Box. That is its purpose."

I quickly found out that this had never been done, and the idea worried the court, not solely for the constant concern for the King's safety, but more because the King behaved so unpredictably. If he became engaged and excited by a performance, there was no telling what he might do. I sensed that thus far, they had been able to contain him and hide his behavior from the public, but a single bad outing at the theater could send rumors flying everywhere. It had been difficult enough with Parliament, according to all the talk I overheard, but the damage there had long been done and was at least advantageously distant in memory. The courtiers, along with the King's sons, had plans in place to keep him from his Parliamentary duties, but those plans would look suspicious if the King were suddenly to appear at a public performance at Drury Lane.

I was escorted from the throne room, a waiting carriage already filled with my clothes and scores to be taken home to Brook Street. The night was warm and the air felt like fine silk. I asked the coachman if we might have a diversionary drive, just to relax from the exertions before going home. The coachman, from St. James's Palace, was obliged to do as I asked. There was a bright moon, so London was not as utterly dark as it normally was, and it was not yet so late, as I could see many house lamps still alight.

I said I would like to ride the Strand to St. Paul's and back through Soho Square to home, a journey that I knew could take an hour or more. I had grown to love the little church of St. Martin-in-the-Fields that stood alone in the marshy area between Westminster and the city. It had become my favorite demarcation, the place from which I most easily found other places. It was also surrounded by gaslight at all times, which I loved. We drove the short distance down the Mall to St. Martin's then the carriage began the long steady climb up Ludgate Hill to St. Paul's. I was not sure why it felt important to visit St. Paul's that evening; perhaps because the cathedral sat on the highest point in London, and felt like a pinnacle I should symbolically visit on that night.

The carriage slowly ascended the darkness of Ludgate Hill, and I reflected on the whirlwind days that had passed. Had they been successful? Who would decide my success? I felt they were triumphant evenings, but it was not my place to call them so. The King, perhaps, would decide, but he was not of sound enough mind to pass true judgment. I would only hear the assessments of musicians I respected, meaning musicians I felt were my equal. As I grew older there were fewer of those, at least in my moments of private honesty. Some writers for the many broadsheets of London might write opinions about the concerts, but would they necessarily determine the success of the three evenings? I knew, as did everyone, that concerts were fleeting things, glimpses of time, but whatever was written about them would often last many years hence, if anyone would later care enough to read it. I hated reading about music, because no amount of reading could bring an experience to life. I noticed that writers in Vienna tended to focus on flaws, or what they perceived as flaws. I had read some of the most ridiculous things about my own music, assessments of the works that were filled with inaccuracies. Many of those people writing could not even tell the key of a symphony without being informed in advance; always the sure sign of a charlatan. I wondered what they might say of my first English concerts, but it mattered little since the King and the upper courtiers knew nothing of the broadsheets.

Surrounded by sleeping families, and a few lingering fires in small camps dotting the fields that embraced the vast building, St. Paul's sat in glorious silence. It felt wondrous to me that people were moved to build such edifices to the glory of God, but also that there were minds capable of conceiving such immensity. St. Paul's felt like a mountain, something that could stand for ten thousand years. I never tired of looking at it, and it seemed to emit an energy, some kind of strange power that entered and restored. I have read of great pyramids in Africa from which emanated renewing energy, but I knew I would never see such a place even if it existed.

I was as tired as it was possible to be on that night, yet the boundlessness of the great building, which stretched in every direction into the darkness, revitalized me. I wondered if it might be the presence of God Himself, more available for intervention near a place devoted to his praise. I felt shame in the presence of St. Paul's, because I had not devoted time to prayer in the previous week when I had actually needed intercessions. And even without prayer, where had my gratitude been? Why had I not offered praise in thanks to God for the many gifts bestowed? Never too late, I thought, so I left the carriage and ascended the steps of the cathedral to offer my thanks for the success at the King's concerts. Energies were lingering now, gathering somewhere out in the dark, and I knew they would somehow make their way to me. God could find me on Brook Street, or at St. James, but my soul needed to be open to Him, and my heart ready for the grand intercessions He had in mind for me. My love for Konstanze and Franz, and the sadness of all I had left behind to come to London, was ever present, but a new happiness was emerging as well, and I knew that both could exist at once.

I instructed the coachman to take me home, driving by the Drury Lane theater this time, and then on to Soho Square. It had gotten quite late into the evening, though many lights were still burning, and the horses flew down Ludgate, achieving dangerous speed for the darkness. I knew that people were forever being struck by horses at night, and I hoped my memory of this day would not be marred by any tincture of tragedy. In the many days of my life, a few remain as clear to me as this moment of writing. My marriage day is one of them. The day I met Lorenzo. Seeing Emanuel as *Hamlet*. The first performance of the C-minor mass. The Romaní woman. My new life. But as the carriage passed the Drury Lane with just enough light for me to see my own *Magic Flute* announced on the large posted playbill, the satisfaction I felt turned to love, a singular kind of love. Not the love of being recognized or the love of being known. It was a love of love itself, a thankfulness that love was available at all.

The Drury Lane behind us, we entered an area of deeper darkness, fields where criminals might reside, and quickly alighted on Soho Square, one of the more populated and elegant parts of London, with each house uniformly lit with identical lamps, creating a proportion I loved, with the four entrances to the square forming perfectly symmetrical pools of darkness, the westernmost of which would take me home. We had stayed near Soho Square on one of my youthful trips, which I knew only from hearing the name, but I retained no memory of that time.

My little house on Brook Street was quiet and inviting. The coachman helped me carry my belongings up the few steps to the front door. I was eager for sleep. There was no fire with which to make tea, and I was too tired to think of building one. I lit two table candles and one lantern for moving about. I took myself to the wall near the mews to retrieve enough water for the night and early morning. I now had two days in which to rest and wait for the next set of ideas to come. Two entire days. I could not remember two consecutive days on which I had no commitments, and they felt like an extravagant gift. Perhaps I could return to Richmond Hill or visit Windsor. I should pay a call of thanks to Sir William to be sure my gratitude was known, and I needed to learn if Sir William had approved of the concerts.

As I was about to ascend the stairs to change from my performance clothes into a nightshirt, I heard a sound I had not experienced in the house before, forcing me to ponder if I had perhaps fallen into a dreaming time. It might be a thief seeking the simplest way into my home. The knocking on the door was timid, like a small animal in search of food. Was I mistaking the sound? I thought it was likely the carriage driver delivering something I had left. I lifted my lantern to the door and opened it.

CHAPTER 51

It took a moment for my eyes to adjust to the moving light, and much more time to comprehend who was standing before me. It was so utterly improbable that I whispered aloud, "Lorenzo? Lorenzo? Lorenzo!"

Lorenzo Da Ponte laughed at the triptych of his own name, and he sang "*Chi? Chi? Chi?*" from our *Figaro*, on the right pitches.

"I would have been less surprised by you actually being Rafaello!" I said.

I cannot describe the joy of hearing his voice again. He said, "I knew you were in London, I heard it months ago, but I had no way of finding you until the King's concerts were announced."

"Were you there?"

"I was not there, Amadé. I cannot be seen at the court."

"Why?" I could not imagine a reason why a man of Lorenzo's talents would not be welcome.

"I'm considered politically dangerous now, Amadé. I have to keep a very low profile here, and I'm just waiting to leave."

"You, dangerous?"

"The revolutions in France and America have shaken this country to its core."

My spirits sank, as I loathed politics. Lorenzo could never keep himself out of political trouble. But I was so happy to see him again that I erupted into tears that were quite apart from the unexpected joy and total exhaustion. There seemed no end to my emotion that night.

Everything that had always been so stimulating about Lorenzo, the deep fire in his eyes, his blazing need for freedom and justice, the deep spirit of *Figaro* himself, came back to me in an instant. I felt as though we were back in a room together writing *Figaro*, and for a moment during my tears I wondered what Cherubino and Susanna were doing at that very moment, as if they were real people like us.

As my spirits soared from shock to welcome, I invited Lorenzo in and offered him wine. My own exhaustion ebbed for a while in the excitement of seeing my dearest friend. Lorenzo was his old energetic, witty, and quick self but I sensed deep distress underneath his giddiness. We talked through the burning of several sets of candles, and for so long that I had at last to go to sleep. I offered Lorenzo my second bed, which he took. We embraced. I put the lanterns and candles out, and silence fell upon Brook Street at last.

I wanted to stay awake to remember everything about that momentous day, as I was afraid of what might disappear in the fog of sleep, but even all of these many years later, my sweet reader, the memory is as clear as something that happened to me yesterday. Lorenzo had returned to my life after years of unknowing silence, suggesting even that he might be dead, so his reappearance was a great relief. But it was also alarming. He had a wife in London, Nancy Grahl, and children both with her and others, yet in our hours of reacquaintance he scarcely mentioned them. He talked to me of friends in France and details of the revolution that I had no care for. He also spoke of levels of danger in London that felt as foreign to my experience as tales of the wilds of America or the Orient. As my head hit the pillow, I wondered if it might be perilous to have Lorenzo in my house. The chambermaid might come in early and discover him there, reporting it back to the Lord Chamberlain. I chastised myself, for how could the girl have any way of knowing it was Lorenzo Da Ponte? I fell away to sleep.

The morning came quickly. I remember saying upon stumbling out of my bedroom, "Lorenzo! You are still here, thank God!" We both laughed. "I was so afraid I would never see you again, just like the last time!"

Lorenzo carried on the conversation as though no sleep had occurred. "I want to take you to see Nancy and go with me to a few appointments. I need to deliver something near here, and then I want to show you a new music store where they are selling all kinds of new instruments. I know the owner and know he would love to meet you. I have many friends for you to meet."

That sounded wonderful. Although I had taken carriage journeys, I'd had little occasion to meet anyone outside the court. We ate some bread and tea before delivering Lorenzo's manuscript to Berkeley Square, where it was slipped into a small bag on the side of the house, there for just that purpose, sheltered from rain by a small hood the enterprising owner had placed there. Walking London with Lorenzo was to walk a new city, because he knew it so well, and he was a natural noticer. Lorenzo walked me through streets I had never seen, to the north, I thought, because we crossed the large Oxford Road with its row of beautiful houses and quiet plots of trees and gardens. I had a dream to perhaps one day live in a grand home like those along the Oxford Road, but Lorenzo told me instead to dream of living in Oxford itself, which he said was by far the most interesting and beautiful place in England. It seemed sometimes that Lorenzo had managed to see every place in England, and I loved hearing about Bath with its ancient Roman ruins, and the great monoliths at Stonehenge, which Lorenzo had actually touched and spent afternoons in their lengthening shadows, writing poetry. After listening to Lorenzo, I wanted to walk under the great scissor arches of Wells Cathedral, and longed to visit the other great structures of the country. Lorenzo had a way of describing them that brought them to life for me and made me want to see them and yearn to have relations in each place with a woman I deeply loved, at least loved deeply for the time I visited.

Lorenzo had always made me want to be in love. Since I arrived in England, I had been working so hard that I had barely noticed a woman besides the royal princesses, and I was feeling in need of a woman's attention. I did not tell Lorenzo about Tamu, nor did I speak of Tamu's clear instruction to have no relations with a woman for a year, and I had not at that moment been in London for even half that time. Lorenzo had always brought to me, as well, not just the desire for women but the women themselves. They always flocked to Lorenzo, and had an unerring sense of what I would like and what kind of woman would submit to me. I noticed every woman on our walk, each a constant reminder that I could not have them. We arrived at the shop dedicated to the sale of musical instruments, and all my thoughts of women dissipated. I had never seen a shop like it before. It had no sign, just a number on a door. Lorenzo knocked and we entered.

In what would have been the drawing room of a substantial house, had it still been used for that purpose, several men were inspecting violins and violas, and near the back of the room, some well-dressed gentlemen were examining flutes. For me it was a wonderland. There were instrument sellers in Vienna, of course, even in tiny Salzburg, but they sold instruments for homes, like clavichords, harpsichords, and small viols of all kinds and sizes. I had seen harmoniums in Vienna that I always wanted to buy but never managed to find the money. But this London shop not only sold instruments for homes but also instruments for orchestras; instruments that only musicians would want or need. Little snippets of music came from all over, including, to my delight, a passage from my own *Eine kleine Nachtmusik*, which flooded me with an unexpected and unreleased joy. Lorenzo knew this feeling in me and had seen it only a few times before.

He knew, too, that the joy was from hearing my music played by strangers. We had once been at an inn together near Praha, en route to *Don Giovanni*, when I heard a violinist somewhere nearby practicing the final movement of my *Haffner* serenade. My lip quivered and my eyes filled as I looked toward the sound and away from Lorenzo. I did not enjoy crying in front of others when I was young, but as I grew older I came to accept it. Lorenzo was attuned to my tears because he took them as signs of joy in the world. Of all my close friends, Lorenzo alone understood that the most productive times for me came with joy.

The shop owner greeted Lorenzo, who introduced me, and the tour of the instruments began. Everything the man sold represented the latest inventions and ideas. I was fascinated by the many ingenious crooks that someone had thought up to give more notes to horns. The possibilities of what pitches they could play were beginning to open beyond the four or five sonorous notes available from all the horns I knew in Vienna. The crooks, curved and beautifully ratioed, were familiar to me, but the new crooks were magnificently twisted and made of several different kinds of brass, giving the crooked attachments enough color delineation to make them easier for players to change them quickly, sending my mind swirling with possibilities. I thought there would soon be no limitations on the beastly difficult horn!

Customers kept entering the shop, so many that I stopped attempting my usual scrutiny of each person, particularly any of the few ladies present. I knew my own desires created various forms of inappropriate looks. I tried to monitor where my eyes alighted, which I always found so difficult. The sight of a woman's ankle across the shop, a young woman trying out a violin, sent my desires racing. Within a few distracted seconds, I could imagine the woman convulsing in spasms of pleasure beneath me. But I was so immersed in the discovery of the instruments that I released the hold of the fantasy. As always when my mind moved between the carnal and the musical, I was left wondering where one went when the other took over. My sexual fantasy of the girl must have gone somewhere, but where? Similarly, my musical ideas must be present within the time I spent several times a day in sexual dreams and self-pleasure. How could I or anyone be two such disparate people at once?

Lorenzo was captivated by the instruments on his own accord, but even more by my delights and playfulness with each one. I could play most of the instruments reasonably well, but in the case of violins and violas, I was more in command than I thought I would be, considering how long it had been since I had practiced.

CHAPTER 52

Two well-dressed men entered followed by two liveried servants each carrying boxes to a nearby table. The boxes were opened, and to my joyous sighs, they were filled with new flutes. I could not wait to hear the tones of the flutes, but I also heard another felicity: the men were speaking in the most educated level of high German. I immediately spoke to them. We exchanged the usual *Hochdeutsch* formalities, through which I discerned that the older of the gentlemen was the owner of the establishment and lived in the large house that was also on the property. The other man was dressed in the cleanest frock coat I had ever seen, and I could not imagine what it must have cost. It was trimmed in a type of fur I didn't recognize, as though it came from an animal from another world. Both Lorenzo and I noted the fur on the man's lapels, and we exchanged knowing looks. Lorenzo's German was excellent, but he had to depend on me for the subtlest things the man was saying, for his German was very learned and cultivated.

I was instantly drawn to the younger of the two men, who introduced himself as John. His German was like that of my father, very fast and clean but melodious and perfectly crafted. He seemed an amiable fellow, and inviting of conversation.

I had not thought much about missing my mother tongue. There was plenty of German, though more French, in the court, even if it was not the German of my childhood. Just at that moment, someone tried a new trumpet in a distant part of the property. Haydn's concerto, the finale, which I had not heard in years and longed to hear all of it right then. I vowed to do it with my court orchestra in the coming days, perhaps for the next set of King's concerts. Meanwhile I kept speaking with this mysterious man named John and learning about his childhood. Then, I heard a little extract from one of my own trumpet concertos. My tears came again, causing John to inquire, in the most poetic way offered by our tongue, if I had unexpectedly been hurt by something he had said. I struggled to explain why I had suddenly become so moved. Only the real explanation was plausible, so after hesitation I finally said what I had been avoiding speaking aloud.

"I heard some of my own music, and I'm away from home and found it very moving, that's all, sir."

John said, "I don't believe I heard your name clearly."

"Amadé."

"What is your surname?"

"Mozart. I am Wolfgang Amadé Mozart."

John looked puzzled, as if the coincidence of our mutual presence was impossible to imagine. "You are actually *the* Mozart, the composer?"

"Yes, sir. Is that surprising?"

John looked dizzy. But he spoke, "I have traveled all over the New World, in areas as wild as can be imagined. I've nearly been killed by Indians on many occasions and have been in the presence of every manner of savage. You cannot imagine the American wilderness. I have spent a great deal of my life at sea, even though I am a bit younger than you, and I have traversed the Atlantic many times. Now I come to this great metropolis, in which I am constantly at business and political functions, with so much to accomplish before I am to report to a ship in Portsmouth to sail back to New York. I am here to purchase fifty to sixty flutes and oboes that I will take with me to sell in New York, not to make money but to bring music to a wild place. I have explicit instructions from the Vice President of the United Colonies of the new United States, the newest government in the world, to do what I can to bring not only business to the nation but also that which enriches and civilizes. And now, by total chance, I find myself in a remote corner of a country in which neither of us was born, and I am standing before the composer of my entire childhood. Are you *really* Wolfgang Amadeus Mozart?"

"Amadé," I said, feeling odd about correcting such a noble man.

"Your father is Leopold?" John asked, surprising me.

"Long departed, more than ten years now."

John went on. "The stories my family used to tell of your father and of you! The brilliance you achieved when you were just a boy. You would not believe it. We were punished with, 'Why can't you be like little Wolfgang?'"

"Your family was, didn't you say, in Walldorf?" I asked.

"Yes, near Heidelberg, where I might happily have stayed had I not come to London as a boy, now so long ago, and been swept up in the whole fever of the place. And then the great energy of everything that was and is still happening in the New World."

Any mention of a new world made my eyes glaze over, as I had spent so much of my life in new worlds and the one thing they all seemed to share is that they were never as new as they thought they were. New countries and new governments inevitably fell to old human frailties, and political ideals bored me. With music, I could achieve an ideal, at least within my mind. Governments were never so easy.

But Lorenzo noticed John's comments. Up to that moment, Lorenzo had remained focused on the discussions of business dealings, any portion of which left my own senses dulled. Time after time, Lorenzo had heard the wild musings of businessmen who promised him a quick way out of his debts, and offered a way for Lorenzo to find a prosperous future. To Lorenzo, any rich person was a charlatan, and any royalty an undeserving usurper of someone else's wealth. But John seemed to have acquired his wealth with the workings of his own mind and so, to Lorenzo, was more deserving of respect and interest. John had experience in the post-revolutionary New World and was intending to return, and anyone who had been to America interested him.

"What is it like there?" Lorenzo asked John.

"An impossible question to answer, of course. New York is very like Amsterdam and the low countries. It is small, and everywhere you go there is water. What homes there are look Dutch in style. There is quite a lot of German spoken, and within the upper classes a good deal of French. But it is a very British place overall, not much different from London except it is much more backward and dirty. There are many opportunities, but much that has yet to be really civilized. I have done well by seizing every opportunity I can find. That is the amazing thing about America: the opportunity. It is a huge land that is almost completely empty once you get beyond New York and into the interior."

Lorenzo clearly wanted to see it all. "How is it possible that it is so empty?"

John continued, "A few savages, but even they cannot compete with the wild beasts of the interior. I have been told by some of my employees about vast herds of bison or other beasts that number a hundred thousand or more. They could never fully be hunted. I've seen flocks of birds that blotted out the sun. And the beavers and other furs are unsurpassed anywhere. The skins and fur trading are inexhaustible. The natives are no match for the wildlife, it seems to me. Of course, I actually know little of them."

It sounded like a wonderland to Lorenzo, but to me felt like a place of terror. I could tell, though, that Lorenzo was eager to leave London and sail to any new world. He exuded desire for another place, whereas I was happy to be wherever I happened to be, and because that was London in that moment I intended to be happy in London for the remaining years of my life. I did not want to find Lorenzo again after almost ten years only to have him leave for America and never be seen again. But Lorenzo had the desperation to get out, as he was never fully content in any one place. I would have to move from room to room when writing and then from coffeehouse to coffeehouse, but I could happily stay in one room or coffeehouse all day, loving the way the light would shift over the hours. In fact, I was hoping to take Lorenzo to a coffeehouse somewhere in London and plan the rest of the day.

By then I had seen everything of the musical instruments. The shop was fantastic and I planned to return because there were instruments I wanted to acquire for the court orchestra, but first I would have to speak to Sir William and others to get the permission. For now I was eager to move about my day and I tried to coax Lorenzo out of his conversation with John. A few others had joined them, and once Lorenzo was engrossed it was difficult to get him away. John, sensing my impatience, stepped away from the gathering crowd.

"Herr Mozart. I will send a carriage for you an hour before sundown. Write down your address for me. Lorenzo and I will meet you at dinner at my club, near St. James."

"I live near St. James," I said, writing my address as asked.

"You will need to arrive by carriage, so I will send for you. Please wear evening clothing. The dining room is formal."

We exchanged farewells as formally as we had greeted each other and I left, the sounds of instruments mixing with an escalating political discussion that Lorenzo seemed to be leading. I was happy to leave it and emerge into the London afternoon. There were so many people out, and I loved seeing the bustle of Oxford Road. I wanted to work, but I knew work would return soon enough. My final *Samson* had not yet been a full turning of the sun, and I could still feel the week of concerts in my body. Until London, I never used to tire. I decided I would stop by home long enough to get a folio to take to a coffeehouse. I had not had time to just enjoy an afternoon in a café, not since Vienna, and it was among my favorite uses of time. I quickly walked home and then to the Haymarket, where I found a lovely spot where I could order a strong Viennese coffee, and start sketching ideas. They came easily. A couple of piano concerto themes. Two new symphonies, and even a symphony with chorus in praise of the King. Coffee always helped my ideas flow.

CHAPTER 53

One of the contraptions at the music shop lingered in my mind. It was not an instrument, but a device with weights and strings that sort of clicked like a clock, but it had no purpose toward the hour. It was meant to give musicians some idea of the distance between notes of music, the tempo. I had longed for a clear way to express the precise rate of my works, which of course varied according to their expression, but there was always a basic ratio of time that made the music seem right. When good musicians played my music, they got close to what I intended. But I had so often heard other musicians play my music far too quickly or, more often, too slowly. But other than telling them, or playing it for them myself, there was no way to indicate with any precision what they should do. I considered returning to the shop to purchase one, but how useful it would really be? For a musician with little talent, no amount of clicking would help them. I always found it astounding how difficult it could be for some musicians to find a tempo. But I also knew that even I often had trouble knowing exactly the speed at which to play music other than my own. I had played some of Haydn's sonatas a particular way, but then I heard Haydn play them himself and I was nowhere near his desires.

It always stayed with me that composers played their own music a particular way. When others played it, there was always just the smallest thing that felt off or, if not off, untrue. If this had been true of Handel and Bach, what could possibly be done about it now? The new gadget at the store might help, but for the remainder of the afternoon I wanted to just enjoy the delicious coffee and the parade of pastries I was being shown. I knew no machine or new gadgetry could convey anything meaningful about music. Only people could do that.

The beauty of the afternoon renewed me, enlivening my heaviest exhaustion. I could tell by the precision of what was arriving inwardly, with no effort at all to search for it, that I had many ideas on the precipice. The intense period of preparation and rehearsal just passed had closed it off for a time, which filled me with anxiety. Any time my flow of ideas was impeded, I was forced to wonder when, or if, it might return. Weeks of trying to get the chorus to sing all of the right notes in time to the complex choruses of *Samson*, a task I thought I would never achieve, was endlessly difficult, real drudgery. The singers were so variable, which made me concentrate my efforts on the more gifted among them, leaving the lesser ones to feel ignored, no doubt.

Perhaps that's what had happened in the court all those years ago, the months of intrigue that appeared to have no reason beneath. I was only able to see it in retrospect, which always puzzled me, being a man who knew things others did not. How could I not see that I concentrated my efforts on the people most capable of performing or understanding me, and rather than fighting with anyone else, I forgot about them. The ignored ones thought me aloof and disengaged, and I left them with nothing to do or say about me except to make up stories. I assumed this was still to come in George III's court, as it was a simple truth about court life: people made up things about anyone they did not understand. Within a court, it was compounded by no one being able to say anything to anyone about the monarch. With that avenue blocked, people had to talk about someone, and it eventually befell me. I tried hard, always, to be friendly and nice to people, and I was not one for tantrums, but neither could I successfully hide my preferences for certain people. There was something about meeting a fellow artist that removed a burden of pretending that a person had talent. I struggled with the entire idea of talent. When I was young and everything was easy, talent was the only thing that defined anyone, and my entire being was inseparable from it. Talent left no option but an entitlement to more talent, and the expectation that one would never have to encounter those of similar talent. Who was the child Mozart without talent?

But talent changed over time, as surely as the light of a day shifted without being noticed. My own talent had moved around, and my passions with it. There were days when I could not wait to approach the keyboard, tune it, and set to improvising before I would shift to composing. But on other days, I wanted to play quartets with my friends, during which many ideas would also begin to come. And I loved to attend the theater, but then felt guilty for the time it took away from music. Plays were very long, which I loved, but there always came a moment in any play, comedy or tragedy, when I imagined myself dying. That was uncanny, as morbidity was not my natural state. But in the theater, always, there it is: death. I assumed that the communal feeling of a play brought death within reach because it brought someone so close to life. But the river that ran through everything was talent, and I had seen many people destroyed by their talent, unable to fully know what to do with it, or what to do next with it. When the next thing I needed was the satiety of private desires, that obliterated all other needs. Copulation had to be next or no other next could be approached. Now I find all desires to be competing so deeply that I struggle with defining the next satisfaction, and every decision is more difficult than when I was young, but that is a story for my old age, friends.

CHAPTER 54

I prepared for a fancy night, lighting a fire in the stove to heat water for washing more than I normally would. One more day remained before I had to return to work and report to the Lord Chamberlain. Any evening with Lorenzo could extend into the hours before sunrise. That Lorenzo and I were to dine in a gentlemen's club, only one sundown after the King's concert, felt like a miracle.

Just as John had promised, a carriage arrived to deliver me to his club. The driver told me he would deliver me home whenever the evening was completed. I knew this meant that the carriage and its driver were John's property, and not simply someone hired for the evening, for only kings and the very wealthy ever made such arrangements. This made me wary.

We arrived quickly to Boodle's, John's club, which was just around the corner. I understood immediately why a carriage had been sent, as there was no way to know a club was at that particular address in St. James, for there was no sign and no identifying number or marking of any kind. I would never have found it. The driver went to a door and gave my name for entrance. The door was opened and I stepped into another world, one far more opulent than what I had seen of St. James's Palace, the home of a king! This was luxury beyond the finest quarters of my acquaintance in Vienna or Paris. I knew that very few men in young America were so rich, so it occurred to me that John must be a special man indeed.

As John and Lorenzo were not present, I was taken to a room designated solely for predinner liqueurs and cigars. These cigars were very small and rolled with exquisite craft for a patron at their request. I rarely enjoyed tobacco but this was nothing like the tobacco I had been given in Vienna or Paris; this was smooth and beautiful, calming to my anxiety, and each puff brought a veil of approaching sleep without being tired.

I heard Lorenzo's voice approaching. He and John appeared to have been friends for years, though I knew they had only met that day. We entered the smoking chamber, a richly decorated room of green velvets and silks. John had a way about him that made people feel they had always known him, which I felt as John greeted me formally with a clink of our glasses, and he told me in high German how happy he was I could join him. Just by looking at Lorenzo I could tell he had consumed alcohol all day, and that he and John had been scheming about something that it would likely take much of the evening for me to pry from him. John instructed that we were to finish drinks before going to the formal dining room.

Though I was in attendance specifically at John's invitation, I felt an outsider with John and Lorenzo. The few hours they had spent alone had bonded them. John held me in a halo of reverence that did not invite familiarity. He was pleasant with me but friendlier, kinder, and more open with Lorenzo. He treated Lorenzo already as a brother, whereas John looked upon me as some kind of cleric. My only hope for the dinner was simply to become part of a trio, to have John consider me less formally. I also wanted to use that precious time to explore more operas with Lorenzo, something I had thought I would not live to see again.

Boodle's smelled like a church. I saw thousands of candles inside the club, so many that the interior came close to daylight. How could they afford such extravagance each night? I was especially sensitive to the smell of candles, as their scent brought strong associations of Salzburg Cathedral and St. Stephen's, but also the years during which Konstanze and I had plenty of money and I bought candles sufficient to fill the room with enough light to compose long into the evening. Soon, though, the expense was simply too great, and I had to relinquish the time after dark. Within Boodle's, I could write all night in any of the rooms. Great chandeliers filled each space, and the many tables were covered in candles. Each man in the club wore exquisite clothing, making me feel more than usually like a servant, since even my best clothing looked disheveled by comparison.

The conversation between Lorenzo and John, which had clearly lasted all day, was coming to conclusion by the time I joined. As we got to table, John finished a thought: "Lorenzo, we are seeing the end of monarchies. In our lifetimes we shall see all of the kings and queens renounced and sent to colonial retirements."

I hoped not to spend the evening on politics, so I said, "For the moment I am quite happy to have a king, for without him I would not have met either of you fine gentlemen."

"It is difficult to imagine that you both wrote those wonderful operas together and then lost touch," John said.

"Lorenzo disappeared. It is what he does from time to time," I said, to the chuckling of the two men. I asked John how he had come to hear our operas.

"I heard only *Figaro* before I left for New York the first time. My father took me. Of course, I did not make it to New York at all in that trip but got stuck in the ice outside Baltimore for days. I may be the only person around who actually walked to America."

"It is amazing that your father took you to *Figaro*," Lorenzo offered.

"Not so amazing. He knew the play. And we would even read it aloud at home. The opera is magnificent."

I offered, "You may experience it again. I hope to perform it here in London. Of course, *Magic Flute* and *Richard III* are to be seen here shortly, but they come from a time after Lorenzo."

"Yes," said John, "I heard about them appearing at the Drury Lane. I shall try to attend but, as I have been telling Lorenzo, I am returning to New York and my business next week. I am due on a ship from Portsmouth."

My heart sank, for I could tell they had already discussed Lorenzo being on the ship with John. And I knew Lorenzo had not been home long enough to even mention the idea to Nancy. I further knew that Lorenzo was one to run from things. I wanted Lorenzo to remain in London so we could write more operas together, even though he might be unable to work again due to his own intrigue. I did not want him to run away from his own life again. I felt all sorts of needs bunch up within me. Though the concerts had been successful, I felt so alone in London, so unprotected, and I wanted Lorenzo with me. I knew the look in his eyes, though. I had seen it many times. Once Lorenzo decided to leave a place, the leaving began long before he actually departed.

John sensed my general unease. "Herr Mozart, rest assured that I am sailing back to America alone."

Lorenzo laughed nervously. John ignored him. "Lorenzo seems more interested in the New World than I expected, but all of his binding ties are in London."

"John, Lorenzo has constant interest in a *different* world, whether it be old or new," I offered, hoping to get Lorenzo to say something, anything.

He did. "Amadé, my dearest and longest friend, and John, my newest, my only interest in life now is freedom, real freedom, and that has replaced even art for me. Amadé, you will find this unsurprising and probably irritating, typical of the many things that have distracted me in the past."

I was indeed irritated by Lorenzo's obsession with anything other than writing. I said, "Lorenzo, it is only your writing that will outlive you. None of your other distracting fixations will last, you must realize that."

The words emerged from me without thought. Kings would be remembered simply for being kings. Even old Schrattenbach would be remembered with a statue in Salzburg that would stand for a thousand years, and probably much else. For people like me and Lorenzo, all that would be remembered of us are our scribblings.

I had to change the subject, as I could see Lorenzo's fears rising. "What have you been happy with in England, John?"

"Your concerts, frankly, gave me more joy than all of the business I have transacted. I am taking back a huge number of instruments to sell in New York, where everything is waiting to happen. New England is quite like London, but without the inherent problems which accompany all large cities. The possibilities are without equal."

Lorenzo was frustrated with me. "That's what I'm talking about, Amadé, the possibilities. I want to live where there is a freedom of possibility."

"You cannot uproot your life again, Lorenzo. Don't do that to your family, or to yourself. You have no idea what might be across the sea. You have never lived outside of what a city offers," I said.

The food kept arriving, and Lorenzo and I reminisced about *Figaro*, *Così*, and *Don Giovanni*, to John's delight. We spoke, too, of the works we thought about but never found time to write, and it was that part of the repartee John most enjoyed, because it was within the unrealized that he felt most able to make a difference. I vowed not to push either man into further thoughts of America, even though something in their conversation made me already imagine them in carriages moving around New York or Boston or Baltimore. John told us again about getting frozen in Baltimore's harbor and walking to America.

By evening's end, Lorenzo and I had planned our next opera, *The Guilty Mother*, as a way of reliving the world of *Figaro* together, it being the continuation of the story by Pierre Beaumarchais.

John said, "Gentlemen, this day has been one I shall never forget. To have met both of you is a personal honor. Lorenzo, I hope I can entice you to my new country, and please know I will help you all I can. Amadé, I could never have imagined being in the presence of the composer of *Figaro*. We are unlikely to encounter each other again, which deepens my gratitude. I ask that we write each other, as I want to hear news of your London career, of all you will write, and of your dreams."

"How can I write to you?" Amadé asked.

"My card will accompany you both in your carriages," John said, as he bowed and left.

CHAPTER 55

"Are you going to America, Lorenzo?" I asked immediately upon John's departure, hoping his fog of alcohol would bring forth the truth.

"Yes, Amadé. I am leaving this dead city."

"What will you do about Nancy and the children?"

"I'm taking them, of course. They just don't know it yet." Lorenzo paused before adding, "Amadé, you should go with us. You will never again find a free passage to America."

"How is it free?" Amadé asked.

"John is sailing home to America on his own vessel."

"How did he come to have so much money? He is no king."

"He told me he made it trading, and buying land. He has a sense of things, and I trust his sense of what I could do there."

"Lorenzo, it was only this time last night that we found each other again. Please do not tell me we will now lose each other again! If you go to America, we will never see each other again," I said, almost crying.

Lorenzo had decided. "I'm going home now to tell Nancy. The day after tomorrow we will be in a carriage to Portsmouth to begin the voyage to America. You could be with us."

I told him I could not leave the King's service so soon after accepting it. The court had been so generous to me, and the King and Sir William so kind, I could not desert them. I said all of this to Lorenzo, though he knew it already.

"You are loyal to everyone but yourself, my friend. You must go where you can have the most opportunity. That cannot possibly be London."

"But Lorenzo, it *is* London. I have my own orchestra, they are putting on my operas, and I have a home and salary that is far beyond anything I've ever had."

"No, you are a servant, exactly like the servant who cleans the chamber pot of George III. You just write music instead."

I said again that I must be loyal to those who had been loyal to me.

"What about me?" Lorenzo appealed. "Haven't I been loyal to you?"

I did not stop to think, though I should have. "No, you haven't. You disappeared without a word. I nearly died after *The Magic Flute* was completed, not knowing if I would ever see you again. Now I am handed the joy of seeing you again only to be told you are going across the sea. I cannot cross a sea. I could barely cross the channel from France, with England visible at every moment! To be surrounded by open sea for days at a time is the most terrifying thing imaginable. I could not possibly survive. My constitution is too weak to even consider it. I would be dead within days, don't you understand?"

I was again in tears. I wanted to stop talking, but could not. A bridge was being crossed. "You don't realize, Lorenzo, how alone I am. You have never had every angel removed from your life, as I have. Papa, Konstanze, Joseph, and then you. And when I decided to start a new life here, I had to do it alone. You know what will happen if I ever found the courage to come to America? You would die on me, and I would be alone there, or you would decide you had to live in Paris and you'd come back. I'll have to be given something to make me delirious for the journey, or I will be sick the whole time. I will likely be sick anyway, no matter what I take. I'm saying goodnight to you, Lorenzo, knowing we will never see each other again."

I rose to leave, still talking. "I will not give you time to say anything, because I do not desire a scene with anyone, especially not in this beautiful club. When I think of what we might have accomplished together, Lorenzo, if you would not make this sudden decision, I am nearly sick.

But until last night you were dead, and now you will die to me again. Who can survive so much loss?"

I left and walked to the carriage awaiting me outside. I could not turn to see Lorenzo even one last time. As I boarded the carriage, I noticed a second carriage that I knew was for Lorenzo. I thought of waiting, but I told the coachman to take me home. There was a small package in the carriage, just as John had said there would be.

CHAPTER 56

The journey was brief and quiet. Above sparkled many stars, though it was a moonless night, which always made me slightly anxious. The moon was a great comfort, wherever it appeared in the canopy of sky, and on those few nights when it went elsewhere I missed it. The presence of all the rest of the celestial bodies without the great orb put my world slightly asunder. I thanked the coachman and entered my house, taking in the heavens for the last time that evening. They were as unutterably beautiful as anything. Not one phrase of music that I had heard or written could compare with a single glance at the night sky. What might the sky be at sea? I would never know, but John would experience that within a few days.

I lit a lantern and readied myself for bed, planning my work for the final day before I would return to the court and plan my next set of concerts. There would be *Magic Flute* rehearsals to attend, and so many things to do. I hoped Lorenzo might knock on the door again, but he was probably by then at home himself, far across London, trying to explain to his wife that he was taking them by ship to America. He would have to tell her something about John, and about the concert and meeting me again, and all of the improbable things that had occurred between the two night skies. I could scarcely believe it myself, and I had witnessed it.

The small packet from John reached out to me when I took the lantern to go upstairs to bed. I decided to wait until morning to open it, when all the day's worries would be less, as I always imagined the night sky somehow summoning the most irritating cares and fixing them while the sun was at rest. Philosophy brought me enormous exhaustion, for was the sun really at rest? Was it not merely high in the sky elsewhere in the world? Many priests tried to explain it to me otherwise, but that is the only explanation. We are on a sphere that mirrors our sleeping and waking. Perhaps the celestial bodies needed to ensure that earthly cares were diminished by making a man so tired he could not possibly worry about them. I put on my night clothes and got into bed, ready for a long sleep.

But curiosity got the better of me: I lit a new candle, and broke the small wax seal on the package. It included an address in New York at his business, and an invitation:

17 August, 1799

Herr Mozart—It was the dream of a lifetime to meet you. I realize I will never likely see you again, nor will I be able to entice you to our fine new world, though I would happily provide the happiest and most generous life you could have. Naturally, it could not rival what the King of England can give you, but you would have every comfort. Your concerts will live with me forever, and I ask that you kindly write to keep me informed of all you are composing, all you are dreaming about. Your dreams, and your music, will find their way to the New World someday, I am certain. Please do not judge dreamers too severely. Lorenzo needs his new dream. Write me. I am just across the seas, hearing in my faulty memory the final moments of *Figaro*, and your symphonies, and forever the sound of your playing just a few nights ago. For as long as I live, the sound will not die. Please write. Yours ever,

John Jacob Astor

If I had heard his full name up to that point, I had not remembered it. John Jacob Astor. I had rarely met anyone so generous and gracious, yet there was something sinister about the man, too. How many men had the ability to meet someone like Lorenzo in a music shop and within a few hours convince him to uproot his family and move all the way across the world? As I put out the lantern, I softened my thoughts on both Lorenzo and John, finding some confidence in Lorenzo arriving home and Nancy talking him out of it. And if not, I now had an address for John and I could find Lorenzo again. The day that had felt like one of the longest of my life was finally over. I blew out the lantern and fell quickly to sleep.

CHAPTER 57

The following morning's sun had fully risen by the time I awoke, and though I had slept many hours, exhaustion still burdened me. I took what breakfast I had in my cupboards, made tea, and quickly dressed. Then I took my folio and walked to the Drury Lane on my day of leisure, to see what I could of my opera. I had learned of a small café just down the hill from the Drury Lane that reminded me of Vienna, full of theater folk, so I wanted to spend leisurely time there as well.

As much as I enjoyed the comforts of the court, it was the theater I missed. I was so eager to hear anything of my beloved two operas in this new language of English. I had been told that they sounded wonderful, and that the translator for *Richard III* in particular had been successful in returning many of the lines directly to Shakespeare. I learned that the area around the Drury Lane was often called the West End, being so far west of London's city. I learned, too, that the West End was crawling with amazing people who knew every line of *Richard III*. The Haymarket was slightly closer to my home on Brook Street, and in both locales there were pubs and cafés where I could sketch should I grow tired of the one I was in.

Two letters awaited me as I left my house, so I packed them into my folio to look at later. I assumed them to be something about the recent concerts. One was tattered and quite long, in French, inquiring about a French premiere of *Tartuffe* and how they might be able to procure materials. I chuckled at the sudden interest in an opera that only months before I could not give away in Paris. I took especial pleasure in writing the person back, saying the premiere would undoubtedly be ordered by the King to be in London within a few months. I knew I was in possession of the only copies of the opera on my shelf at Brook Street. The thought of finally hearing *Tartuffe* made me laugh into the silence of the café, causing many to stare at me. The opera was the funniest thing I had ever written, and I could not wait to cackle through the first rehearsals and hear audiences roar with laughter, to rival that heard at *Figaro*.

The second letter was from the Lord Chamberlain, asking me to call on him at his earliest convenience before the next day's rehearsals. I thought this surely a courtesy to reiterate the King's gratitude for the success of my first concerts, so I decided against visiting the palace that very day, thinking it best to wait until the following morning and to spend my day sketching ideas.

I had known for quite some time that I wanted to create a completely new opera for London as soon as possible, and my greatest memory of Emanuel on stage was *Hamlet*. It would be incredibly bold to write *Hamlet* for a London audience, the most learned of whom knew every word. The challenge for the play, as Emanuel and I had often discussed, was what to remove. I had an idea that had never been tried before, of writing an opera in more than one part—not just acts, but entire full-length operas that told a single story. I deduced from what I remembered of *Hamlet*, in which I saw Emanuel appear more than a dozen times, that I could write a full-length opera that ended with the arrival of the Players and the idea of them performing *The Murder of Gonzago*. A second opera could then be written, and I could already hear great portions of it, beginning with "To be or not to be..."; Ophelia's return of Hamlet's tokens and letters; and ending with the death of Polonius. Then—and this I thought the most unprecedented of all—a third opera would begin with sending Rosencrantz and Guildenstern to England with Hamlet, instructing the King to murder him, the graveyard scene, Osric could make a wonderful appearance in an opera, followed by the battles, poisonings, and the end of the Danish royal family. I could see it all, though I was sure I would be considered as mad as Hamlet himself to conceive such a large work, the length of three operas to tell the story of one, though I knew each opera in itself could stand on its own. No one had dared to conceive of a single musical work stretching over so long a time, and I knew it would be met with incredulity at first, but my imagination was already experiencing it.

Maria Stuart would make an excellent property, and Schiller had recently written a play of it that I needed to find and read. I knew the premise, with the two monarchs meeting and Mary being sent to her death. George III would likely not allow such an opera to be performed in his court, but since it was possible to make Elizabeth into the honorable one, depending on one's view, perhaps it would be allowed. Schiller was, to me, the greatest poet in Germany, but perhaps he was not to the taste of the English. I sat that afternoon and wrote Schiller, penning a lovely letter to Goethe in the process. I needed to write them both. Writing them in my native tongue showed me how far I had traveled. I kissed the letter.

CHAPTER 58

I walked into that beautiful London morning toward the Haymarket, where I found no one yet at work. I proceeded to St. Martin-in-the-Fields, where I left a donation from my recent earnings as alms for the poor. It was not my church, but I loved the peace of it. It was a country church doing so much for the many poor who populated the fields. I could not fully enjoy the success of those days without leaving a gift of gratitude for those less fortunate. The short walk to the Drury Lane brought me back to the world, and I entered the small café next to the theater to await the day's rehearsals. It was a lively crowd, like the cafés of Vienna, each person buried in their daily sheets so popular in London. I found a sheet in German as well as several in French. That was one of the wonders of London, that so many languages could be found.

I read what news I could find, though much in the sheets were opinions on politics around the world. I was proud that I could read with considerably more understanding in English than when I arrived from Hastings. Around me, I overheard some talk of *The Magic Flute*, and upon introducing myself as the opera's composer, I was invited to join the people's table. They were actors, though none were involved in the production. However, they had heard much about it, particularly the lavish nature of its settings and the extraordinary difficulty of the music. Although I could follow much of what they said, they reminded me of Emanuel, sharing his special ray of inner light available only to those who act upon the stage. I felt most at home in the presence of those who spent their lives in the theater. I asked this group if they had heard anything of Schiller's *Maria Stuart,* and they all seemed to know it intimately, describing scenes that I had only imagined.

One of the actors, a particularly lively fellow, pulled a folio of papers from his satchel and handed me a play called *The Fairy of the Lake,* not yet published, and there was great excitement around the table for it. I wondered how they all knew so much about this play and, according to their conversation, all plays. They said I must meet the poet John Thelwall, the most radical in London, and they felt nearly certain that *The Fairy of the Lake* would be banned from public performance on the stage. But perhaps with my music and in the ecstatic forum of opera it might be thought more acceptable.

I was immediately thrust back to *Figaro,* as the conversations were similar. Lorenzo had been radical in his way, as certainly Beaumarchais had been, but it wasn't their politics that attracted me. Thelwall's play did indeed sound promising, but I was, then as now, wary of the term *radical* because of its associations with that devil Voltaire. Someone had suggested that I write an opera based on Voltaire's *Candide.* I had managed to read the novella in German, and I could not possibly countenance a work like that for the stage. There was too much hectic action, all of it broadly satirical, suitable for a music hall, certainly not for an exalted form like opera. Voltaire used *Candide* to needlessly attack one of my heroes, Gottfried Leibniz, whose natural optimism I shared. For me *Candide* was an attack on optimism. What good for the world could be justified in that? I wondered how to make a plausible opera from such a mess. I had hoped to discuss it with Lorenzo someday, but he had again fled to a "better" world. My anger at him arose, knowing he was likely approaching Portsmouth and getting ready to sail to America with Astor. I wondered how Nancy took the news that she and the children were being uprooted again.

CHAPTER 59

Natura non facit saltus. These were the words upon which I was raised. "Nature does not make jumps." They were the words of Leibniz, one of the great men I wish I could have met. Leibniz was worthy of everything to me because he was not one of those dangerous thinkers who ignored God. He assumed the world to be basically good, and that God had created the best possible world for us at this moment. This was exactly how I felt for the greatest bulk of my life. I despise people who look darkly on the world, like a devil having taken over their soul. We are born to laugh and love, and there should be little more to life than that. Moments of laughter and love are what I most remember about my life. True, there have also been times of fury and hurt that I struggle to make disappear. It infuriated me that Voltaire, in addition to all his other muckraking, used Leibniz as the butt of his jokes and the object of his satire. If more of the world followed Leibniz's thoughts and ways of living, life would be better for everyone. I was sure that Leibniz must have been a Catholic, but I never found out for sure. Who could doubt the best of all possible worlds when one could sit in a café and talk about wonderful things?

I wrote letters to both Goethe and Schiller about my arrival in London. Schiller was always a more touchy personality, so I trod more gingerly with him. Goethe was a mensch, so I put forth a proposal for *Faust* to see what he had to say about it. I wanted to let them both know that I was established in London with a home, and ready to hear about their plans in Weimar. Goethe was one of the greatest men of my young life, and I longed to write an opera with him. Every word we shared together immediately turned itself to music. He had so much knowledge and wisdom, even as a young man; yet unlike many educated men I met, he was kind. Schiller was frillier and grander, and he could never overcome how he felt about himself. Both men were of intense feelings, and when I was at my best, they both brought out the best in me, just as Lorenzo and Emanuel had done. How I loved people who made people feel alive, and how I loathed those who tried to diminish. Men with such sensitivity are often perceived as weaklings, as was I, often. I find it extraordinary that we meet thousands of people, most of whom mean nothing to us at all. Then you meet one or two, like Schiller and Goethe, and they change you forever.

I excused myself from the actors to attend rehearsals for *The Magic Flute* at the Drury Lane. One of my table companions told me there was to be no rehearsal because they heard the performances had been canceled. I pointed to the Drury Lane and the great broadsheets announcing the performance that were hung all around its perimeter, worn from the weather but still very present. They must have heard incorrectly, I said, and thanked them for their company, with an especial thanks for my copy of *The Fairy of the Lake*, which I vowed to read as soon as possible.

I entered the Drury Lane and immediately my suspicions were quelled, as there was a rehearsal going on exactly as planned. I toyed with returning to the café to correct my new friends' opinions, but I was too excited from seeing all of the singers to take the time. They were to rehearse the three boys with Pamina, her attempted suicide, and then move on to the finale. The boys began, "The sun, the herald of the morning… will rise above us all." My English had reached the point that I could understand every word! I found the settings beautiful and opulent. The Lord Chamberlain had not spared expense on the settings. I thought the music was being taken slightly too slowly, and also felt it was slowing slightly as it progressed, something that always bothered me. When I played my own concertos, I was forever trying to get orchestras not to slow down. The *tones macht* scene was beautiful, and I loved hearing it in

English, as the singers were excellent. I was excited for the premiere the following week, though the date had not been set. I asked when I could see a complete run with the music in order, and they said they had only ever rehearsed my opera in fragments.

At that moment I had two operas rehearsing in two different London theaters at the same time. I was exhilarated! I decided to walk home via the Haymarket, in the hopes of seeing a similar rehearsal of *Richard III*. I could not remember ever before hearing parts of two of my operas in a single day in two different theaters. I was as happy as I had ever been.

The birds were particularly glorious that day, making me miss my birds in Vienna, particularly my very dear bird, Kelly, whom I named after that rascal Michael Kelly. I wondered how I would ever see Michael and Nancy again. I knew there must be a fine bird seller in London, probably even some exotic birds I was unfamiliar with. I needed to find another starling or finch to keep me company as I had in Vienna. My dear little bird!

To my surprise, the Haymarket was closed. There were no rehearsals of *Richard III* as I was told there would be, and immediately my chest constricted. Had the men at the café been right about a cancellation, but simply misheard or misremembered which opera was the victim? I suddenly missed *Richard III* terribly, having looked forward to hearing part of it that day. There was nothing to be done, so I walked home to Brook Street, enjoying more of the birds.

At home, I sat to read *The Fairy of the Lake*. Although the English was formal, I could now almost fully understand it. Arthur, Guinevere, Rowena, and an incubus, exactly like our word in German, *Inkubus*. A chariot pulled by swans emerges from a lake. Sorcery, jealousy, and the triumph of majesty and virtue, a crowning of the King. The story excited me tremendously, and as was usual when I read a potential opera, I could hear music immediately. *The Fairy of the Lake* felt like the perfect first opera for me to write in English. The music was unfolding in my mind before I even finished devouring the poem. My spirit soared as the opening music of sorcery came to me, and I retrieved some manuscript and began. I could scarcely move the quill fast enough.

Within a few hours, I had sketched an opening sequence as well as a chorus conjured by Rowena to receive information about King Arthur. I wanted to do nothing else at that moment but write my new opera, but I had the responsibility of returning to the court the next morning and resuming rehearsals. Rowena and Guinevere would be the greatest female roles I had ever written, I felt sure. Vortigen and Arthur, too—up there with *Figaro* and *Idomeneo*. And the great deus ex machina Fairy appearing at the end could be the rival of the commendatore's appearance. I was furiously writing when I heard a carriage stop on Brook Street. I assumed it was the messenger from the Drury Lane with a note to tell me when I might see a complete rehearsal of *The Magic Flute*. I knew the next weeks were going to be endlessly busy.

There was a knock. It was an equerry from the Lord Chamberlain.

"The Lord Chamberlain wants to ensure that you received his message that you are to appear in the palace at the earliest potentiality."

I was unsure of that last word, but I understood the request.

"I assumed it to mean I could see him before my rehearsals in the morning," I told the equerry.

"Assumptions on the part of any servant of the court are ill-advised."

I heard only the word "servant," and was immediately transported back to Salzburg, being forced to write music I did not love. I asked if I should go to the palace at that moment, acknowledging that I was not dressed for the Lord Chamberlain. I was advised to appear at the palace as soon as I could manage it. The equerry departed.

I felt a terrible foreboding. I lit a fire to heat enough water to clean myself properly for the Lord Chamberlain's office. The joy of the three King's concerts suddenly seemed a world away, and I feared I had done something horribly wrong without knowing it. I thought over the previous few weeks, hoping my memory could be roused. Perhaps I had said something untoward to someone and it had been reported to the court? Perhaps I had said something to the King in my audience that in reflection had upset him?

I dressed and hurried to St. James. My heart was pounding in my chest. I was admitted immediately and sent to an elegant room, which I knew was near the Lord Chamberlain's quarters. A courtier told me to await a summons. The palace was silent. I waited for what felt like hours. The light through the window shifted to indicate evening was approaching. I was hungry. I thought perhaps someone had forgotten I was waiting, so I timidly walked down a hallway, trying to hear the presence of anyone I might ask, but the palace appeared to be empty. I wondered if I should leave and return the next day. I found my way to the door and was stopped by a palace guard, who told me I should wait where I was told for the Lord Chamberlain to call. I returned to the room where I had waited all day. And I waited longer. The day turned to night. I did not ever wait with patience or temperance. Sitting in silence was the most challenging thing to ask of me, but I sat for hour upon hour. Finally, an hour after the sun had dropped in the sky, an equerry came to tell me that unfortunately the Lord Chamberlain would be unable to see me, and I should return the following morning.

I left and walked out onto the darkness of the Mall. I was dazed with exhaustion and frustrated by this purposeful wasting of my time. Something was wrong, but what? I would have to wait a sleepless and worry-filled overnight to discover what I had done. Gloomy, I walked home, following the gaslights that took me slightly out of the way and past the front of Boodle's, where just the night before I had been given a feast with John and Lorenzo and talked about the New World. I was sure I would never see either of them again. I wished I could go inside and have another roast. I weighed going to a pub and drinking to calm my mood, but I decided I would rather return to work more on *The Fairy of the Lake*.

CHAPTER 60

Once my opera emerged again, my spirits lifted and I hurried home to reunite with my Arthurian opera. I lit a fire and lit my torches so I could continue where I had left off. I poured wine and set to work. Each character told me clearly how they wanted to sound, and I loved listening to each of them. I was tired but decided to push on until morning, enjoying my time with such a wonderful play. I wondered why it had been banned. Surely the Lord Chamberlain was not already aware of my possession of the play, but what if he was? Would that be the reason for my summons? It had only been handed to me earlier that very day, and the request to come to the palace had arrived before I left for the theater. It was all so confusing.

I thought perhaps that the King, having loved my concerts so much, wanted to create a regular series, necessitating a new focus and schedule to accomplish. This gave reason to the urgency. King George III was known to regularly cause havoc with the caprices of his needs, and no doubt the court had been brought to many standstills by his wishes. *The Fairy of the Lake* would be, I already knew, one of the greatest operas I would ever compose. Everything in England had gone so well that I felt sure my gratitude to God for my constant industry would be looked on with favor.

I wore out several quills and an entire bottle of claret that night. By the time dawn fully arrived, I had filled more than twenty pages of sketches, though these were not my usual; they were more finely developed as I wrote than anything I had yet put down. There was something about constant frenzied work that made one more finely tuned. Logic would deduce that a person's output would decrease over time; Haydn's certainly had. I had always thought the most productive time of life would be youth. Each time I entered a new composition into my thematic catalogue, I would leaf through a few pages and remember each composition. Often just a few thematic notes would send me into a memory that would have had no other starting point without those few notes. I could remember where I was sitting when I wrote in the catalogue, where I had thought of it, all of its origins, and I could recall whatever I was feeling at that time. So many memories. I assumed that someday there might be a use for such a catalogue, but for now I simply kept it in a fine leather book Konstanze had found for me in Vienna. I longed to finish *The Fairy of the Lake* so I could enter it into the catalogue. What a marvelous opera it was going to be!

I had some bread and made a strong tea to prepare for a return to St. James to await the Lord Chamberlain. I retraced my route from the day before, my stomach again churning from nervousness and dread. Soon I was sitting again in the outer chamber where I had spent so many hours the day before. The same equerry arrived to tell me to wait until called. I asked about my rehearsal and the arrival of the orchestra, but was told there would be no gathering today, and to please await the summons from the Lord Chamberlain.

More hours passed. At one point I noticed there were no shadows cast from the windows because the sun was directly overhead. More hours passed. I resented losing all the work on my opera that I could have completed during the endless silence of those hours. Rather than getting stuck again, at least I brought along my sketchbook so I could do something besides sit in silence. The themes I wrote that day are too painful for me to hear now! I tried to calm myself, but each time I closed I eyes I saw the bridge, as it seemed just on the other side of my being, lying in wait with a terrible force enticing me toward it.

The sun was at its late-afternoon angle when distant footsteps came toward the chamber, then the equerry finally told me to enter the Lord Chamberlain's quarters.

"Herr Mozart, I do apologize for keeping you waiting. We have had rather chaotic days at the palace, to say the least that might be said."

I bowed and smiled. "I take it my concerts did not please?"

"Your concerts were very successful, so it is with sadness that the wish of this court is that you leave us."

"Why? His Majesty was excited by the concerts."

"That, Herr Mozart, is where the problem lies. His Majesty's health is such that he cannot be subjected to the excitements of music or the large gatherings required to bring the concerts to fruition."

"Was he displeased?"

"I am not at liberty to discuss His Majesty's feelings. But on the day following the concert, his mind descended into a terrifying madness. He did not know Queen Charlotte. He did not know even himself. He kept singing phrases of your music and imagining he was actually on the stage performing. He would not eat. He would cry at voices only he could hear, reacting to them as though they were actually next to him. His doctors found him to be inconsolable, and because he sometimes hears the court orchestra rehearsing, it is now thought to be poor for his health to have music in the palace."

CHAPTER 61

D arts of lightning went through me. "Surely there is another place in this vast court where we could rehearse? You do not mean to put all of the musicians on the street? And me? I have just moved to your country and left my wife and children to be in this position which is the greatest in the world. I have so much to write and to accomplish for the King. I am his humble servant. Please, Lord Chamberlain, I beg you."

Even as I committed the act, I could not believe it. I had long told myself I would never again do this, but I knelt before the Lord Chamberlain to beg him to change his mind.

"Herr Mozart, we will naturally pay for your passage back to Vienna, and there will be court assistance in packing your house for the journey."

I remember my words all too clearly. "I cannot return to Vienna. I have no home there now. Please! No! I have imagined the remainder of my life in London. I have operas and symphonies all for the glory of His Majesty. Sir William has promised me so much. Are you releasing him from his duties as well?" My voice sounded childishly desperate.

"Sir William is to retire from the court and move to Oxford."

"Will I be able to say farewell to him?"

"No. You will need to return to Brook Street and begin preparations to return to Vienna. You will have use of our carriage to take you to Hastings, with an overnight stay at an inn convenient to the occasion. You will leave at dawn tomorrow."

I tried not to cry but I was helpless to stop. "But *The Magic Flute* and *Richard III*."

He explained that as His Majesty insisted on attending a public performance of *The Magic Flute*, it was easier for the courtiers to tell him it simply wasn't being performed. The court decided it was best to cancel the productions and potentially do them when the King felt better.

"But if you send me home to Vienna, I will never be able to return here."

"I assume that the talented artists preparing your operas will be able to do so without your presence. The theaters report that you were quite satisfied with their efforts," the Lord Chamberlain said.

"Of course, sir. But as Sir William promised me, I am already at work on an opera for the court, an original opera specifically for London."

"What a shame. Perhaps the wind will blow differently in a few years. No doubt you and Signor Da Ponte will have something you can cook up together."

I feared I might vomit. The Lord Chamberlain had spied on us at Boodle's. Or he had followed me around London as I walked with Lorenzo. He probably knew something about Astor. But the court had known about Lorenzo all along.

I knew it was best to say nothing, particularly as I could not know what kinds of political craziness Lorenzo had gotten involved in. Had he not had such a unique poetic mind, I would have ranked him with the Voltaires of the world, but I knew Lorenzo was a poet first and everything else after, and this made him a forever person to me. So, to the Lord Chamberlain I said nothing.

"Herr Mozart, we have enjoyed your enormous success in these months at the court, and we wish you a peaceful journey back to your home."

I was again out on the Mall, now for the last time. The sun was not far over the grand palace at the end of the Mall, the Queen's House. My heart was so rapidly pounding that I gasped for breath. Everything seemed to be caving in. My gaze darted from one end of the Mall to the other. I looked back at St. James where I had triumphed only days before. It was over. I had failed. Lorenzo had done me in. I said aloud that if ever saw

Lorenzo again, I would strike him. The bells at Westminster pealed the hour. The Abbey drew me back to it one last time.

CHAPTER 62

I followed the sound of the bells. I had to find Sir William to tell him, to thank him, to say farewell. I thought of all of the dear musicians in the orchestra who would think I had simply abandoned them. The Lord Chamberlain would find a way to blame me, to say the decision had been inevitable. Was the news of the King's health true? I had no way of knowing. I thought back on my audience. On that evening George III had not been a man in charge of his own faculties. But would the elimination of my music, or all music, really help him? His spirit was calmed by the presence of sound. I knew things that others did not know, so I knew the story about the King was false. They were using the King's precarious health as an excuse for economizing. Sir William was being retired like a faulty horse. I was considered suspect because I spent the day with Lorenzo. I longed to return to simpler days, days when my heart did not pound like timpani.

I entered Westminster Abbey and asked everyone I passed if they had seen Sir William Parsons. The organ bay and choir were empty. I approached a priest, who told me Sir William was already on his way to Oxford and he knew of no way to reach him except to take a carriage there. "It is only a short day's ride. Beautiful," the priest said, blessing me as he walked away. I rushed from the Abbey to Brook Street. I had compositions scattered everywhere, and many trunks of my belongings from Vienna that had mercifully not yet been unpacked. I had no time to absorb the emotion of being sent away so soon after arrival, and I had no time to write Konstanze that I was returning. Would she even allow me back into our home?

I wondered if I could possibly find Tamu in France and take him home to Vienna with me. I knew of no slaves in Vienna, though in Joseph II's court there had been liveried men, but I had assumed them to be members of the court. Since meeting Tamu, it bothered me that I did not *know*.

I packed my trunks, haphazardly throwing in every music sheet I could find, knowing I would sort it all out at some point. I felt a deep pull toward sleep, having had none during my writing frenzy on *Fairy*. I threw it all into a trunk. My clothes and a few wigs were packed into their own trunks. There was no time to reflect on what had happened. I fell asleep for a few moments. To my surprise, I woke only when the knock on my door came at dawn.

It was the same coachman who had driven me from Lewes to London, and the familiarity made us both laugh. The man said something about being surprised to see me so soon. We loaded the carriage and began our journey with the sun still not fully risen. I watched my beloved little house on Brook Street disappear behind me, sure I would never see it again. "Good-bye, dear home," I said quietly.

Our journey took us past St. James where King George lived, and past the Queen's House. The sun was rising to the left of the carriage. An idea struck me.

I asked the coachman the distance to Portsmouth instead of Hastings. The coachman told me the two ports were almost equidistant, but going to Portsmouth would be a punishable offense for him, as he had been instructed clearly to deliver me to Hastings, and the journey to Portsmouth would require a completely different route out of London than the one he had planned in the direction of France. He told me I could also get to France from Portsmouth, but those boats were likely to take longer, and potentially deliver me to a part of France which would unduly lengthen my journey home.

I am still unsure how, but I convinced the man to take me to Portsmouth instead of Hastings, promising never to tell anyone. How could anyone find out he went somewhere other than Hastings? Only two days had passed since John and Lorenzo left for Portsmouth, and John said it took a few days to prepare the ship. Perhaps I could arrive in time to gain passage with them, just as John had promised. I dreaded taking such a risk, but of all the things I could not know in having been dismissed by the court, I was certain of one thing: I could not return to Vienna. I thought of going to Paris, where *Tartuffe* could possibly have a premiere and I could begin life anew, but Paris was filled with composers and dark memories, so it would not be so different to Vienna. *Tartuffe* had also been rejected, so I was unsure that it would ever be accepted.

The road toward Portsmouth was well traveled, and there had been so little rain that it felt we arrived in Milford shortly after we departed London. It had naturally been many hours, but I found the journey pleasant, being outside of London and so quickly into the fields of sheep and cows. As a child I had brought laughter from my parents because someone at Salzburg Cathedral asked me where I lived, expecting me to point toward our house across the Salz, but instead I had said I lived in our carriage. I felt as though I had spent most of my life in one.

Still, the trip to Milford was beautiful, and much of it looked like we might be near Lewes again. I could not be sure, but it did look familiar. I had grown up amid great mountains, but here it felt like all of England could be seen from the downs of Surrey. Milford was lovely. Lewes was truly beautiful, a place I could live. We stayed at the only inn in Milford, and I had not realized my hunger until I caught the scent of the available feast of pheasant and boar. London already seemed far away.

CHAPTER 63

The next morning's journey began an hour before sunrise, and by the time the day was in full light I caught sight of the sea. At that my fear began to rise. I had been terrified merely to cross the channel from Calais to Hastings; I could not imagine being on a ship for days, even weeks, and not knowing when I would arrive or what might happen along the way. Still, John offered the only opportunity for a new life that I had at that moment. I could write music anywhere, but there had to be a use for my music. Vienna had used me already and was moving on toward their new sounds in which I had no interest. At least if I went across the sea to the New World, I would never again have to hear of Ludwig van Beethoven. That alone might be worth the journey! But I could also hear Papa's voice telling me that I could not run from my problems. Whatever I feared would pursue me wherever I went. By that reckoning, I should return to Vienna.

Should I return to Salzburg—God forbid—or perhaps join my son in Italy? There were an increasing number of provinces in Italy ruled by Austria, so I might well find a position as a court composer and write what I liked. In Italy there would be the gorgeous weather and beautiful women. Women. How I missed women! London had been completely dry of sexual pleasure. I'd had no time and no opportunity to meet a woman besides the royal princesses, who were both flirtatious, but I would have been terrified to impregnate one of the royal line, as that would have meant not only banishment but probably imprisonment. To think now that I once considered myself a potential royal consort!

After lunch, the sea drew closer and the carriage driver said we were within an hour of Portsmouth. I had to soon make a decision that would last forever: returning home to Vienna or finding a way to go across the sea, hopefully with John and Lorenzo.

There were so many ships in Portsmouth Harbour. I asked the coachman to drive the horses as hard as he dared, as time suddenly felt scarce. I knew that if I had too much time for consideration, I might make the wrong decision. My best moments of life had been the ones I had no time to weigh, and my first thought was always better than my tenth. The carriage reached the quayside. I asked the coachman to wait. I started yelling toward each ship, "Astor?" running among the many docked vessels. Their masts were bobbing side to side out of time with one another, which distracted my purpose. "Astor! Astor! Lorenzo!" I yelled, drawing attention but no response from each ship. There was a man near the end of the quayside who said, "*Grüss Gott*"—the first time I had heard a Viennese greeting in my many absent months. I asked the man about Astor, and if he knew him.

"Of course. John Jacob is a legend in Portsmouth."

I was frantic. "Where is he? He promised me passage to New York."

"I'm sorry, my friend. You see that ship?" The man pointed to a ship far distant, rounding a head on which stood a castle.

"That is Southsea Castle. Once they pass it they will be in the channel and shortly in the open sea. You have missed them, my friend. I'm sorry."

"Could we drive my carriage to the castle and try to yell for them?" I said, desperately.

"They would never hear you, with the wind as strong as it is today."

I had to try. I began yelling toward Astor's ship. I ran back to the carriage and told the driver to head toward the castle and to get as close to the sea as he possibly could. I swore I could hear Lorenzo's laugh aboard the ship, and if I could hear Lorenzo, perhaps I could make enough noise to be heard on the ship from somewhere near the castle. I hoped my desires were not deceiving me.

The carriage drove us quickly toward the castle, and I could still see the ship. The wind was strong, which I hoped might carry the sound of my voice. I went to the shore and yelled endlessly for Lorenzo.

Incredibly, Lorenzo replied. Far in the distance, and with a sound I had to strain to hear, Lorenzo said it was incredible that I was there. I begged him to bring the ship back for me. Lorenzo said it was impossible, that there was no way to return, and that John was sorry. Lorenzo yelled "Farewell!" and something about coming to America. The wind carried the ship away, and I watched it disappear into the mist, the voice of Lorenzo fading with it. My hopes dissolved in the wind. I had to turn my attentions to finding passage to France from Portsmouth, so I had my poor carriage man drive me back to the quay. I found the German-speaking man again to begin to explore what options might appear.

"Portsmouth is quick if you want to get to France or to Lisbon, but if you want to get quickly to America, you need to travel to Liverpool and speak to a man names Rodney Brookes."

"How am I to get to Liverpool?"

"Have your carriage take you."

I told him my carriage had to return to London.

My new Austrian friend said, "I can get you a carriage passage with three others who are leaving this afternoon for Liverpool. It is a four-day journey."

"Four days!"

"Yes, sir. Let me know what you would like to do and I will help you arrange it."

I returned to my carriage.

The carriage man asked me what I would like to do. After an unusually long silence, I told him I would like to unload my trunks and accept the passage to Liverpool. It was an impetuous decision, but I had to follow it. Liverpool it was.

CHAPTER 64

The ensuing days have always been a blur in my memory, now as then. The wait at Portsmouth was trivial, but the three men with whom I shared a carriage were roughly hewn, smoking heavily, chewing and then spitting tobacco, a habit I had once indulged but which I found a unique disgust in others. The men filled the carriage with smoke even with the windows open. The days were horribly long, dawn to sunset, and the roads were the most horrendous I had experienced in all of my years of travel. For days the carriage tossed as if on rough water, giving me tremendous sickness, further wearying me to consideration of an ocean voyage. Mr. Rodney Brookes, I thought, had better have a solution to my predicament worthy of the vile days in the carriage with three brutes. And forever there was my thought: what would I do in Liverpool if I did not find passage? From there I would have to find my way back to Vienna, and that would be even more arduous and likely take me through London, which would be mortifying.

Some respite came when we stopped at inns for the nights of rest, and I felt lucky to briefly not be moving. The inns on the way to Liverpool, though, were not as nice as the inns in the south, in Milford or Lewes, and nothing close to what I experienced on the continent throughout my life. These inns were dirt floors and filth, though the final night, at Stoke-on-Trent, was almost acceptable. I remember little of these days other than their discomfort.

We arrived at the docklands shortly after lunchtime. I had been all over the world and seen everything from royal palaces to tents in the Austrian forests, but I had never seen any place so revolting as Liverpool. There was drunken vomit everywhere on the already-filthy streets, and lame dogs picking at whatever they could find. Men huddled around fires examined the new arrivals, and I felt my three traveling companions fit in with them. I felt out of place and terrified, especially when unloading my trunks from the carriage following us. I was stuck on the docks with four huge trunks, requiring assistance to move them, and I had no idea where to find Mr. Rodney Brookes nor anyone else who might be able to help me. I felt that I had to immediately get to America in order not to spend even one night in Liverpool. I asked a few men about finding Mr. Brookes, but no one was willing or able to help me.

I had seen prostitutes before, in Vienna and Paris, even in Naples, but this was the first time I had heard such vulgarity in England.

"Dock that cock here, mate," one of them said to me, making me shudder. She was covered in small cuts, making me nauseous, which only caused her to laugh at my disgust with all of her friends.

Though often tempted with opportunity, I never had relations with a prostitute. Within the truth of this quill, I must admit that I certainly indulged in many women. But by the time I was living England, with illness having long pocked my face, I felt uneasy with women. I could always feel them staring at my scars, or intentionally looking elsewhere to avoid them. Most of the fun of relations in bed lay in staring into a woman's eyes, and lacking that, the act felt like empty exercise. At that moment in Liverpool, I thought nothing could make a man think less of pleasures of the flesh than these women on the docks. They were the most vulgar I'd ever seen.

I feared going too far astray from my trunks, since wherever there were so many prostitutes there were also thieves. Scanning the docks, I noticed a small establishment with open doors and windows. Brookes and Roscoe Trade. I thought this might be the Brookes I was told to seek, and to my relief, Mr. Brookes greeted me, of sorts, upon entrance.

"I'm Wolfgang Amadé Mozart from Vienna, and I would like to go to America."

"Where in America? Nice to meet you, whatever your name is," he said, unable to pronounce my name properly, though he attempted something like "Mohzart." It was too much to expect anyone in Liverpool to know who I was.

"New York," Amadé said.

"I might be able to get you to Baltimore, but that is a far sight closer than you are now," he said.

"Where is Baltimore?" I remembered that John had mentioned the place.

"Not far from Philadelphia, which ain't far from New York."

When I had heard all of these names before, they were just exotic words. Suddenly they became actual places. I asked Mr. Brookes the price of passage and if I would be allowed to take my four trunks.

"What are you running away from, German wife?"

His question was impertinent. I said, "I'm sorry? I'm not running from anything. I want to go to the New World."

"Why?"

"Because John Jacob Astor invited me." I was sure even this Brookes creature would know the name of such a wealthy man.

"You want me to believe you know John Jacob Astor?" He laughed.

"I worked in the courts of Kaiser Joseph II and King George III," I said. Even all of these years later, I wonder why I allowed that to enter a conversation on a dock in Liverpool. Idiotic!

"Then why didn't you get the King to give you passage to the New World. How in hell did you find your way to Liverpool? Something doesn't add up here, German man." The foulness of his breath made me wince, but I said nothing.

"Are you a German or Hungarian man?" Brookes yelled.

"Almost. I am subject to the Archduchy of Austria," I said, "but I have been in the recent employ of King George III."

"Well, we have plenty of your kind going to the New World. Sixty pounds sterling." He pushed a wad of tobacco into his mouth.

I had to ask him to repeat the price because it was so far beyond what I had ever considered for passage. People bought homes for less. "That is outlandish, sir," I said.

"Fine. Then hike it back to London and Vienna, mate." The horrid laughter of Mr. Brookes ignited laughter from others in the room overhearing us.

"I will pay you ten pounds sterling," I said, knowing I would pay twenty.

"Fine, mate. I've got a ship leaving at sunset tonight, probably to New York. We will see. We've got lights all the way to Holy Island and then it's open sea for a month, mate. It is yours for ten pounds."

"And my trunks?"

"Yeah, you'll have a room on the upper deck and you'll have to fit them in there. The trunks will be ten pounds each. The lads there will help you load them. Ship is over there, the *Gregson*."

"You are charging me fifty pounds sterling!" I screamed.

"Take it or find yourself a place in Liverpool."

I paid the recreant fifty pounds.

CHAPTER 65

My anger at this horrid man blinded me to my own terror. I was relieved to find my trunks unmolested, and Mr. Brookes did indeed send a group of young men to help him load them onto the ship. Even in the calm of the harbor, the ship heaved and groaned to such a degree than I could not imagine how I might survive any kind of voyage. As I awaited instructions as to how I was to function on board the ship, I tried out my small bed in a cabin located just below the main deck, a few steps down and then a few steps looped in the other direction. There did not seem to be many aboard besides crew, but I, having never been on a ship of this size before, thought there might be all kinds of hidden compartments aboard. Ships were mysterious, and some elements of my fear had been swept aside in the rush to arrive there, the sudden need to find Astor and Lorenzo. I was already so exhausted by the journey of four lost days from Portsmouth, and I felt half a lifetime away from London. Never before had I been so far from where I started. I longed to work on *Fairy of the Lake* but that, too, felt a world away. My bed was comfortable, but I was alarmed by the ropes and pulleys in the walls, because I feared there might be days at sea when I would need them just to stand up. My dread was tremendous.

The ship was being constantly loaded with goods, the lower hold filling with iron, alcohol, woolen goods, some of it so heavy that I marveled that the ship could stay afloat at all. Captain Phillips came to greet me, and he seemed a kindly fellow, much nicer than that devil Mr. Brookes, and the first mate came as well, even speaking a few words of learned German to me. He told me when and how food would be served each day, at the large dining table belowdecks, and that the cooks would serve soups and breads. He explained my daily ration of water carefully: if weather permitted bathing, the captain would designate an anchoring within sight of shore to allow for safe swimming to clean the body. In the days of open sea, though, there would be no bathing and no stopping. Weather allowing, when we got to America the captain would pull into an inlet for cleaning up and bathing before arrival in our final port. It terrified me to hear the words "open sea."

Sitting in the relative calm of the port, I thought I might be able to work on some music, but even the slight rolling of the ship made writing impossible. At sea I knew this would be many times worse and last much longer. I had seen maps of the great sea, but a map provides no conception of size or power. I went to the deck as the sun was setting, and was surprised to see the ship unmoored from the dock and already some distance from the shore. There had been no warning of departure and thus no sense of ceremony for what was one of the profoundest moments of my life. I had lost track of days, but I knew it must be nearing the end of August, or perhaps it was already September. This is one thing that memory will never restore to me: I do not know on which date I left the Old World. I had imagined waving back at crowds on the shore, but there was nothing back there in the darkness except the glow of a few fires. A faint silhouette of low-lying hills were all that remained of that day, and everything I had ever known was behind those darkening forms.

The wind flapping the sails created a perfect little rhythm on which I could focus and I surprisingly fell into a deep sleep. I did not wake until morning, when the first mate summoned me to see the view of Holyhead, "Probably the last you'll see of Britain, unless we have a view of Ramsey at some point, and sometimes Ireland is visible as we pass into the open sea."

CHAPTER 66

The open sea. The words were such a horror that I chose not to hear them, or to turn them into some other words, like Swansea or Battersea...I just heard *opensea,* as though it was a city. I went on deck and the breeze was a balm, beautifully cool and salty. The coast of Wales was ravishing, so verdant that it appeared to be growing before my eyes. The sea was calm and soothing, not at all a thing of terror. I was brought a cup of weak tea and a small amount of toast, and it sat well on the tenderness of my stomach. If this was to be the journey, I thought I might be able to actually compose, and for the first time I thought the trip might be enjoyable.

That first morning was a delight, and the air felt wonderful. I could write a symphony that expressed the beauty of the sea. The entirety of my first day was fine, but land was always visible. I cannot explain why that was so reassuring, because the land was obviously too far to reach should the boat slip from under us owing to some malfunction or accident, but there was always that vague comfort. On the second day out from Liverpool, however, there was no land to be seen. It was the first day of my life in which I was fully at sea, the first day in which I felt as small as I knew all of God's creatures must be. Still, the terror I expected did not come. The sea was slightly roiling, in long slow waves that felt more soothing than I had expected. Our weather was beautiful. Another entire day passed in high winds, moving us along quickly. It amazed me how the captain and his sailors knew how to arrange the sails to use the unpredictable wind.

At the end of our fourth day at sea, land became visible again far off to the left—the "port side" as Captain Phillips had taught me—and this was most confusing. I had been told we would be weeks at sea, yet here was land only days after our departure. I rushed to find the captain or the first mate for an explanation.

I found the crew of the ship preparing to anchor, and we were nearing a shore. I was confounded. The songs of the birds were unlike anything I had ever heard before. I wondered if Captain Phillips had perhaps diverted our ship to France. But the birds told me we were not in France. I was definitely in a new world but I did not know where, not even I, who knew things others did not. I knew we could not possibly have sailed to America in so short a time. In the melee I could not find the first mate, but I could see Captain Phillips near the front of the ship, directing officers to guide the ship toward an anchoring area from which he was yelling that tenders would row into shore.

I yelled, "Captain, where are we and why are we stopping?"

"Not now, German. I've got a ship to anchor!"

"Captain! I demand to know where we are and why we are here," I yelled again.

"You'll see."

I surveyed the shore trying to figure out something, anything, even where on God's earth I was.

Captain Phillips yelled again, "And you are not to leave the ship, German! Stay on board. You are not to disembark."

I was unsure what his last word meant, but I felt no desire to go ashore. The birds fascinated me, as their songs carried some weight of fear at the presence of the ship. I could hear that they were warning one another of great danger. I knew those tones, but I had never heard those precise birds before. I could see nothing but trees and could not imagine why we were stopping at all.

I heard the voice of the first mate. "Captain, do not anchor! There is a channel into the lagoon. I have just looked again at the map." The first mate pointed to what appeared to be a small opening in the shoreline, barely visible. I was riveted to the scene, as though I were watching a painting in a palace.

The captain ordered the hoisting of certain sails. There was a strong wind behind the *Gregson* that took us into the channel in moments. Soon we were within a large lagoon, and there was a fort with cannons. I was cold with fear, and so far from any world I knew. For the first time in my life, I had no idea where I was. Had I not written great operas and concertos? At that moment I no longer knew that man.

I tried to sound brave. "Captain! You must tell me what we are doing here!"

As the crew prepared to anchor alongside what looked like a large settlement on shore, both within and outside the fort, the captain came over to talk to me.

I looked at him sadly, as something in his face made it dawn upon me what was happening. Still, I had to hear it aloud.

The captain spoke. "Yes, Amadé, your ten-quid passage to America is aboard a merchant ship, and we have goods to trade before we sail for America."

"Why didn't Mr. Brookes explain this to me? I have been tricked."

"Would you have come aboard if you'd known you were coming to the Kingdom of Dahomey?"

I had never heard the word. "Dahomey? Where is that? Where are we?"

Captain Phillips's voice originally had held kindness, but it now sounded harsh and mean. "You're on the slave coast, German. We have goods to sell here and we will acquire goods that will be sold in America. How did you think you had a cabin to yourself on such a huge vessel?"

I asked him what goods our ship was trading.

"You can see them getting lined up at the fort right now."

"Slaves?" I saw large groups of blacks being assembled. They were in chains. Had I not seen it with my own eyes, I would never have believed it possible for humans to be treated in such a way. I said the word again: "Slaves!"

"Of course. What did you think?" Captain Phillips said.

"I cannot possibly be aboard a slave ship. I demand you return me to Liverpool this instant."

"Hah! For ten pounds! Hey mates, German here wants us to take him back to Liverpool because he's upset that we ain't in New York yet."

The crew laughed at me in a humiliating way.

"How many will we have, First Mate?" the captain shouted, forcing me to hear.

"Five hundred, Captain. We'll bring them aboard as soon as the crew has unloaded our hold. I have the ship's manifesto done, Captain."

"Well done, First Mate."

I tried to reason with him. "Captain, I was not told I was aboard a slave ship. I cannot possibly go to New York like this."

"They will all be belowdecks, German. You won't have to get dirty. Stench can be bad, though."

"Captain, I cannot!" I was near tears. "I am a court composer to George III!" I knew, of course, that I was no longer the court composer to anyone, but I was so frantic I was sure I was going mad.

"Well, court composer, I can leave you here and you can wait on a ship to return you to Liverpool or Bristol, but I couldn't tell you when that might be. I can see about them keeping you at the fort. You wouldn't be safe anywhere else."

"But I am to get to New York to the employ of John Jacob Astor!"

"Sure, you know John Jacob Astor…and my mum is Queen Charlotte. I have more news for you, German. We are not sailing to New York. We will likely anchor in Baltimore." I remembered that I had heard this before.

"The *Gregson* is a slave ship?"

"For years. They aren't going to tell you that. Brookes just wanted to get you gone before you made any trouble for him, and he wanted your fifty pounds." The captain's voice sounded even more sinister.

"I have left behind everything I have ever known. How could you all do this to me?" I said, knowing I had done it to myself.

"Look, German. You've made your choices. Nobody made you get on this ship."

"And slavery is abhorrent. Unspeakable," I said.

I was surprised the word escaped me, as I had never used it before… abhorrent—*abscheulich* in my language—and both words were apt for slavery. Who could possibly put shackles on a child? Until I met Tamu, I had never given thought to slavery, because it was something I thought would remain far from me, something that would never directly touch my life. I had been a servant, though never a slave, and slavery was the provenance and right of royalty. The noble class surely deserved the right to slavery, particularly as just punishment for unspeakable crimes. This was all I had ever known of slavery until I found myself in a ship on the slave coast.

In Salzburg, London, or Vienna the rights of the noble class were never questioned. I had myself lost jobs, such as I had to the court in Salzburg, simply for asking a question or for refusing to write a work I had no wish to compose. Though it felt so at the time, I had certainly not experienced slavery, but I had also never questioned the right of the Archduke or Emperor to make their judgments against me. They had been born into the nobility, and with that birth came certain rights. I, lacking nobility, had been able to live and work in courts because I had unusual abilities. Slaves, so I had always heard, had particular abilities that I did not possess, but they lacked the mental possibilities of other people, yet I had never questioned whether or not this was one of God's truths. This was the way of the world as I had known it; but still, humans surely could not be owned and traded like tea or spices! After all, it was Tamu who had cured me using only a few plants, and his French was better than mine, so of course I knew that there were no differences of any kind between our noggins. What nonsense I had been taught!

CHAPTER 67

The teachings I had learned since birth stated that we are all God's children. I believed this then as I believe it even more now, but at St. Stephen's there were black servants, and even in the court of George III, busy as I was, I noticed black men in positions of menial service. There must have been slaves but I shamefully had not taken notice; I simply accepted what was. Emanuel and I had talked about Pamina being made a slave in *The Magic Flute*, and we had talked often about the black heart of Monostatos, and how he could not be trusted with the virtue of Pamina.

I thought of my character Osmin, and wondered if I had unthoughtfully written a slave character in him. Osmin is a bloodthirsty Moor, but a buffoon. How could that be anything but charming? Moors in Vienna terrified people, so to laugh at them was to make them more human. Suddenly, that of which I thought myself innocent became a source of guilt. Before I was tricked onto a slave ship, I thought laughter was everything. But there was no laughter to be had in Dahomey. I could smell a few fires and a dense wet forest, but there was nothing familiar to me, nothing at all. London and Vienna were out there somewhere, but it was difficult to imagine they inhabited the same world as Dahomey.

I had no choice but to remain on the *Gregson*, as I would not have long survived were I to be left in such a place. The crew unloaded goods for many hours, as the sun passed over and descended. Papers were signed between Captain Phillips and officials in the fort.

What next occurred was the most unspeakable thing I had ever seen, like what I had always imagined it must have been like to watch the Crucifixion. The cruelty with which hundreds of people were herded onto the *Gregson* in shackles and sent to the underdecks of the vessel, naked, was something that even in a nightmare would have lived within me forever. But on that day I saw it with my own eyes, mostly men but also women and children, and it nauseated me. I had arrived in a hell of my own choosing, yet I had been given no choice. I had sought only an escape from London and a promise from John, and I had been tricked. As I began to pray, an even greater horror emerged: as the groups of eight slaves all shackled together kept being forced upon the boat, one of them, identified as insubordinate, was led to the deck in front of the others and flogged. It was clearly a warning to the others not to attempt to fight or disrupt.

I could not watch a man be flogged. I went to my cabin and tried to erase the sight, but there was no escaping the unutterably horrific sound of it. The whip sailed through the air with terrible swiftness and landed with a horrendous crack, followed by a scream that felt like the gate of Hell itself. I tried to sing to drown it out, but there was nothing to be heard besides the poor creature being relentlessly beaten. I could not believe the ferocity of the beating, and the captain allowed it to continue, even encouraged it. The lashes must have numbered more than one hundred, yet the man continued his screams, proof of a powerful life force still within him. I screamed into my cabin in hopes of being heard on deck. I screamed continually for the beating to stop. My screams turned to cries. My own spirit felt like I was receiving the lash. The flogging finally stopped.

The captain came to my cabin. "You are not going to make it on this vessel if you scream at the imposition of every punishment. You need to find some backbone, German."

"What has the man done to deserve such violence against his body?" I cried.

"I have no idea. It is the job of the overseer to maintain order on this ship. Do you want a mutiny belowdecks and have those hundreds of inferiors come up and kill us all?"

"Inferiors? They are being taken from their homes. We are all equally inferior in the eyes of God."

"The eyes of God don't see Dahomey, I can assure you. And it is God who made the slave, not man, not me, not you. Have you not read your Good Book?" The captain laughed at me.

"I cannot be on this ship if men are to be beaten and tortured." I had never in my life been so distraught and ashamed of my fellow man.

"I've sailed with this overseer before. He has no mercy on these people. He keeps order, and one of the ways he keeps order is to flog. I'm not going to stop him. I have a job to do, which is to deliver this cargo to Baltimore where they can be sold. And I'm not going to have some fancy German crying every time we do it. It is the captain's prerogative to keep order on the ship, so I advise you to keep your German mouth shut unless you want to get flogged yourself."

The captain left. Alone in my cabin, I began to cry again. It was an uncontrollable wrenching of some part of me I had never before known. I struggled to stay as silent but I wept more than I remember ever weeping in my life, great wracking sobs that left my body depleted and in need of water and nourishment. Many hours later I went to the deck to find whatever food might exist. To my surprise, the first mate, overseer, and captain were enjoying a feast on deck, as if to celebrate the successful boarding of their cargo.

"German! Have some food while you can. We are going to try to make it last. If we catch a good wind, we will be in Baltimore in three weeks, but the food can get pretty scanty near the end. Enjoy it while we have it," said the captain.

"Where is the man who was beaten?" I asked.

The men laughed. The captain said he was belowdecks with all the other cargo. "You'll hear no more from him tonight."

The strange bird sounds caught me again, and the early lighting of day was beginning to the east. I asked if we would leave Dahomey on that morning, and was told we would leave as soon as there was enough light.

"German, you heard about the *Zong*?" the captain asked me.

I admitted that I knew not of this word.

"The *Zong* was a slave ship like ours, about twenty years hence, I believe. They got lost in the great sea and the slaves started dying. You see, German…what is your name again?"

"Amadé."

"I'm-a-day…" The captain laughed. "Yes, you are a day, and a week, and month, German. Well, Imaday, we don't have insurance on the slaves, so any of them what dies will come out of my pocket. So we will be exercising them up here on deck most of every day. You want to stay alive, you stay above the barricado, that wall there, with us during each day, then you can safely get to your cabin at night. The crew will do their best to keep the odor away, but if we have hot weather, it can get smelly."

"Where do the passengers below deck shit?" I asked.

"The same place you do, Imaday."

"I have a chamber pot, and I can piss off the side."

"They don't have chamber pots, and let's be clear—they are not passengers. They are cargo."

"If they do not have chamber pots, then they shit belowdecks?" I asked, horrified.

"Of course. We try to get them to wait until they need to go and go off the side up here, but sometimes they can't wait or are too stupid to understand what we are telling them."

"It is not stupidity if they cannot understand your language," I said. "And who could possibly understand being taken from their home?"

"You have no idea what you are in for, Imaday. Anyway, the *Zong*… the slaves started dying and the captain knew he had no insurance for them unless they were drowned. So he threw them all overboard and collected his insurance. Court ruled in his favor, too, because all of our living cargo must be protected, and if they are going to make the ship sick they should be tossed to save it all. That was in 1781. The next time you are in a library, if you ever are, you can read about it, if anybody is dumb enough to have written anything about it. Caused a fury of articles in Liverpool, the idiots. Have to make trouble by raking muck everywhere, never leaving well enough alone. On this ship we leave well enough alone, got it, Imaday?"

He said a French word I believe I heard as a child, but had a never heard to describe a person. He was demeaning and juvenile. For me, they were passengers, just like me. I was in an ocean of cruelty from which there was no escape.

CHAPTER 68

The sky was rapidly moving from soft to deep blue. The captain ordered the crew of the *Gregson* to the ready, and our loaded ship departed the lagoon, eased down the short channel, and we were in open ocean within an hour. Within three hours, all land had disappeared. It was a cloudless day and quite beautiful, with a relatively calm sea. With land gone from the field of vision, our ship was alone in the vast ocean. I was told to get behind the barricado, as they were going to bring the prisoners to the deck for their meals and exercise. I was also told they were to eat only once a day, just a watery slop of rice and beans. The passengers were brought to the deck two by two, shackled in pairs. So, I deduced, part of the reason it had taken so long to board them was bringing them on in groups of eight, removing those irons, and replacing them with pairs. The crew brought the women first, and with them what few children were on board, each of whom stayed close to their mothers, terrified. I noticed that the children, at least at that moment, were not in chains. I do not believe I have ever seen anything more heartrending than those children, torn from anything they had ever known, and already witnesses to such extraordinary cruelty. How could anyone do this to children?

The men were the most heavily guarded and chained with the heaviest irons. I could already see that the irons around their ankles and wrists had torn through the skin and were caked with blood. I thought they must be horribly painful already, and we had only just departed. I wondered how they would look in a few weeks when we neared America. Two by two, their shackles were removed and the men forced to dance to entertain the crew. I watched them all closely. There were certain personalities that I noticed were happy to dance, happy to try to bring a smile to one of the women or outdance their male companions. But most did their duties without enthusiasm, willing to do just enough to not be punished. Still fewer, I noticed, always young men, were unwilling to do anything, and these young men were to learn on this first day the consequences of not following orders. The overseer would bring the lash down at the slightest provocation, and one young man defiantly stared him down. That young man was tied to a post to receive a flogging. The overseer did not immediately punish the man. He used the threat of the flogging to get all of the other passengers to follow their orders, which they did. But then, as the sun was dipping low and all of the food had been cleaned up, the overseer gave the young man one last opportunity to dance for the ship. He spat on the overseer.

The flogging commenced, and I had no escape, as my cabin was just barely on the other side of the barricado. I looked away, but still the nightmare of sounds began. The boy was so young that he did not cry out for the first twenty strikes. Then his screams began, and they were more horrible than the flogging the night before. I tried to concentrate on the sound of the sea. I thought of the captain's story, 1781, the *Zong*. At the moment that mutiny was happening somewhere in this part of the world, all of that horror, I had been in Munich preparing *Idomeneo*, a sea story. If only I had known! But I had no idea, and what could I have done?

The beating was so detestable, so abominable, that I thought of throwing myself into the surge, knowing I would be dead within minutes. But I could not jump off the ship, for a netting surrounded the *Gregson* to prevent the enslaved cargo from choosing the sea over bondage. That this netting had been installed at enormous expense and ingenuity proved to me that many passengers had previously thrown themselves overboard. The *Zong* prisoners had no choice; their choices were made for them by the captain. But if the prisoners aboard the *Gregson* were to want to leave, they could not.

The overseer continued through more than one hundred twenty lashes even though the boy stopped screaming, having passed out from the pain. Women and children were crying, and the overseer screamed at them to be quiet. He said he would flog anyone who made a noise, but they could not understand a word he was saying, so how could he expect them to follow his instructions? I knew what it was like to be unable to understand a language, but I'd had patient and loving teachers to help me.

The prisoners were all shackled again and taken two by two to their hold below the deck. Finally I was allowed to cross the barricado, have my own dinner, and return to my cabin. The cruelty I had witnessed was beyond anything I could properly write in this testament, dear reader. I had read in church for years of the scourging of Christ, and there were statues and paintings all over Salzburg Cathedral, indeed in every church I ever visited, but they were works of art. They had no sound or smell. There were no cries of agony in the learnings of catechism. What I had just witnessed was as torturous as Golgotha, and that boy had done nothing but refuse to dance. He was used as a lesson to the others. The overseer was, for me, crueler than Pontius Pilate, who had only sentenced Jesus to death, knowing what he would suffer. But Pontius Pilate did not have the courage to watch his suffering, nor did he mete it out. The overseer had free rein to decide how any single passenger was treated, anyone he considered to be cargo, and also to dispense the punishment himself, deciding on its severity as it progressed. The sustained brutality this boy had suffered probably killed him. I would ask after the boy, though I felt part of myself die in thinking what he had suffered.

There was no sunset, as the ship was sailing into a wall of clouds. The captain, surveying the western sky, said to expect rougher seas in the coming days.

I retired to my cabin. The stench from the lower decks caused me to retch, but I had nothing left to vomit. As bad as the odor was already on this first night out from Dahomey, it was the cries that I could not withstand. The wailing was constant, and the cries of the children slayed my heart. I could hear one child uttering a single word nonstop, a word I could not understand but which I was sure was simply the child calling for his mother. I thought of my own mother in eternal rest in a Paris cemetery. I wondered if Konstanze was still alive. I was sure she was, but it had become difficult to think of anyone I had known as still among the living, for I felt completely dead to my old life. Aboard the *Gregson*, sailing into a storm, I thought of my *Idomeneo* and the lifetime that now separated me from it. I was in the surest hell, with no escape.

CHAPTER 69

My fever started that night and had risen alarmingly by the first sunrise at sea. The ship was heaving violently, and rains lashed my cabin. The seas were too rough for anyone to be on deck, and through my delirium I could tell that passengers were not going to be allowed out of their beds. The crying was horrible, worsening my fever and mixing with it toward something that felt to me like death, a feeling I knew.

The overseer would shout to the pitiful creatures, and crew members tried to take them enough food and water to keep them alive. I heard many of them vomiting from the roiling seas, and I wondered how long my own body could endure this suffering, even knowing that my torment was far lesser than just a few feet below me. Their cries were constant. I thought it must be what God hears of the world whenever he listens to the anguish of our prayers. In all that God hears, could he not hear these poor souls aboard the *Gregson*?

I fell into the worst sickness I had experienced since the night the Romaní woman came to save my life after *The Magic Flute*. How I wished I had her on board, as I did not feel I would be able to live much longer. Surely I would not make it to America.

Days passed in endless fever. My body would freeze for what felt like a day, then it was so hot that I felt I would never cool. I lost track of the boundaries of night and day. The first mate brought me eat and drink, and I occasionally could stomach small amounts. I took water when I could, but often would vomit it. My fever boiled on.

The ship calmed for what felt like many days, during which I tried to sit up but was too weak. I heard the slaves on deck dancing. I heard more floggings. I cried. I cried for Leopold, for my own children. I cried thinking of all of the music I had composed. I was often at the bridge again, and there again was the terrible dragon pulling me across. I fought to stay away from it, but it was strong and inviting. One entire day passed in which I stared down some creature at the center of the bridge. The bridge itself seemed to wobble, which it had never done before in any dream.

I noticed that my heavy trunks had moved all over the room. The sea seemed steady for the moment, so I tried to use the chamber pot, but I could no longer walk. I must have been in bed for several days, and had to stay there. Crew members came to check on me, especially the first mate, who I thought had some measure of affection or pity for me.

I think I recall the captain coming, too, but I am no longer sure of anything that happened in the latter part of the voyage. I kept singing fragments that came to me, but then they escaped as though they were running from me. I remained in bed all the time by then, much like the night of the dragon years before when I almost died. I was in and out of sleeping and waking. I had no idea how much time had passed, but one day I knew beyond doubt that I was near the end of my journey, no matter where the *Gregson* was. The dragon was closing in, and I had lost what strength I had to fight it.

I remember telling the first mate to inform someone on shore that I had died, and I tried for an entire day to give my address in Vienna to him so that he could have someone write to Konstanze. I told him repeatedly that if I died, no one would know. I asked where my body would go if I passed, and the first mate told me they would bury me at sea. "No, anything but that!" I begged, as being lost at sea seemed the worst of all fates. Death was at hand, and though I had been there before, this was the first time I fully accepted the fate of the gods. I longed for an end to my pain. Others on the ship seemed to share my wish, for their cries went on without cease. I was reaching a place of strange peace.

CHAPTER 70

Presently I came aware that the ship was gently rocking, which I assumed meant I had reached the portal of death. Soon my soul would rise to be with my father and mother, and I would be able to look back upon my body, its suffering completed.

Instead, the captain came into my cabin with a man, who said, "Sir, can you tell me who you are?"

I had not heard this man's voice before, but I managed to answer, "I...I am Wolfgang Amadé Mozart from Vienna."

"You are the composer Mozart?"

"I am," I said, barely able to speak.

"What are you doing aboard this vessel?"

"I...bought passage in Liverpool. I was...tricked."

The captain spoke up. "He wasn't tricked. He just didn't listen to what was told to him."

"That is a lie!"

The dragon retreated. Then the man spoke again. "I am a doctor. We will take you to a place where you can recover."

"Where am I? Where are the others?"

"You are in Baltimore, Herr Mozart. The slaves have all been removed and taken to their holding area where they will be sold."

"They are all gone already?" Belatedly, I realized I had not been addressed as "Herr" since London.

"Yes, all gone. According to what the captain has told me, you've been in a deep sleep, what we call morbidly drowsy, for two weeks or more. You need vast amounts of water immediately. I have help coming to carry you on a stretcher to our hospital. You will not be able to walk for a few days." The man had a kind voice.

"And my trunks?" I asked.

"Yes, we will remove those from the ship as well. Let us concentrate on your recovery."

"Farewell, Imaday," the captain said.

"I must have been a great trial for you, Captain. I am sorry. But thank you for keeping me alive."

"If I did. You may still have some trouble carrying on. I know a slave ship isn't what you expected. I'm sorry if you feel we tricked you."

"I will not say I was not tricked. But thank you."

"I'm returning to Liverpool in two days, if you feel like going home," Captain Phillips said. He surely could tell from my eyes that I would never step foot onto a ship again.

I was carried a short distance to a small brick building, a quiet room from where I could see Baltimore Harbor. I was fed chicken broth and given so much water that I thought I might never stop pissing. I had taken the waters at Baden Baden one year with Konstanze and Aloysia, and I wished I could be there now. The same doctor who boarded the ship to help me occasionally visited, and I always had questions for him. Within two days, I felt considerably better, and this made me curious. Having spent so much of my life in illness, I knew that my normal recovery often took weeks or months. I asked the kindly doctor why I was better so quickly after being so near death.

"There is a lot we do not understand, Herr Mozart. But I have seen cases of extreme sensitivity to motion at sea, putting some into a comatose state similar to yours. No doubt you came in and out of your spell occasionally, but somehow your body knew enough of itself to shut down, in its way, and force you to wait until the motion ceased. Once you arrived on land, your condition improved rapidly. You will need some care to learn to walk safely again, but I imagine that will return just as quickly."

"What about all the slaves? Where are they?" I asked.

"They will be sold at auction. Presumably they are at the auction house by now."

"But many of them were sicker than I. Who will care for them?"

"I don't know. The auction house has provisions for keeping the slaves healthy. It is to their advantage as a business, of course. No one will buy a sickly slave."

"Doctor, how can you countenance such a thing? The passage from Dahomey was an earthly hell. I cannot in my wildest imaginings have thought such cruelties were possible. Human beings cannot be treated in this way. You are in a healing profession. How can you accept it?"

"It is the law, Herr Mozart. I cannot say I approve of slavery, but neither do I think our country could survive without it. We depend on slaves for the wealth of this nation. The captain of the *Gregson* told me you needed to seek John Jacob Astor. Is that true?"

"Yes, sir. He invited me to work for him. He is in New York, but I do not know how I can get there nor how I can find him." I realized I had lost Astor's precious letter to me.

"You will recover here for a few more days. I suggest you write Mr. Astor a letter which we can deliver from here. I then suggest you take a ship from here to New York, which is the fastest way to get there. It is probably a four-day journey, possibly less."

"What about going by carriage?"

"Probably more than a week. I'm unsure, having never been farther than Philadelphia."

"How far is Philadelphia?"

"Two days at the least. From Philadelphia to New York, there are many rivers and obstacles for a carriage. I assure you that a ship is the easiest way to get to New York."

"I will never go on a ship again." I said. Staying on land for the rest of my life was my only comfort at that moment.

"Herr Mozart, your name is familiar here. You have been written about in the dailies and broadsheets. But how can you imagine that operas and symphonies will have a place in America? They are entertainments designed for European sensibilities."

"You do me honor in saying my name. I believe music to be a natural language for anyone. The songs I heard on board ship from those forced to come here. Their music was magnificent! I've never heard anything like it. Has no one ever written down their songs?"

"Write down the songs of Negroes? Why would any composer, much less one of your stature, care about music as lowly as that?"

"The songs are not lowly. I loved them."

"You have written *The Magic Flute*! That is very popular here in this country."

"How can they have performed *The Magic Flute* here? They have no materials, no score, and no permission from me to do so," I said, thinking how furious Konstanze would be if she heard of someone performing my music without paying for it.

"Well, I've heard of it being performed in large cities. Not Baltimore, of course, but New York or New Orleans," the doctor said.

"Where is New Orleans?" I asked.

"Creole country. Weeks from here, in the south. You will never find John Jacob Astor there."

CHAPTER 71

As I recovered, the doctor and I had several nice conversations, and he recommended that I write Astor, which I did immediately. Though I was unsure of Astor's address, as I could not find the letter he wrote me, I gave my small scribblings to the doctor, who said he would try to find a way to get it to New York and to Astor. My baggage was in the room with me, all pieces battered from the journey, and I had to wonder how many of my belongings remained among my possessions. I suddenly panicked that my letter from Ludwig had somehow been lost, but I still had the bag in which I had packed it away. The doctor suggested that I move to an inn in Philadelphia for recovery, particularly if I had the money to do so, which I did. I learned a great deal from the kindly doctor about my new country, and I am mortified now that I cannot remember his name. I wrote John that I arrived in the same place he had years before, in Baltimore, but I wrote nothing of my hazy memories of the *Gregson*.

I wanted to punish Mr. Brookes in Liverpool for tricking me, but I had no way to even find him. I knew I was recovering when I harbored new anger at the Lord Chamberlain for dismissing me without explanation. What treachery had been hoisted upon me in London, worse than any I experienced in Salzburg or Vienna, and after I had placed so many hopes upon the opportunity! I was angry at myself for accepting the dismissal without insisting on seeing the King. I also needed to write Konstanze. There were so many I needed to write. Everyone in the Old World would assume me dead until they heard from me.

I assumed someone in America who could write for the broadsheets might say I had arrived, which would at least allow John Jacob to know I had come across. My windows were opened to let in the freshest air. The bird sounds were magnificent, incredibly complex. Within them I heard sounds within sounds that I had never heard anywhere else. The birds in Dahomey had been fascinating, but there were so many horrors to absorb there, and it was such a short time, that I'd had no time to reflect and listen. The birds in England had been lovely, too, but if the bird sounds in Baltimore were any indication, there would be constant music available. I longed to have manuscript at the ready to take down the Negro songs I had heard while I could remember them so clearly. Already the memory of them was fading because my mind was trying to escape the horror. I knew none of their words, of course, but I could remember every melody clearly, and if I could just write them all down, I could have someone put words to them someday. Even as I write, I worry still that remembering the *Gregson* might bring on madness.

Within a few days, the doctor said it was time to leave the hospital. A carriage was ordered to take me to Philadelphia with an overnight stop at an inn in Elkton. I usually dreaded carriage rides, but this was a delight. The roads were smooth and the birdsong incomparable, changing each hour as we progressed toward Philadelphia. This new country seemed to belong more fully to nature than to man. We passed many carriages, but the settlements were few and small. Everywhere, though, was wildlife, and the great vistas of lakes and the enormous rivers we crossed on barges renewed me. My lungs filled and felt clear for the first time in months.

The inn at Elkton far surpassed establishments I had experienced in Austria or France, and most certainly it was superior to any of the revolting places I had been forced to patronize on the unfortunate trip from Portsmouth to Liverpool. The innkeeper was kind, and she brought me a feast. Not since the night at Boodle's had I eaten a proper meal, as the hospital allowed only bland offerings. I had a fine cut of beef with sweet wine and extremely hearty potatoes. After some time passed, she brought me a breast of chicken and, knowing I was from Austria, a dish that resembled spätzle, followed by more wine. I was afraid of eating, having been so ill, but the food and wine enlivened my spirits from within. I fell into the deepest sleep I had experienced in weeks, and I woke feeling energetic for the first time in recent memory. What I wanted more than anything was to get to know Philadelphia and spend a few days working if I could find a place. I wanted to finish *The Fairy of the Lake,* though by then it was a painful memory. I had heard, though I was not sure how, that there were many Germans in Philadelphia, so hopefully one of them would be able to get me quickly to New York, where I could be in the employ of Astor.

CHAPTER 72

It had been years since I had been forced to worry about money. In truth I had been unable to understand money for most of my life. For me, money was but a means to an end, and the end was pleasure or comfort. Money was the energy to do something, to take a chance on living. But money always disappeared with shocking swiftness. I tried to get my employers to pay me properly, better than a servant, but not until St. Stephen's did I achieve that, and then my appointment to the court of George III saw a tripling of what I was making in Vienna. I carried a tidy sum within my satchel, but I did not understand how my British coins would be spent in the New World. Were I unable to convert it properly into the currency of America, then I was poor indeed, where I had thought myself rich when I arrived.

What a miracle that my money and trunks had not been stolen while I was in the morbid sleep. I assumed the horrible men on the ship would steal my money, as money seemed to be the only thing they lived for, certainly it was how they justified to their God that the forced slavery of Africans was their right. Were it not for money, there would likely be no slavery. Why was it impossible for governments to act like Joseph II? Putting everyone on a living stipend allowed people to get on with their lives. If this new country was founded as I had read, on the principles of life, liberty, and an attempt at happiness, then how could they possibly make the object of life be the making of money? And more important, how could a country that saw itself as a beacon of liberty sell slaves? I thought that if I had as much money as John Jacob Astor, I would simply employ all of the slaves and educate them so that within a generation they would be free of their bondage and would likely repay Astor many times over for generations. But Astor was not a government. Probably even he did not even have that amount of money. It was too large a problem for me or anyone to solve.

All this reminded me of how much I hated politics. A government that collects taxes could bring an end to slavery immediately if they wanted, and could send all of the slaves into schools that would educate them out of slavery forever. Or, better still, they could send them home to rejoin their families. I thought then as I think now: schools and churches and music were the only things worth spending money on, because schools free the mind, churches the heart, and music liberates the spirit.

I was interested to learn about my new country, as I knew the churches were important, but I could not understand which church was the most important. Surely they would make a choice, having gained independence from England, to adopt their own national church. But in my new nation, all kinds of worship from the Old World made their way to the New. One of the problems in London had been that I did not attend church. I wanted to find a Catholic place of worship, and that had been a most unpopular point of contention in the royal court.

Philadelphia was so superior to Baltimore that I thought I had entered some kind of paradise. I was delivered to an inn sitting aside Southwest Square, where the proprietor told me the price of a stay of one month. My British gold was heartily accepted, and I handed her two coins for the duration of my stay. My trunks were unloaded into spacious accommodations. I paid the carriage driver and watched him drive away. My quarters comprised two large rooms, a bedroom with a fireplace, and a drawing room with a stove. The inn offered no meals, but because I had only just arrived there was freshly baked bread awaiting me, which the innkeeper hoped would tide me over until I could do my own shopping. I was offered wine as well, which I happily accepted, as always.

I opened my windows onto the square and delighted in at last being somewhere that felt safe. I had so much to catch up on and a new life to begin.

Finally knowing where I was, I needed to gather my mind to knowing *when* I was. Konstanze and I had traveled from Vienna at winter's end, and by the hottest days of midsummer I was in London. The ocean voyage, though, was beclouded with fever and nightmare. I could not remember when the ship had departed Africa nor when I arrived on American shores. The trees were still with leaves, but they had lost their deep green and were beginning to herald the coming of another winter. I loved this season, but I was desperate for news from home, news from London—anything. I unpacked my music trunk first to retrieve my manuscripts. It had been so long since I had placed quill to page, but I returned to my work as though nothing had intervened, writing the next measure of *The Fairy of the Lake*, and sketching out the music of some Negro songs. I had enough paper to last a few weeks, and the quills I had purchased with Lorenzo and John were still in their wrapping. I began a list of things to explore in Philadelphia. I would need to find quills at some point, of course, and potentially manuscript, though I knew John would have fine papers available to me once I made my way to New York. For the moment, I was not restless to travel again. I needed the security of a few days of work, and I had a new city to discover.

The sun descended quickly, and I fell into a peaceful and dreamless sleep, not awakening until the sun had fully risen on what was my first full day of actual freedom in my new country. The cool air through the window brought a host of ideas rushing in. My idea of an opera on *Hamlet*, which had felt so potent in London, suddenly felt too ambitious for a country that had no opera. I first needed to discern what this new country needed and would allow, as all I knew were the many dreams of which Astor had spoken. I wondered if there were even any theaters suitable for opera, a query solved on my first walk.

The doctor had been right in telling me that it would take a few days to find the strength to walk again, but the morning was so lovely that I felt up to it. There were merchants all around Southwest Square, giving me confidence that I would be able to easily purchase food and wine on my journey back to health. The air was cool and calm and everywhere the scent of fireplaces, not a new sensation for me but the scent itself was different and delightful. The Philadelphians were burning a different type of wood than they had in London, and certainly different from Vienna. My first stop at a merchant was for wood for my own needs and I was astounded to learn that the merchant would actually carry the wood to my inn. No merchant in the Naschmarkt had ever offered to personally bring purchased goods to our home, at least not without an exorbitant payment.

I felt strengthened by the air, so I walked further afield, out of sight of the square. Philadelphia looked to me like London, with beautiful brick homes, the finest of which had marble steps like I had seen in Westminster and Whitehall. Also, like London, the streets that were not made of dirt were of brick, something I had not seen in Vienna outside the grounds of a palace. Vienna had cobblestones, which were terribly dangerous. Here in Philadelphia, the street names were beautifully painted, or in lavish instances were carved on the sides of the corner houses. This pleased my eye, and I knew that it had also been borrowed from London. My heart thrilled at a sight on Chestnut Street: a theater, the first I saw on American shores. The placards on the front offered some type of revue performance, and another offering I did not quite understand, but which I assumed was some sort of play. The theater was a smaller version of my favorite in Vienna where I had seen Emanuel in so many performances and where I had myself enjoyed performing. The doors were open, though it was not a theatrical time of day, so I entered. The lobby was small and lovely, drawing me into the theater itself, where a rehearsal was under way. Everywhere were candlelit chandeliers of amazing beauty, and I unexpectedly felt a tear slowly descend my cheek at the sight of a theater again.

CHAPTER 73

Inside the theater, the pianist had a strong left hand and the song being rehearsed was simple but appealing. What fascinated me was the piano! How had they managed to get a piano from the Old World to this new country? Surely it had not come aboard a ship, so there must be someone nearby manufacturing pianos. John would surely know. This piano had a completely different sound to any other I had heard. The frame of the instrument was incredibly ornate, with candles built into the music stand, which I had seen on the grandest instruments in Vienna and Paris. This piano, though, stood upright, and the sound was heavy. The singer was quite loud, but I was overjoyed to hear anything. I still recall this moment, the first music I heard in Philadelphia, and the song was so simple it could easily be remembered. It had only eight measures of actual music, and the rest was repetition. It was a simple song in what almost sounded like E minor, though the pitches were obscure. The song was sad, about a woman crazed, a woman named Jane.

They finished rehearsing the song. I applauded, and though they thanked and noticed me, they were busy with many aspects of rehearsing their performance. There seemed no organization to what they were presenting. A man was calling names to ask for the next portion, which was a man throwing balls in the air in a way I had seen along the Seine as a child, a *Jongleur*. I never imagined needing to know the word in English, but I was certain there was one. The *Jongleur* was excellent, creating a windmill effect with a set of red balls that was most pleasing.

He did a few other tricks as well, to which I applauded and, for the first time in the New World, I found myself laughing with joy. The theater was busy, a feeling I knew well. I felt at home. A scene from *Hamlet* followed, which I felt was a good omen. I had seen the play so often in German that I remembered the situation of the scene, though the English was too difficult to fully understand. It was the scene between Hamlet and his mother, with Polonius behind the curtain. Their sequence ended with the stabbing, and I thought the poses to be well done. I could already hear the duet I might have composed. Hamlet would be a tenor, Gertrude a lower soprano.

What followed at the Chestnut Street Theater would long live as one of my greatest memories, and an unexpected welcome to my new country. Two singers and the pianist with the strong left hand performed my duet between Don Giovanni and Zerlina in English. I knew that scores of *Don Giovanni* had been printed in London to an English translation, and someone must have imported the scores and they somehow found their way to Philadelphia. The singers were decent, though the soprano seemed to slow each of her lines, and generally the tempo was a little lugubrious. The second portion, that in the 6/8 meter, was beyond their abilities. Each phrase seemed to take on its own tempo, sometimes too slow, often too fast. When the duet ended, the man yelling for the acts to arrive and depart gave the pianist an instruction to actually go *faster* in the 6/8, and I could not help myself.

"Sir! The tempo is already too rapid for that section. Please do not instruct them to make it worse. It is the first half of the duet that needs to go faster; the two sections should proceed at the same tempo, and the number of notes in each measure itself achieves the written change to allegro," I said.

The room became silent.

"How in hell do you know?" the man said.

"I'm sorry. I am a stranger to you, but I do know this music," I said.

"No one knows this music. It is being heard in this country for the first time in *this* act," the man said.

"I mean no harm or disrespect, sir."

"Please, show us your expertise, since you thought it fit to correct us," the man said.

Except to fellow musicians, I did not like being known. I found it humiliating to be introduced to strangers as a composer or a pianist, because such an unusual profession would always be greeted with more queries, always forcing a conversation in which I had no wish to participate. But I had been unable to stay silent, so I had to comply with the man's wishes. The pianist stepped aside as I approached the piano, replacing the music to the opening page. I returned the score to him.

"You don't require the printed music, sir?" the pianist asked.

"I think I will be fine," I said.

I began, singing and playing in Italian, "Là ci darem la mano," significantly quicker than the singers had done it, and the 6/8 section, though the same tempo, felt slower to them because of their memories of their faulty tempo. As I progressed, though they were skeptical at first, it gradually dawned on them that what they were hearing felt more natural than what they had been doing. They thanked me for my help. The man running the theater asked my name, but I was too embarrassed.

"I'm just an interested visitor. I hope you all have a wonderful performance. I will try to attend."

I was told the hour in which the presentation was to begin and they asked again for my name. I simply said I had appointments to keep, and I found myself out on Chestnut Street moments later. I thought of all of the words I knew for unique joys, and thought there needed to be a new one for what I felt that morning. To hear even a small portion of *Don Giovanni* on my first day in Philadelphia was too great a wonder to be imagined.

Philadelphia held many wonders. The Schuylkill River was particularly beautiful, and near it I saw a building signed as a "Deutsche Bank," German Bank, so I entered to ask if my gold British coins could be exchanged for American currency. Indeed it could, a gentleman told me, but then asked why I would want to trade in British gold when British gold *was* the standard. I did not understand this at all, but I thanked the gentleman for his help. In some distant part of the bank, I heard German being spoken, which drew my ear. I asked if I could speak to the German man I was hearing, and he was summoned.

I immediately discerned from his accent that the banker was from Leipzig. I asked him about Astor, and he knew the name but could not offer further assistance. I also asked him if there was a shop for musical instruments in Philadelphia, and the man kindly wrote down an address. He also told me that the best place for instruments was a short carriage ride away in Germantown. "It is a very musical place," the man said. The banker explained the value of keeping my gold coins, and he asked when and how I had arrived. I was too embarrassed to tell of being tricked onto a ship, or to explain the unusual circumstances of being released from the court of George III. It was so improbable that a servant of the most powerful court in the world would be standing in a bank by the Schuylkill that I decided to simply say I had just arrived and leave it at that. I stopped at a butcher and a greengrocer for a day's provisions, before arriving back home to Southwest Square at nightfall. I had so much music I wanted to write, though I was curious to see Germantown. I asked my innkeeper about a carriage for Germantown, and she was kind enough to arrange it within a few days. As always, I set goals around appointments like the carriage ride to Germantown, and so I vowed to finish a new symphony and a new piano sonata before the carriage ride, and not to spend too much time out and about. What I knew my spirit needed more than anything was to compose.

I set to work that very night. My symphony had been gestating for weeks in the far reaches of my horrific journey. The illness at sea had unleashed some unseen part of myself, and the music came to me in ways I had never before experienced. I used to write down a bass line over which all of the other parts would quickly reveal themselves. Now, though, I pictured a new type of music, and that is the only word I can imagine, gentle reader: it was actually a picture. I could see it on the page before I had written it. This symphony, which I would call *Tempest*, had been written in my mind during the heaviest parts of my fever, and writing it down made me recall parts of the journey I had already forced myself to forget. Many of the Negro songs came to me within this writing, and I knew I could play with these tunes in such a way as to make them palatable to ears accustomed to a different music. Many of the Negro songs had a Moorish feeling, and I was curious to find out why that would be so. I wondered further why *any* song would feel Moorish, for what did that mean?

Years before, I was obsessed with Janissary music. I first heard it, I believe, in Italy. The Janissary bands had tremendous energy and they had affected me deeply. Their music could be remembered instantly because it was worth remembering. I had never known an actual Janissary, but I knew many people who did. They had terrified Salzburg when I was a child, so the opportunity to poke a little fun at them was not unwelcome in Vienna a few years later. Their perfect uniforms were an indelible memory, and I was old enough to understand that adults constantly seek the comforting familiarities of childhood.

I remember a visiting Ottoman diplomat to Salzburg for whom I played the piano. I was quite young. The Moorish man spoke in a tongue I had never heard, and he had with him a man to whom he spoke, who then uttered his thoughts in German to the Archbishop. It was fascinating to witness. The silks the Ottomans wore were of the richest colors I had ever seen, and their great silk turbans looked like clouds when they walked. But my strongest memory was of the elaborate ceremony after I played, in which the Archbishop was presented with coffee from Turkey, not only the drink itself, in but beautiful porcelain cups and plates as colorful as their clothes, perfectly embroidered napkins made of the finest cotton. The Ottomans had clear instructions as to how coffee should be consumed, as though the way of drinking it was as important as the liquid. I never forgot the extraordinary taste of the coffee, so different from the thickly bitter drink so often served in Vienna. Their coffee had been prepared to perfection, and was smooth and inviting. From that moment I became fascinated with anything Turkish or Moorish, which always meant to me something like that coffee: an art that was cultivated to beauty.

CHAPTER 74

I loved Philadelphia immediately, and I finished my *Tempest* symphony in a matter of days. It was the first symphony I could recall writing that stretched the tonal centers so deeply, almost beyond the conventions I had been taught. The sonorities that came to me were unlike any I had heard from any composer, and I had never before written a symphony making use of so much percussion. I remember hearing Haydn's great G-major symphony that had a military band that always made me cackle, but this was something different. I combined a bass drum with pizzicato cellos and basses. I was sure that if played as I asked, quietly, the bass drum sound would punctuate but disappear inside the tones of the low-stringed instruments, creating a new effect in music. Much of my new symphony was in D minor, but it strayed far from it as well. Musicians on first reading would certainly think me crazy, but as I pored over the new symphony with the orchestra of my mind, I was proud of the industry of my first days in America. I longed to hear the work.

I unpacked the music trunk that had not been opened since Vienna. I had hoped in London to remind myself every day of what was in there, but I had never found the time. Konstanze had done most of the work of packing this trunk, though I had thrown in a few things while I'd been consumed with the writing of *Tartuffe*.

The trunk, I discovered, contained orchestral materials in the hand of Süssmayer for *Figaro*, *Don Giovanni*, *Così*, *Seraglio*, and *Magic Flute*. I found many of my symphonies and at least twenty piano concertos.

And there was my old thematic logbook, long out of date, and naturally missing all of my London music. No copy of *Idomeneo* or even *Clemenza*. No trios or cassations or divertimenti, no serenades, none of my newest horn or trumpet concertos. Still, there were enough materials to get some of my music played, and I could probably rewrite any of my works from memory if necessary, possibly improving them besides.

I was relieved to find my original copies of *Richard III* in the trunk. I organized the music into stacks in my bedroom: opera, symphonies, concertos. Unsurprisingly, the stack for opera was the largest, and I had *Tartuffe* packed away somewhere to add to it all.

By the time the carriage came to take me to Germantown, I had finished my first symphony in America and a sketch for a piano sonata. The carriage driver said Germantown was not far and the ride would be pleasant, as indeed it was. The countryside was gentle, with many small farms between Philadelphia and the German settlement. We were into the colder months and shorter days, and Christmas was approaching. I was delivered to a main street that greatly lightened my spirit, as I not seen much of my native language in months. Many of the buildings looked like they had been brought from small towns in Bavaria and Thuringia that I had seen as a boy. I was not sure what I was seeking in this small village, but it was pleasing to know that some portion of my homeland had transplanted itself along with me. There was a coffeehouse and a restaurant. Having enjoyed the memory of extraordinary Moorish coffee in my Salzburg youth, I decided to patronize the coffee establishment first. Though the coffee in Germantown could not compete with my distant memory, ordering in German and reading German news sheets made up for the lack of taste. I read of a war with Ottoman provinces in the Barbary States, a news item I would not have noticed before coming into such violent contact with Africa myself. I was not sure where the Barbary States were in relation to Dahomey, but I knew they must have some connection.

In the density of one of the broadsheets in the café, one name jumped off the page at me. There was a notice that a symphony in C major by Ludwig van Beethoven had been played in Vienna to enormous acclaim.

I pictured the performance, which I was sure had taken place at the Burgtheater. Konstanze would have been there. Everyone I knew in Vienna would have been there. Papa Haydn, Süssmayer, all of our friends. They would have enjoyed sweet breads after. Ludwig would have invoked my name. I thought for a moment that Ludwig might still be in love with Konstanze, and thinking of the candlelit hall for a new symphony and everyone together made me ache as though I was ill. But what I longed for was love itself, not Konstanze. At that moment I had lost everything and everyone I had ever known, but I had not yet felt that grief, not until reading about Ludwig. Grief comes of its own accord in whatever season it chooses, and it returns at will. Konstanze had not yet been mourned, as I had not yet allowed it. I longed to hear the symphony itself, which must surely be Ludwig's first, and I wondered how it might compare to my own. I reminded myself that I had completed nearly seventy symphonies by that time, so I was slowly catching up with Haydn.

I left the coffeehouse. The air was cool, and the remaining leaves were a rich set of colors. I loved the smell of the season, the scent of wet leaves and fires. I saw a sight that I initially found frightening but it turned quickly to something very beautiful: a hot air balloon. I had heard tales of such balloons all through my travels, and I had seen small balloons carried aloft in the Prater, but this was four times the size of a man, maybe more, larger than any building. It carried a small basket and was connected to the ground by a rope, but still it soared higher into the air than any creation of man I had ever seen. I walked quickly toward it, my legs still weak from the crossing, but the balloon had a power over all who viewed it. Everyone in Germantown was leaving their buildings to move in its direction.

As my steps drew me closer to the bright red bladder hanging in the sky, I heard a glorious sound: an orchestra playing the great minuet that ends Handel's *Musick for the Royal Fireworks*. I was overjoyed to hear any music, but especially the music of Handel, and for them to be playing it meant there were enough musicians in this place to play some of my own music. After some time, I found myself in the middle of a crowd gathered beneath the huge red balloon, each person mesmerized by its unnerving presence in the sky. As beautiful as the balloon was, it was the orchestra that thrilled me, and they played reasonably well. I could not expect them to be as accomplished as my extraordinary orchestra in London.

I made my way through the crowd to see if I could find the leader of this music, and just to see the musicians. They were large in number for a such a gathering. I overheard several people near the orchestra say this gathering was actually a rehearsal for some sort of regatta to come in a few days. The balloon was to be hoisted over the river as the orchestra played for what they were all sure would be a large crowd. I thought the accidental crowd was impressively large, as everyone was fascinated by the balloon, and I vowed to return for the regatta itself.

When the rehearsal ended, I complimented the orchestra leader, and expressed my curiosity about the musicians. The leading violinist immediately responded to me in German. He was from Leipzig and had emigrated along with many families, most of whom were musicians. I was fascinated, and loved hearing the distinctive Saxon accent, so different from my Salzburg tones. The man asked my name, a request that would normally embarrass me, but the company of musicians brought safety.

"My name is Mozart," I said. "Wolfgang Amadé Mozart."

The man laughed. "You have the same name as the famous composer."

"I am the composer Mozart," I said, joining the laughter.

"It can't be." The man summoned the musicians around me, each of whom were preparing to go home.

"This is Mozart. The actual Mozart."

The musicians were stunned, having heard my name for their whole lives. They told me so much so quickly! For them, Mozart was not simply the name of a person, but a whole era. They waited for each new work of mine to come available in the music sellers of Dresden and Leipzig. They had packed my violin sonatas and other sheets into their trunks for the journey, sure of the unavailability of my music in this new world. They had fled intolerance of their religious beliefs in Leipzig, and they wanted to live simply as musicians, making music their devotional gift to the church, but their abilities to rouse emotions were cause for suspicion. William Penn had promised them a haven for their artistic talents, and that promise was fulfilled. They explained that musicians had freedom in Germantown, and even in Philadelphia there were churches allowing instruments to be played within, unlike so many churches at home.

They invited me to return for Sunday devotions in German, and I told them I had a new symphony to show them, as well as several other works they might not yet know. They let out a cheer at the idea. I was overjoyed to learn that I might be able to actually hear my works so soon. I asked if there was a pianoforte and was told there was a fine instrument in the German church as well as an organ. They invited me to visit it that very day.

On my way back to meet my carriage, another shop caught my eye, a furrier. I thought of Astor's comment that a great deal of his fortune had been made selling fur. Surely, then, this shop would know Astor. I inquired.

The shop was stacked with pelts of various animals, any one of which could be made into a coat or muff. The owner of the shop, discovering that I was new to the country, told me that winter could be harsh and was always bitter coldness, and that I should consider a new coat in preparation. I told him I would consider it, and since I would be occasionally in Germantown, I would likely buy the coat as winter approached. Then I asked after Astor.

"John Jacob! Of course he is quite well known to me. There is not a furrier in the country who does not know him."

I remembered John writing me and leaving his address, but I had not yet found the paper among my belongings. I pictured it possibly still sitting in the London house, unless it was in one of my large trunks.

I asked the furrier how I might reach Astor, and the man wrote down John's address on a small card. He knew the address without consultation. "John Jacob Astor, Vesey Street, New York City."

I thanked the man as profusely as I knew how.

On the carriage ride back to Philadelphia, I composed a letter to Astor in my mind. I had loved Germantown, and had I not already paid for an inn at Southwest Square, I would prefer it to beautiful Philadelphia, but the carriage ride was easy and, like the journey that morning, very enjoyable.

That night I set to paper all of the letters I needed—to Astor, to Lorenzo, to Konstanze, to my sons, to Sir William. I needed to write again to both Goethe and Schiller, as I had heard in London that they were about to undertake the direction of the theater in Weimar. My letters to them were now woefully out of date. I decided that my first new opera in America, after completing *The Fairy of the Lake*, would be *Faust*, as I had long contemplated Goethe's great novel. I remember hearing from Emanuel that Goethe himself thought I should write it. *Hamlet* could wait, as I would need the right circumstances to realize it, and *Hamlet* filled me with doubts. *Faust*, though, I knew to be exactly the type of opera that would appeal to an audience of Germantown patrons. With some additions, I could develop them into a fine orchestra, and I felt sure singers could be found. As darkness fell, I sketched a theme for a new piano concerto as well. Life was returning.

CHAPTER 75

The days grew shorter, and my planned first month in Philadelphia quickly became three, passing the Christmas season. Christmas was a day of quiet thanks, with a lovely goose at the inn provided by my kindly innkeeper. I spent each Sabbath in Germantown and made many friends there among the musicians. Once the novelty wore off of having me in their little settlement, the musicians of Germantown came to expect and grow accustomed to their new Sunday routine, which was to see me at church services, followed by a fine German meal, and then hours of reading and rehearsing whatever new music I brought them. They found my new *Tempest* symphony a terrific challenge, but they kept at it. In the months since my arrival, I had written a spectacular new piano concerto that I shared with them, and they delighted in perfecting its many quicksilver musical responses and inventive dialogues between wind instruments and the solo piano. I also honored the musicians of Germantown by writing works specifically for them, for precisely their strengths, and I called these works, which were not full symphonies, *American Serenades*. They loved playing them, as they had just the number of challenges to surmount, and I gave them the joy of referencing some of their native songs from Saxony, all of which gave me enormous joy to recall. The Sundays in Germantown were filled with music and food.

Though they would not openly say so, some in Germantown were alarmed at some songs I presented to them shortly after that first Christmas. It was clear that I had labored over them, being as foreign to me as they were. The best singer in Germantown, I learned, was Adelaide Hette, and she had learned them for me, in some version of a language known only to her. They were my twenty-five Negro songs, for which, because they had no words, I simply placed English words from a hymn book into the rhythm of the songs. It puzzled them why a German composer would take such "primitive" music, as they called it, and attempt to bring it into the world of artistic song. They had to admit that the result, however, was exemplary, the most beautiful songs they had ever heard. I had never written many songs, so I found the labor beautiful indeed, and to this day I cannot recall being prouder of such simplicity. With simple additions and clarifications of harmony, I turned childish songs into music that wanted to be heard again and again. It thrilled my musician friends to be the first to hear my songs, even as they questioned my judgment in writing them.

These songs had never been heard by white men, nor had they ever been written down, so the residents of Germantown privately found it implausible that I could have remembered these songs, especially since Negroes sang, as far as they knew, in a primeval kind of language. They questioned that I could have been anywhere I might have heard them. The songs were in English, which they knew was imperfect for me; and because they were not in any style of German or Saxon language, they assumed the songs to be false. I assured them the songs were authentic as I heard them. Still, the songs could be understood on one hearing, and they were a small way I could honor the sufferings of those poor souls with whom I came to America.

Adelaide had a beautiful voice. She sang five of the twenty-five songs for the Germantown residents one Sunday afternoon in the new year, leaving them all in a conundrum. I had presented them with exquisite songs, but to bring the Negro into such prominence was not to be understood by my new friends. I am sure it was much discussed outside of my presence.

A few Sundays later, I was asked to play the small organ in the church for a service, which I was happy to do. I quickly composed a processional, fugue, and recessional, though in truth I improvised quite a lot of the recessional, having run out of time to set quill to paper. I was seated at the organ to listen to the sermon, in my native German, when I noticed the priest directing words specifically toward me.

"Too much sympathy with the Negro race is against the teachings of God. As the Bible clearly tells us, the Negro is born into slavery. It is not man who enslaves, but God. If Jesus Christ, who suffered so grievously for us, did not condemn slavery, how dare we do so? Are we to ignore the Apostle Paul's Epistle to the Ephesians 6:5-7, my dear parishioners?"

> Servants, be obedient to them that are your masters according to the flesh, with fear and trembling, in singleness of your heart, as unto Christ; not with eye-service, as men-pleasers; but as the servants of Christ, doing the will of God from the heart; with good will doing service, as to the Lord, and not to men: knowing that whatsoever good thing any man doeth, the same shall he receive of the Lord, whether he be bond or free.

I could take no more. Before the priest finished his sermon, I opened the organ to its loudest registration and drowned the sermon with music. An act so brazen had never before seen by anyone in Germantown. The priest demanded I stop the music, screaming into the dense chords that I was improvising. I thought he might incite some violence against my person, so I stopped. As I created a sudden silence by pulling my hands and feet from the organ, many in the congregation were angrily yelling at me. The priest silenced the building and addressed me.

"You are insolent and you will leave this church immediately."

I said to him, to them all, "You cannot condone the enslaving of our fellow man. You cannot."

"The Bible condones it, not I. You have the audacity to bring Negro songs into this community and present them as art? I have reported you to the authorities for this sedition."

In my highest German I said calmly, "I will not hear from the church of my birth that God is the reason we enslave."

"It is the law of much of this land, Herr Mozart."

"This is a free state for the Negro," I said, to the surprise of us both.

"True, they cannot be enslaved in Pennsylvania, but that does not mean we are to mingle with them and taint our souls with their songs. You cannot write a Negro song, Herr Mozart. What you did was dangerous to this community and this church. We have enough free Negroes in this state already. Imagine what we would have if you make their music popular!"

I was embarrassed to have brought the service to a stop, but I knew I could not stay. I thought of Tamu in the bracken in France. I thought of the unspeakable tortures I had seen on the *Gregson*. This man of God was using my beloved Catholic church to justify what I had seen on that ship, a horror from which my memory would never be free. I wondered where each of the slaves on the *Gregson* was at that very moment. How many had lived?

I retrieved my music from the organ and packed my satchel. I slowly departed the silent church, my friends in Germantown all staring at me, wondering what I might next do. The priest's eyes followed my journey toward the door. Before departing, I turned to speak.

"My friends, you have given me a home and a welcome to this country and I am grateful to you all. Leaving my home, I did not know if I would ever hear music again, and you gave me music, God's greatest gift, and for that I am grateful. But we know in our hearts that all men are equal. We are brothers. People stolen from other lands, some of them even princes and queens, cannot be owned because a country says it is so. And you, Most Reverend Father, to be able to look in your own morning glass and live with yourself, you have decided that our holiest book justifies our unholiest act. You accuse me of what you like, but I will never enter a church again if this is the teaching."

"Apostate!" the priest yelled. I heard cries of "Heretic!" and other names as I left. The unrest continued as I entered my carriage and told the driver to return me to Southwest Square. The episode had weakened my body as much as my spirit. Though it was likely still morning, I felt exhausted, and even before departing I missed the fun times I had been gifted in Germantown. They had so embraced every piece of music I brought them that it never occurred to me that the Negro songs would be thought heretical. We had all grown up on the same Bible, but in this new country they had decided their Bible taught that slavery was acceptable, even expected, ordained by God. I wondered what my father would have thought. My fever on the ship kept me from seeing the full extent of what the slaves on the *Gregson* had suffered. God had protected me with illness, so why would God not protect the slaves? I cannot imagine the priests at St. Stephens saying such nonsense, but perhaps they did not know what I now knew. Having experienced it, I could never escape the memory of the sight and sound.

CHAPTER 76

All the while, I awaited a reply from Astor that did not come. Privately I wondered about John's health, and I eagerly checked with the innkeeper each day for mail. Long after I had sent a spate of letters to my old life, the two replies I most wanted were the two I did not get. I had miraculously received a wonderful long letter from Goethe, embracing and encouraging the idea of me writing an opera based on his *Faust*, and sending me welcome news of happenings in Weimar and many friends in Berlin and Vienna. My most cherished day in Philadelphia was the chilly afternoon on which a letter arrived from Konstanze. She must have written me immediately upon receiving my letter. I could hear her voice in the gentle handwriting, and I thought I could detect a slight scent of her still on the paper. She had written the hospital in Baltimore, so the doctors must have forwarded it to me. *Unglaublich!*

4 April, 1800

Wolfie,

For all of us in Vienna, your letter arrived like water in a desert. I am so happy you arrived safely in the New World, though I know I will never understand why you took yourself to such a place just because it did not work out as planned in London. You have been through this sort of thing before. Why were you so frivolous in your thoughts? Why did you not come home to Vienna, to me, to your son? I cannot imagine your fragile body surviving the horrible weeks at sea. Franz is very smart, quite like you, and he is showing a lot of musical promise. He loves to compose, and he is playing some of your sonatas and very well, too! Haydn is in frail health, but he is still the pride of Vienna, and he is very proud of you. We heard Ludwig's first symphony, and though he owes everything to you, it was a beautiful and successful evening. The other Franz, the one you don't want to hear about, is attentive and sweet. He takes care of me, Wolfie, and he is not so tempestuous a person. He is a flat road where you are a mountain crossing. Of course, mountains are more beautiful, but they are also sometimes dangerous, as we both know.

I have organized all of your music and arranged for publishing. You know that this is the only income I can have, but you should have your share as well. I don't know how I can possibly send you money, and there has been quite a lot come into the house in the past months, as *Magic Flute, Richard III*, and *Don Giovanni* have all been revived in Vienna and Munich. I am told there are plans for *Clemenza* and *Figaro* in the warmer weather, which will bring in more funds.

It is difficult for these words to loosen themselves from my quill, but we must face that we will not see each other again. You have crossed an ocean, and I cannot follow you there. I do not have the means or the strength. Young Franz may be able to find you someday, but at this time it is difficult to imagine how he could make his way to you. How are you going to make a living in America? Are you planning to write music in a country with no music? How will you stay alive? And if it is true what they say, that there are huge fortunes to be made in that new world, will you be sharing those riches with your wife and young son?

Until you wrote, I had never heard of Philadelphia. Is that where the revolution happened? I had letters from friends in London who told me you simply disappeared overnight. I thought you dead, Wolfie, and though it was joyous to find you alive, it is not so happy to discover that you are in a place so far away that you are dead to your family. I cannot understand your actions, but I hope you will understand mine. It feels to me that we should ask the church to annul our marriage, since we will not be together again, my love. Yes, I love you with all my heart, but I could not follow you to London. I had to follow my heart, as you will have to follow yours.

Your loving wife, **Konstanze**

I wanted news of Karl Thomas in Italy before too many months passed, and her letter mentioned nothing of him at all. Always, with Konstanze, there was something that was not quite enough. She would say too much of what needn't be said, and not enough of what should. By those early months of 1800, I was excited by a new century, and Konstanze was in spirit quite dead to me, the strangest feeling in the world. How can someone be dead when they are sending me letters, and when we have two children together whose lives are still ahead of them? I saw others, all my life, in great conundrums about their wives, but until that moment it had not occurred to me that I shared their experience.

CHAPTER 77

The late-spring snow was heavy and wet, like the snow in Vienna that hung on as spring was trying its best to break through. Working diligently on initial ideas for *Faust* one morning, I noticed out my window from Southwest Square that a magnificent carriage had stilled in front of the inn. I rushed downstairs. Standing just inside the inn was John Jacob Astor!—and suddenly, all of my waiting ended in a single moment. John had brought his own carriage to Philadelphia to take me to New York, just as he promised he would, and he had come himself to be sure that I was in good health. I was overjoyed to see him. Indeed, I doubt I was ever again in my life happier to see a single person. Well, perhaps. Read on, friends.

Seeing John again was the most wonderful gift. We immediately spoke as though no time had transpired between us and no ocean had separated our last unity. John apologized for how long it had taken him to respond, but he explained that he had been on a furring expedition and had only received my letter upon return. He had no need to apologize, as I told him that I would have found my way to New York eventually once I was fully recovered from my crossing. Even as I said the words I didn't believe them, for the ocean crossing had taken all of my nerve with it—I could no longer do brave things like find New York City on my own. In my experience, many men promised things they did not actually mean. John was a rare person who kept promises.

He said, "What people perhaps do not understand about the fur industry is that the most productive months are the coldest. It is grueling work, Amadé, but so worthwhile. It has given me the means to help the greatest composer in the world."

"Herr Astor, I knew I would eventually find my way to you somehow, yet here you have found your way to me instead." I was nearly in tears.

"I read your letter and could not imagine the circumstances by which you arrived in Baltimore. Except, of course, I can imagine them because I arrived myself in Baltimore years ago. I am perhaps the only person in history who walked to America." John laughed heartily, repeating the story he told to someone nearly every day of his life. Having now lived so long, I know that people often repeat themselves. When I was younger, all stories were new and interesting, but as I have aged I realize it is not so. There were only a few stories that people kept embellishing and repeating. Still, since I had last seen John, much had occurred, and I knew that at some point of my life, I would begin to relay to many people the stories of my arrival.

At that moment, though, I shared only with John the incredible tales of my arrival, sparing no detail. For the first time, I was able to say aloud and be believed that I had just missed their departure in Portsmouth, been tricked aboard a slaving ship bound for the New World from Liverpool, that I had been present in Dahomey as slaves were loaded on the *Gregson*, then traversed the middle passage in a morbid fever only to arrive in Baltimore to be removed from the ship by a doctor, sent to a hospital, and only then brought to Philadelphia, a place I had barely heard of before. John could tell from the length and emotion of my tale that I had been gravely affected by the journey.

"Amadé, we are all lucky you survived. I should have been home for your letter. I am sorry that your welcome to this country has been less than ideal. Sarah and I are eager to welcome you." I owe absolutely everything of my American life to John Jacob Astor.

"No, John, please understand. I made amazing friends in Germantown, and we have made music together." I wanted to forget my journey and for John not to feel guilty for it.

"I should have been here to welcome you, as I promised. But your arrival was so unexpected. You seemed not of the constitution to make the passage, even on the most luxurious of ships. To imagine the horrifying conditions you endured stretches my abilities. Those slaving ships are horrendous; I have seen them in various ports."

I was sure John had seen the ships before, but I could tell from his voice that he had never been aboard one. At all important moments of my life, I became a child again. I asked John if I could still go with him to New York.

"Why do you imagine I am here? I have come to take you to your new home."

I asked the question that I had asked of so many in the past. "What will be my duties?"

"The best plans are not made known," John said.

I trusted him implicitly. I told him I had promised to write *Faust* for the Germantown musicians, but that it had not gone as planned. I did not yet want to bring Astor into the entirety of what happened in Germantown.

"Then *Faust* can be the first opera you compose for New York, your first opera in America. I will build a theater for the purpose," John said.

I asked about Lorenzo.

"I do not know, Amadé. He disappeared, as you probably predicted. I have not heard a word from him."

"He will reappear, John," I said, happy to not carry anger toward Lorenzo, at least for a time. If I thought about him long enough, my love would turn to hatred.

CHAPTER 78

The preparations to move me to New York took several days, as my departure came as surprise to everyone at the inn. The innkeeper needed to know my address in New York in case mail arrived, and Astor told the innkeeper that my address would be Vesey Street in New York City, the same as his own, leaving me to wonder if I was to be living with John and Sarah.

Astor paid the remaining expenses I owed to the inn, which were not extravagant. I felt I had been rescued from a lonely bondage, though I knew I would always miss Philadelphia, the first place in America that I had known as well as I had Paris or London.

Astor stayed in the nearby home of a friend from the fur-trading business, on Spruce Street, a house that was itself considerably larger than my inn housing at least twenty inhabitants. John told me that his house in New York was considerably larger, which at first I could not believe. I began to have enormous expectations for the new life into which I was entering.

John and Sarah's generosity overwhelmed me, and I expressed my worries to John about how I might ever repay them.

"My payment will be in the works you will compose in this country, Amadé," John said many times.

But one unspoken fear lingered: had John earned his fortune from slavery? He said he thought the slave ships horrific, but had he profited from their industry? If so, I knew I would be powerless to stay silent and might thus jeopardize my own good fortune. And I knew no easy to way to find out, for circumstances prevented me from asking John too directly. Perhaps it would become clear once I moved to New York, but it worried me enormously in those early days.

CHAPTER 79

A t last the day came for our departure. A separate carriage was summoned for my trunks, allowing John and me to share his luxurious
carriage unencumbered. It was magnificently appointed, with beautifully
carved jugs of water and sweet breads for our journey, even flowers to
pleasantly scent the cabin. Our journey required an overnight stay in
Princeton, where John had arranged to stay at a home on Nassau Street
that was more sumptuous than any king's palace I had known, one which
made the home of his Philadelphia friend look like that of a tradesman.
The wealth of my new country astounded me, and John lived in a world
of luxury that I liked, but which ignited worry that I would grow too
accustomed. I had seen many people take on lives they could not sustain,
and it often destroyed their spirit. Even Konstanze and I had at one time
lived beyond what I knew we should, and the difference became something
we had to carry, a heavy weight on us both. John and I were served dinner
at the home that evening by liveried black servants, causing me to observe
John closely. I wanted to discover if the servants were or were not slaves, for
we were in a free state of Jersey, if I understood correctly. I knew nothing
of how the states laws might differ, though I knew Pennsylvania had been
free, but the Negroes I saw in Philadelphia certainly did not appear free;
they seemed like slaves in all but name. Mostly no one spoke to them at
all, as though an unwritten set of rules prevented discourse.

At the end of our enormous meal, we retired to the smoking room
for cigars and brandy wine. I observed John give one of the servants a

great deal of money for their help with the meal. I thought John surely would not have given money to slaves, so I deduced that they must be free blacks. I wished I understood their situation, but I did feel that I understood John's generosity and kindliness as proof that he felt as I did about the great evil.

Everything was so different from anything I had known, even shitting. The fancy house in Princeton, the owners of which were not there even though John and I were given permission to stay, had a special outdoor area expressly for shitting. We were to shit into a special bowl that had a mixture of sand and water and spices, and my shit disappeared within it without a trace of odor. It was so remarkable that I tried to make as much shit as I possibly could just to experience it again. I wondered if John and Sarah's house had this great extravagance to get rid of shit. It was a marvel! It is quite common in homes now but was completely new to me then.

Over brandy wine, John explained more of his idea for me in New York. He wanted to build a theater suitable for opera in a part of New York City where John also planned to build a grand new home, on Lafayette Street, which meant little to me then. He explained that there were theaters in the city, but none of a level of grandeur and beauty fitting for opera. Further, he wanted me to compose an *annual* opera, something that would bring the attention of the world to New York.

"In what language, John?"

"I think you can do as you like. Surely your *Faust* will be a German opera. Who will be the poet?" he asked, forgetting that I had told him about Goethe.

The question filled me with joy, because opera was what I wanted to write more than anything, and I had never had such perfection of opportunity.

I told him of my brief correspondence with Goethe, and said I would write him again to ask him to write it. I explained to John that he had been working on his *Faust* idea for many years, and I remember saying, "He surely has it done by now." Little did I know.

John said, "Imagine, an opera by Mozart and Goethe for our first season!"

He then asked me the subject of *Faust*, and though I explained the simple plot to him, I quickly realized there was no way to adequately describe the depth of Goethe's idea. *Faust* was, is, about everything.

I was overwhelmed with the profoundest gratitude, which I repeatedly expressed to John. Secretly, I wanted to write more than one opera per year, and felt that if I worked with diligence I could compose as many as three, particularly if I found a poet capable of the right combination of industry and inspiration. Where on earth was Lorenzo? He and I could create three operas a year easily. Were I to be blessed with ten more years of life, that could be thirty operas to follow *Richard III*! I had to wonder if it would really be possible. As I look back now, I realize I did not quite make that, but I was not far off.

I awoke the courage to tell John of my idea of writing four separate operas on *Hamlet*. John assented to every idea I put forth, though he wondered to me if *King Lear* might not be more suitable since "neither of us is a young prince any longer, we are getting on with age!" It was clear to me that John loved *King Lear*, and that it was a play I needed to know better.

The following day, traveling from Princeton to New York City, several of my earlier piano concertos were all over my memory. The day was one of the most beautiful I could recall, and spring arrived as we did. The leaves were budding with new green, which I loved, as they were at a similar time of year in Salzburg. John's carriage was carried across every stream or river by ferries who all seemed to know we were coming—yet these ferries were there constantly to accommodate the many travelers. The country was so alive! The ferries fascinated me, because they delivered us downriver to a dock that was easy to miss, especially if the river was a large one like our final ferry crossing of the Hudson. Our driver clearly had driven this journey many times before. John explained to me that he traveled often to Philadelphia, and at least once a year all the way to Washington. He knew this terrain well, and he always used the same carriage men. John was loyal to those in his employ.

I loved the wide grandeur of the Hudson River, which we entered at Hoboken, and the ferry delivered us to the lower portion of an island,

Mannahatta, that was so large one could not tell it was an island at all. John lived only a short distance from where our ferry alighted on land. I recall with complete clarity the day I first set foot on the rocky land of my new home. We arrived at Partition Street, and the ride from there to John and Sarah's home was brief. The scent of spring was everywhere, and it brought London to my mind, though the light was softer and the scents more delicate. One felt so far from the countryside in London, as though no city could ever be larger. Mannahatta, though, still felt like countryside, and enormous fields were visible even in the fading light of the day. The memory of my piano concertos kept coming, the D minor in particular, mixing itself in memory with my earlier D major, one of the concertos I especially loved. I loved them all, of course, or I would not have listened to the dictates of my mind, but my second D-major concerto was a favorite child. I was able to place within it the most beautiful feelings of my own childhood and all sorts of crackling little discoveries. The final few minutes of our carriage ride, the short distance from the Hudson to John's house, brought with it what felt to me like every note of D major that had ever exited my quill.

CHAPTER 80

John's house on Vesey Street was made of stone, like a castle. It reminded me of how the castle at Heidelberg might have looked had it not been destroyed by lightning. There was even a small tower connected to the central home, sitting high above it. John's enormous property included many other dwellings, such as a kitchen house that was larger than any home in which I had ever dwelled. I was taken immediately into the main house, as a small army of servants set to work on my trunks and preparing the horses to rest from their exertions.

The house smelled of roses and honey oil candles. Damask curtains and rich wallpapers caught the light of huge whale oil chandeliers, each of which glowed like sunrise. Outside of Schönbrunn Palace, I had never seen the like of it. John said, "I'm going to work for a few hours in my office. I will have the staff prepare anything you'd like for your evening meal. I will see you tomorrow, and you can meet Sarah and the children. Welcome home, Amadé."

I was actually *home*. After all the months of uncertainty and change, I was actually *home*. My body shook slightly from unexpected tears. I could only marvel at a house that was so large that the Astor children, who I would not meet for another day, were somewhere within it, along with Sarah Astor and dozens of servants, yet the house was completely silent. How was it possible?

I was shown to my quarters by one of the young men charged with bringing my trunks up the many flights of stairs, as my bedroom and personal area were at the top of the home's tower. I was to live in a tower, just as I had wished years before as a boy in Salzburg, an image brought to me in a dream that I had forgotten until that moment! My bed was the most ornate and luxurious I had ever seen, even searching my memories of when I had stayed with Papa in palaces. At the Vesey Street house, heat filled the room from the small fireplace and iron stove that had been ignited for hours. Within moments I was alone in my new home within John Astor's house in New York. From Vienna to Paris to London to Africa to Baltimore to Philadelphia and now, home, the place where I would stay, I hoped, forever.

I opened a window to fill my lungs with the new air of this new place. Everywhere was the smell of the sea, though there was no actual sea to be heard. Gulls circled the house as though guarding us from something. I could see distant fires across the river we had just crossed, and I knew that upon the next sunrise I would have a magnificent view from this new promontory. I was at the top of a new world.

CHAPTER 81

A t dawn, I arose for my first glimpse of bluffs across the river and even distant low mountains far to the right. I descended to the breakfast room as requested, following the scent of cinnamon and baking sugar. John introduced me at last to his wife Sarah, who said, "Amadé, at long last you are here. Welcome to our home." The children were eating in a separate breakfast area, and many more days transpired before they were brought into our adult world.

Sarah was both kindly and serious, and her greeting to me, though warm, was also distracted, because she was busily discussing the new Astor Music Store with John as though she was also a businessman. She had a vivacious laugh, all allegro and staccato, and I liked her tremendously from the start. She asked me about my journey, to which I simply said, "I'm very happy to be here at last." She acted as though she had always expected I would be there with them, as though it was the most natural thing in the world for me to have crossed an ocean and to have approached death on the journey. Sarah was one of the people who made things better, and even my haunted memories of the *Gregson* softened in her presence. What a gift to be able to heal wounded souls.

Sarah said, "Amadé, I'd like you to go with me today to the instrument shop, as we need your help with a few things. And that is where John and I would like you to work on your compositions. Our old apartments are above the shop, and you can have them as your studio. It is very nice, very spacious, and you will have privacy that won't be possible here."

I was thrilled. I offered that I would be happy to both live and work at the shop, in order not to crowd their home. And I also thought that a clavichord could easily be placed within my tower and never be heard anywhere in the vast house, but that idea was rejected. Sarah had decided that I was to work in the studio over the shop, so that became what I would do. And it was clearly important to both John and Sarah that I live at Vesey Street.

"As you can see, it is not crowded here. We are soon to build a large farmhouse a few miles north of here and when we do, this house will be even quieter than it is now. We will likely leave you here if your quarters are suitable. The children are in their own area so that they don't bother us, and William is a firebrand, Amadé! You will see! Children can be so noisy, as you well know." Sarah laughed a laugh that would become very familiar to me.

The instrument shop on Wall Street, just past Federal Hall, seemed much like the one in London where John and I had the fortune to meet. Everywhere was the smell of wood and lacquer, as the shop made viols for private sale, a multitude of which were available, and many more being made right there by a set of craftsmen to whom I was introduced. The flutes that John had purchased in London in my presence were displayed on a beautiful wooden rack. There were fortepianos and harpsichords, each of which I was eager to play.

Sarah said, "If you see an instrument you want moved upstairs, just tell me. You can have whichever one you want."

I was taken upstairs to a spacious set of rooms nearly empty except for a few instruments stored away, a writing desk, plenty of paper, and a fortepiano. I could already imagine the volume of music I would compose in the place. Sarah said she could send someone to tune the fortepiano whenever I liked, and I was proud to tell her I knew how to tune it myself.

Sarah had a number of questions for me about the quality of certain instruments, which I tried my best to answer. But she sensed that I was eager to get to work, so she left me with a key to my quarters upstairs, and asked if I knew how to get home by foot or if I wanted a carriage. I told her I had no need for a carriage, as the Astor house was practically visible from the store, and I wanted to grow accustomed to my new city by walking. New York was considerably smaller than London, making everything more readily available.

"The best plans are not made known," John had said to me back in Philadelphia, yet I was eager to know one part of the plan: my salary. I had been given so much already—a home, a studio, and the freedom to do as I wanted—it was a dream come true. But I also wanted to be able to send money to Konstanze for little Franz if there could be any way to do so. John was a big dreamer, and I was already far in his debt. I needed to bring up the subject of a salary, either with Sarah or with John, but I did not know how.

My first day in the studio was productive, in that I started earnestly sketching further my ideas for *Faust* that I had begun in Philadelphia, at least as much as I could without a libretto. I had Goethe's original idea, but no doubt he had expanded greatly on it by the time I got to New York. I knew that any letter from Goethe would take months, so I was getting concerned about *Faust* as a first opera for New York. Goethe had been working on the book for as long as I had known him, therefore most of my recent life; and it remained more of an idea than a completion even when I had departed Vienna. I remembered another play I had loved and had seen several times, Schiller's *Die Räuber*, and I thought it would make an extremely exciting opera for a new country. Thinking back on it, I saw no reason the action could not be set in young America, as there were undoubtedly aristocratic brothers vying for inheritance even in a youthful country. I wrote down that I would inquire with Sarah or John how I might be able to obtain a copy of *Die Räuber* in New York. Perhaps there was a bookshop that could find it for me? In memory it was ready to be set to music with little adaptation.

Eager to use my new freedom, I began to play long passages of several of my piano concertos, skipping from one to the other. I had concertos in almost every key, something I had not consciously tried to create. At that point I had written no concerto in B minor, so I wrote an idea in my notebook that might work. I was playing one of my very early F-major concertos, one I always loved, when I heard the downstairs door of the shop open. The instrument shop, I would quickly learn, was busy with the making of instruments, but few people actually came into the shop, as one needed purpose to enter a shop selling musical instruments. Each opening of the door in those early days, I learned, was an event.

I stopped playing and heard the man introduce himself to the downstairs shopkeeper as Mr. James Hewitt, who was inquiring about the purchase of a violin. The information and prices were given to him. I was about to begin playing again when he heard Hewitt ask a question.

"Who was playing the fortepiano a few moments ago?"

"I'm not at liberty to say, Mr. Hewitt," the shopkeeper replied, precisely as instructed by Sarah.

"He was playing so expertly. I know every musician in New York. I would endeavor to know his name, please?"

"He is a composer in the employ of the Astors, sir, and I am not at liberty to speak his name."

Unsatisfied, Hewitt went to the base of the stairs and yelled, "You, up there on the fortepiano! Who are you?"

I froze, frightened. No one besides the Astors had spoken to me in New York, and I suddenly felt insecure about my English. I wondered if my playing was somehow violating a rule I might not understand. The shopkeeper could not restrain James. I heard her leave the shop, presumably to find help in case Mr. James Hewitt might cause her or even me some kind of bodily harm. I could hear her fright in the slamming of the door.

James repeated his question. I could detect something kindly in the man's voice. I told him to come upstairs. One of the workmen building violins downstairs followed him up, concerned about my safety, but I told him it was all right.

The sounds of voices never lied. Looking at James Hewitt, one might think him something of a bully, but his voice was tender. I never once trusted the Lord Chamberlain's voice, but I always found comfort in the voice of Joseph II. Mr. Hewitt complimented me on my playing.

"You must be new in the city. Please tell me, who are you?"

"My family is Mozart. I am Wolfgang Amadé Mozart, from Vienna." I thought my statement was unkind to the little town of my birth, so I amended, "From Vienna, born in Salzburg more than forty years distant, far back into the time we both know."

Hewitt took off his small eyeglasses and stared into my eyes. "You are actually Mozart. *The* Mozart?"

"I am my father's son, sir—and you are?"

He said, "I am James Hewitt, also a musician, though I feel I can hardly claim that profession in front of you. Did Astor get you here?"

"He did. I am so fortunate."

His gruff figure softened. "I can share with you my sonata, *The Battle of Trenton*, but it would do me the greatest honor to hear *your* work, sir. The stories we have read of your accomplishments as a child are the wonder of the world. I cannot believe I am meeting *the* Mozart!"

I reminded him that I had not been a child for many years, and that I left Vienna nearly a year before to become the court composer for George III, where I met Astor. I told Hewitt that Astor invited me and that after an arduous journey, I had finally arrived just in recent days.

"Do you have plans to publish your music in New York?" Hewitt asked.

I did not know how many of John's plans should be disclosed, nor did I know if John had plans to include music publishing as part of my duties. I confessed to Hewitt that I had not been in New York long enough to know such things, and that business did not interest me. I offered, "I do not know how to answer that, Mr. Hewitt."

"Please, call me James. I have published volumes of your piano sonatas, as well as *Figaro* and *Magic Flute*, in English of course. There is a great demand for your music in this new country."

"You have scores of my operas in English?" I asked, delighted to know of *two* translations of *The Magic Flute*, and that I might not have to write to the court of St. James at all.

"Oh yes, though there are few singers here capable of performing them. Still, some of us like to play through them and dream."

"These operas are old. Might there be interest in my new works?" I asked.

"Of course! How did Astor convince you to leave London? That man is amazing." Hewitt had a kindly voice that pleased my ear.

"Yes. Amazing." I was too embarrassed to tell him or anyone that I had not immediately taken John's generous offer. And how my life would have altered had I only gone with him the day after we dined together at Boodle's. Life in London seemed far away indeed.

"I leave you with my card. Call on me anytime for anything," James said. "I do not live far from here."

Trusting him immediately, I said, "And I will be here each day working. Sometimes downstairs in the shop, more likely up here composing." I was so happy at that moment to say out loud what my new life would be.

Hewitt continued, "I would love to meet Mr. Astor. He has done a great thing for New York by convincing you to come here. Please play something for me, Herr Mozart. It has been the dream of my life to hear you play."

It had been so long since I had been asked to play. Given what James had told me, I thought I should play one of my older sonatas, and I had heard several times that the *Turkish* sonata that I had composed many years before was very popular around the world. There was never any way of fully knowing the truth of popularity, as it was often simply a feeling in the air that could not be seen. But something about the *Turkish* sonata seemed always to have been in the world, even before I placed it upon paper. So, for Hewitt I played the final movement of it, the only part of the sonata that had a Turkish flavor. Having not played it in years, I had forgotten how challenging it was, both the filigree within the middle A major but also the complicated octaves together with the drum effects in the bass line. What used to be so easy was now a labor within my fingers, causing me to laugh as I finished the difficult coda.

"Your notes are spells, Herr Mozart, and you use every note like a wizard," the kindly Hewitt said.

CHAPTER 82

I was unclear what he meant. But I thanked him and James descended the stairs and left the shop. I loved recalling my old A-major sonata. Alone in my studio again, and the shop seeming to have calmed from the appearance of James Hewitt, I returned to the beginning of my old sonata, remembering the sweet siciliana tune I had used as the opening music, one of those melodies that lingered like an illusion within my mind for years before that morning when I had put all the notes down on paper within a few hours. I could have written two hundred variations on that pliable and simple tune, but I chose whatever came to mind that day, as I always did. I thought it best never to amble through ideas; better to write them down and move on. As I played, I knew that some of my variations were now different from what I had set down on paper two decades before, or whenever it was. I found it odd then, and odder now, that there are works on which I devoted many hours, only to realize I can no longer remember them. There was a time when I held everything in memory all at once, and I could call upon any one of my creations with just a thought. But memory changed. So much has now happened to me.

I heard the door of the shop again and I stopped playing. Sarah Astor ascended the stairs calling my name, followed by the shopkeeper, who was still shaken by Mr. Hewitt. Sarah inquired how as to how my first day had been. I calmed the shopkeeper, who went back to work. With excitement, I told Sarah about James Hewitt.

"I know he has tried to begin an instrument shop as well," she said.

"And he has published music. He asked about publishing mine."

"I believe, Amadé, as this city continues to grow so fast, that we should start selling more printed music. Perhaps Mr. Hewitt could help us if we were to employ him. I will discuss the matter with John. We have enough room to sell bins of printed music," Sarah said. "We certainly do not want him going into business to compete with us."

I thought it would be wonderful to have a place for printed music, as it could be a gathering place for all of the city's musicians, helping me get to know them.

"There are several already," she said, "but there are no others where Wolfgang Mozart works, are there?" She smiled and told me I was done for the day and that she wanted to stay and deal with some business.

My first day completed, I walked home. Thousands of people were doing the same, going around to the many small shops. I entered the Vesey Street house, still feeling like a guest, and I had constantly to remind myself that I lived there. Preparations were being made for dinner when I noticed a woman arranging flowers for the table. She was the most beautiful woman I had ever seen. My cherished reader, you will have realized by now that I was never one to look away from beauty. Indeed, I lived for the beautiful and was highly susceptible to it. I had looked closely at every beautiful woman who ever came within my sight. She noticed me looking at her, and she drew her eyes to mine. The light from the newly lit lamps was shining through her eyes. I had been in love many times, perhaps too many, as I was in love with love, but this was a different feeling. Lingering on her eyes, I waited for the other servants to leave her alone with me in the room.

CHAPTER 83

"Are you Mr. Astor's new composer?"

I said yes, and that my name was Amadé.

"I am Alice."

"Are you in the regular employ of the Astors?" I asked, hoping she might be, so that I could see her often.

"I am. They are so kind to me. I work in several households," Alice said.

I loved the sound of her voice. "You speak so well. Far better than I. My English is so poor."

"I can help you."

I believed her. I was very fast with languages, but English took longer than any language I had ever learned. I was proud of my improvement, though, and I could speak to Alice.

"Your English sounds like Mr. Astor's, like you learned it in the old country." She laughed.

"I did, mostly. I lived in London for a short time, as did Mr. Astor," I said.

Alice. I said her name several times in my mind before saying it aloud to her.

"Mrs. Astor told me you are a famous composer," Alice said.

"Perhaps to the few people who care about such things. In this country, I am no one. I have just arrived and must prove my worth here. Fame means nothing," I said, my view of myself having changed in that single moment. Only minutes before I had not known Alice; then everything changed.

"Will you play music for me, Amadé?"

"I will happily play music for you, Alice. And I will also write music for you. Has anyone ever written music for you?"

"No one!"

She had the most beautiful smile I had ever seen and laugh I had ever heard. Alice was unlike any other woman, and I lack the words to describe her. Although her skin was dark, she was not a Negro nor did she look like European women. I did not want to ask her origin, because I could sense that the question might be a source of pain. I had not loved Konstanze upon meeting her, but had grown to love her over time. Alice immediately seemed to have always existed in my life and heart, and I wondered how I had ever been alive without knowing her. I longed to know everything about her, and I asked when he could see her again.

"You cannot be seen with a servant of the household," Alice said.

"But I, too, am a servant of the household. We are the same." I laughed.

"We are not the same. Look at me," she said.

"I have to see you again. Please Alice, let us take a walk together, anything."

She said, softly, "You cannot be seen in public with someone like me."

"Are you betrothed?" I asked, not having yet considered the idea that other men might have noticed her. Yet how could they not? She was as completely beautiful as a season or a mountain.

"I am not. Amadé, please play music for me," she said.

We went to the large drawing room where there was a fortepiano. I played sonatas for her, music that had never been heard in my new country, but which I now played solely for her. She had never heard such sounds, never even thought of their possibility, and by the time I was into the second variation of my A-major sonata, I could tell she was falling in love with me.

We began talking between my selections, and I would have spent hours with her had not her duties called her back to the preparations for dinner.

"You must not put your position in jeopardy, Amadé, by cavorting with me," Alice warned me, running back toward the dining room.

"I do not understand your meaning. It is you cavorting with me!" I teased her.

"I am a mulatta. The laws of this country forbid you to be seen with me," she said.

I did not know what a mulatta was, and I could not understand a law that would keep her from me. In time, Alice would explain it to me, always trying to get me to understand why we must resist each other. Trying to stay apart became the focus of our lives for many months afterward.

In that one single day, I met a man of influence besides Astor, and then the most gorgeous and profound woman of my life, all unexpectedly. I had to wonder what other fortunes New York might bring.

CHAPTER 84

I could not restrain myself where Alice was concerned. My energies returned and I felt healthier than I had felt for years, like a child again. Every day I woke early, walked to the instrument store to tend to whatever business was necessary, went upstairs and composed until the sun tilted in a particular direction, after which I returned to Vesey Street, sometimes taking dinner with the Astors, absent John, who was usually away on business expeditions, often taking dinner myself in a small dining area off the main hall. But dinner always allowed me to see Alice, and within months we began dining together in a more secluded room near the kitchen house that sat at the back of the property. We found we were able to be alone there, and we did not rouse suspicion. Over the months, as I completed my operas on *Die Räuber* as well as *The Fairy of the Lake*, I was also composing pianoforte sonatas to be heard only by Alice. She became my muse.

After meeting Alice, I wrote a large amount of music in D major and A major, always the keys of my happiest times. In 1784, my happiest earlier year, I had completed a concerto in D that I loved beyond most of my others, and I was sure at that time it was my greatest, finishing it only a week after the concerto that preceded it. I tried to explain it to her, and she delighted me when she said that keys don't mean much to most people. I explained that keys were just a way to organize music, and they didn't have to have meaning outside of musical circles. Keys, of course, had enormous meaning to me, meaning that was mine alone.

"But don't you realize, Amadé, that talk of keys makes many people feel inadequate in speaking to you, and keeps them from music instead of inviting them in." As usual, Alice brought new thoughts to me.

"I will take an idea and put it into every key, and the best key will reveal itself. It is the easiest way to remember works over the long course of my life," I said, laughing, having never considered that keys might be daunting for anyone. They were so much a part of my life that I could not picture them not being central to the lives of all musicians. Did not every musician think in keys? Also, it was important to remind myself that Alice was not a trained musician, even though she had a musician's soul, a soul I recognized when I saw it. Perhaps Alice was right; perhaps there was a better way to title music, given that I was in a new country and new place, with none of the conventions of Vienna or Paris being necessary or even desirable. Might the public feel less daunted if my symphonies had names rather than numbers? I wrote the thought in my notebook that very evening.

CHAPTER 85

Consummation with Alice became my entire world, for I was not only on a new continent but also in a new century, starting a new life. I had obviously committed the act many times before, but Alice was my first in the New World, and the intercourse itself felt very different in this new place. Alice did not feel like my previous comfortable conquests, even the ones who had cost me a great deal of emotion, and at least one back in the Old World at least six seasons before who had cost me an excruciating rash that took months to heal. Some women I simply had to experience once, and then the bloom of their fascination quickly waned. But with Alice I could not experience enough of her. With her I was able, in the moment of passion, to play a role I never played with anyone else. I was able to bring in a degree of dominance that we both knew was false, but which pleased us both. In truth, Alice was the dominating presence in our relationship, but at the peak of sexual passion she ceded that role to me, which I loved.

Our early weeks of love stretched into the months of my first winter in New York, as 1800 turned to 1801. Alice never came to the instrument shop and thus never to my studio. Because she lived in a small house behind the Astor property and worked in the main home, it was not noticed when she was with me in my secluded tower room. I began to suspect that Sarah Astor knew of our union, but she said nothing. I did not harbor fear of loving a fellow servant of the household, but Alice's slightly dark skin did give me pause, not because I loved her less but it made me love her differently, though I still do not understand why. I heard the talk all around New York, and often in the instrument shop, of the problems of the Negro, problems that would not have naturally occurred to me. Outside of our household, Alice continually explained, our union was illegal and would result in jail, absolutely for her, and possibly also for me.

"Why do you not understand this, Amadé? You are such a brilliant man," she said to me one evening.

I replied that her skin was different from mine, but that was all.

"That is enough," she said.

"You are so beautiful. I want to touch every part of your skin."

"And you have, my darling Amadé, haven't you?" she said, exciting me.

"How could your skin be wrong? It is not of your choosing. Look at my skin, covered with holes from the pox—it is my skin that should be illegal!" I laughed. I was always embarrassed by my scars, even knowing there was nothing I could do about them.

Alice said, "My skin reminds the white man of what he has done. I am the color of their late-night whims."

I loved learning about Alice, who was born in Mannahatta not far from where she and I now lived, yet she would never allow me to know much of anything about her earlier life. She had been in the employ of the Astors since she was a child, which meant she was also far younger than I was. The concern for the gap in our ages should have been mine, yet Alice alone worried about it. I should have worried that she would still be young when she had to care for an aging man like me, but she said it was precisely this possible care that drew me to her.

"Alice, I want you to marry me," I said, not having planned to ask her.

"It is impossible, Ami, you must not ask." I loved the music her voice made of *Ami*.

I did not ask again, and though I wanted her to stay with me in the tower, I learned to accept the situation of living separately but nearby. She brought my mail each day, which was part of her task for the household, because she was among the few servants able to read. I wanted to ask her how she came to have such an education, but that always seemed like something I should ask later. I longed to wake up with her, but accepted that it was not yet possible. I tried to imagine this being so in Vienna, but also did not believe there were any women like Alice in Vienna. I loved her beyond any love I had ever known. I still do.

Sarah left me a note that she expected John to return to New York within a few days and he would want to meet with me as soon as possible.

I chilled reading the note, for fear that John had found out about Alice and was going to inform me that I was no longer in the employ of the Astors or worse: that I could no longer see Alice. I felt I was being summoned before Leopold for a scolding, or that the Lord Chamberlain would again be informing me that I was no longer the court composer.

Hours after John's return, I was summoned to his office, a part of the house I had not yet seen. There was a passageway and a secretive doorway through which a servant guided me. John greeted me kindly, and because his journey had taken many months, and already winter had set in, a vast fireplace was blazing near John's desk. My eyes were drawn high above the desk because the upper part of the room was a pyramid. This was not visible from outside John's home, so he must have purposefully tried to conceal it. He was talking about his travels, which were interesting enough, but the pyramid room told me something John had never disclosed. He was a fellow Mason.

I had worked so hard in America and then fallen so deeply in love that I left my Masonic life across the ocean. It made sense to me that John was a Mason, as he espoused every tenet of the order, and I felt foolish that I had not deduced it before.

"Can I attend Lodge with you?" I asked him.

"Of course you can, Amadé, with great pleasure. We can go this week. So much of my business success is due to the Lodge. As you know, the Masons are dedicated to the success of everyone within the brotherhood."

I had not heard the word before in English, *brotherhood*, the same word as in German, *Bruderschaft*, and I loved hearing it. My Masonic order in Vienna, where I was quickly promoted to master Mason, had been my place of peace in the turmoil of my life there. John reminded me of Ignaz, our Lodgemaster, though it bothered me to forget the surname of Ignaz. I knew the name would come to me at some inopportune time and I would suddenly blurt it out, confounding everyone present. As John was speaking, I kept pondering the name, before finally grabbing my own mind back to where it was supposed to be. John said he wanted to speak to me about an important matter.

I was certain an ax was about to fall, but I tried to remain calm, as all conversations with John were opportune. My early months in New York stretched into several years, years of enormous happiness for me: Alice and our young love, work at the Astor Music Shop and getting to know new musical friends in New York City. John said an extraordinary thing.

"Now, though, there is the matter of the theater that I wish to bring up with you. I have secured land far to the east of here, where there is currently almost nothing. It may seem a folly to build an opera house in the middle of a field, but I know we will be patronized if we make the theater spectacular enough. I am building a farm home even farther to the north, and when Sarah and I move there, you may be able to stay at Vesey Street and perhaps expand your quarters a bit. We can discuss that. I expect the opera house will take about a year to build, and I have the design here to show you. Tell me what you think."

My mind skipped over the opera house to the exciting idea of having more room, but feared that Alice would be moving to the farm with the Astors. My worry grew from that moment, like a complicated fugue, and the longer I waited to tell Sarah and John about Alice and me, the greater my anxiety. So often, I reminded myself, my mind floated back to Bach's Preludes and Fugues in each key, the well-tempered, and I noted that I often wanted to write my own set of preludes and fugues, updated as modern music, and I wanted to start working on them the next time I was at the studio.

"Amadé, what do you think of the plans for the opera house?" John prompted, amused that I was lost in thought.

I bent over the sheets he spread before me. I had never seen the plan of a theater before, despite spending my life in them, and the Astor Opera House looked enormous, ornate beyond comprehension. The plans showed plush curtains and gold bunting and chairs of the finest woods from the eastern forests. I could not imagine the expense of such a place, but Astor was determined to build his opera house to rival the greatest theaters of his experiences in Germany and Italy.

"John, I think it looks like the most magnificent theater in the world, if you are able to build it," I said.

He asked what operas I had chosen for the opening of the theater, and I told him he wanted to perform *The Magic Flute* along with its sequel, *The Labyrinth.*

"Marvelous! What about *Faust?*"

"I will shortly have a surprise for you on *Faust,* John, but I need more time."

I also told him of *Der Räuber,* knowing his love of Schiller.

John told me it was time to form an orchestra and give several concerts in smaller theaters around Mannahatta to get the New York public accustomed to fine music. John intended to hire a manager for his new theater, someone who could help me plan orchestral rehearsals and deal with all of the many arrangements I would have to make. Once the theater neared completion, I would need to plan the scenery for the operas, and John would employ whomever I recommended. He emphasized that the operas must be the most magnificent things ever seen in New York. This opera house was to be the symbol of everything John wanted to achieve.

It captured my dreams, too, yet all I wanted to talk about was Alice. Instead I told John that I had received in the mail a complete libretto for an opera on *Faust,* accompanied by a long letter from Goethe about all of the happenings in Vienna. I asked if I could utilize *Faust* for the second season in the new theater, and John suggested we do the opposite: open the new Astor Opera House with *Faust,* followed by *The Magic Flute* and *The Labyrinth. Der Räuber* and *The Fairy of the Lake* could follow in the next season. John wanted to expand to several operas a season within a few years, and he wanted me to be thinking about what operas by other composers to seek.

I delighted in thinking about operas by other composers in addition to mine, and I thought we should perform plays and concerts as well, as was done at the Burgtheater. John asked if I might be willing to do some of my earlier operas like *Figaro* or *Don Giovanni*. He thought that within a few years the New York public would be ready for strong winter seasons of opera. He planned to speak to a number of his New York business friends about developing a set of subscribers to the new opera house, so that each could own a box they could use for business and enjoyment. One of the things John noticed about New York was that there was so little to do for leisure. It was a wonderful city for making money, but John felt one of the best uses for his money was to give me the artistic freedom I had never before possessed.

"I am forever in your debt, John. I don't know how I can ever thank you," I said, tears forming in my eyes.

"My payment will be opera finding a place in this country, my friend," John said.

CHAPTER 86

I did not feel I deserved such generosity, not from John nor from anyone. There was so much for which I needed to atone, not the least of which was falling in love with one of John's servants. I thought him more magnanimous than any king or emperor of my acquaintance. Haydn had known more security than any musician in history. Jesus Christ Bach, too, back when the dear J.C. was still alive. Nearly all of the composers I knew, though, produced stack after stack of quality music, yet every priest and every learned person I met outside the Lodges thought it was God's will that artists should always be suffering and starving, as though that made an artist better. I knew an artist could use the ills of life that happen to every person blessed with a long enough time to feel pain and joy, but the real work of life is in creating something that others can feel. In this, I felt my work as important as anyone else's, and it is something John alone seemed to understand without being an artist himself. There remains no one in my long life like John Astor, who kept me from so much adversity.

He said, "You see, Amadé, when I was only sixteen, I went to work for my uncle George in London at his shop that sold flutes and pianos, right where you and I met up. George was so difficult with me, so exacting, that I probably learned more about the work at hand than I had when I worked for my father as a butcher and milk seller. I learned the trade of musical instruments more thoroughly because I was so frightened of my uncle. He was ruthless, and not afraid to hit us if we did something he did not like. I swore I would never be that way with my children nor anyone in my employ."

I was fascinated that John applied what he learned from selling instruments to dealing in furs. I admired anyone who was able to make a living out of business, because I had no way of knowing how that was done. I was eager to learn about the instruments in the shop and the musicians who came to buy them, but I would prefer to give all of the instruments away, as I didn't know, nor care to know, how to make enough profit to keep a business open. I told John how much I admired anyone who could make money.

"Amadé, how did you learn your craft?" he asked me.

"I learned from my father, at least at first. But my real learning came from Johann Christian in London, when I was a boy. I could never tell my father this, of course, but J.C. knew how to bring out my instincts, and not just to follow rules. Meeting him so young sent me toward his father's compositions, J.S. Bach, and when I fully committed those to memory, I realized that no matter how good any of us thought we might be, Johann Sebastian would be better. His compositions are the greatest music any of us will likely ever know. What he could craft in just a few minutes puts us all to shame. The tragedy is that he did not have any interest in opera; what operas he could have written! His son made up for it, of course, but I cannot imagine how great the composer of the *St. Matthew Passion* could have been had he darkened the door of a theater." I realized I had talked rather longer than what likely interested John.

"I have so much to learn from you, Amadé. I thank you for that. I know very little music of Herr Bach."

"You must! I will play some for you, as they are the works I often study. I will struggle to remember them all, as they are quite complex," I said, continuing, "What are to be the terms of my compositions for the opera house?"

"Yes, of course. Your terms. I had hoped for you to write one opera per year, work in the shop, and write whatever concert music you care to invent."

"Yes, sir, but on what terms?" I felt bold to ask, but I needed to know.

"On the terms that you live in our home free of charge, where you can eat and drink at your will."

"I must be able to send some money to Konstanze for my child, Franz. I'm sure you understand."

"Of course. I have my business associates in the fur industry in Vienna who can forward money to her. You just tell me how much you believe she needs and we will take care of it. This should not be a worry for you."

I thanked him, but John's generosity set off a quandary that altered my sleep. I could keep Konstanze and Franz supported, perhaps quite generously, and John would probably not notice whether the sum was high or low. But what if he did? I knew that if I asked too high an amount, I could be thought an ingrate. But if I requested a sum that was too little to support Konstanze, it would be a constant source of worry. I produced a number to John's office a few days later, and no one ever questioned it. I was told to write to Konstanze to tell her the address in Vienna where she could retrieve the money each month. With this weight of worrying about supporting Konstanze lifted from my shoulders, I was able to have peaceful sleep again, and more productive work. Money is such a constant distraction, whether too little to too much! (Though I would not mind having the problem of too much for once in my life.)

Goethe and I maintained a heavy correspondence during those early years in New York. Long before I left Vienna, he had shared with me a fragment of his idea for *Faust*, and I thought it brilliant, perhaps more suited for opera than for the kind of long verse *roman* he was conceiving—something they called a "novel" in this new world. *Faust* contains all of the higher secrets of mankind, and one must always bow before such thoughts. Goethe also caused a flood of news from home, as he must have talked about my letters with others in Weimar and Vienna, wherever he was, because I began receiving almost daily missives from friends once Goethe made his own writings to me a habit.

It became more widely known among my old circles that I had fled to the New World, and the extraordinary news of the new Astor Opera House was making a memorable impression everywhere. Everything one had always heard of George III's American colonies was that each was more savage than the other, without any kind of life approaching what we had in Vienna or Paris or London. I knew little about the colonies as a totality, then or now, and though it felt like I had seen so much over more than twenty years here, I have known intimately only a small hillock in Virginia where I spent a few memorable days, and a small lower portion of a huge verdant island where I lived for so long. I never counted Baltimore or Pennsylvania because I knew them only when I was recovering my health, and I doubt anyone in Germantown remembers me, which is absolutely fine. But with the realizations of an opera house and new compositions vibrating the air of the New World, musical works quite different from the Old, the opinions of friends in Vienna and elsewhere were forced to change.

For many, opera houses are places of great civilization. Little did people know that gentle savages are often found within these theaters, where cabals and jealousies are rampant, and a whole range of people who know nothing about the art long to be seen as though they do. Outside of the *Gregson*, which was like entering Hell itself, the most pointlessly silly behavior within my witness was to be found in opera houses. Even my beloved *Figaro*, of all of my works, was greeted with hisses and booing—the bastards!—each time it appeared in the civilized "old" world. Not here! Everyone suspected Salieri for *Figaro*'s first cabal, but it was actually just a bunch of miserable German singers who were against the Italians in the cast. *Cretini!* All you had to do was listen to them sitting around farting and complaining.

Sebastian Winter, dear friend, wrote often to me all through the years, and I kissed each letter a thousand times, as he was someone I missed beyond measure. He was the valet to Prince Joseph Maria Benedikt in Donaueschingen when I met him in my happiest years in Vienna around the time of *Figaro*. How I wish I could have convinced him to come to America, where he would have had a wonderful time. I knew he and Tamu were cut from the same cloth, even if they came from completely different worlds. The New World would have suited Sebastian, yet some people feel they must always remain where they always were. Why is that? It was in letters to Sebastian that I poured out my heart, so I hope he saves them, because I have been more honest with him than with anyone else in my life.

It became a rare week that I did not have a letter from Goethe; and not long into this pattern, I began receiving whole revised scenes of a German libretto on his *Faust*. He seemed unable to ever finish it. Even scenes I had long completed, he would send anew. I could kiss his hand a thousand times a thousand for each letter he wrote! As far as I could tell, he still planned to publish a novel of his *Faust*, but it had not yet eventuated. And who would read such a novel, so long and so tedious? Only other people like Heinrich Faust. I wanted to engage with stories that many people would like, at least the educated people. For a long time I thought there was no entertaining the uneducated, yet everyone I ever met who saw *The Labyrinth* or *The Magic Flute*, whatever their station in life, had something to say about it, and not a single one of them failed to feel *something*.

I imagine Goethe worked without cease on his book, because he was even more excessive a person than I. He actually did as I had hoped: he agreed to write an opera with me though we were miles and months apart, and could only communicate via messages within the mail that arrived aboard unpredictable ships. This was cumbersome, to be sure, but it made me far less impetuous than I might have been had we been together as normal, where our two personalities might not have had the most profound effect on the other. I felt sure we would drink a lot if we were working together. I did not, after all, know him well in the sense that I knew Lorenzo, and Lorenzo and I drank a great deal of wine. It is incredible to me now that the best parts of our operas often emerged when I was on the drunken side of a day. Drinking kept the dark side of the bridge at bay.

Because of this strange arrangement, *Faust* was to take the longest of any opera I had ever penned, yet Goethe finished his poem for me quickly, almost as if it had been lying in wait for years. He wrote the whole libretto at least four times, yet I could only set it once! What a gift *Faust* was to the world, all from the silent thoughts of a brooding man. It frustrated Goethe no end that we in New York should be the first to hear this opera, and it would take years before he had opportunity to hear his own opera in Berlin. I loved getting letters from all over Europe about performances of my works, though I would have been considerably happier had they instead just paid me.

For many years I considered an opera on Gottholt Lessing's *Nathan the Wise*. I had seen the play years before, and it was a joy to read it again. Once Lorenzo returned to New York (patience, dear ones!), he was forever scouring the city for books, perturbed that so few of them were in Italian. Though I never succeeded in finding any such places, he claimed there were all kinds of hidden treasures in shops tucked away on side streets on the lower eastern side of our island. Because there was a market, books in all languages appeared in New York especially, he assured, in German. He was much more willing to go into shady shops and down alleyways than I. He was Venetian, after all, and unless you were willing to travel into the darkness of Venice, you would never find anything.

What an opera *Nathan the Wise* would make!—but it was not to be, as I had too many other ideas to pursue. I also was not sure how Americans might take to an opera that placed a Jew at the center of a parable that equated the Islamists and the Christians. I met Gottholt somewhere, perhaps Mannheim, I cannot remember, and found him amazing. I twice saw his play *Die Juden* and it left a major impression on me as well, but there was no way I could propose such a work for New York, as there was such intolerance for the Jews everywhere. After traveling on the *Gregson*, I could not countenance hatred toward anyone for any reason other than retribution for the cruelty they wrought on others. I did not share the views of the Jews in those years, because I was still then firmly a member of the church of Rome, but I never felt they should be persecuted for refusing to accept what I believe. I had been guilty of hatred myself many times in my life, and I even once passed the persecution of a Jew in Stephansplatz and I am filled with shame to say that I did not even turn my head. I not only should have stopped, but also I should have yelled and demanded they stop torturing the poor man.

Nathan the Wise was an opera that needed to be written and a story that needed to be told, and perhaps I can still get to it, except, of course, that something else besides this overdue testament has become the obsession of my life.

No one would believe that Goethe and I could write an opera when separated by the great ocean, and I could not have achieved it with anyone except him. Actually, I loved to call Goethe not by his childhood name Johann but by one of his baptismal names: Wolfgang. Each time I wrote his name I could hear his tremendous laugh. I missed him as I missed so many others, but writing *Faust* together gave us a way to still be together even under such a terrible reality. To my sure knowledge, no one in the world except me called him Wolfgang. I giggle even as it leaves my quill, for he did not look like a Wolfgang at all; he was as fully a Johann as anyone could be.

When he had allowed me to read his *Faust* idea many years before in Vienna, the experience of his words stayed with me. I understood his great invention of the Faust character because I understood my own dear Leopold. Now that I think back on Papa, I realize he was very like Faust, though there is no possible doubt that Faust was Goethe himself. Papa was as learned and fastidious as Heinrich Faust, thinking that all of his ballast would prove somehow worthwhile if he were to acquire all the knowledge and respect of the world. Even when Franz d'Ippold wrote to tell me of Papa's death, there was within it worry about money, always money. My little starling died only days after Papa, and Konstanze thought I was more heartbroken over the bird than my dear father. No, Stanzie, I could simply utter words about my little darling that I could never say about Papa.

Papa, may God always keep you within his bosom. You were in a constant state of waiting, like an alchemist who has put all of his elements together but had yet to know their outcome—you waited, always, for gold. You accused me so often of impatience or intemperance, but it was you, Papa, not anyone else, who awaited the arrival of something that would never come. You longed for me to reflect you like a looking glass, though you disapproved of whatever image I produced. You wanted me to be whatever I was not, and I could never be pious or frugal enough. I would happily forgo some of these current happier years if I could have one more moment with you, but you would not have approved of any single moment of my life now, though I am shortly to have lived the same number of days as you. I know, Papa, that you would never have uttered the words, but you privately blamed me for not caring more fully to Mama in Paris. I could never get you to understand that she was overtaken by a demon of disease that no priest or doctor could vanquish. I had not seen anyone before or since who was as ill as she, though I suppose in those weeks following *The Magic Flute*, years ago now, buried in my own sickbed and the dragons coming for me at every opportunity, I came close to such illness myself. I made a bargain with God, just like Faust, but as my quill passes swiftly across these pages of my long life, I seem to have lost my need for the past, the very place where I thought I would find comfort in my final years.

There is still great joy in life, but enormous pain as well. When one lives a long time, as I have, memories accumulate and weigh down upon themselves. Papa, Ludwig, cousin Bäsle—so many I will never see again. That is what I fear I have come to believe now.

Schiller was flowery compared to Wolfgang Goethe, but I do remain in deepest love with my opera on Schiller's best play *Die Räuber*, though I saw many other of Schiller's plays in Vienna that I also felt to be fine indeed. *Die Räuber* was the first opera I wrote for America, though I strangely have little memory of actually writing it down. I remember completing it, and naturally I remember its marvelous performances in the Astor Opera House, but I wish I could recall more. My mind and spirit were still recovering from the terrible journey, and I composed as a way to keep my mind from the horrors. All of my *Tempest* was composed at the same time, and by the time we got around to performing it, our singers were beginning to reach their full maturity. The performances were marvelous, and I can recall for the purposes of my testament that they were among the best performances I had experienced in my life. It made me think at the time how I wanted to write other operas on Schiller's work: *Maria Stuart*, I always thought, would make a most marvelous opera, but that would have been impossible in London for obvious reasons, and no one in America cared a whit about a wronged Catholic. I was not allowed a long enough stay in London for my Catholicism to become the issue it undoubtedly would have. *Faust*, dear lonely reader, was my long roadway away from the church of my youth, though I do not think I realized this as the music was taking its shape within me. Dear Papa in Heaven, forgive me!

Gretchen in *Faust*, my greatest soprano role up until my last opera, was a woman so like Konstanze herself, easily swayed by jewels and riches, and disapproved of by Leopold. All manner of trials are heaped on Gretchen's head, and the *gran scena* in which she drowns her own child made me weep in the composing of it. I found an ingenious way of portraying her endless spinning at the wheel, and only recently did I find the great titan Schubert having conceived a lovely song in D minor that displayed Gretchen's plight quite differently from mine.

I long still to meet this young Schubert, and only hope that someday it may be possible, but I cannot imagine how that might be so. Would he ever make the long journey across the sea? He was, of all places, from Himmelpfortgrund, right in Vienna, where we used to send our mad; and appropriately enough, Ludwig lived there when I first knew him. Schubert, though still just a boy, has written the most magnificent symphonies. The earliest one I knew about is a B-flat major that gave me tremendous delight, as it is full of the musical qualities I thought Vienna had lost in their relentless fascination for Ludwig's insanities. I actually led it at the Astor Opera House and the orchestra loved playing it.

Schubert had every advantage over me, being right in the center of Vienna from the beginning, instead of stuck in the provinces of a beautiful place like Salzburg, but unlike so many he seems to be taking advantage of his advantages. I have heard about him since he was just a boy of ten, first from Haydn, when Haydn still had wits. The way Haydn—and even Konstanze—wrote me about him made me think they were worried he might be another little Amadeus. As grateful as I am to have seen the world, I would have been more grateful to be born in Vienna, where I could have instantly and easily learned what it took me a lifetime to acquire. Oh, to have been born at a center of music instead of in Salzburg, where the mountains keep the world away and the people isolated.

Thinking of this mysterious Schubert brings to mind other ghosts. Ghosts are everywhere, and unlike me, to my enormous surprise, they are undaunted by oceans. Will Ludwig ever stop coming to me? I cannot write of him yet, and I wish I could stop thinking of him, but there are many days in the quiet of this beautiful place where I have trouble thinking of anyone else.

Before Goethe and I met as adults on his return home from Italy, I met him in Mainz when I was but seven years old, and he was only a teenager who spoke with the thick Frankfurt accent that always made me laugh. I felt none of the affection held by so many for his *Sorrows of Young Werther*, and I thought him a blasphemer for a long time, proving something more of myself than of him. Werther could not accept that a woman with whom he was obsessed did not love him. This is not a failing of love but a triumph of the mind's sickness that I felt had no need for romanticizing. If a woman did not love me, I moved on to the next! Goethe initially had wanted me to write an opera on his *Werther*, but it could not hold my interest so strongly. Such things should not be put in an opera, or anywhere else, for that matter—or so I thought in those years.

I had dark dreams on the days when I would compose *Faust*'s devil, and most especially on the day I wrote the church scene; and as I confess these words to my parchment, I still cannot believe that I wrote that entire long scene in a single passing from morning to night, but I did.

After six months, it became clear that John's hope to open the opera house within a year was a delusional ambition. Indeed, he explained, the building of the Astor Opera House would take at least an additional three months. I feigned disappointment when actually I was relieved to have the extra time to identify and train the singers and prepare the settings. John had suggested a set of scenic artists who painted wallpapers and copied paintings for American markets, and I found them fine enough, but there were so many scenes in both *The Magic Flute* and *The Labyrinth*, and the designs had to be made in such a way as to change the scenes in a relatively small amount of time. The capabilities of the Astor Opera House, though not yet known, were said to be the most advanced in the world. But these scenery artists questioned what that meant, as they had little idea what theaters in Europe were capable of achieving. Could they hang two painted settings close to each other? How close? Their unfamiliarity took up time, so very much time.

The lighting of the opera house was ordered from London and arrived far before it was needed. It comprised a complex set of whale oil lamps surrounded by mirrors, quite a number of mirrors for the candles which would light the stage itself. Music stands arrived for the orchestra, with sconces for two whale oil candles on either side.

I was disappointed in the wait to open my operas, but the delay gave me time to train the necessary singers and, truth be told, to finish my ideas for *Faust*. I find it quaint now that we all thought the Astor Opera House would open in 1803, or that I would have so enormous a work as *Faust* completed in so little time. At least we were able to form the Astor Orchestra and give concerts from just after my arrival until the Opera House eventually did open, and it staggers me to this day, in 1805. It took a full three years to build the vast theater! It also amuses me that we held on to *Faust* for so long, knowing I would need many more years to finish it. I decided we would open with *The Magic Flute* and *The Labyrinth*.

CHAPTER 87

When I had trouble understanding a problem, whether in a composition or within my love for Alice, I took myself to a small field north of John's house from which the great Hudson River could be seen. In all my early years in New York, from 1800 until well into 1805, I slowly walked a Chartres Labyrinth that I had worn down over time. There was no labyrinth on the ground there or anywhere else in America that I knew of, but with my memory that knew things that others did not, I could conjure one in the recesses of my mind, and it never failed to calm me. I used precisely the same number of steps I had used in Chartres as a child, and slowly the labyrinth wore itself into the ground. All my life, the dearest places that lingered in my memory were exactly like my new labyrinth in the grassy meadow in New York: places that had been worn down by their use.

The places in Salzburg where Nannerl and I had played as a child had their own little pathways worn down by us and other children. When I returned years later, I found the reclaiming of the pathways by nature to be bittersweet and moving. I knew that someday my labyrinth in the field looking at the Hudson would be given back to the forces that always govern such places, but for now it was my favorite place in my new city. In those early years with Alice, there was much that required resolution. As far as I knew, John either knew all about me and Alice and did not care enough to mention her, or he truly did not know because Sarah decided it was best to keep it from him. As the winter approached, I found myself at the open field tracing the labyrinth on more days than not. My love for Alice caused much inner and outer turmoil, but my love only increased each day. Nothing could diminish it.

I suspected that Alice had training in medicine, for like Tamu she always knew what herbs and salves would speed the healing of minor ailments. She shared very little of her past with me, as she was as content to hear the details of my life as I was to speak about myself. She adored hearing of Vienna and Prague particularly, and she said they felt as exotic and foreign to her as America must have long felt to me. She shared that she had been raised in New York, which was itself an exoticism, as I rarely met anyone in New York who was born there. I wondered how the city could possibly continue to grow, as it felt already to be as large and as busy as it was possible for it be. It was an island, so would run out of space eventually. I asked Alice discreetly about her childhood, but she was always reticent. I was so bold as to ask if I could meet her parents and ask for her hand, but she said that would be impossible. I asked if she knew both of her parents and she said she did, but always she would turn our speaking back to something about me.

It was only in the summer of 1804 that Alice revealed anything to me about her parents. She told me she was being called to a nearby household in Greenwich Village to care for a man who had been shot. "My father has sent for me urgently, to care for a man who has been shot in a duel in Hoboken," and with that she informed me that her father was a doctor. Alice received his letter from a carrier on horseback, and she instantly joined the man to ride all the way up to Greenwich, the farthest reaches of the city before it turned to open fields. I wanted to join her to assure her safety, but she would not allow it. Alexander Hamilton's injured body had been brought to a house in Greenwich, and he lived less than a day. Alice attended him from his arrival in the house until his passing. She was the only person with him at the moment his soul passed on. I knew that Alexander Hamilton was important to the nation, though I had not followed why, but I was proud of my gorgeous Alice for tending his soul on its passage. After Hamilton died, I learned more about him, and

I mourned all of those who, like Hamilton, were not known until they died for their country.

Alice never spoke of him again, but it became clear to me that the world turned on those few people who could ride away on a moment's notice to care for someone. These are the truly brilliant people of life, not musicians or creators. People who knew exactly when and how to apply a poultice to ease someone's suffering, or what herb to administer and at what moment. These are the silently brilliant.

This is what I testify to be the most remarkable thing about Alice, and she alone has provided this profound lesson of my life. She lives her own life in silence. I have been paraded in front of people for my whole life. Even all these years after my name became world renowned when Nannerl and I were children, people even of the uneducated classes seem to know my name. I am aware of eyes peering at me whenever I walk to the opera house in lower Manhattan, just as they had in Vienna. Even my short errands in Vienna would be noticed, and I could hear people whisper as I passed. But not Alice. She has never been noticed by anyone, nor has she sought their attentions. Papa scolded me for years for never thinking of anything except being noticed. I never listened to him, but he was right. I did everything in my life to get noticed, and Alice has shown me the quiet way. Now my days are mostly filled with the sounds of the forest around us, interrupted occasionally by a carriage. The great Potomac River never makes its presence known. It is as silent as Alice. But as always, dear ones, I am ahead of myself. Patience.

CHAPTER 88

My biggest worry as our first season approached, so I thought, was how to find singers. In a country that had yet to develop a tradition of singing, there were very few of my hearing who were capable of singing the great roles in *The Magic Flute*, and those few I found needed constant training. The roles I created in *Faust* were very demanding. I wrote to the court in London to see if any of my fine cast at the Drury Lane would be able to make the crossing to appear in the first season at the Astor Opera House, but, unsurprising, I received no reply. I wrote to Konstanze about singers she knew in Vienna who might be willing to travel to America to appear in the first operas produced in our young country, but it had been months since I had heard anything at all from her, even though she knew my new address on Vesey Street. I made it clear to her that *The Magic Flute* would be performed, and she knew *The Labyrinth* as well as anyone. She would have heard about *Faust*, at least, from Goethe. *Magic Flute* and *Labyrinth* could utilize the same cast, but almost none of those singers could also appear in *Faust*. We needed a great many singers.

I had heard no one yet in New York of the quality of Nancy Storace, one of the greatest singers of my experience. I wrote Nancy, to whom I had not spoken in years. I knew it was a distant possibility but I could not fail to try to find her.

25 July, 1804

Nancy Storace, King's Theatre, London

Dear Nancy—You won't believe it is actually me, your old Wolfgang, writing you from another world. Yes, I did it. I came to New York, in a way that you would not believe even if I confessed it to you in church. How are you, my darling Nancy? I have a question for you and that new husband (I assume you have married John by now, you brazen woman!).

Would you be willing to come to New York to teach singing? I have been given the dream position here by John Jacob Astor, and the man is both crazy and rich enough to build an opera house in New York and to have me prepare a production of my new opera *Faust* as well as *The Magic Flute* to open it. Can you believe it? On many days I cannot.

John has said he will spare no expense to develop opera and fine music in New York. If you were to come here to teach, you would be virtually the only teacher of singing of real distinction and accomplishment in this large city. There were a group of singers I met near Philadelphia who were very fine, and there are many interested and talented singers in New York, but they need your training. Would you come, please? Join me in New York and we could have the most wonderful time.

Kiss your ass, **Wolfgang**

I remembered the exercises Nancy used to sing before rehearsals, and the remembrance brought other memories to mind. I could recall so many of the exercises I used to employ as a pianist, those to limber up the fingers and set the mind to work in various keys, in counterpoint and then retrograde counterpoint. I loved them because they were fun little puzzles. I knew it would not take me long, so I set to work writing down all of the exercises I knew, as well as ways to embellish and improve them. All of my own keyboard tricks might be an interesting tool to publish someday to help people teach.

Singers began pouring into the music shop, having heard that I was offering lessons in how to improve their voices. I longed to have Nancy with me, or any number of other singers, to help me train the singers we needed in New York in those years who could be equal to the available singers in London or Vienna. It was the tallest of orders, dear friends.

So great was my worry that I went to Sarah with a proposal to open a singing school. Though not a singer myself, I had taught the basics of musicianship to many singers, and I understood the basics of singing well enough to take a talented voice to its potential. A whole generation of singers was going to have to be created, and I expressed my fears to both John and Sarah, who explained that all of their own successes were born from just such seemingly impossible situations. John had been told that so few people could afford furs that it was an impossible business in which to invest so much of his own time and money, but as it turned out he made a fortune from his own instincts. So it would be, John said, with opera in the young country of America. John believed that opera could change the landscape of the nation, because his own love of singing had taught him so. John loved to sing, and his favorite nights at his home on Vesey Street were gatherings with his growing children around the fortepiano and singing songs that I taught them. My "Das Veilchen" was John's favorite, and to hear his own children sing it, though it was very challenging for them, was something he said he would remember far into his old age. John encouraged me to open my singing school, and he put Sarah in charge of it.

CHAPTER 89

On the very day John and Sarah agreed to opening a singing school, that man named Paine walked into the instrument shop and greeted me. He said he wanted to hire a small orchestra for a funeral service. I could not immediately recall the first I had heard of his name, but the smell of the particular tobacco coming off him took me back to Lewes, and the many remarks that I resembled a man named Paine. Looking at him across the counter of the Astor Music Store, we did indeed look similar.

Paine was one of the few people I met in America who knew who I was before I got there. Lorenzo and others, including the kindly man in Lewes who had given them to me, had tried to get to me to read the writings of Paine, either in German or in French. But I had resisted, bored as I was by anything political. Paine was all politics. By a certain point of life, though, I knew that the politics of the moment were the reason I had risked the horrendous trip to America, and politics provided the reason John had the money to give me the life I had always dreamed. It was always complicated for me to think about people like Paine, because he was a reminder of that rascal Voltaire. Men of his type liked to stir political feelings without knowing what they were doing, without offering solutions to actual problems; yet friends I deeply respected thought Paine had paved the way for the American Revolution. I knew the need of revolutions, but I wanted them to happen without having to know about them. Still, standing in front of him, he was impossible to ignore.

"Herr Mozart, I have heard your name from my youngest years. It is an honor to meet the man who wrote *The Marriage of Figaro*," Thomas said.

"Where did you hear *Figaro*?" I asked.

"In Paris, during the best years anyone will ever have in Paris," he said.

I asked what brought him to New York.

"It is identical to what brings everyone to New York. Everyone here is running from something. This is a new start, is it not, Herr Mozart?"

I did not like his tone. I had refused to read Paine's *Rights of Man* because I thought the title impertinent: man had no rights of any kind to give to another, for all rights came from God. But since arriving in America, and seeing what the rights of men actually were, I was beginning to think differently about politics. I was beginning to see that the actions of a government affect the lives of real people like Tamu, like those poor people on the *Gregson*, and that the rights were not what I had been taught they were to be. I took it as something as real as the Gospels that men were born free and remained that way unless they committed a stinking act deserving of punishment. Alice made me feel very differently about the rights bestowed by men.

Paine knew a lot about music, which impressed me, but with him standing before me, I found it difficult not to blame him for the revolution that destroyed France. I liked the old regime before it decided to revolt, as they loved my music and paid me handsomely. The revolution in France took away all of the beautiful things and made everything that remained uglier than it had been before. Great operas and paintings made possible by the royal family were all taken away. What was France to do with no royal patronage? I had found out, not so very long before, just what France had become.

I asked him when he was last in France.

"It has been a number of years now. Why?"

"You do not realize the terrible effect of the revolution," I said, irritated.

"Terrible? There was no choice. Just as there is no choice here. There will be more revolution here, I can tell you, and probably not too long from now. Fifty years at the most, probably much sooner," Paine said.

"I do hope not. I have seen quite enough of politics."

"*Figaro* was the best play in history, and you made it into the greatest opera. How I wish you could have written a work directly with Beaumarchais instead of using that rascal Da Ponte," Thomas said.

"Lorenzo was, and remains, the greatest poet for the theater, so I do not know why you speak against him, especially in these first few moments of meeting each other. Beaumarchais would never have allowed what I did to *Figaro*, because he wanted it all to be about politics," I said.

"*Figaro* is entirely politics, Herr Mozart."

"*Figaro* is entirely about love, Mr. Paine."

"Were there no politics, none of the love would be interesting," Paine said.

"Were there no love, none of the politics would have any purpose," I said, sure I was bringing our tense discussion to an end.

"Da Ponte merely took the best of Beaumarchais and arranged it as poetry," Paine said.

"Merely? He translated an entire libretto from German, not French, into Italian, and wrote a libretto in rhyming couplets. Every sentence is a rhyme, and all of the characters rhyme as themselves, yet one is never aware of Lorenzo. I know of no one else in the world who could have achieved such a feat," I said to the impertinent little shit.

He tried again. "Perhaps my Italian is not brilliant enough to discern the subtleties, but it seems to me it is your music that makes *Figaro*, not that rascal's mimicry of Beaumarchais."

"No, it was I who outlined what of Beaumarchais we were to keep and what to excise. I wanted no revolutionary scenes of any kind, except Figaro saying no to his master. I wanted an opera about people, not governments," I said, never having articulated it before. "It was I who decided the progression of the long finales, but Lorenzo did everything else."

"Well, we shall get nowhere on the subject of *Figaro*. Did you enjoy Lewes?" Paine asked.

"I thought it one of the loveliest places I have ever seen. Windy and sweet." I enjoyed the remembrance.

"It is hell on earth. Dirty and small-minded and dull. I could not wait to get out of that White Hart horror."

"Would you like to buy a viol?" I asked, hoping he would leave.

To my shock, Paine indeed purchased a viol, testing it out and surprising me with his proficiency. He thanked me for our conversation and vowed to see me again now that we were both living in proximity.

I thought Paine to be well-named, but there was intrigue about him as well, like there had been with Lorenzo. I silently hoped I would not have to experience such a disagreeable man again. Still, Paine was important, and he was a writer. I wondered if he might be willing to be the poet of an opera, if he could do so without getting too political. I liked that Paine was against slavery, and I remembered hearing some writings of his about the Indians of America, reminding me that I knew nothing about them at all.

I enjoyed the company of people who were not like me. But too much difference filled me with fury, as I could not countenance Lorenzo's behavior, nor his constant disappearances and his lying. Writing operas with him was not easy, as it was difficult to get Lorenzo to concentrate. Swaths of time would pass when he would do nothing, and then suddenly he would bring me half of a completed act. I had similar periods of inactivity followed by frenzy, so I needed someone who would be predictable and steady. If my partner's work flowed evenly, my own erraticism had balance. Because balance was the one thing I never could achieve, it was the one thing I most desired. And here it was again, balance, showing itself as a desire in a new nation. My old devils followed me across the sea, yet I had been so sure they could be left behind.

CHAPTER 90

The opera house had begun with just a tiny building, a small hut with a wood stove, where John would occasionally visit the architect and builder who was overseeing the massive building, one of the largest in New York, probably one of the largest in the world. I often went out of my way to walk by it, though it was far from my normal New York pathway of Vesey Street to the Wall Street shop. John approved the hiring of hundreds of men to build his opera house as quickly as they could manage. From the laying of the foundation stones to the installation of the lanterns and curtains was to be the span of only four seasons, little more than a year, but everything took longer than John anticipated.

The year 1804 became the busiest one of my life, because John desired a set of concerts to get New York excited about my music. We had to get an orchestra ready for a new opera house and, eventually, we would have to train a chorus—but that required many more singers than we had. Because of the Astor Music Store, I got to know nearly every musician in New York, so I convinced Sarah to allow me to have small concerts in the upstairs studio where I worked.

"This is the only way I know, Mrs. Astor, of discerning how well a man may play one of the instruments purchased here," I told her.

"It will take you many months to find all of the musicians in New York," Sarah said, understanding my predicament.

"I will do it in weeks, Mrs. Astor. I promise you."

I was always unrealistic about how much time a task required. To Konstanze, this had been the single most frustrating thing about being married to me. I would plan a few hours for work that would actually take several days. I always refused to accept deadlines and schedules, but because John and Sarah had made their needs so clear, that I produce an initial New York concert, I set to work quickly. I had met several violin teachers in the store, and over the ensuing weeks I arranged to play some of my own sonatas with their students. To my amazement, Sarah had acted quickly to get music publishing to be a part of the store, setting a builder to the task of creating enough bins of the right size, and word quickly spread that the Astor Music Store had the largest selection in New York. James Hewitt, to my delight, was hired to oversee the printed music, and he discussed many issues with me about how to get more of my own music published. I handed James what music I had, the compositions for which I had fair copies, and I explained to him the contents of my music trunk.

I enjoyed the company of Hewitt, and he and I pored through the printed music that seemed to arrive in great bundles on each arriving ship. I was as grateful to find a copy of Bach's *Well-Tempered Clavier* as I was irritated to find a collection of Ludwig's early sonatas. So much new music was being printed, much of it from composers right in America, and I longed to meet them all. I found Hewitt's own compositions to be interesting and tuneful, fun to play, and it seemed to thrill John to hear me play them. I found quartets by someone named Giovanni A-T-S, the most bizarre name I had ever seen, and they were lovely, if a little simplistic. Hewitt told me "Giovanni" was actually John Antes who lived in Pennsylvania, an immediate warning to me that I might not want to meet him. I finally told Hewitt about what happened to me in Germantown.

Hewitt said, "I assure you, John Antes is not like those people. He is in a beautiful community of Moravians. We must visit there sometime."

I told him I did not wish to see Philadelphia again.

"John, 'Giovanni,' is often in New York. You will meet him. The man you must meet most immediately is John Moller, the wonderful organist of Trinity Church. He is also one of the great violinists in the city, and he will be overjoyed to meet you."

This was most exciting to me, meeting more and more musicians. I was starting to believe we might actually be able to assemble an orchestra.

"There is another young man of great talent, I think: Anthony Heinrich, not more than twenty, who you must meet. He is from Bohemia, just arrived from Boston, where he was stranded by an uncle who lost everything. He is somewhat of a lost young man, but I think he could be a great help to us in forming the orchestra for Astor."

"Where is he?" I asked.

"He is currently living in our home, helping my wife with our little one, Sophia, who is already showing promise on the fortepiano. You should hear her!" A great glow came over Hewitt when he spoke of his daughter.

"I would love to hear a talented youngster. We have so much to do, though, to get this orchestra put together, do we not?" I said.

"We do. Let me arrange for John Moller to come to the shop. And you should hear him at Trinity Church. Such a wonderful instrument there."

"Really? Has he played any of my organ music?"

"I'm sure he has. Have we any of your organ music in the shop?" James asked.

"Not that I have seen. Most of it was never published. I wrote more organ music for St. Stephen's than Bach wrote for St. Thomas!" I wasn't sure if I was fully speaking the truth, but I knew I had written a vast amount.

"How can we acquire it?" James asked.

"I have written Konstanze, though all of my organ music must still be at St. Stephen's. I don't know if they would allow me to have it." I never imagined a need to sell organ music.

"Organ music is very popular all over the country. There could be a market for it, especially if we are the only shop in the country selling it."

I admired that James always thought about business, as I had no head for it at all.

The concert planning happened quickly, as it had in London, and I was busily meeting new musicians each day. Alice never visited the shop so as not to arouse any suspicions, but we spent each late night together in my quarters before she would go to her own home to sleep. It nagged at me that I needed to write Konstanze, made all the more difficult by having fallen in love with another woman. I was never one for confrontations, particularly by letter, as I hated disappointing anyone. Still, I needed what I needed.

17 October, 1804

My darling Konstanze,

A lifetime seems to have passed. I am at home in New York now, and John and Sarah Astor are the angels I have always sought and needed. No king or emperor has been so generous to me as they have been. I have private quarters within the Astor home, which is itself the size of a palace. I can scarcely believe that your letter asks me for still more money. As you well know, Mr. Astor has agreed to provide a stipend for you and little Franz each month, which you can retrieve from the furrier shop on Weihburggasse 17. Let this be enough for you, please, and do not ask me again.

I have a studio above the instrument shop where John and his wife Sarah have asked me to work to earn their generosity. The shop is fascinating, and I am meeting all of the musicians in New York, as they all come in to see the wares but also, it must be said, to meet me. I was surprised at how much my name seems to be known in this new land. How can it be so?

What is to become of my darling wife, Konstanze? You will never come to America, I know. And I am within a rare dream, able to compose operas that will be seen here in the New World and, I hope, at home in Vienna and in other places I am unlikely to see again: Prague, Berlin, Milan, Naples, Paris, London. This is my new life, my darling, and I am sure you are having a new life as well. We know what this means. For our own health and love, we must each marry again. We must ask St. Stephen's to break the bonds of our marriage, just as you have described. Can you do this? You walk by the church every day, and you must still know everyone there.

I know this will not please you, but I need for you to pack my remaining music and mail it all to me. I know this will be a great trouble and expense, but I will find a way through John to get money to you. Also, could you ask at St. Stephen's for my organ and choir music to be mailed to me here?

There is so much interest here in America in the music of Mozart, and I really must have all of it here with me. There is so much chamber music and so many sonatas that I'm sure I've forgotten. In truth, I am longing to see all of my old friends that I wrote long ago. Please send them to me at Astor residence, Vesey Street, New York, America.

I miss you and little Franz, and I kiss you both, especially you, on your little pink ass. I can understand many things, my darling, but I can never understand how we can never see each other again.

Ami

Outside of composition, I had not seriously played the fortepiano since leaving London. I started arranging small concerts in my studio above the store, two a week, including one with John Moller, the only violinist capable of playing my second-oldest A-major sonata, the one I always loved the most. I wrote it as Lorenzo and I were writing *Don Giovanni,* and I was able to use material I had rejected for the opera within it, so to me if to no one else, it was my *Leporello* sonata. The opening movement contained all the music I had hoped to use for the catalogue, but the scanning of Lorenzo's Italian did not work well in it. The middle movement was my original idea for the trio between Elvira, the Don, and Leporello, but I thought it not quite right and changed to music in three instead of four beats per phrase. The final movement of my sonata was its own world, one of the most challenging for all fingers involved, and I always loved its little tricks to the ear. John Moller was amiable and kind, the first violinist I met in New York who could really play.

Often I ventured to Trinity Church to hear Moller rehearse on the organ. John and Sarah occasionally attended services at Trinity, always inviting me to join them, but since arriving in New York I had been unwilling to attend a church service. I held lingering pain from what happened at Germantown that I knew I would have to examine someday.

In Vienna it would have been unthinkable to go to Lodge without also attending church, but in New York I was able to have the solace of Masonry without the burden of also attending church. John's Lodge was a beautiful building that many passed without even knowing what it was. It sat on Wall Street not far from the shop, and it looked somewhat like the large stone banks in London. I rejoiced in my new Masonic brothers in New York, though there is obviously little I can say about them and remain true to my order. They were the finest men in the New World.

Besides admiring John's playing, I enjoyed that John never implored me to come to services in the way so many church musicians usually did. I found time to compose a new prelude and fugue especially for John, calling it *Trinity*, which John loved. It was my best work for organ, I feel sure.

I noticed that John Moller was especially attentive to me, in a way that reminded me of many other men I had met around churches. I knew that Moller probably had a secret, but so did I: Alice. It did not bother me, though I could not understand John's feelings, which he was making more and more clear to me. I hoped that Moller could find some way to feel for someone the love that I felt for Alice, or what I felt at one time for Konstanze. My love for Alice made me realize how difficult it is to fulfill a love that has something forbidden about it. It made me sad for Moller, as he seemed to love me in some way I could not return, though it was nothing we ever discussed.

Within a few days of rehearsing together, I felt close enough to Moller to tell him about my trip from Liverpool. He was shocked by it, and kept saying that he wished he could have comforted me somehow, or wished I could have joined him, as Moller's trip from Hamburg had been so different, relatively comfortable and exciting, and his ship had excellent food. Moller and I had been born nearly at the same time, and he was the first musician of my acquaintance in New York who felt like the musicians I had known in Vienna. I knew Moller could be an enormous help in forming the orchestra for the concerts and then for my operas. I asked him if he would serve as my Kapellmeister, the principal violin of the orchestra, and he cried when he accepted.

"Moller, I am eager for you to meet Alice. I am more in love with her than I have ever been with any woman in my entire life. She is the most beautiful woman on God's planet!" It felt good to say the words aloud.

"That is wonderful, Amadé. I am delighted for you." That's what he said, but he seemed more sadly happy than delighted.

What amazed me about Moller was that we needed very little rehearsal together, even for my difficult A-major sonata. Many of the other musicians I had met, and with whom I was rehearsing, required a great deal more time, but Moller and I rehearsed only twice, both times at Vesey Street, and he was confident from the start. Moller said he had occasionally come into the shop to buy organ music, but I had no memory of seeing him there. As I had long known, the more two musicians think alike, the less the need of rehearsal. Of course, when works get to be very large, like *The Magic Flute*, there is no choice but to rehearse and rehearse, because it takes so long simply to get so many people to play music together. Moller remarked, too, on how little those who enjoy music think about its execution. I recalled to him instances in which I had felt like two minds thought as one, but more often I was dismayed at how difficult music was made by so many musicians, many of whom played things at wrong tempos or insisted on focusing on meaningless details. The heart of music back then remains to this day, the great *line*, and it was not something that could be taught or explained. The line was everything, that slow river of tone through which music moves. The line never stops; we just occasionally join it. Many musicians can play notes, but only artists have the *line*.

CHAPTER 91

Since I had divulged a secret to Moller by telling him about Alice, he returned the favor to me, but it was an uneasy secret. He told me that his rector at Trinity Church, Benjamin Moore, entered the sanctuary one afternoon to question him about his friendship with me, saying I was not known to attend church regularly, and that I was raised a Roman Catholic.

Moller reported being asked, "What is your business with him?"

Moller told him, "Reverend Moore, Herr Mozart has brought so much music to life for me. We are nearly the same age, and from the earliest time I can remember as a child in Germany, I have heard about him. Any child interested in music will have heard of him. Besides royalty, Amadé was the most famous person in the world when I was growing up. He is my first friend in New York who feels like a musical brother."

Reverend Moore then intimated that Moller's fascination with me went beyond the usual bonds of friendship. Moller knew immediately what the reverend meant, as did I. All of Moller's attempts to conceal his feelings for me, or any number of other men in New York, had been unsuccessful. Moller confessed to me that he thought the reverend had him followed, and then he confessed something shocking: tales of his late-night meanderings around the South Street Seaport, where the simplest of his desires could be satisfied anonymously, without consequence, as the sailors who momentarily were pleasured by him inevitably were gone by the time he returned. Moller thought it far enough away from Trinity Church not to be seen, but wondered aloud if Reverend Moore had assigned someone to follow him. Moller was suddenly terrified, thinking back just on his previous few nights.

I could see that Moller was in terrible turmoil, and though I repeated to him that I held no understanding of such desires, I suggested to him that he try to imprison his affections. He should pray earnestly each day and night to be delivered from desires which might destroy him.

I further suggested that perhaps Reverend Moore knew of Moller's escapades along the sea front not because he had him followed, but because the good reverend was there seeking the same thing. Moller laughed at that, though I was not joking. He was being pressured to confess where he spent his evenings, and trying not to implicate me, so I asked Moore about becoming the Kapellmeister of the Astor Orchestra. Apparently the rector was not satisfied with Moller's answer, so he confessed to me the lie he told Moore.

"Amadé, I am so sorry, I told him I had been seeing a woman, and I told him it was Alice, the girl in the employ of the Astors. Your Alice."

This startled me at first, having known many of the machinations of reverends and archbishops and thus hoping he had not put Alice in jeopardy. But I knew Moller well enough to know he was just trying to end the interrogation. It apparently worked, as Reverend Moore told Moller that any of his impure desires would disappear once he found a nice Christian woman, which is how Moller described Alice.

"I am sorry, Amadé. I was desperate to come up with a name fast, and the first who came to mind was your beloved Alice. I hope I have not endangered you or her, and I hope my lie will not make its way to Mr. Astor."

I told him that neither John nor Sarah was likely to listen to such rumors, and I told him not to worry himself about it. I had worries enough of my own, trying to keep my relationship with Alice a secret. And there were further secrets to Alice than her just being a mulatta. She confessed to me that her own religious faith was not Christian, and in those moments when she felt the liberty of telling me her feelings, her words were heretical. Had they come from any person other than the woman I loved above all others on Earth, I would likely have yelled that she was a blasphemer. But any words that came from Alice were beautiful to me. I assumed that my terrible pestilence, the rash of which had long departed, prevented me from fathering another child. This was a comfort.

CHAPTER 92

In the many small concerts I arranged at the Astor store, and with the help of Hewitt and Moller, I assembled enough musicians capable of playing my compositions. I was then able to go to the Astors to arrange our first concert at the Royal Amsterdam Theatre, not far from the store, and the only theater John and Sarah considered to be of fine enough quality for their desires. John Astor paid each of the musicians a small sum in gold bullion that he personally brought from his bank. No musician in America had ever before been paid in real money for their labors, and they were astounded that John paid them in full at the end of each rehearsal.

For the concert, and on Moller's advice, I chose music I thought would best train my new orchestra. We began with the overture to *The Magic Flute*, which they did not yet know was going to help them when they had to learn the entire opera, plus another overture, to *Figaro*, that was significantly more difficult. I then played two of my own piano concertos, the B flat from years ago, which I had numbered in my logbook as my twenty-seventh, and one I had written since arriving in New York, in E flat. I had lost track of the numbers by then. It was perhaps my fortieth piano concerto. I then selected two symphonies, one earlier, my Symphony No. 40 in G minor, and my more recent *Tempest*.

The rehearsals were arduous, for while the musicians were each willing and capable, as a group they had never played anything so difficult as these works. The symphonies were initially nearly impossible for them, particularly the *Tempest*, and I found it challenging to get them to play the correct fast tempo of my G-minor finale, as they kept slowing down to make it easier to play.

"Clarinets! When you have to sustain chords, please do not slow down. You must keep feeling the pulse inside of them!" I must have said this a hundred times.

"We are just following the string players!" the first clarinetist spoke back to me.

"My friends, please. I simply ask that you keep an inner pulse with me. I am playing continuo, but you can sense me from where you are, where we all are."

The clarinetist spoke up again. "We cannot see or hear you, Herr Mozart, so what are we supposed to do?"

I implored, "Please just do your best to stay with me. I will try to do more than play and nod. I will use my arms in those places, but you must follow and pay attention! Do not have your head buried in the music all the time." I was annoyed to find clarinetists just as much trouble in the New World as in the Old. If only they could all play like Anton Stadler, but it seemed unlikely anyone would ever master the new instrument again as he had. Stadler could sound like the greatest singers, often even better, and I loved how quietly he could play, always with the sweetest spirit in the sound. So many of these other clarinets sound like some kind of duck, sending their tense squeaks and squawks all over everything and covering every other sound. Nothing agonized me like clarinets, and yet I kept writing for them. Where is my sense?

"I wish I could hear Stadler again," I said to myself.

"Herr Mozart, we are just trying to stay together with you," the clarinetist said, not making the situation easier.

"I shall do my best to make it easier for you," I said, wondering when a clarinetist was someday going to make it easier for me instead of me for them.

Clarinetist aside, mostly our new orchestra was amiable and hard-working, and many had never played in such a large ensemble before. None had ever played a complete symphony, much less two, and these were both very difficult and long works. I worked them hard, going home each night to Alice, who dutifully heard my long stories of worry about the concerts, how I felt my life with the Astors depended on the success of this single event, as though I had never done a thing of worth before. John had been so generous, I told Alice, but might he stop or change his mind if the New York public did not take well to my concert? Might he regret building his opera house, or put a stop to it? He had spent so much already that it was probably too late to turn back, and I also knew that the whims of the rich were unpredictable. I had seen it all too many times.

I found, too, that our new orchestra was unaccustomed to playing piano concertos, and they found it difficult to hear me playing. The instrument was small but had a penetrating sound. I asked the maker if he could do anything to make the quills sharper to create more sound, but he could not understand my request. I thought often of my dear London orchestra and how quickly they had come together for the King's concerts, but I had been given many weeks to prepare them. For the New York concert, from the first orchestral rehearsal to the performance, I had only a little over six weeks. The concert was announced. The finest seats were reserved for John and Sarah and their friends, and the theater staff placed roses over their seats to keep others from occupying them. The remainder of the seats would be open to whoever heard about the concert's occurrence. John had large posters printed and put up on the side of the theater and at many corner shops where they could be seen by passersby.

CHAPTER 93

My fear for the concerts was a fear shared by all musicians, that either no one would attend, or that those who attended would not understand the music. This was an audience who had likely never heard live music of any quality in their lives, excepting John and Sarah. So I experienced more than my usual amount of fear before performing, particularly about playing two of my own concertos, because it had been so long since I had performed at the keyboard. I had seen many singers suffer from the fear of performance—"stage fright," I had heard my colleagues in London call it—but I had never experienced it myself. I had played for kings and queens and demanding archbishops and rectors and the Lord Chamberlain and André Grétry and all kinds of important people, so I was astounded to feel nervous about performing in a country that had no idea what it was hearing in the first place. Were there any order in God's universe, it was the audience who should have been nervous, but this never seemed to be life's reality.

I suggested to John and Sarah that they allow their household staff to attend the final rehearsal for the concert, which they initially resisted. They explained that the concert was so sought that they were certain I would have to perform more than one concert to satisfy the demand. As the night approached, the household staff were not allowed to come, but Sarah brought Alice to both concerts, given on consecutive nights, ostensibly to help her with her belongings, to act as a lady-in-waiting. I took the meaning of this kindness to be that Sarah understood what was transpiring between me and Alice, and Sarah was giving us her private approval. Had Alice tried to simply purchase a ticket, she would have been refused, and though the Astors and I knew there must have been huge resistance to Alice's presence in the auditorium, no one would dare say a word because she was seated with the Astors.

To my surprise, and I thought even to John's, the New York public reacted with extreme joy and appreciation of the concerts, as though they had been longing for exactly the kind of experience my music gave them. They applauded enthusiastically after each movement, thinking each to be the end. But when they discerned that the concertos were musical designs of three movements and the symphonies of four, they applauded even more at the end of each work. I loved applause between movements, and even during, as I had experienced years before in Mannheim. If an audience hears something that pleases them, they should just applaud. At the end of the New York concert, their applause overflowed, shaking the small Royal Amsterdam Theatre on that cold January night. Theaters were wonderful in the cold weather, because the crowds heated everything but not too much. All my life I have loved winter performances.

In the weeks following, all the talk in New York was of the opening of the Astor Opera House and of my music. I was a child again. Patrons began pouring into the music shop simply to get a glimpse of me, so much so that I had to stop going downstairs at the shop altogether, and I no longer noticed the opening of the front door, for it never stopped. Patrons at the music shop were drawn by the knowledge that the famous Mozart was upstairs at the fortepiano composing music they might soon hear in concerts, or in their opera house. So many shops in the New York were noisy and talkative, but in the Astor Music Store, the clientele was respectfully quiet, like they were in a church, uttering their questions in hushed tones so as not to disturb me in my work upstairs.

John and Sarah were so thrilled that they gave a celebratory dinner for me in the formal dining room on Vesey Street. Alice, of course, had to work to serve the guests, when I actually wanted her at my side to celebrate. Each time she entered the dining hall our eyes met, and Alice gave a slight smile. I wondered how long I could manage to live secluded away in my tower. I was ready to live in my own house, however small, and have Alice join me there. When the Astors gave a dinner, it was a feast. Though they lived like royalty, they did not act it. Sarah had such a hearty laugh it almost embarrassed John.

Over dinner, John explained that the new president of the country, Thomas Jefferson, was preparing to purchase New Orleans from the French, and that John expected the enterprising new president might also manage to purchase as much as he could of the Louisiana Territory, an area that required explaining not only to me but also to Sarah and the few other of John's guests that night who had attended my concerts. John said that the size of the country was about to double, having enormous implications for his fur-trapping business, particularly as the need for fur was increasing in England and France and beyond. John believed his profits could be so high that he could expand the musical instrument business to stores in the old cities of Boston, Philadelphia, and possibly also in the young Washington in the District of Columbia, where the United States government was building their capital. Few people lived in Washington, John said, but what few were there would surely want to have music. I admired that John could speak for a long time to his guests, all of whom stayed silent to hear him; and when John spoke, it was as interesting as being at a play or an opera. You could not stop listening to him, and no one liked when he stopped. I admired this quality, because I was terrible at speaking to groups, even to orchestras. I loved for people to hear my music, but speaking terrified me. Even giving a toast after dinner, as was the custom at the Astors', just as it had been at Joseph Haydn's, was a painful source of fear for me.

CHAPTER 94

In the following months, in every broadsheet all over New York, the talk was of me. "Boy Genius from Salzburg, Now Living in New York, Stuns the City with Concert." I read this headline and laughed that I was still being called a boy genius even as I approached my fiftieth year. The success of the concerts led to many more, two a month, and this gave the opportunity to rehearse the orchestra regularly and move them toward a routine. Moller was a boon, able to help his fellow violinists immediately by making suggestions of fingerings and bow pressure and speed that always made everything go more smoothly. I had worked with many different Kapellmeisters, and Moller was up with the finest of them. I told him that he was as fine as the Kapellmeister I had in London, and because I had so often spoken to him about the high quality of the court orchestra in London, this was the highest compliment I could pay.

Alice's reaction to the concerts filled my heart, for she told me repeatedly that my music had moved her to tears, and it brought up many questions for her. One of the things she most enjoyed about coming to my quarters, even though she had to sneak around to do so, was that it gave her a time to read. I had so many books, most of which came from John and Sarah's collection. But one afternoon, as we were both quietly reading in my tower apartment, I heard her humming a tune of mine, the slow movement of my B-flat concerto that I had played in the first concerts, and then a bit of the E-flat concerto as well, which she had heard me rehearsing in the Astor house. She was singing them in the right keys, which I remarked to her as a little joke.

"You know keys don't mean anything to most people," Alice repeated to me.

"You may not know what the keys mean, but you are singing in them, so you remember them, and only fine musicians can do that," I said.

I hummed one of the tunes from my Negro songs that I had transcribed back in Germantown. Alice did not know the song, but she learned it quickly. I asked her to sing a bit louder, and I tried to teach her the words to the simple song. She was embarrassed to hear her own voice vibrate the old wood of the house, but she told me it felt good to set her voice free. She said she had loved singing as a child, but was always discouraged from drawing attention to herself. I tested several scales on her voice, and she completed each of them in a way I found outstanding. Alice had a ravishing voice of such melting beauty that I asked her repeatedly to sing certain phrases of my music, like the opening of my long-distant "L'amerò, sarò costante," or "Ruhe sanft," and the richness of her sound made me erupt in tears. How had I not heard her voice until that moment? Such a voice should never be silenced!

I made love to her that night in a way I never had. Something in hearing her voice had liberated me as much as her. I had not discovered her voice at all; it was *Alice* who had discovered it. The voice was hers and hers alone. Alice was always enormously giving and generous in the sensuality of our bed. Her natural shyness, and the fear brought on by our illegal relationship, made her seek the solace of our amorous pleasures. Everything built up within her could be released by my touch and kiss, and when I entered her, particularly that night, I felt her body might burst into a million stars, only to have it brought back beyond a peak neither of us could understand but which we knew we needed. Her voice would grace the operatic stages one day, and I felt it would be soon. I would have to find a way to make it possible.

I was teaching Alice some scales, but had moved on to singing the pitches of one of my simpler songs, "Die Verschweigung," which I knew was one of John Astor's favorites because he mentioned that he had heard it as a boy. I decided to teach Alice "Ah, vous dirai-je, Maman," because it was taught to every educated child to help them learn French. Alice seemed to already know it, even singing words to the famous tune. I sang variations to it, and she sang them back to me perfectly.

I prepared and played a concert a month with my new orchestra in the time leading up to the opening of the Astor Opera House in June, and it thrilled me to play as many of my own concertos as I could practicably make possible. The public stood in line for hours to ensure entrance, and John and Sarah were dutifully at each one. For John, the concerts were an investment in his opera house, giving the public a small taste of what their eventual meal would be. Sarah found the concerts to be inordinately expensive, but John always assured her that on balance, they were not costing them very much. Indeed, within three months John was able to increase the cost of tickets to a point that they even turned a small profit, pleasing both of Sarah's eyes, one of which was always on the purse.

I conducted my favorite symphony of Haydn's, one of many he wrote in his beloved G major, and one I heard at the Esterházy palace when Haydn introduced it, shortly after I arrived home from my initial *Don Giovanni*, a time which began my decline into the ill health that might have taken my life but for my good fortune and the grace of God. Teaching the work to the orchestra, I was able to feel their growth, and it was also like sitting down to dinner with Haydn himself, as though we were talking as we always had. It pained me to know I would never see Haydn again, one of the many griefs I had not considered upon leaving Vienna. Having his music on a program of mine, though, which John said must have been the first Haydn performed in the new country, was as big a success as my own music had been, which gave me courage to program other music that was not mine.

As it was told to me in various letters, Ludwig was working on another opera about the constancy of women, an opera called *Leonore*. He had so criticized my opera on the same subject that I could not help but chuckle at the idea he would write such a work. To my knowledge at that time, Ludwig had harbored no relationships with women at all, yet he had the temerity to call our *Così fan tutte* "immoral," as though he knew anything about the fairer sex! He seemed one of those men who preferred aching for love rather than providing it. I was eager to hear his opera if he ever wrote it, but something told me he would never finish it.

My teaching increased greatly in those early years, most especially my teaching of Alice. She was a naturally born singer, able to absorb music quickly. She was an excellent mimic, which is always helpful at the start, but she did not remain within mimicry. She had her own voice and ideas. I began teaching her the duet between Papageno and Papagena in my *Magic Flute*, and my favorite moment of any day was singing it with her. My voice was constantly hoarse and raspy from all the teaching, and my singing voice was nasal and unattractive to my own ears at the best of times, but I *could* sing in my uniquely ugly way. Having heard the duet many times in life, I had naturally heard it sung wonderfully, terribly, and, most often, too slowly. But Alice sang it as I always imagined it, with purity and clarity and the *line*…everything in music is about the line.

Alice sounded better than dear Anna Gottlieb, whom I talked of constantly and loved, and it always delighted Alice that I compared her favorably to Anna. Anna had been so young, only seventeen so she said, though I was always suspected she was considerably younger as she was so inexperienced. Indeed, I had to write out for her what more veteran singers might have improvised. I thought often of writing to Anna, as I wondered how she was, along with so many others, but never did. Alice easily learned the two difficult decorations at the end of the duet, assailing the little turn with the clarity of a violinist, and her highest notes were meltingly beautiful. It should not be possible, but her voice was even more beautiful than she was.

I learned to love *The Magic Flute* in English because Alice could learn it quicker. "We live by love, by love alone!" ended the first stanza, and she would look into my eyes as she sang those words, filling my heart to bursting. "Man and wife, when joined by love…rise to join the gods above," ended the duet, and when Alice sang those lines my voice choked with tears. I realized that although I thought I had felt love many times before in life, I had not. Alice was the first person in my life that I ever fully and completely loved.

CHAPTER 95

I wanted to find a way to place Alice onto one of my concert programs and, eventually, to perform Pamina in either *The Magic Flute* or *The Labyrinth*, probably the former as it was easier for an inexperienced singer and the second Pamina required a huge amount of vocal strength and agility. I knew there might be resistance to Alice singing, and I purposefully did not talk to her about it, knowing the idea would make her tremendously nervous. She had only ever sung in front of me, but hers was a voice that should not only be heard by one person.

I had slowly been teaching her one of my earliest arias, "Voi avete un cor fedele," because it was not too long and the Italian was simple. I had to write it all down again, as there was no score among my luggage and Hewitt had never seen a score to it, but it came back to me quickly. It amused me that I could remember every note and harmony but not the circumstances that originally accompanied its composition. I heard many sopranos perform it over the years. The fast notes in the second half of the aria, such an insurmountable challenge for many, held no difficulties for Alice. I had always loved the longing little melody, and to hear Alice sing it brought it to life in new ways, and with an ecstasy that accompanies the beginning of any life.

One night in my tower room, after Alice had retired to her house, I wrote down on a parchment my desired program for the next concert at the Royal Amsterdam. It must have been for April of 1805:

- A new march by James Hewitt
- An old canon written by Johann Pachelbel
- A new piano concerto of mine
- A new symphony of mine
- "Voi avete un cor fedele," an old aria of mine, sung by Alice Reynolds

No program like this had been done before, and I was especially happy to honor James by performing his music. Pachelbel's Canon was a marvelous work in the old German style, much like the works I learned as a child. Certainly it was old-fashioned, but very beautiful. The Pachelbel score arrived in New York practically unused, having been stored away in a church in Charleston, South Carolina, and it found its way to Hewitt at the shop. I could not imagine the circumstances that got it onto a ship bound for New York, but Hewitt had been contacted from the docks that there was a shipment of music. It would remain a mystery. Was perhaps Pachelbel's son or grandson still in the southern colonies somewhere? I hoped not, because I knew that everything from Virginia to the south was dependent on slaves, and I did not want to think of this music in that way.

The program went to John and Sarah, who both said to me in passing one day that they thought the new program looked "fascinating" and they "couldn't wait to hear it." Hewitt prepared all the orchestral materials, and it came time to rehearse. I had prepared Alice to sing my aria, and she accepted the idea of singing in public with no fear at all, which surprised me. Singing for the first time with an orchestra is a significant challenge for any singer, but most singers have time to work up to such a feat, making me adore all the more that Alice harbored little fear. The only thing that seemed to worry her, as she said to me, was what to wear, as she had no fancy clothing that she knew women wore to the theater.

Sarah helped her with clothing for the rehearsal, placing Alice into her first whalebone corset, and gave her a simple white linen dress and a lovely small hat in which she could conceal her voluminous hair. Sarah advised that Alice's hair be washed the morning of the rehearsal and tucked tightly under the hat, "as no one is used to such an expanse on the top of a lady's head." This in particular made me smile, for one of the things I most loved about Alice was when her hair was set free, when it expanded into a great wavy field of black wheat. I would bury myself within it, loving her scent, and never quite being able to grasp that anyone could have such an abundance of hair on top of them, especially since my hair had long been thin and gray. Only in recent months had I resumed wearing the wigs I had long worn in the Old World. Wigs were expensive in New York, and the few I brought in my trunks, made of goat hair, had not weathered the trip well. But near the music shop there was a wigmaker, and I felt it was time to live more like a gentleman again. John Astor wore no wig, as he had a full head of hair that was the envy of many men. James Hewitt wigged from time to time; Moller never. I was long accustomed to covering my fallow head, and the heat of the wig did not disturb me. I felt more confident with it upon my head, just as Alice felt better having her own hair hidden.

CHAPTER 96

The orchestra was improving, which was a big source of pride. Alice came with me to the theater a week before the concert, and she sat just offstage, waiting for her turn. I took the orchestra through the rigors of "Voi avete," warning them always to maintain tempo. They struggled, strangely, with the last allegro, which I felt to be the easiest part of the aria. One never knows. I could see Alice offstage, listening to the aria she would soon sing, and she smiled at all the new sounds she was hearing. I felt that were Alice to suddenly have her arm accidentally cut, it would not be blood that poured forth from her, but music. Everything about her countenance breathed sound and amity, and I longed to be more like her. I had too quickly become too much of a businessman in America, too focused on getting the details finished. Alice, though, reminded me of the purpose of the work, the *why* in the *how*.

It came time for me to call Alice onstage. The orchestra had experienced no one but me, so to have a singer at all was new—but for that singer to be a Negress was a startling novelty. They had no collective way of reacting. Individually, each musician would have told me that yes, absolutely, they would perform with a Negress, but collectively they were duty bound to be shocked. They looked to me, wondering why I had not told them of her color, but I simply introduced her as Alice Reynolds, and they greeted her with shocked silence. I was careful not to portray my own love for Alice, greeting her with cordiality but nothing more.

I began the aria, leading from the fortepiano, and during the short introduction I glanced toward Alice to see if she yet revealed any nerves, but she did not. She began to sing.

I had known from the start that Alice possessed a voice of unusual beauty, but I had only ever heard her in the great room of the Astor house. Though quite a large room, it was nothing like the Royal Amsterdam. The watery way in which her voice enveloped the entire large space, blooming ever outward, was a marvel. I had heard every great singer in Vienna and other musical centers, but I had never heard anyone equal the beauty of Alice's voice. I knew from that moment that my emotion about her voice was not simply because I loved her, but because she actually was in the possession of a miracle.

The men of the orchestra, initially wary of Alice, were so stunned that many lost their place in the relatively simple early moments of the aria, with bass players plonking their downbeat G's into many upbeats. As the work progressed into the faster section, it was clear to them that they were in the presence of a fellow artist. Alice's highest notes rang out with power that none of them had heard before.

When the final note of Alice's first rehearsal cleared, the orchestra applauded her with both hands and feet. She looked to me, and all I could see was a person who had just done what they were born to do. I also realized something else: that when the forces are right, music is not a struggle to create. It feels effortless and weightless at the keyboard, or in whatever small sculpting of the air as is needed to keep things together. In the presence of a great voice, orchestras play their best, because they want to match her. I had heard it a few times before, with Düssek of course, but also with Nancy, with Anna, even with Emanuel in his funny way, but too often it had been middle ground. I wished the Astors had been at that first rehearsal. Hewitt was there, and he came to me at the rehearsal's completion, awash in tears.

"Amadé, I've never heard anything like that in my life. What an incredible voice she has!"

"Yes, once in a lifetime," I said.

"And you taught her all of that in a few weeks?"

"I did. But when one has a gift such as hers, the teaching is easy."

"The audience is going to lose their minds. They've never heard a sound like this," Hewitt said.

Alice sang the aria at four subsequent rehearsals, improving on it each time, gaining in confidence. When time came for the final rehearsal, I asked John and Sarah to attend. I wanted them to experience her in the large theater. I loved that John called the street in front of his new opera house, *Himmelfortgasse,* the Gate of Heaven Road, even though he knew the real street to be called Lafayette, which struck me as an unusually pedestrian name for a street. Sarah and John loved Hewitt's new march, and they thought Pachelbel's Canon to be a lovely trifle. My new piano concerto was, they thought, an absolute delight. They came to visit me at the interval before the second half of the concert.

"You are writing much more complex music since you came to this country," John said, quite correctly.

"Really?" I mulled over his words. John had been at the London concerts, which were not so very long ago in terms of the calendar, but which felt to be from another lifetime. I knew that the big change in my life was not so much America as it was Alice.

John continued, "Yes, Amadé, I don't know of a more heroic and uplifting piano concerto, do you? It almost brings you out of your seat and makes you feel you can fly!"

Hewitt came to tell me they were nearly ready to begin the second half and that all of the musicians had returned from their pause. A man rushed in behind him. I had seen him before around the Royal Amsterdam.

"Where's Astor?" the man asked all of us.

"I am John Astor, if you please. Who are you?"

"Simpson. I'm the manager of this establishment."

John remained calm. "You seem troubled."

"You bet I'm troubled. No negress is going to sing on the stage of this theater," Simpson said, his face bloated with fury.

"I have rented this theater, sir, for a sizable sum, and we will present who we like," Astor said, making me proud of him.

But my heart sank, because I knew that Alice would be prevented from singing. I wondered how I could tell her such a heartbreaking thing, but then I noticed her behind Simpson. She heard everything.

"It is against the law for her to perform on this stage. You want to ask the police?" Simpson said.

"I've heard of no such law. This woman is a gifted singer and she should be allowed to be heard. She will proceed. Go on, Amadé," John said.

"If you put that woman on, I will bring the police in here and arrest the lot of you. I don't care what you say, the law is the law. John Astor is surely not going to break the law," Simpson snarled.

"If the law is unjust, it is one's duty to break it," John said. I always wished I could think of such words, but my fear kept them hidden.

I could see Alice crying.

"I also hear she's a quadroon and a runaway slave to boot," Simpson said.

I did not know what a quadroon was, but I had never heard Alice speak of being a runaway.

John was getting angry. "That is a lie. Alice Reynolds has been in my employ since she was a child, and she is going to sing on this stage at Herr Mozart's concert or you will not receive a shilling or sixpence for your theater."

"You've no right to break the law," Simpson said, noticing Alice crying behind him. Simpson pointed to her. "Is this the negress singer?"

My chest was tight, but I had to speak up. "Please do not speak of her with such cruelty."

"Cruelty? I need you all cleared out of here right now. I'll take you to court, Astor, and you know very well the court will side with me."

John said, quietly, "Amadé, maybe this just is not the moment. Perhaps we are moving too quickly."

"John, I cannot bear to deprive Alice of this. Her voice is the greatest I've ever heard."

Sarah said, "Amadé, it could risk Alice being jailed. We don't know what could happen."

Simpson spoke up, gleefully, "You bet she will be put in jail, and I will not have this theater associated with such goings-on."

"Amadé, I'm sorry. I promise you, we will find another place for Alice to sing, perhaps at the Park Theatre," John said. "The Park is small but could be nice for a solo singer."

"John, this orchestra has been inspired beyond reason by Alice. We have to go forward. What is the worst that could happen?" I asked.

"The worst that could happen would be that Alice is jailed, and it could harm the prospects for the new opera house."

Sarah quietly said, "John…"

John took Sarah's words. "We have to think about the future. There is only so fast life can move."

Simpson couldn't hold back. "The future ain't gonna be her singing on this stage, I can tell you that."

"You needn't keep talking. We heard you," Sarah said.

I was heartsick. "John, I'm in no position to quit, especially after all you have given me. But this cannot be allowed. This is the silencing of a brilliant artist."

"I know, but I cannot change a whole country," John said, sadly. He looked to Sarah for comfort, and he looked so heartbroken.

John looked at Sarah a long time in silence, and she seemed to give him a strength he had lacked. "Amadé, I ask that you perform the rest of the concert, since there is so much interest and excitement."

"Including Alice?" I asked.

"Including Alice. I am sad to say, my friend, that the world is full of profound wrongs. We have to deal with what we can when we can."

Simpson was furious. "I'll have the police in here, Astor."

"You go right ahead. This theater is sold out for two nights. Are you prepared to pay me all that money back?" John said.

Simpson finally left, yelling about the police, as John and Sarah went to their box for the second half of the concert. I went to Alice to try to explain.

I was afraid Alice might too upset to continue, but I could not have been more wrong. Her voice rang out truly and perfectly, even better than at any of the previous rehearsals. The few people present gave her a taste of that crackling sound of people clapping and the sounds of their feet hitting the floor in appreciation, a sound I was used to in Vienna and had noticed even in London. The audience in their seats would hit their boots on the floor as though they were running, creating a huge roar of love that came toward the orchestra. There were very few people at the rehearsal, but I was thrilled that two of those people were John and Sarah, because I needed them to believe their own ears and not just hear my thoughts about Alice.

They returned backstage after we finished. Both Astors were in tears of joy. They told Alice her voice was the most beautiful they had ever heard. Alice was thrilled. It is so difficult to describe a voice, dear reader. Alice's voice was both large and powerful like the trunk of a tree, while also possessing vulnerable and beautiful leaves that floated on the wind. I knew Alice had the potential to be one of the greatest singers in the world. We returned home together, hoping we had not been seen.

CHAPTER 97

The next morning, the day of the first concert, one of the worst nightmares of my entire life ensued, almost equal to the *Gregson*. I thought I was still within sleep as I heard Alice's voice far in the distance. She was screaming my name, screaming for help. But it was no dream. She was being carried off by the police. John and Sarah were begging the policemen to be gentle. I put on a long coat and went outside to see if I could help. They were hitting my Alice, for no reason other than her crying. John kept asking why she was being taken away, and a policeman said she was not to be allowed to perform. Alice saw me, and her eyes looked so desperate, so heartbroken.

"All she has done is have a beautiful voice!" I yelled, but they would not be moved. Her hands were tied and I could tell she was in pain. "Amadé, help me! Mr. Astor, please!" Her cries were horrible, and they sent me into a strange trance where I could scarcely move my body. John said he would accompany them to the jail and take care of it, and he followed the police in their carriage. Sarah tried her best to comfort me, assuring me that all would be well and that John would fix everything.

"What if John had not been here? What then?" I sobbed. "John cannot fix what made the police come here and take her from her home."

Sarah said she was sure it would be impossible for Alice to sing at the concerts, and I knew she was right. To the credit of John's eternal soul, he returned with Alice within a few hours, and she rushed into my arms. I asked if she had been hurt, and she said she was unharmed, but something within her spirit had been rendered immobile. I could tell. She was not the same. Just the night before, this eternally beautifully woman had vibrated the air of an entire enormous theater and filled it with gorgeous sound and emotional stirrings. And the very next day she was carted away and humiliated simply because of the color of her skin.

John asked that Alice go to her little house so that I could concentrate on doing the concerts. I wanted only to be with her, but I had to respect John's wishes. He explained that he would do everything he possibly could to be sure Alice could sing at a later time, but that the only way he could get her out of jail was to promise that she would not perform at that moment. Simpson's threats had been right, and John had to admit that Alice would be breaking the law and what he wanted to do was work on the law itself rather than risk putting Alice in any more danger. Although distraught, I understood, and I agreed to John's request. The carriage came to take me to the concert and John went with me, leaving Sarah with Alice.

Waiting backstage for the concert to begin, every time I thought of Alice my mind went blank. It was like the bridge of my dream, except I was awake.

I never liked waiting around for concerts to begin, because it gives one too much time to get nervous. Of course, if one isn't there, it makes everyone else nervous, but one must take care to preserve one's concentration. And I had to remember the larger purpose of this and all of our concerts, which was to prepare the public for the work of our opera house. John's and Sarah's deepest wish was to establish opera on the American continent, and through that to establish the teaching of music as central to the fabric of the life of the new country. John knew that whatever was not established early would be difficult to do later.

Even recalling it now, it is a challenging to describe my level of nervousness. I had performed for royalty, but who knew what music would mean to my new country? The orchestra was nervous as well, but they pulled themselves together wonderfully.

I can say that at no point before or since have I ever heard such appreciative and enthusiastic applause. The audience was delirious for us, for music, and there could be no doubt from that first concert that we had done the right thing, and had trained in the right way. They were an orchestra that could nearly have sat beside my court orchestra in London and felt only slightly inferior. My poor sweet Alice.

CHAPTER 98

Back in Vienna a decade before, I had already written what I thought was going to be my opera, *The Labyrinth*, and I had sung long passages of it to Alice, but in those days of her first concert the opera had taken on a different conception for me. I needed a kind of music I had not written because I now needed scenes and themes that differed from my original version. With Alice forbidden to sing, the only way I could focus on the concert was to focus on *The Labyrinth*. I decided to completely rewrite it. My imagination was expanding on what Emanuel originally gave me, and I wanted to include all kinds of Masonic images, especially for my new American audiences where so few would likely be Masons. I could embed wisdom and musical imagery within *The Labyrinth* that I had not in *The Magic Flute*, nor even in the Viennese performances of *The Labyrinth*, because nearly everyone who came to Emanuel's theater was a Mason, so why hide anything?

Thanks to the voyage across the great ocean, and the journey of John finding me again, and now a new horror with what happened to Alice, a wholly new music was forming itself in me, something that went further than the original *Labyrinth*. In moments before waking, moments when I always dreamed, my dreams had changed since meeting Alice. My heart had always yearned for something I could not name, and I finally felt I could express it in *The Labyrinth*—the new *Labyrinth*. I was feeling a rare communion with a creator, not something I had often thought upon. Catholicism had been so focused on what I *did* rather than what I *believed*, yet I felt a deep connection with the wisdom that comes from believing in something greater. This was the problem with Paine and Voltaire and all those dreadful revolutionists: they wanted to make everything an accident, as though it was not always for the best. I had to believe everything was for the best, for I simply had no other way to live.

I wanted to bring the listeners to *The Labyrinth* into the world of the Lodge, the Temple, into a drama that assumes a supreme being and a future existence. I wondered why it had taken me so long to notice that belief in the next life informed everything about this one. I had never thought so clearly about being done with Catholicism, because I had not allowed myself time to think about what had happened in Germantown, and how it was not so different from what had happened in Salzburg, nor at St. Stephen's. Catholics who believed in the tenets of the church were one thing, but so many were busy policing other people that they forgot what they were to believe. I knew there was an inherent need in men to be initiated into manhood. For women, knowing when they became adults was easy, for their bodies bled and their bosoms produced milk when they became with child. Men, though, had no clear idea of when they moved from boy to man. Men lacked any kind of moral or ethical guideline to find mature masculinity.

The Labyrinth had to have an initiation scene that my first version lacked. But after being on a slave ship, I could not have a silly stage trial that was as simple and predictable as in *The Magic Flute*. The initiation scene in my new opera would have to be more realistic, something more akin to what actual people actually experienced as a trial in their lives. I wanted to write an opening scene that involved Tamino and Pamina reading from a cipher book, trying to figure out what the code within the book meant, and where it was trying to lead them. We must always be trying to decode one another.

Though I was unsure it would be allowed, I decided to have the first act of the opera set on or around King Solomon's Temple, on the portico, then in the middle chamber, and the culminating scene of the act taking place in the Temple's holy inner chamber, for which I could create the most ecstatic and intimate music I had ever invented, and Alice could sing it. If I created music for these initiating scenes, it could be based on geometry, just as any finely produced building is, but I had deduce how to make the repeated ratios of buildings re-create themselves in music. Geometry was the greatest symbol of a supreme being, because geometry was something someone had to actually think about. There is nothing random within it. My many fugues for *The Labyrinth* were, then, the perfect expression of the work itself. I thought of a way to increase the complexity of the opera's final fugue by overlaying a retrograde version of the fugue in four parts, creating a simultaneous eight-part fugue, four parts times two, that lasted for the whole of the opera's finale. There had been nothing like it in music before. Writing *The Labyrinth* again turned it into the most complex and most satisfying of all of my operas, in that it was as much fun to dream about and write as it was to hear rehearsals of it. I longed to rewrite *Idomeneo* as well, to give it a modern style.

"As above, so below," I had heard John say to Sarah, and I had heard it before at the Lodge. But I thought it should be reversed—"As below, so above"—because what mattered to me began down below, starting with the inner light of beingness, and it radiated outward into the musical works themselves. Too many composers, myself included, concentrated on the outward meaning of a work. Masonry had taught me that the degrees of understanding and initiation through which every man must pass…well, it was a divine puzzle, how to write an opera that illustrates "As above, so below," or its reverse, and I knew there must be a way.

In memory, most of the big ideas of my life carried great fear along with them. Even just the idea of going to London had been terrifying, but I always composed through the fear and created something to take its place. For those long minutes leading up to the concert, I walked in my mind the labyrinth in the small field north of the Astor house, and an idea came to me that was so strong and so fully formed that I did not fear it. No one had ever come up with this idea before, and it strengthened and clarified as I worked through it. It was not just the complexity of the final fugue that came to me, but an opera just like my labyrinth: exactly the same going forward and backward. I could actually hear it fitting together, a gigantic palindrome. Music could be conceived that worked the same in both directions, as many small works had proven, but not an entire opera. I worried at first that it might too complex to figure out, but as I kept imagining the musical ideas of my earlier version, many of them fulfilled this idea already. There would be no recitatives in this opera, except perhaps in the scene of the nine vaults. I thought through the vault scene, and it could also be made into a palindrome. If each number could be the same forward and backward, then the entire opera would be so.

Finally the time for the concert came, and though I was highly distracted by my new idea to recompose *The Labyrinth*, and also worried about Alice, the performance was highly successful.

CHAPTER 99

After the concert John and I hurried back to Vesey Street, eager to see Alice, but she was not in her house. I feared the worst. I heard no one else at home as I went to my tower room. Happily, Alice was awaiting me in my bedroom.

My heart filled to hear her voice. "Amadé, I know how upset you must be, but you must realize the gift you've given me already. I did not need to have all the rest of it."

"I am here to comfort you, dear one—you should not have to make it easier for me," I told her. "We will find a way for you to sing, I promise."

"As long as I get to sing with you, that will be enough."

"You will sing for more people than just for me. Alice, dear, you know that the time we have here is not infinite, but our life, our feeling of being alive, is the same feeling that Jesus felt, or Handel, or any girl born in Africa. We are all the same," I said, not sensing I was giving her much comfort.

"The feeling may be the same, but we are not all the same, Amadé. You will harm your life by thinking so, because you will create so many expectations for yourself that will only create disappointment."

"I have great belief that much of our life, perhaps all, is a preparation and trial for something more infinite. You will sing, Alice, both here and now, and forever with the angels, forever at my side."

"I want to believe you, dear Amadé, but I am not sure that I do." She gave a sad smile.

"You see, Alice, whatever it is we are made of, not our bodies, but the real people, is something that cannot be created or destroyed." I had never formed the sentence exactly that way before, and never in English.

"You do not believe we are created?" Alice asked.

"Of course, *we* are created, but we are made of something infinite. Our Creator has only the infinite with which to create. That is what makes these disappointments like today bearable, at least for me." I hoped this idea helped.

"And because of this infinity, you believe we will be together always?" Alice asked, and sounding like a young girl.

"I know it, my darling. We will be together beyond our deaths, somewhere in Heaven. Let us stay with that part of ourselves that does not die, my darling…the part of you that sings."

"I've never known anyone who talked as you do. I thought your symphony was so beautiful, really."

"Not too long?" I asked.

"Maybe a little in the final movement," she said, the first time she had ever expressed an opinion about one of my compositions, which made us both laugh. I knew that if we could laugh on such a tragic day, then we might heal and make music together again.

"Alice, Alice…I've come up with so many ideas for *The Labyrinth*, and I believe it is going to be the greatest thing I've ever done, if I can achieve what I hope."

"I can tell from the sound of your voice that you will achieve it. What is it? You've already sung so many of the airs and melodies from it."

My voice spilled out allegrissimo. "None of them are good enough. I hear a whole new kind of music for this opera. It will drive me mad if I cannot achieve it. You see, Alice, I want *The Labyrinth* to echo the book of nature itself. There must be four seasons in the opera, just as there are four quadrants in the labyrinth, as nature rules us all. Do you understand?"

"Do I understand that nature rules us all? I know only how nature made me. There is nothing else in my power to know," Alice said, which did nothing to silence me.

"There is a code of ethics by which we must live, and what happened to you is far outside of it. I want to do what I can, Alice, to make that known. I feel I can place things within *The Labyrinth* that will make the right and wrong apparent. I can only hope. There is a Lodge of Perfection, and I feels it's my duty to try to bring opera to that place, and to try to bring our little world into that place. I cannot change everything, but I can make the world around us safer and better, perhaps."

For Alice, I know, I lacked realism. She did not think the world capable of change, not in the same way I thought it so, and why should she feel this? I had changed her world, to be sure, with a totality she might have thought impossible before meeting me, but I had not changed the larger world at all. She had changed my world completely, but not *the* world. Martyrs are always thought to have changed the world, but did they, really? What changes did Joan of Arc actually bring about? She was burned at the stake for no reason. Hers was a story I knew Alice loved, not because of any redemption she might have attained, but because she died for nothing.

But my words spilled onward. "The first scene of *The Labyrinth*, Alice, is going to be totally different from what I originally thought. A sword has been lost, and the men are raising a stone for the first temple in Jerusalem. We are at a funeral service for Master Hiram. This must be the opening scene, and I have already conceived how it can play identically both backward and forward. Then a character named Enoch, a baritone I'm sure, shows his brothers the nine vertical vaults crossed by nine arches; he shows the constant refinement available to us through study and discipline. Enoch is concerned about preserving what might be lost, and he has been entrusted with ensuring that the wisdom of the world is enshrined in the nine vaults beneath the first temple. They will be the vaults of Enoch, and the crypts of Solomon which cross them. Are you following?"

Alice smiled but said nothing.

"Alice, I will make Enoch a Knight of the Rose Croix—the Red Cross—and he will have his initiations of silence, fidelity, obedience, all like Tamino has in *The Magic Flute*, but he will emulate Jesus himself, not as a Son of God, but as an example, as a great teacher. None of that redeemer nonsense, or the silly trinity. Who in their right mind would believe those things?"

I was surprised at my vehemence, for I was speaking heresy.

Alice said, "Amadé, you have always believed Jesus Christ to be the Son of God. You've said a thousand times you were raised on it."

"Yes, I was raised on it. But I was raised on Jesus Christ as the example of everything. But what if this is wrong, Alice, and we just see him as a figure of great teaching? Then everyone can learn from him, not only Catholics, not only those who believe. I think belief is deeply important, but I do think I have been very lazy about what I believed. We can't just take what we are taught as children and believe it for the rest of our lives. What if we learn something that contradicts that teaching? Is it not important to be able to change your mind?" I said, as if talking to myself.

"Ami…I was raised to believe that our lives are given to us and whatever our lot, our job is to accept it and pray for freedom and peace after death. It was too much to hope to have everything in life."

I blinked at her, for Alice had never said those things to me before.

"But Alice, you are paid by Mr. Astor. You are not a slave." I realized I had not used the word in her presence before.

"I am not a slave, but I also have no available freedom, really. There are all kinds of slavery, Ami. I have learned to keep my mouth shut, and I am sure I have said too much right now." Tears came to her eyes.

"There are all kinds of slavery, yes, but there are all kinds of life and all kinds of death. Not being able to sing today is a death, there is no doubt. But there are all kinds of ways to life as well. Jesus Christ was like the Hiram legends that we learn about at the Masonic Lodge. Hiram was and is a shining example of the perfect man. I am going to present Hiram near the end of the first act of *The Labyrinth,* out of nowhere. He must rise out of the floor, already a master, having been long initiated already."

I was speaking so fast no one could keep up.

"Your opera is getting longer every minute," Alice said, laughing. "And what about *Faust?*"

"It is all within the legend of Osiris, my darling. And *Faust* will get done, I promise you!"

"Osiris?" Alice asked, surprised at this new word.

"Osiris. Sarastro sings about him in *The Magic Flute*. Osiris and Hiram are likely the same person, with Hiram being brought into our own time, a name we can better understand. Osiris was the King of Egypt, killed by his brother Seth, who cut up his body and spread him across Egypt. A faithful wife, and there is nothing greater than a faithful wife, my darling…"—I kissed Alice, then kept talking—"his faithful wife collected all the pieces of him and put him back together. He couldn't live as he had lived, having been torn to bits, so he became King of the Underworld. You see, Alice, when you can no longer live as you have in the past, you have to be the king of what you can. What I have seen today is evil, and I will not stop until it is gone. Hiram and Enoch will build this labyrinth…oh, Alice, I can hear it all already. There has never been such an opera!" I yelled.

Alice said, "It seems that the gods themselves are speaking through you. There is more to our lives than this mundane world, I know that."

I must have looked crazed. "Alice, I will have a scene, and it is already finished in my mind, at the Egyptian Court of the Dead, with the chorus calling upon Anubis, Thoth, and Osiris. We are to build the Temple of Solomon by the opera's end. Enoch attaining the third degree has to be one of the central scenes. Oh, Alice, I am so excited! The gods themselves will weigh into the worthiness of entering the afterlife."

"Oh, Amadé, you are amazing!"

"I am not amazing, Alice. Life is amazing, even a life that would silence your voice for a day. I am going to make you a Master of the Royal Secret. I have not done enough to help you."

"What more could you have done?" she asked.

"We spend so much time explaining music's meaning…and then this happens. I don't know what to do with it."

Alice looked at me quizzically. "My darling, I don't know how to help you write your opera, but I know you must just begin now and write every day until it is completed."

"It will not take long. As long as a journey from Babylon to Jerusalem, so a few long days of writing instead of riding. The rubble of the first temple, darling Alice, that is the rubble of our lives…I have to make reference to the Lion, Ox, Eagle, and to Man."

I began to hum and then loudly sing my *Haffner* symphony's first movement. Alice recognized it instantly.

"We have to be seekers of light," I said.

"Ami, are you going mad or are you drunk?" Alice had never seen me in this state.

"Alice, my love…my gorgeous one…I am neither mad nor drunk. I am on that side of the bridge that demands I sit and write for the next many hours, at the end of which will emerge my new version of *The Labyrinth*. I have been here before. I wait and wait, gathering ideas. Holding them. Witnessing them. I am like a dam I once saw in a low-lying area near where I grew up, somewhere near Salzburg, where a rare animal built a dam from stray wood and mud. They were called beavers, but they had somehow invaded from Asia or India; someone had brought them back for their pelts. And they built dams. They were the most extraordinary things. I went to see one, and the little animals, so clever, could dam the water while still allowing it to run. Yet they knew when the water was running low due to lack of rain or from the heat, and they would fill in the remainder of the dam. The water would pool behind it, sometimes for many days, and of course the water found its way out as it always did. The dams they built made me believe in God." There seemed no end to my talking that night.

"You didn't believe in God until you saw beavers build a dam?" Alice laughed.

"Alice, my darling, there are some things you cannot understand until you have lived as long as I have. There are things you see that simply demand you think differently about everything you've ever known."

Though neither of us expected or planned it, I made love to her that night in a new way. There was a happening between us that we each felt in a different way, that we were able to convert into a different meaning between us, one in which I searched for a sensation rather than simply striving for one I knew I would eventually reach. There was no expectation that night of release or fulfillment; everything was contained in the journey of our enjoinment.

When we finished, together, I said to her, "Magic is so important, my darling. It is so vital that we believe in magic, not in the darkest of magics, but in the real magic, the alchemy that finds its way into the best of what we know. This is why we live, my Alice. We almost got there today, but not quite. I promise you, we will arrive there together someday." The final words escaped me before I drifted into sleep.

CHAPTER 100

My dreams from that night are as vivid to me today as they were then. What I would always recall of my dreams the night after Alice was silenced, and the night I fully conceived of *The Labyrinth*, was a braid. I dreamed of a braid that resembled the ropes on the few ships I had unfortunately experienced, especially the ropes of the *Gregson*. In my dreams, I saw myself approach a mirrored glass, trying to discern the great braid that was attached to my head. My braid was a part of my own hair, like the long tails I used to have as a youth, but this braid was right in the middle of my head, and it was multicolored, which I found strange both in the dream and in my remembrance of it. The braid was beautifully crafted by someone, and it was twice the length of my own hair, or the length my hair might be if I had never shorn it. The remainder of my hair was just as it was in my waking hours, thinly clumped together and growing in every possible direction, the individual hairs having no interest in ever lying down together. It was thought in my dream that the cutting of the braid might be painful or harmful, and pulling it out would cause a wound from which no one could recover. The braid was cut, though, by someone else while I was looking in a mirrored glass, yet it caused me no pain. The braid was beautiful by itself, and I expressed a wish within my dream to keep it, but I was not allowed. It had to be taken away.

The concert the next afternoon was another huge success, but I could not get my heart into the music that day. I missed my Alice, missed what her voice would have added to the concert. All through the entirety of the other music we performed, I kept hearing "Voi avete un cor fedele," even slipping the main theme of it into my first cadenza of the concerto, which every member of the orchestra noticed. I had not had time to assess how the orchestra members were feeling about Alice, and I purposefully did not arrive at the theater early so I would not have to be upset again by anything. The Astors attended the concert and did their usual socializing with their rich friends, but they did not come backstage afterward, which I knew was because they felt guilty about what had happened to Alice. Alice stayed home, of course, and was asleep in her bed by the time I returned from the second concert. I longed to see her, but I knew she needed her rest after the ordeal she had endured.

Late that night, John came to visit me in my tower room, a part of the vast house to which he rarely came.

"Amadé, I want to apologize to you for what happened with Alice. The concert was stunning, but I know how disappointed you must feel."

"Her voice is among the greatest I've ever heard. I hope she will be allowed to sing another time. Or will it be this way always, even in your opera house?" I asked.

"I believe I can insist she sing in our opera house, but you must realize it will cause a great deal of scandal, and we are getting close now to the time when you must decide who is to sing for the opening of *Faust*. We are within six months of being able to launch this amazing theater unto the world."

"I want Alice to perform Pamina in *The Labyrinth*, John. Please," I added quietly.

"I will do my best, and congratulations on your concert tonight, on all of your concerts. They have been amazingly successful, and the world seems ready for this new venture."

"It is very exciting, John."

"Tell me about you and Alice," he said, giving me no warning and thus no time to prepare.

I was happy the subject had finally been broached, but I was flummoxed as to what to say. Honesty was what I desired, but I knew that if I said too much I might shock my employer, but not disclosing enough would be untrue to Alice, and John had always been honest, so he deserved truth from me.

"John, I know how complicated this has become for you, and we are doing our best to keep it quiet. But I have to tell you, not as my employer but as my friend, that Alice is someone I love more than any other woman I have ever known." It felt good to finally say it aloud.

John asked me about Konstanze.

"I have written to ask her for a dissolution of our marriage, for the sake of both of us. We had no time to decide what to do with our lives. She simply left me on the shore of France and returned home. Had she gone to London with me, perhaps it would have turned out differently. I do not know."

"You certainly cannot marry Alice while you are married to Konstanze, and I'm not entirely sure you can legally marry Alice at all. The scandal alone might sink our venture with the opera house, and ruin you in this city. I wouldn't be able to protect you from gossip. It may be legal for you to marry Alice in New York, once your marriage to Konstanze is suspended, but I will have to discreetly find that out for you."

"Thank you, John," I said, nearly in tears.

"But even if it is legal, I cannot imagine a world in which it would be acceptable for you to be seen in public together, or even for her to sing under your direction," he said, sadly.

"But she is perhaps the greatest singer in this country!"

"I've heard her. She is indeed astounding, but the world is the world, Amadé. There is only so much you can do before the scandal takes over the work and drowns out all you have accomplished."

"Is there a way to keep our union silent? If Alice were to live with me here, would it not be possible? Your friends know that we are both in your employ."

"We've bought a farm north of here, far up the island. If I move you and Alice up there to a house, along with a carriage, only the horseman would know you were there together. I can build several houses there, to make it appear that Alice is working for you. And I'd like to have a house for me and Sarah eventually, just so we have a quiet place to get away from the noise of this busy place."

"How far away is it? I have so much work to achieve."

"It can't be more than five miles, near where the broadway ends. There is absolutely nothing up there. It is remote, but there is water in streams everywhere, and we will dig you a well, just like here. We could put your studio up there instead of at the store. The carriage ride would take you perhaps thirty minutes. It is beautiful up there. Sarah and I are toying with building a very large house, but for now we just want a cozy nook to get away. We are looking at perhaps building a large house on the East River, but we would still want a getaway. If we move you up there, it might give us the chance of keeping your relationship quiet." John was thinking aloud as he spoke, which I had rarely seen him do. He was always calm and considered.

He asked if I had ever lived in the countryside.

I admitted that I never had, but I found the prospect exciting, mostly because I could be alone with Alice, alone with a fortepiano or a clavichord, and alone to write music. So much of my life had been within cities that I often longed for the peace of the countryside.

I had to tell him, "John, I'm overwhelmed by what you have given me, and now you are poised to give me more. I do not, or don't, know what to say. Is that how it is said: 'don't'?"

"There is a great deal of work to do, my friend, and I find that I've never regretted money spent on beauty. I am frugal, really, compared to most people, which may strike anyone as humorous since I am spending a fortune to build a theater that can probably only lose money. What I've found, Amadé, having means I never had before, is that the money I spend that makes me grateful is never a waste of money. The large tract of land I bought a few miles north of here stretches across the island, from the river we crossed together to get here, to the eastern river. It doesn't feel like it on most days, but we are a huge island. I've never been to the upper reaches of it, but many have. My Dutch friends all speak of a stone mill far up the river, a place they are calling something like Yonkeers. There is apparently a Dutch manor house up there that would rival Vesey Street.

If I build the manse on the East River, it should be the finest home in the country, up there with Jefferson's Virginia estate. And if that happens, you and Alice can already be living up in one of the outer buildings of the western farm."

It seemed at that moment that John had deduced it all. "Whatever you think best, John, is what I will do. I want to focus now on finishing *The Labyrinth*. I have decided to take a whole new direction with it." I was eager to get to a keyboard and paper the next day to start working on it. "And I promise your beloved *Faust* will be done, as well. It is easy by comparison."

He asked me when both operas would be ready.

"I may have both completed within a month if I work hard. It is finished. It just is not yet written down," I said proudly.

Shortly after the concerts, as I was immersed in finishing and revising *The Labyrinth* and getting *Faust* committed to paper, Alice began experiencing regular bouts of illness, leaving her often unable to work. Sarah decreed that Alice was to remain in her small house on the back of the property, in case Alice had a contagion. For days I was not allowed to visit her, days in which I would hear from various others in the household that Alice was no better. I remained hard at work on *The Labyrinth*, and occasionally on Goethe's opera, but I moved my desk to a window from where I could see Alice's cottage, and observe anyone who went in or out. I asked about Alice all the time, and was always told that she was resting.

Sarah sent for a doctor, and besides him, only one of the other girls working in the Astor home was allowed into Alice's cottage. The doctor initially stated that Alice should quarantine for a fortnight, which I quickly learned meant fourteen nights, but even after that time and after the administering of medicines, Alice was no better. The doctor returned, and I saw Sarah summoned to Alice's house. I was strictly ordered to stay away. I knew something was transpiring, but I was not allowed to know what. Sarah and the doctor emerged from Alice's cottage, and I saw the doctor leave.

I went to Sarah's drawing room, where she was at work at her desk, having seen the doctor off. "Mrs. Astor, could I inquire as to Alice's health?" I asked.

"Of course, Amadé. You can go to see her now. She is still ill and quite weak, but there is no contagion. You can go now. I'm sure seeing you will pick up her spirits."

I rushed to Alice's cottage, where I found her so weak she could barely speak. I kissed her forehead, which was soaked with perspiration.

"My darling. I want you to feel better. I have—I've had so many sick days, and I can't bear the idea of you feeling so bad. What is wrong? What did the doctor say?"

"I am with child," she said, breathily.

CHAPTER 101

"Darling, I am so happy," I told her. And I was happy. How could I be otherwise? There I was, just short of fifty years old, and I was to experience the joy of fatherhood anew.

"How can you be happy? This baby growing inside of me will be taken from me, will be taken from us. We both know that." Alice was crying.

"We will find a way. No son or daughter of mine will be taken from us."

"Do you promise?" Alice had never asked me to make a promise of any kind.

"I promise, Alice. Stop your tears now," I said, caressing her.

I was consumed with finishing *The Labyrinth*, and with this news of Alice being enceinte, as they always said in Vienna, our lives went into a new level of secrecy. Alice was confined completely to her cottage, and I worked every lighted hour on *The Labyrinth* and *Faust*, using them to distract from my worries about being a father again so late in my life. The idea of another young Mozart thrilled me, though I wondered about little Franz, my son who would be nearing his teenage years at that moment, and would likely have no memory of me at all. I'd had only one letter from my older boy Karl since arriving in America, stamped from Livorno, saying he would likely move to Milan within the year. He was working in business. I thought Karl should try to come to America to work for John, and I wrote to tell him so, but I had no reply as yet. Karl had been a puzzle to me, another labyrinth. He inherited a great gift at the piano, and he had even played some concertos. I longed to play the piano with Karl, and there were plans for us to try out the concerto for two pianos that I had written for Nannerl. Such memories, especially when I played it with Josepha, one of my prize pupils. That girl's hands could play anything. Josepha Auernhammer...I wondered if she was still alive and where she was.

What puzzled me about Karl was that he seemed to have so little interest in playing, even though he was so gifted for it. I wanted to get Karl interested in women, too, especially one of the many gifted singers who came within our circle. But Karl resisted each of them, leaving me to wonder if my son was like Moller...or one of those men I tried to fight off at Salzburg Cathedral, one of the buggers as they called them in London. A man in London, too, back when I was a child, had tried to kiss me. I had told Leopold about it, but my father didn't believe me, saying, "You just misunderstood the English customs." But I knew I had not misunderstood anything.

Karl might be one of those men, but I desperately hoped not, because those men were so often destined for endless unhappiness. There were many singers and actors of my acquaintance, safely protected by the theatrical communities and out of the reach or eye of the church, who managed to live seemingly happy lives as buggers. There were even women who seemed to have little interest in men, and I found all of them very curious, because I could not imagine ever kissing a man, and thus could not imagine a woman kissing a woman. Still, I had once seen Konstanze kiss a woman as romantically as she kissed me as her husband, and I found the kiss strangely arousing, as though Konstanze had hidden depths within her that might become available to me at any moment. I hoped that Karl, whether he was in Livorno or had now moved to Milan, would find some circle who would make him happy.

The Labyrinth kept calling me, day after day, hour after hour, often stretching into the night with the aid of my favorite lamps. Those lamps were superior to those I'd had on Brook Street in London. I found that of late, with Alice sick in bed, I was also waking early in worry for her. Sometimes I sneaked to her cottage before dawn, before Sarah or John might see me, to ask about her progress. Having witnessed all of

Konstanze's pregnancies, I had learned certain guideposts, and it felt like Alice was getting close to the end of her confinement, as her belly was large. I was so eager to meet our child. But Alice said she was still at least a month away, and she found it almost impossible to leave her bed, as the slightest exertion left her completely exhausted. She had little appetite, but was doing her best to stay nourished. The chamber pot, she told me, was the most activity she could muster in a day. She slept many hours a day, and she told me her dreams were strewn with strange visions that she hoped weren't presentiments of the type of life their child might have. We both wondered what color skin our child would have. And would he or she have a singing voice like hers or a musical talent like mine? She loved to ask these questions of me each time I visited, each time unaware that she had asked them before. I learned just to listen and give her the same answers each time, and the predictability seemed to bring her a measure of comfort.

Even with Alice ill, I experienced one of the most joyous days of my life when I put the finishing touches on *The Labyrinth*. It was the most satisfying work I had ever composed. Before turning the score over to Hewitt for copying, I checked that I had achieved what I set out to do, that the opera would be exactly the same if reading from the end, and indeed it was. At the exact middle point, I ended the first act and began the second act with the same chord, and this middle point was like the summit of a mountain, when water would run in different directions on either side of the highest point. The whole of *The Labyrinth* was like that. I vowed to tell no one, to see if any clever musician would figure it out, as I knew it was challenging to find something that was hidden in plain sight. I wouldn't mention it to Hewitt and see if he noticed. Moller, I knew, would likely be the first to find it.

CHAPTER 102

The opening of the Astor Opera House was finally set for June 15, 1805, and I threw myself into rehearsals. It was one thing, of course, to rehearse one opera like *The Magic Flute* with an orchestra struggling to play it at all, but to prepare two of the same length, with *The Labyrinth* being even more complexly difficult than *The Magic Flute*, seemed to be an insurmountable challenge. In addition to this, of course, we had another completely new opera in my *Faust*, which was being copied and we were forced to wait for it. The orchestra had trouble even holding the same tempo of Papageno's first aria, much less the second Queen of the Night in the *Flute*. But the Queen's two arias in *The Labyrinth* made those in the first opera feel like child's play. I had not been moved to write so many challenging notes for a soprano since Josepha Weber or perhaps Cavalicri. The soprano roles in *Turtuffe* and *Richard III* had not been so treacherously high and filled with fast notes, but the Queen inspired me. I took inspiration from my own arias for the *Flute*, highly embellishing them in *Labyrinth* and filling them with dense quick fugues for the Queen, a solo flute, oboe, trumpet, and bassoon, a combination I had never tried before. The arias in *The Labyrinth* would have challenged any orchestra in Vienna, even my extraordinary London ensemble, so it was particularly difficult work for my New York group, which we called the Astor Orchestra, though I'd had no official permission to call it so.

I grew to love them, as they were earnest and hardworking, and the finest among them knew they were part of something historic, bringing operas to a continent for the first time. One of the musicians told me of having heard there had been a showing of *The Magic Flute* in the distant city of New Orleans, as far away from New York as was London. I wondered if this was somehow true, for how could the materials have made their way to such a place? There were French settlers there, from long before either the French or American Revolutions, and perhaps the French scores from ten years before had found their way into a trunk leaving on a ship from Le Havre or Marseilles? I was unsure, but nearly certain that it could not be true.

"Besides," I said, echoing Sarah, "this is the first *Magic Flute* in America with the composer conducting!" which made my colleagues in the orchestra cheer. We worked seven to eight hours a day, while I also tried to fit in rehearsals with the singers for all the other operas.

With Alice confined completely during her pregnancy, I thought it best to have a great deal of work to do, so I did. The singers needed hard work each day, especially to cope with the careful execution of all of the opera's many ensembles. The final dress rehearsals of the two operas, set two days apart to allow the singers time to rest, arrived with terrifying swiftness. There was always more to be done, and never quite enough time. The days leading up to the opening blurred into a pattern: I would wake early enough to check on Alice, go to the new opera house to rehearse, and arrive back at Vesey Street around sunset so exhausted that I fell into my bed, only to repeat the same thing the following day. And all the while, as we worked away on *The Magic Flute* and *The Labyrinth*, it was announced that *Faust* was to be our premiere, though I had yet to finish it. I knew it would be the third, not the first, opera in America.

I had been able to get to know the theater very well, as I wanted to see my productions from as many vantage points as possible. The only opera house I had ever seen to rival it was La Scala, and it felt bigger to me than even that vast Milan theater. I had seen all the major theaters of Europe, and this was its equal. I found the decor thrilling, all gold and red, and so much dark mahogany wood. The oil lamps emitted no scent, so the Astor lacked the odor of so many of the large opera houses in Europe. But as beautiful as it was, what I most loved was the sound of the place.

There was so much wood that it felt like being encased within a giant violin, and music was resonant within it. The first time I heard the opening chord of *The Magic Flute* in the Astor Opera House, I feel immediately in love with it, and I began to imagine all the operas I would write for it.

John and Sarah came to see me before the performance, before they went to greet the arriving crowds, finding me outside the entrance the orchestra used to go to their seats. The orchestra sat in a special area between the audience and the stage, an area slightly lower than the seats. No one in New York had ever seen such an arrangement in a theater, but they also had never seen any building so opulent.

John wished me "all the best" for the performance, and Sarah told me they were proud of what I had accomplished. Before going to their seats, John had one more thing to say.

"I wasn't sure I should tell you, but I am sure you will hear it anyway, and it is best you know."

"What is it? Is everything suitable and to your liking?"

"The president is here. He did not inform us he was coming to New York, and when he found out about the opera house and especially when he found out you were here, he insisted on attending," John said.

It seems impossible I could be so stupid, but I asked, "The president of what?"

"Amadé, the President of the United States. Thomas Jefferson is here."

CHAPTER 103

"We will need to play 'The President's March' since he is here," John added. "Is that possible?"

"Will the orchestra know this? How is it possible to have materials to play this on such short notice?"

Several of the musicians overheard our exchange. They had worked so hard to prepare *The Magic Flute*, and it worried them to think that their initial sounds might be compromised by being so thrown together.

"What is this song, John?" I asked.

"Everyone here knows it. I'm sure," John said, and Sarah concurred.

I looked to a few of my musicians standing around. One of them started to hum. John picked up the cue and sang in a voice stronger than I had imagined he possessed. I had never heard him sing so lustily before, and I thought it always such a special moment when a man's true singing voice is heard for the first time, especially a man so well known.

Hail, Columbia, happy land!
Hail, ye heroes, heav'n-born band…

More of the musicians gathered in, recognizing the tune and remembering the words, having heard it since childhood on more occasions than they realized.

Who fought and bled in freedom's cause,
And when the storm of war was gone
Enjoy'd the peace your valor won.
Let independence be our boast,
Ever mindful what it cost;
Ever grateful for the prize,
Let its altar reach the skies.

John asked me if we could have this song played to open the performance, adding, "It would please Jefferson to no end, and do us no harm in the circles of Washington, I imagine. Thank you all, and we are so eager for *The Magic Flute*!" And with that, John and Sarah left.

I asked the musicians to sing me the tune again. It was simple, in two parts, episodic, better than many military marches, but just as predictable.

I asked for some manuscript and quills.

Less than an hour remained before the performance was to begin. To the amazement of the musicians who watched me do it, I wrote individual orchestra parts, one by one, for exactly the winds and brass of *The Magic Flute*'s orchestra, two each of flutes, oboes, bassoons, and I thought basset horns would be preferable to clarinets for this song, plus two trumpets, two horns, three trombones, and timpani. Sixteen separate parts in all, hastily written down. No string parts, I said as I handed out the parts to the musicians minutes before they were to begin *The Magic Flute*. Word was sent around that Jefferson was in the house, and this anthem needed to be played in his honor.

No time to rehearse. Just before we began, as Jefferson was about to be announced and ceremonially brought into the center box to sit with John and Sarah, a horn player came to me to ask if he was to be crooked in E flat or in F, as the ink of their part had slightly smudged.

"In *es*—E flat, as you say," I replied calmly.

"The anthem is in E flat, or we are crooked in E flat?" the player asked.

"Both!"

The player would relay the tale for many years to come, because none of the musicians in my orchestra could imagine that anyone was able to hold in their mind, with no score, all of the orchestral parts of a melody heard only moments before. "Hail, Columbia," as I arranged it, would become part of the lore of *The Magic Flute*'s opening night in New York, and the beginning of the Astor Opera House. But what they did not realize was that I had been holding such information in my mind for half a century by that point. It was not an ordeal for me.

CHAPTER 104

I had read and heard stories of Thomas Jefferson as an ambassador in Paris, and Grétry had told me of Jefferson's love and knowledge of music, which we both found so unusual for someone from the New World. It was one of the few things on which Grétry and I agreed. Grétry had heard Jefferson play the violin and found him more than competent, which was more than I could say for Joseph II at the fortepiano, or for Grétry for that matter. I had been shown Jefferson's Declaration for the country in which I now stood awaiting the first performance of one of my operas—and, for all anyone knew, the first performance of any opera in the young country. Actually, I had been shown Jefferson's Declaration of Independence years before in a German broadsheet, on a day when it was read in a café in Vienna by a young man I considered rather too revolutionary. Lorenzo admired all the revolutionists, but I found revolutionism distasteful, if only because every hour spent on anarchy and freedom was an hour in which I felt less free.

I once had a dream so powerful that it felt as real to me as an actual happening: that I had written an opera about Marie Antoinette, and there was a presence in the dream of Jefferson, and the entirety of the dream was about the presence of a man inappropriate for the station of the woman, or was it the opposite—a woman who was ill-suited for the position of the man with whom she was conjoined? I was reminded of the dream in those moments before *The Magic Flute* began in the presence of all of New York's notables led by John and Sarah Astor in the center box, in the unexpected presence of the President of the United States, Thomas Jefferson, surrounded by what looked like courtiers, in this land that was supposed to lack them.

Having finished leading "Hail, Columbia" to welcome the president, I began *The Magic Flute*. For days I had worked with my new orchestra on the precise attack of the opera's first chord, as every moment of *The Magic* Flute grew from it. I had told them many times, "I can tell from the quality of this first assail how the entire performance will commence," and I meant it. I had experienced it so many times, both in leading *The Magic Flute* myself and in attending many performances. One time I had decided rather late to attend a performance. It was shortly before my terrible sickness, and I had not had time to tell Emanuel I was coming. Standing outside the box where I would watch the performance, I could hear the audience being silenced. I had myself led the first performances, before my health left me too exhausted to contemplate them, so Süssie led in my absence, which is who I thought I was hearing. As I removed my overcoat to enter the box, the first chord of the opera sounded. I was alarmed. "This can't be Franz!" I said, because something about the initial entrance didn't sound right. Sure enough, when I entered the theater and noticed the orchestra in front of the stage, a young man I did not know was leading the performance. Just the initial chord made all the difference.

On that night in New York, the first chord of *The Magic Flute* began, and a spirit of something I recognized but could not name came over me. Jefferson and Astor were forgotten, the months of preparation accepted and moved beyond, the horrible journey to America now distant. The performance progressed with simplicity and ease. The large audience laughed particularly at the antics of Papageno, as Mr. Thomas, the youngest member of the cast, had a perfect ability to project his lines far into the auditorium. He was an immensely comic person and I found him very clever. Mr. Thomas loved to come into the orchestral area of the auditorium and watch the performance unseen to the public, standing next to the trombones, sometimes almost missing his entrances. He simply loved being a part of it all.

Upon completion of the opera's first act, I left the orchestral area and took a goblet of fresh water and a small glass of wine, to calm my nerves.

The applause came in different places than it had in Vienna, which interested me. To my complete delight, the American public seemed to take my opera to heart. The character of Monostatos was booed, just like in Vienna, but given what I had lived through in the time since Vienna, this was something I decided I would change about *The Magic Flute*. The blackamoor character of Monostatos was suitable perhaps for the Viennese, but in America he was a figure they recognized differently. As the scenes progressed, I wondered how I had never thought of this: the character who has dark and evil tendencies, the overseer of Sarastro's temple, implied that he is all of these things by his nature as a black man. This cannot stand, I thought, and I began rewriting it immediately. Monostatos would be not a blackamoor, but an evil person. I immediately conceived a new aria for Monostatos which made his evil not about being black, but about being a person mistreated. These terrible caricatures that were so common in Vienna should not be the new way of opera, especially in America. There was so very much work to do!

CHAPTER 105

President Jefferson was brought backstage to meet me and the cast. Introduced to me, Thomas Jefferson said, "When I saw the three doors of the Temple marked 'wisdom, reason, and nature,' I could not but think of 'Life, Liberty, and the Pursuit of Happiness,' Herr Mozart."

I could not believe that the President of the United States was speaking directly to me.

"It is our honor that you graced us with your presence tonight, Mr. President," I said.

"There is no grace in the presence of another person, Herr Mozart, not in this country. We are graced only by nature, as it feels your Tamino and Pamina must be," Jefferson said.

"Thank you, Mr. President." I was unsure of what else to say to his perfection of words.

"This opera, this opera house, your presence here in our country, Herr Mozart, changes what we might become. I am reminded of my years in Paris, nights at the opera I never imagined would be possible in my own country. I congratulate you all, and most admiringly I commend Mr. Astor for his generosity in building this splendid monument to art," Jefferson said, to polite applause.

"You honor us tonight as you honor the nation as our president," John said, needing to say something.

Jefferson continued, "I invite you, John, and your wonderful wife, Sarah, as well as Herr Mozart, to my home in Virginia where I am to spend the next two months. Please join me, and we can discuss whatever future opera and music may have in this new world. Herr Mozart, have you a wife?"

"My wife, Konstanze, remains in Vienna, Mr. President." The words did not feel right as they left me. I thought of Alice, and I glanced at John, who smiled.

"Very well, then, you can travel in procession, perhaps, with John and Sarah. It is two full days by carriage from here, I believe," the president said, departing. "You will love Monticello."

There was a small party outside the theater following Jefferson's departure. I was restless at the party, wanting to get home to Alice. John Astor stood to speak.

"Ladies and gentlemen of the cast, and my friends who are here: Sarah and I want to congratulate you all for the superb performance that opens this new era of fine music and opera in New York City and, I hope, for the entire country as well. Even our son William enjoyed it, and could probably hum all of Papageno's tunes! We will see you all back here for *The Labyrinth* and eventually, we hope, the premiere of *Faust*. To Amadé, to Wolfgang Amadé Mozart, now an American in name at least, I salute you as the greatest musician of our day."

John raised his glass and everyone drank a toast, followed by applause for me. John and Sarah asked me to join them in their carriage for the ride home.

"A huge triumph, Amadé. I congratulate you again," John said as we pulled away from the opera house. I thanked him.

"I can report to you, and it is fine to talk about in front of Sarah, that the three houses on the farm are nearing completion. You'll be able to move in once we are back from Monticello."

"We are going so soon to Virginia? What about Alice?" I asked.

"Alice will be just fine, and there is not a thing you can do for her. It is not often that an invitation comes from the President of the United States, so we will not linger over it. We will go within a few days. Once Alice has given birth, we will move you all up to the farm, where privacy will be assured."

Perhaps from the relief of having the performance finished, I began to cry tears of joy. The thought of living away from prying eyes with Alice brought too much bliss to hold back.

I was forever saying how thankful how I was. And I reminded John that I had not yet attained my dissolution of marriage from Konstanze.

"We know that, Amadé. But with you away at the farm, we don't see many ways for people to find out. Though it is on the island we are now riding along, there is little chance that there will be visitors there, because it is simply too far away from where the city's busy machinations happen. Now, what are your future plans for the opera house?"

"I need to finish *Faust*, and I believe its premiere will be a major event. We can give *Faust* within two months, I think, slightly longer depending on how long we are to be at Monticello. Then I thought we would perform *Figaro* and *Richard III*. And depending on how successful these performances are, perhaps we will revive them next season?" I could scarcely believe my own words.

"Very good. Excellent idea. How are you actually proceeding with *Faust*?" John mentioned it as if no time had transpired since Philadelphia.

"I have Goethe's complete libretto now, and I can make it the next work if you like. I thought I might surprise you with *Baron Munchausen*, but I know from Sarah that it won't be much of a surprise." I laughed.

"Oh! Please write them both. It would be wonderful to have a serious opera and a comedy. Can you write them both?"

"I believe I could. *Faust* is essentially done already, and the Baron will write himself, I have a feeling. Few things will ever take as long as *The Labyrinth*. Remember, too, that we have *Tartuffe* and *The Fairy of the Lake*."

"You are the busiest composer in the world. I cannot keep up!" John laughed.

"Can Moller be your poet for *Baron M*?" Sarah asked me.

"That is a wonderful idea," I said. "I will ask him to try it out."

We arrived quickly to Vesey Street.

John ended the evening with, "Amadé, I think we should take a small orchestra to Monticello with us so we can impress the president. A short concert of your works would be wonderful. Please arrange it."

CHAPTER 106

The caravan that departed Vesey Street that late June day was something I had only ever seen in royal processions, as when Joseph II departed for Schönbrunn Palace. There were at least forty carriages, one of them usually used only for funerals to carry the fortepiano being gifted to President Jefferson by John and Sarah, and on which I was instructed to play a newly composed work during the first dinner upon our arrival. I shuddered at what the jostling journey would do to the instrument's tuning, but I would set it right in time. I had in the previous days composed the *Monticello Sonata in F Major* expressly for the president. There were carriages filled with pelts and fur hats and coats, all as gifts for the residents of Monticello, for whomever it was decided by Jefferson should have one.

The journey was the first time in months I'd had a chance to talk at length to John about anything.

"Where, John, do you suppose Lorenzo is? Or do you think he is living still?"

"I imagine he is in the German or Italian settlements of Pennsylvania somewhere. This is enormous territory, you must understand. Pennsylvania is the size of the Holy Roman Empire, at least the one we grew up within," John said.

"Will he return to New York? What did he say to you?" I had wanted to utter the question for months.

"The valley of the Susquehanna River is reportedly one of the Edens of our country, and he did say he had reason to take himself there. I could send you by carriage from Monticello to there if you desire to find him."

"No, I cannot imagine the idea of traveling alone in this country. There is too much unknown, and I am so happy with my life in New York, thanks to you. You have made my every dream come true, John."

I wanted to bring the topic of Alice into the conversation but didn't find the courage. Sarah looked upon me as though expecting it to come up at any moment. Finally she said, "Alice will be fine, Amadé, I promise you."

On our first night out of New York, the Astors and I and a few other service coaches stopped at a luxurious inn between Philadelphia and Baltimore. My quarters were as beautiful as what I had in the house on Vesey Street. During dinner at the inn, we spoke more about Lorenzo, the arrival in Pennsylvania having aroused John's memory, and Sarah asked me about Konstanze and what had happened between us. Something about being away from New York made her more inquisitive, and the wine made me freer to talk.

"I love her still. I love everyone I've ever met with the same passion I had when I met them. My affections don't change, but something within her changed over the years. She became so critical of everything I did, so unhappy with anything I said, and I think she even grew to dislike my music, and music was the one place where we were always able to meet. When we left Vienna with Franz, it was fully my expectation that we would go to London together and be there still, had it all gone as planned. The night before we were to leave France, she took our son and went back to Paris, leaving me forever. I had no time to grieve, no time to even think about it. She just left. We have exchanged a few letters back and forth since that time, but for any reality we are both dead to the other. There is no possibility we will see each other again. I want more than anything now to marry Alice." I said the words aloud at last.

"We will deal with that in due time. Let's get your baby born and your operas birthed as well. We can't do too much at once. You are certainly an industrious man!" Sarah laughed.

It was a thrill to see the countryside again, though I was happy we did not enter either Philadelphia or Baltimore.

CHAPTER 107

We departed early the next morning and arrived at Monticello with still a few hours of sun left in the day. The remainder of the caravan had arrived hours before, having traveled all night. The man who greeted us at the base of the hill told "Mr. Astor" that all of his servants were currently asleep at an inn at Three Notch'd Road, but they would be summoned now that we had arrived. The Astors would be placed in Mr. Jefferson's guest quarters, and I, "Mr. Mozart," would have a small room in the house as well, "though not as luxurious as the Astors'."

The carriages proceeded up the hill toward the manor. Thomas Jefferson was standing on the portico of his house to greet us, along with some of his children, and many servants.

"Welcome to Monticello!" Jefferson yelled once we were close enough to hear him.

"We are thrilled to be here, Mr. President!" John yelled back.

"Thomas!" the president yelled.

Sarah was greeted first once the carriage came to a stop, which I thought unusual. Then John, then me, just as it should be.

Jefferson said, "I never imagined that I would have the great Mozart in my very own home. You do me much honor."

I said, "Your home is the most beautifully sited I've ever seen. It is a palace." I meant it. It seemed as though one could see the entire world from there.

Jefferson replied, "Oh, no, my friend. Property is but a pathway to human happiness, not an inherent right in itself. I have been gifted with this glorious patch of earth from my father in order to bring happiness to myself and others."

"It is my honor to be in the home of the president," I said, and John echoed similar sentiments.

"The President's House is my temporary home. It is the people's house, but this is where my heart lies. I wake up early in Washington and I imagine myself here," Jefferson said.

John announced, "Mr. President, we have taken this rare opportunity to bring you a special concert of Amadé's orchestra, some of whom have come along with us on our journey."

"Splendid! It is such a beautiful day that we should set up here on the west lawn. Can we get all of that arranged in time for sunset?" Jefferson said to the crowd of people behind him, who all dutifully dispersed to enact his wishes.

We entered Monticello. Crossing the threshold of the house, I noticed a beautiful woman, slightly older than Alice, who was of a similar look, as though the blood of a white man flowed within her. I thought of my own child at that moment growing in Alice's belly, and I wondered again what my new baby might look like, what color skin the little child might have. Was this a bad thing to wonder? This woman clearly had a special type of role at Monticello, but all the servants there seemed different from the household staff on Vesey Street. It dawned on me that we had traveled to the south, and it must mean that Monticello was peopled by slaves. How could it be? How could the President of the United States, this new world founded on liberty, own another human being? I hoped it was not so, but I feared that it was. I knew that if Jefferson held slaves, I would not be able to hold my tongue, and that might embarrass the Astors or even harm my position in America. Jefferson was, after all, the president of the nation.

Astor admired the home, and he thought it right that the President of the United States should live in a fine home, but Monticello seemed to him something more. It approached what was owned by the monarchs of Europe. It was not so much the home itself that John seemed to envy, but all of the land.

"You aren't afraid that the poor of Virginia will rise up against you, Mr. President?" John asked, despite Sarah's advice not to bring up politics.

"Call me Thomas, Mr. Astor. I am attempting to avoid something akin to the third estate, sir," Jefferson said.

"Would you have prevented my fortune, Mr. Presi—Thomas?" John asked.

"Certainly not. You've earned it honestly, I'm sure. That is the miracle of the country, that clever men can be rewarded for their ambitions."

I meant not to speak but could not help myself. "You seem to have been rewarded by the toil of others, Mr. President."

"What do you mean, sir?" Jefferson drew back defensively.

"I mean, with all respect, Mr. President, that the man who wrote that all men are created equal feels that some are more equal than others."

Sarah looked as though her blood had been drained away. John was silent, but looked as eager as I to see what the president would say.

"I'm glad you asked, Herr Mozart. I am opposed to slavery, but I also recognize that a country can only do so much at once. I had to find compromises, as did Washington and Adams before me. I can't tell you how many fights Samuel Adams and I had about slavery, as he could not countenance the owning of another person. But you see, our sixteen colonies, now states—oh sorry, seventeen, as Ohio is now seated at our fine table—will soon be more than doubled in size, as Mr. Astor knows. The slave markets in Louisiana, quite far from here, are the fuel for the fires of the south's economy."

"But if you can only make money by enslaving people, how is that the freedom you and Adams and Franklin, all of you men I so admire… how do you look at yourself in the glass knowing money has been made from others?" I said, trying to control myself.

"Astor here, don't you think he has made money from others, Herr Mozart?"

John spoke up, "Now Thomas…I have never owned a slave."

"Yes, neither has Adams, as he keeps telling me. But you've still made money because slavery exists. Who do you think skins all of the pelts you sell to England and France?"

Sarah intervened, "Tell us more about the purchase of the Louisiana Territory, Mr. President."

Jefferson took the hint to change the subject. "I approached them only to buy New Orleans, you see. Because without a southern port, France would have had no way to trade. The slave rebellions in Haiti scared the life of out everyone in France. It scared me, too. I feel the more compromises we can make with the slave owners, the more we can encourage humane treatment, the less likely we will be to see a slave revolt here in this country. With so much land now, we will be able to spread our wings and not be so reliant."

"Do you really think that is how it will work, Thomas?" Astor asked.

"France is an ally of this country, unlike our mother country, who would like to see us all enslaved, John. Are you a Sarastro or a Queen of the Night?"

I laughed at Jefferson's reference to *The Magic Flute*. Following Sarah's introduction, as I always tried to do, I said, "It appears to me, Mr. President, that our orchestra is set up and ready for you."

"Splendid! Let us take ourselves to the lawn."

CHAPTER 108

I greeted my musicians, and we began the *Paris* symphony in honor of Jefferson. The first movement was loud enough for me to notice that the fortepiano was terribly out of tune. I spent all of the first movement quickly tuning it well enough to play my D-major concerto, the other piece we had brought. D major was the best key for playing outside. I remembered Alice scolding me for thinking in keys, and I wondered how she was faring.

Jefferson was delighted by the concert. "I never dreamed we would have such music at Monticello, Herr Mozart! Would you do us the honor after dinner of playing the violin with me?"

"I would be honored, Mr. President!" I said, recalling how long it had been since I'd played the violin.

"We play a lot of violin here at Monticello, but of course never with the famous Mozart. We shall prepare for dinner now. Please join me inside and let me show you my home."

We were guided through Monticello in more depth, and it surprised me how small it was compared to Vesey Street. John had called it a palace, but it was modest in size, even as it looked large from the outside. I immediately discovered optical illusions within the home, ways to make it appear larger than it was, though it all looked very gracious and beautiful to me. Soon we sat down in an informal dining room, which somewhat irritated Sarah, who had brought special clothes for dinner. Jefferson, sensing her unease, said, "Mrs. Astor, we will have a more formal dinner tomorrow night. The night of your arrival should be leisurely."

As soon as the water and wine were served, John asked, "You were made President by Alexander Hamilton were you not, Thomas?"

"I had not thought it common knowledge. But Hamilton was so loud, as a rule, that one could never harbor secrets with the man. He held no discretion at all, blurting out whatever he wanted to say with no thought of the godliness of his words," Jefferson said. "Were he here tonight, he would probably turn into an expert on Mozart, knowing more about your life than you do, Amadé." Jefferson laughed.

I noticed that Jefferson bristled when speaking of Hamilton, and I was happy simply to know who the man was, since Alice had tended him in his dying hours. I longed to have Alice at my side to hear Jefferson speak.

"One thing is sure," he said. "Hamilton would have loved your new opera house, Mr. Astor."

"Hamilton broke the tie between you and Aaron Burr?" John asked.

"Yes, sir. He did. Hamilton made me President, since that is what you seem intent on me saying."

"And then Burr killed Hamilton?" John pressed.

"Yes, sir. He did, and I am forever sorry for it. Two impossible men, but I loved Hamilton then and love him now. We saw two different countries, and I'm happy to say that the country of farmers that I believe is our best way forward is coming to pass, particularly as we have so much more land," Jefferson said with pride.

"But New York City is growing very fast, Thomas." John said.

"Washington is as well, and I think Boston is the largest in our nation right now. I do not think the cities should continue to grow, though, as it is very bad for the health of people to live so close together. Look at the terrible poverty in France, poverty that brought them revolution."

I asked, "Why are all men not allowed to vote?"

"Landowners vote, Herr Mozart, as it should be. It is the ownership of land that makes a worthy citizen."

"But sir, your farm here, while very beautiful, is toiled by slaves."

"Here we are again. You seem to have a soft heart for the black race, Herr Mozart." Jefferson was clearly getting irritated with me.

"As a young man I read your own writings, and they were most inspiring. Life, liberty, and the pursuit of happiness, apparent truths, all men being equal in the eyes of the Creator. I hope I am not saying too much."

"My belief is true even if it appears my actions are not. You see, the words in the Declaration, if they are not entirely true now, will *become* true over time."

"But you *own* human beings," I said.

Jefferson raised his voice slightly. "You must agree with me that black men are inherently inferior, as exemplified by your opera, *The Magic Flute*, Herr Mozart." Jefferson said.

"What?"

"It is all there. Your slave Monostatos is beaten. There is not a slave here at Monticello who has ever felt the lash," Jefferson defended.

"I do not believe any man is inferior to me," I said.

"You played for kings and queens as a child. Anyone who did not do so is by nature inferior to you," Jefferson said, silencing me.

CHAPTER 109

The meal was served by four women, including the woman I had noticed upon entering Monticello. Jefferson served a feast of pheasant, boar, and chicken, and he explained a range of vegetables that had been chosen from his own garden at Monticello, including a vegetable I had only ever tasted in France, *Spargel*. Jefferson called it asparagus, and John and Sarah seemed to know it.

After dinner, the woman who looked like Alice came to Jefferson's side and said to him in perfect French that she had mixed his favorite ice cream in the sabottiere.

I asked her in French how the ice cream was made. She looked startled to be addressed at all, and she looked to Jefferson to see if it was suitable to speak to me. Jefferson assented. She explained that the ice from the icehouse was mixed in the sabottiere, an inner canister, with eggs and sugar. I loved how she spoke, though it was clear that she wasn't French, as she had an accent I could not recognize. Jefferson seemed perturbed that I spoke French, erasing his private code with the woman.

Jefferson turned the subject back to my opera. "Before we retire to the drawing room to play our violins, I would love to hear more about what you are planning for the magnificent new opera house in New York City. I can scarcely believe that such a beautiful theater is in our country. It rivals the great theaters I attended in Paris years ago. Herr Mozart, you had been there a few years prior to my arrival, but you were still the absolute talk of the court. London, too."

I ached to hear about Paris and London again, as they both represented colossal failure for me. It was between Paris and London that my whole odyssey had begun. My whole life to others was defined by success, but for me my life had been a cascading set of failures, and my mind drifted off into all I had not done.

John spoke up on my behalf. "We plan to produce at least four operas each year, and I want to have Amadé put together many concerts as well. I have the Park Theatre, as you know, but with the addition of this new opera house, there will not be an entertainment anywhere in the world that could not appear in New York City. I plan, eventually, to have all of the greatest entertainment from Europe visit New York City. We can be a center for art, Mr. President." John said, with a pride I had come to know.

Jefferson seemed pleased, but his words did not match his actions. "This country needs art, to be sure, but what we most need right now is land, so that every white man in this nation has his own farm. Otherwise, we will have a nation dependent on the government for everything."

"That is your beloved France, is it not, Mr. President?" John said, trying to joke.

"Music is a necessity of life, Astor, but it can sometimes be a vainglorious spectacle, which no country needs."

"Did you find *The Magic Flute* to be just a spectacle, sir?" I asked.

"Not at all, but not everyone is a Mozart," Jefferson said. "Tomorrow, my friends, we shall ride in landaus around the property, and I have some special events for you in the afternoon. Specialties of the plantation."

We retired to the drawing room and I was handed a fine violin. On the music stands were French editions of my own compositions for two violins.

Jefferson said, "I've played these duets for years, always badly I'm sure, but I never thought I would be here in my home playing them with the man who wrote them. I hope I can keep up."

"All men are created equal, Mr. President," I said, tuning the violin.

I had not thought of these duets in decades, and they reminded me of Nannerl, as I had written them for the two of us, and I had always given her the more challenging elements to play, which made me smile to as I prepared to play them with the President of the United States.

The woman to whom I had spoken French came into the room to listen, which made Jefferson take notice.

"Sally! You are a good fiddler. Come here and play the next movement with Herr Mozart."

Sally looked like she would rather not have all of the eyes of the room on her, but she took Jefferson's violin and took her place at the music stand.

"We are at the second movement, Sally. I am Amadé," I whispered to her.

"*C'est un plaisir*," she said to me, adding, "and don't go too fast for me."

I loved her voice, which was soft and sweet, like Alice's. Sally was older than Alice, but she was still very beautiful, I thought. I longed so deeply for Alice.

And *magari*, she was a good violinist. I wasn't at liberty to say that she was a much better player than Jefferson, and she was playing the same violin so it could not be blamed on the instrument. Her intonation was perfection, and I realized just how long it had been since I had played anything but the fortepiano.

We played violin together for more than an hour, through most of my duets, but Jefferson had an extensive library, so we kept going far past the time Monticello usually settled into sleep.

Jefferson said, "We have a crowded tomorrow, so we had best all be off to bed."

John gave a final toast to the evening, and I was shown my quarters at last, where all of my luggage had been placed by the staff. The bedroom was small, with a door to the outside and a path to an outdoor privy. The lamp in my room gave off a lavender glow, and everywhere was the aroma of mint mixed with rosemary. I noticed on the table in the corner there was a small vial over a candle, and the scent seemed to be coming from the small cup of oil. Monticello was filled with such touches, small things that made the home seem more spacious and luxurious than it might otherwise be. I drifted into a deep sleep.

CHAPTER 110

After sleeping peacefully in such comfortable quarters, I happily devoured great heaps of food from the luxurious buffet of breakfast items spread across the dining room the following morning. Sweet meats, boiled eggs, baked radishes, toasted breads, confits of every description, sweet baked beans like I had seen in London, thick slabs of ham, corn bread, sausages, boiled potatoes made into a delicious hash that I had never tasted in any other country. The teas at Monticello were smooth and earthy, though some of the breakfast guests chose coffee that smelled so much like Vienna that I could not bear to taste it without missing my homeland.

I felt for my poor orchestral musicians, as they had to leave for the return trip to New York, but I was comforted knowing the Astors allowed them an overnight stay this time at the same inn near Philadelphia where we had stayed the night before. I knew that some of the best nights for musicians were when they were touring, because the rules were lax and great fun was had. My fondest memories on tour with orchestras were the nights of travel. I remembered a night journeying from Vienna to Prague, a quick trip, and the whole orchestra stayed at an inn sited next to a beautiful lake. The orchestra began a game in which the only possible outcome was throwing me into the lake. At the time, I thought it such an inconvenience to be thrown in the lake, but as I aged it turned into a joyous C-major memory.

I was sure that the characters of musical keys were in decline even when I was a child. By the time I got to Monticello, I thought they probably meant nothing at all. C major was the key of innocence and simplicity. A child's first conscious view of the world is always in C major, as I said many times. There were certain keys in which music could smile but not laugh, and some in which they could quietly sob but stop short of weeping. D minor was the key of faithless women and the melancholy that followed their realizations—did anyone notice that the only D minor in *Così* was a comic moment? There was so much about *Così* that people refused to understand. True conversations with God came in E-flat major and its relative, C minor. Deep grief was always expressed in F minor, the key that longs for the grave. Divine dispensation always came in B minor, and when hearing that key I always awaited the announcement of my own fate. I thought there were too many associations to write down, because I never felt anything in life that was absent one of the keys. A major was the key in which trust in God was expressed, and I turned to it only in times of utmost peace that my own guidance was aligned with the reality of my own actions. There is an entire testament to be written about keys, my dear and patient readers, if I ever am blessed with the time.

Monticello felt like a wonderland, and it was difficult to believe that anyone lived in such a place. After breakfast I was taken in a landau with President Jefferson to a neighboring hill where the most amazing sight had been arranged. The vista was beautiful, and Jefferson told me it faced west, and with the sun directly behind us at that moment I believed he was right. Jefferson told me to keep my eyes trained on a particular area nearby, and within a few minutes four hot air balloons appeared. I told Jefferson about the balloon I had seen in Germantown, and about the air balloons since I was a child in Paris.

"How do you keep them from sailing away?" I asked, feeling ten years old.

"You can't see because of the trees, but there is a pathway down there, worn down by horses and partly by me taking long walks, and some of the staff are holding on to the balloons and walking them along that path. They will float all the way back to the house," Jefferson said.

What amazed me was how something so enormous as those balloons could be so silent. Jefferson's balloons were three times the size of what I had seen in Germantown. They were a gorgeous sight, floating silently among the trees. The balloons were brilliantly colored and decorated.

"Who painted them?"

"I have a fellow here at Monticello who is a brilliant painter. He painted all four of the balloons," Jefferson said.

"I must meet him. He must do the decor for our operas."

"I do not think that would be possible, Amadé."

"Because he is a slave?" I said, feeling my anxiety rise.

"He is having a better life here than he would be having in Africa. I know you are an abolitionist, which I understand."

"How can you know what his life would have been in his home?" I asked.

"There are crops that are grown here that cannot be grown anywhere in Europe, and as everyone knows, Africans have immunity to the diseases of the south."

"Then pay people to work your crops," I said, "as we pay people for our scenery."

"There is a great deal you cannot understand, Amadé. There is absolutely no pathway to our agrarian economy, at least not now, without the use of slaves. Your Bible outlines this order very clearly, does it not?" Jefferson said.

"A man cannot be *owned*," I repeated.

"Maybe you should write your own Bible if you don't like the real one, as I did," Jefferson said. "And you don't realize that my slaves are not mistreated. I consider them family. There is a legal code called *partus sequitur ventrem*, which means that in this country a child born to a slave is a slave. I have freed the children of my slaves. Did you know that?"

"That is admirable. But I have seen something you have not seen. I came to this country on a slave ship," I said, having rarely said it out loud before.

"How on earth was Mozart placed on a slave ship?"

"I was tricked. I tried to get to Portsmouth to come to New York with Astor and Da Ponte, but I didn't arrive in time. I went from one disaster to another, and I was tricked onto a ship in Liverpool, told the ship was coming to America. They failed to tell me, though, that it was stopping in Africa. I have seen the horrors, Mr. President. It cannot be defended." I felt uneasy at confronting the most famous man in the world, but I had to do it.

He replied, "My secretary of state lives not far from here, and he owns many more slaves than I, yet no one says a word about Madison's slaves on his plantation, which is considerably larger than Monticello."

I decided to ask the question that had burned in me since playing the violin the night before. "The girl, Sally, who played the violin so beautifully with me last night. Is she a slave?"

"She is. She has grown up on this plantation."

"How did she come to play so well?"

"I taught her to play, and all of her children."

"If a slave is able to play the violin as well as you, how can they be thought inferior?"

"Amadé, you see, if I were to give you abolitionists what they want, and free all of the slaves, they would have to be sent back to Africa, because it is an unthinkable that they could ever mix with society in this nation, especially in the south. You only know this northern area of the country. It is very different down south."

"You are the president. Change the country."

Jefferson sighed. "We have lived through upheaval after upheaval since before the Continental Congress. If the slaves were to be freed, the violence that would erupt would be devastating. We must avoid it."

"I pray to God for an end to slavery," I said aloud for the first time. I thought of my dear Alice, who might at that moment be giving birth to our child.

"God made the Africans slaves, did he not? Who are we to change it? If their freedom in this nation is meant to be, then it will be made apparent to us all. But now, it is not at all clear."

The balloons disappeared around the hill, and Jefferson said he wanted to show me something else. We boarded the landau again, and the horse was restless.

We pulled up to a set of large cages that were practically hanging from a small cliffside. A group of slaves was tending four large birds of a type I had seen from a distance around Salzburg, falcons.

"Tamu! Bring the best-trained falcon here for Herr Mozart!" Jefferson yelled.

CHAPTER 111

Neither of us could believe it. I'd thought I would never see Tamu again, having left him in the reeds in France. I moved to hug him, but the falcon on his arm was protective and would not let me approach.

"Tamu! By what grace of God am I seeing you again?" I sobbed as I had not sobbed in months.

"Herr Mozart! Have you recovered?" Tamu asked, causing me to laugh through his tears.

Jefferson spoke. "Recovered from what? How can you possibly know each other?"

"Mr. President, Tamu is a doctor. We met in France the night before I sailed for England. He healed me." I cried more.

The falcon was impatient, so Tamu unchained it from his arm and set it free. "He will return, Mr. Jefferson."

Tamu looked to Jefferson to see if it was suitable for him to hug me. Jefferson nodded assent.

"Herr Mozart, I am so delighted to see you again," Tamu said, hugging me, and I was still crying.

"Tamu is a man of many talents at Monticello. He has learned falconry very quickly, and is the best falconer we have. He also painted the balloons you just enjoyed," Jefferson said proudly.

Just as Tamu said it would, the falcon returned to his arm, on which he wore a thick covering. The bird terrified me, as I had fascination with wild animals but little experience being near them.

I asked him how he learned to tame such a creature.

"Reward," said Tamu. "No punishment. And patience. They are actually very gentle birds if you are gentle with them. Don't look her in the eye, Amadé. There is something about the eye that makes them afraid."

I asked Tamu if he lived at Monticello.

"I do, Amadé. I was captured near where I said good-bye to you, brought to England, and was sailed out of Bristol to New York, where Mr. Jefferson's overseer, Mr. Bacon, purchased me."

I hated hearing the words "purchased me" come from Tamu.

"You should be with your family, being a doctor," I said.

"Show us the other falcons," Jefferson said to change the subject.

The Astors spent much of the day with James Madison, Jefferson's secretary of state, at his plantation nearby. John said he had much to discuss with Monroe, whose views on Astor had altered considerably over the years. He had apparently thought Astor some kind of magical criminal, as nothing else could explain to him the vast fortune he had acquired so quickly. By the end of the day, armed with knowledge that only a secretary of state could have shared, Astor disclosed to me a way how he would become still richer. Be patient, dear reader.

After lunch at Montpelier, Madison's plantation, the Astors returned to Monticello. John relayed to me that Madison had asked him, "What is this I'm hearing about you opening a second theater in New York, one for opera?"

"Mr. Madison," John replied, "I've brought the greatest composer in the world to America, and the opera that the president attended only a few weeks ago was deeply enjoyed by him."

"It must be costing you a fortune," Madison said.

"And worth every dollar," Astor said, making Sarah smile.

"A fool and his money are soon parted," Madison supposedly said—or was it Sarah?

"Wouldn't it show the world a civilized country if we were to have a national opera?" Astor asked him.

"You want our citizenry to pay for Italians to come here to sing?" Madison was incredulous.

"A national opera would show the world that America is here to stay, that we respect the traditions from which we immigrated," Astor said.

"The traditions from which our parents escaped! I was born in Virginia, sir. I am no Englishman."

"Don't you believe the teaching of music would help soften the harder edges of this land?" Astor asked.

"That is possible, but opera is not the language of the American soul, I assure you."

"I've seen more of this nation than you, Mr. Secretary, and I can tell you that music is very much at the heart of the American soul."

"Yes, but not music from Italy. Perhaps your Mozart can develop something for your money." Madison laughed.

Astor said, "Mozart is no Italian. He writes operas in German and English now."

I dressed early for dinner so that I could tune the fortepiano that had been brought from New York on a bier that looked like a casket. I hoped the journey had not harmed my favorite instrument, and I was surprised it was not more out of tune than it was. I got the instrument ready for my concert after dinner, though I was still unsure what I would play.

CHAPTER 112

That evening's formal dinner at Monticello began with whiskey punch on the west patio, and I, unaccustomed to spirits, soon felt slightly dizzy. The Astors regaled Jefferson with tales from Montpelier, and Astor told him about the fur business and his burgeoning business at the music store, so unexpectedly a success with the arrival of me—"the very Mozart," as he described me. Jefferson, though, wanted to hear all about the funding of the opera house, what it was actually costing Astor, and how he intended to sustain it. Astor would not disclose the amount of money he had spent building the theater, as he thought that might discourage Jefferson from considering the proposal he made at the start of the dinner.

"I propose the first toast of the evening to President Jefferson, whose hospitality is matched only by his generous heart," Astor said, as Jefferson, Sarah, and I raised our glasses. There were more servants in the dining room than diners.

"And I propose to you, Mr. President, that Sarah and I build an additional opera house, a national opera, placed within sight of the Congressional House, and a short carriage ride from the President's House, right in Washington's heart."

Jefferson laughed. "We barely have adequate buildings for the nation's business. I cannot be seen to be building a place for entertainment within the government. Besides, we have theaters already."

"But Mr. President, imagine foreign dignitaries coming to the new city of Washington and taking them to see *The Magic Flute,* as you did in New York just recently," Astor said.

"Yes, that was splendid, and you make an excellent point. It would show our best to the world. Monroe and Madison and Adams would slaughter me for even mentioning it."

"I will donate the cost of building the theater, Mr. President. It could be the grandest theater in the world. We have learned a great deal about building theaters from putting up two in the last ten years."

"I will give it some thought. You really cannot imagine the opposition one would face to such an idea, even if the building costs taxpayers nothing. We risk looking to our critics like the very aristocrats we declared independence from, do we not?"

"Like business, Mr. President, there is an American way to do it that needn't copy the Old World," Astor said.

"What this country needs is farms, not opera houses," Jefferson said, already preparing for the arguments he knew would be forthcoming.

"Mr. President, this country could be great enough to have both. And if a private citizen wants to fund a national opera, which could also be a national theater, wouldn't that be an opportunity to create excellent plays and operas that would be ambassadors for the nation?"

"I don't view *The Magic Flute* itself as an ambassador from Vienna," Jefferson said.

"I believe I do, respectfully," Astor said.

"Herr Mozart, what say you to this astounding proposition?" Jefferson asked me.

"Mr. President, I am honored beyond measure to be in your home, and my reuniting with Tamu today was such an unexpected moment. I am speechless with gratitude," I said.

"Come now, tell me your thoughts about a national opera."

"I have not had the pleasure of visiting the new capital city, but I do know that if there are to be two opera houses in this nation, it will require training. It might serve the country well to have a conservatory of music," I said.

"We do not even have a national bank yet!" Jefferson laughed. "And we are still paying debts from the Revolution. How can I justify entertainment?"

"I would not view it as entertainment, Mr. President, but investment. It could alter the course of your nation," I said, surprised at my own words, which sounded rather like John.

"Nations are not altered by operas, with all respect, Herr Mozart."

Astor spoke up. "Are they not, Mr. President?"

"Thomas...please...call me Thomas," the president said, perturbed.

CHAPTER 113

During our two more days at Monticello, I spent much time with Tamu. I would always remember the days as a fond memory, though it distressed me to see Tamu enslaved. I wanted him to return to New York with me, but I could not find a time to ask Astor. Jefferson and Astor were in heavy consultation with each other during those days, walking in the gardens for many hours and meeting in Jefferson's study. I could tell that subjects of great import were being discussed, and I was nervous to interrupt John to ask him what to do about a single person, when they were probably discussing the purchase of the Louisiana Territory. On the last afternoon before we were to depart for New York, I saw Sarah sitting on the west patio awaiting the punch hour. I asked if I could approach her.

"Of course, Amadé!"

She asked how my trip had been.

"It has been miraculous, Sarah. I have found a friend I met in France, Tamu, who Mr. Jefferson purchased for Monticello. He is such a wonderful man. Is there any way he could return to New York with us?"

"We would have to take that up with Mr. Jefferson. If he owns Tamu, he would have to give him to us. Mr. Astor will never purchase a slave, Amadé." Sarah talked of Tamu as though he were a piece of furniture.

"Would Mr. Jefferson give him to you? Do people ever give away slaves?" I was trying to puzzle a way to get Tamu freed to be with me, then I could conspire to get him home to his family.

"I'm sure people do, but my understanding is that your friend is new here and is young and strong. That makes him quite valuable," Sarah said.

"Would Mr. Astor purchase Tamu if he could work at the new opera house? Tamu can do anything: paint, make balloons, train falcons, and he is a healer. In France he healed me from a dreadful pestilence."

"I can bring the subject to Mr. Astor, but I feel certain he will never purchase Tamu, not for any reason. But if we can convince the president to give him to us, then of course it might be possible. For that would mean his liberation." She added, "But I don't want you to get your hopes up, and I ask that you not say anything to Tamu, either."

I could not abide the idea of returning to New York and Tamu being left behind as a slave. I had said farewell to him once already and could not bear it again.

The final dinner at Monticello was informal, and Jefferson thanked the Astors for bringing me to America. When I returned to my room, there was a parting gift waiting on my bed, a beautifully wrapped little package. I was unsure if should unwrap it so I packed it with my things to return to New York.

There was a letter attached to the package.

4 July, 1805

Dear Amadé,

It was an unimaginable pleasure to welcome you to Monticello. My little hill is like our young country: unfinished and full of promise. Hearing you play both the fiddle and the clavichord was such a joy, and I'm sure the tones will be soaked into the timbers of the home.

Hearing your glorious *Magic Flute* and then enjoying your company, I was reminded of a book I was given years ago by a German friend in Paris. I'm afraid my German is not competent enough to enjoy it in your native tongue, so I feel better gifting it to you. The book has enjoyed enormous fame. I read it not long ago in its original English, strange as it was to read a book by a woman. It is a fanciful and beautiful story. As I was recalling it, it struck me as the type of story you might conjure into a beautiful opera.

It is touching that you found your friend Tamu again. Mr. Astor spoke to me about releasing him into his employ so that Tamu could come to New York. I cannot at this time do without him at the plantation, as he has made himself indispensable to life at Monticello.

I do hope you enjoy reading *Oronooko*. And I eagerly await our next meeting.

Thomas

The return journey from Monticello to New York passed so quickly for me that it was finally possible to feel the size of the American nation. Imagine me, a boy from Salzburg, receiving a gift from the president of this new nation! Our stay in the inn was predictable, the first time I had been able to predict anything in my new country. We crossed the Hudson by ferry just as I had with John when we first saw the city, making me nostalgic for those early days.

I expected to return to what had become normal life in New York. We had been away only eight days, yet what awaited me upon arrival at Vesey Street was staggering, unbelievable, and joyous. Never had so many gifts arrived in my life at once, and so unexpectedly, like a river meeting a dam that sends it back on itself before bursting. Several of the servants of the house approached the carriage excitedly to tell me and the Astors that Alice had given birth to a healthy baby boy.

"When can I see him? When can I see Alice?" I asked.

Sarah said, "Let me go to Alice and give you a report. Ladies are not at their best after babies come, believe me." Sarah went off with the servants, laughing.

I could not immediately grasp what else greeted me, for they seemed at first like ghosts, only silhouettes in the doorway of the great house, yet they were not dead. They were standing right before me as though no ocean had come between us.

CHAPTER 114

Nannerl, my beloved sister, was weeping in the entryway of the Astor house, and as I hugged her I could smell the lavender soaps she had used since childhood. The scent of her brought back the entirety of my youth, and I could not stop weeping long enough to introduce her to the Astors. John Astor said something under his breath about the perfection of seeing the famous siblings reunited. He had seen us perform together as children. And there was a child, Babette, Nannerl's youngest daughter, whom I had never met. She was about the age of our little Franz. Two relatives, where only moments before I had been so alone! Babette even greeted me with a little a cappella song she wrote for me. Imagine the joy!

The woman behind Nannerl greeted Astor, and I was so overcome with seeing Nannerl that I did not immediately regard the other woman.

I heard her voice speaking to Astor, and all I could do was say her name.

"Nancy? Nancy. Nancy? Nancy!"

I could scarcely believe Nancy Storace was in front of me. My dear Susanna, the heartiest laugh I had ever encountered, the woman who had been present to witness the greatest triumphs of my midlife, was standing before me, her eyes brimmed with tears. She remembered our beloved *Figaro*.

"Rafaello..." she sang to me in a whisper as I embraced her, my laughter turning to tears.

"Oh my darling, darling, Nancy. I am so overcome with happiness to see you. Oh, God is a great God!" I said.

"My darling man. It is a miracle to see you again!"

"Wolfie, Johann has gone to Heaven," Nannerl said.

"Your husband is no more?" I asked.

Nannerl was weeping. "He has passed on, leaving me to come to see my dear brother who I never thought I would see again. Why did you not tell us you were coming to the New World?"

"I did not know myself!" I laughed my secret laugh to my sister.

Nannerl and Nancy—I kept repeating their names and embracing them. I knew that my life in America would now be completely different with them present in the country. I knew it would take days, weeks perhaps, to fully understand what had been awakened by their presence at Vesey Street.

John and Sarah, always accommodating, welcomed both women into the house, vowing to place them into new quarters as the new farm being built to the west of Longacre was being constructed. Within a few minutes of our return, John had already received a report on the buildings at Longacre, which were going up faster than he had expected. The large house that John and Sarah and the children would occupy was naturally taking longer, but the other houses were not far from completion.

As in several instances in my long life, I could not stop crying. How I would ever compose again with the two most beloved women of my life having arrived in my new country to distract and delight me? But I knew the spark would return. I just needed the time afforded by distance to relearn the love of their presence.

The surprise was not only Nancy and Nannerl. I was handed a parcel from Vienna, from Konstanze, which included a letter from her as well as new editions of two symphonies by Ludwig, in C major and D major, sent directly to him from my own wife. The letter was a lengthy one, so I did what I often did: I put it into my satchel to read in the daytime.

Sarah came to the main room of the house where I was still greeting Nannerl and Nancy to report that Alice had indeed ended her confinement with the birth a few days before, and Abraham Mozart was sleeping comfortably by her side. Abraham...my son was Abraham. I longed to see Alice in person, but Sarah advised waiting a few days. Nannerl and

Nancy, hearing of the birth of Abraham Mozart, had many questions that they knew would take many days to answer, and the moment of reunion did not seem to be the most opportune time to ask me how I had become a father again with Konstanze awaiting me in Vienna.

Their questions were set aside when a servant brought little Abraham to us, and they said that the sight of me meeting my child was worth the long trip across the ocean. Though the baby was but days old, I thought him the hairiest child I had ever seen. Our boy had a full head of hair, more than I had at any time in my life, and hair on his arms and back as well. He was beautiful, all the more so because he had qualities of both Alice and the Mozarts. His skin was dark, like the scrumptious women I met in Naples as a child, but his features were mine. I had always had trouble looking on infants as future humans. I understood the obvious, that *die Kinder* were little blanks pieces of manuscript awaiting composition. They could be formed into whatever their parents imagined for them, and I knew fears were inherited.

It was reported to me that Alice was recovering well from the birth, and I could possibly see her within a week. Little Abraham, though, was to be brought to me every morning, and every morning I would weep at the sight of our beautiful boy. I had never imagined that I would be shaping another life. By the time little Abraham was born, my little Franz was becoming a man.

Time was the most terrifying prison of all. That prison always set itself upon me near the end of a composition, demarcated by deep dreads within my spirit that dragged me toward some dark image. During the prison of time, every interruption, no matter how trivial, felt like it could ruin everything about the composition itself. In whatever way I tried to stay focused and get everything written down, something always interrupted, and it provoked fury in me, and fury was the one thing I could never understand.

CHAPTER 115

Nannerl, Babette, and Nancy were shown to bedrooms they would occupy until the Longacre farm was completed and we moved north. I finally made it to my quarters in the tower of the Astor house. I was exhausted from the journey and from the arrival of Nancy and Nannerl, and I had the letter from Konstanze to pore over. It had yet to dawn on me that I was truly again a father. My first surprises had been awaiting me at the door of the house, but this surprise was resting in my room, lying on my bed. My eyes adjusted to the dim light of the bedroom, but I could not trust my sight. Nancy and Nannerl were likely already asleep, so it couldn't be either of them. Who was lying with his back to the door in my own bed? I moved closer and was dumbstruck. It was…yes…could it be so…yes…

"Lorenzo?" I said, loudly enough to wake the sleeping man.

"Tutto è disposto: l'ora dovrebbe esser vicina…" the *bastardo* sang, and in the right key.

It really was Lorenzo, the arsehole, and I called him every filthy name I knew. My life had been a series of entrances and exits of Lorenzo Da Ponte, but at least this was an entrance. I had just become a father, at an age most become grandfathers. I was still absorbing the arrival of my sister and the best singer I knew. I had yet to understand how they arrived in New York, what their plans were, but no one came to the New World only to visit; one only came to start a new life.

"Amadé, I last heard your voice, the voice of voices, somewhere in the fog of Portsmouth. For a long time I wasn't sure it was you. When I started reading in the broadsheets that you had arrived in New York, it dawned on me that it really was you back on those shores of England. It occurred to me that you must have found your way to the New World."

"Where have you been, *bastardo*?"

"The valley of the Susquehanna River is one of the only heavens on the Earth. I must take you there."

I made it clear that I had no interest in visiting a river, not any river. The summer of 1805 was a momentous one indeed!

Lorenzo ignored me and said, "I have two librettos ready for you, and I've worked on them both for over a year, hour after hour of refinement and rhyming. My friend, I offer to you the two operas that will sit on either side of our greatest work: *The Barber of Seville* and *The Guilty Mother*."

I took the pages from him. On sight, the librettos looked much like *The Marriage of Figaro*, and I got the same rush of excitement and readiness upon leafing through Lorenzo's two proposals. I knew there was already a very famous opera on the *Barber* by Giovanni Paisiello, popular since my youth, and in certain circles it would be impossible to compete with an existing opera. But in a new country without knowledge of Paisiello's popular opera, it was an opportunity rarely found.

"I also suggest we think of a couple of rewrites of pieces we both saw and knew weren't very good, like Stephen Storace's *Gli equivoci* or Salieri's *Axur*. You loved those librettos and talked about writing both."

"I've moved on from those kinds of operas, Lorenzo. But there is no doubt I am going to compose our two Beaumarchais operas! You ass-licking prick!" I was crying with joy.

"You will notice, Amadé, that each opera has a slightly altered version of 'Tutti contenti saremo così,' so there can be unity between the three works, and in the final opera it must be written quite differently, with irony. You will find the way, I have no doubt," Lorenzo said.

"I have so many works to compose now, most especially *Faust*. Astor has made this a dream come true. But you, how could you just leave me stranded in Portsmouth like that? You cannot imagine the hell into which I was then forced."

"I could hear your voice but there was no possible way to turn the ship back. We had been late leaving as it was, searching for the right wind or something. Our journey was quite fast, under thirty days, and incredibly pleasant, I must say. Astor travels like Joseph II."

My anger at that moment was of an unusual kind. Normally, I would just blurt out whatever angered me, like the geysers at Baden Baden, but this was too enormous. I decided instead to move on with Lorenzo as though nothing had happened, because I knew if I began to release the well of anger, there would be no stopping it, and no more operas together. We ended up talking far into the night before he left to walk home, far to the east of the lower island.

CHAPTER 116

Those days after Monticello were the fullest of my life. I spent days reading Lorenzo's new librettos for *Barber* and *Mother*, and immediately the music began its journey to me, though this was time I should have spent on *Faust*. Here were words that music could bring to life, and every ensemble was already there, perfectly placed for what I needed. All of the fun we'd had writing *Figaro* all those years ago returned to me when I read the words. Words were worlds.

My little Abraham was my daily happiness, and Alice was recovering toward herself each day. Nancy and Nannerl were learning their way around our part of the island, and I immediately set them to work teaching at the music shop, where our students quickly began to grow in number.

Lorenzo had decided to move back to New York, largely to be with his fellow Italians who were arriving in ever-greater numbers, as Sarah often noted. The Italians were mostly gathered in settlements far to the east from Vesey Street, by the eastern river of the city, and I had rarely been over there. That part of the city was undeveloped compared to the area around the store and the new opera house, but I knew that Lorenzo did not care about such luxuries. I thought he had lived in unnecessary squalor in Vienna and, for all I knew, in Venice as well. What I saw of Lorenzo's part of London had been alarming, but I had never known anyone so capable as Lorenzo of interacting with kings and nobility while going home to a dirt floor. I admired his adaptability, in a way, because life would be infinitely simpler if I had not been so accustomed to physical comfort. I knew I could never afford the life I had always been shown, but I felt I must have been shown it for a reason. God was not such to show a man something he could not attain.

Despite the brief sojourn to Monticello, there was an inordinate amount of mail in the weeks following. I had a letter from the German Society of the City of New York, apparently only just now aware of my presence, asking me to write a piano trio and a string quartet for an event at their new building near the Astor Opera House.

Near year's end, I finally got to the package that had arrived from Konstanze. I recognized her scripts and also the special ink she used for certain types of paper. I disliked that she was using it for packages, as it was expensive to use for something so ordinary. I opened the package and found a letter from Konstanze and a set of scores. The little witch—she'd sent me not only scores to Ludwig's first and second symphonies but also the parts for them, parts I could tell had been played because they included markings that only players make. This meant she wanted me to perform them.

1 June, 1805

Dear Wolfie,

I hope this reaches you, as it has valuable music within it and you will be the only person in America in possession of it. Ludwig's symphony has caused a sensation in Vienna, as so many of yours did. Franz and I attended the first performance and I then returned for several more. I think it would be wonderful for Ludwig if you were to give the first performances in the New World.

I am grateful that you've arranged for some payment through Mr. Astor, but I wonder how you expect me to live on only that. You've asked me to send all of your scores to you, but how do you imagine I will then have an income? I have been working with your publisher and arranging performances, and now you are asking me to remove that meager income. I cannot understand it.

As to the other matter. There is no kind way to put it: we are no longer married. The Archbishop of St. Stephen's contacted Salzburg. All of this took many weeks, you understand, and under the circumstances they consider us to be married no longer.

I wasn't going to tell you, but I was with child. At my age this is a significant worry, of course, and the child did not live. I know you will worry about it, so you must realize that Franz and I have continued to be together. He is such a fine man, and he loves you so. It gives me the feeling of you and I still being together, the best of us remaining through the separation.

I have left my sin within the capable hands of my confessor, and I am slowly coming to penance.

Stanzie

I was stunned by Konstanze's adultery, before turning the cold eye upon myself, as I had done precisely as Konstanze had. But, I reasoned, I had been forced to go to London alone and thus was tricked into coming to America, whereas Konstanze had *chosen* not to fulfill her commitment to me. Now she had been untrue to me with Süssmayer, someone who had vowed fidelity not only to his own wife, but to me! Süssmayer had seen me at my most vulnerable.

I finally opened Beethoven's C-major symphony only to see that the first chord was lifted right from a Haydn quartet in E-flat major, if memory served. A standard lyrical opening followed, like several of my symphonies and nearly all of Haydn's. I had to wonder again who this kid thought he was. Still, the first movement was solidly constructed, if somewhat conventional. From the second movement onward, though, it was stunning. This was one of the great symphonies that had been written, up there with the best of Haydn and, though I hated to admit it, surpassing anything I had yet composed except, perhaps, *Tempest*, and Ludwig would have no way of hearing that. Giving a performance of this new symphony in New York would be the magnanimous thing to do, but it risked exposing my own musicians, having been immersed in my own compositions for a long time, to a work that was superior. I imagined them playing Ludwig's work and asking me to bring him to America. What then? President Jefferson would be obliged to be as accommodating of Ludwig as he had of me, possibly even offering to pay for it. And publicly showing my jealousy was a humiliation I could not risk. What to do?

Ludwig's second symphony awaited my perusal, and it was a huge and ambitious step forward from his first. The slow movement was one of the most beautiful possible, even as many of the ideas were slightly stolen from me but, again I hated to admit it, improved and personalized by this upstart. The length he achieved in the slow movement was extraordinary, as though he had simply mined it like ore. His D-major symphony was an absolute miracle. Every idea that to my mind had ever surfaced in music was attempted by Ludwig within it, and he reached ever onward toward the infinite, bringing the symphony to an amazing conclusion.

Other scores arrived in the shop, including two piano concertos of Ludwig's that Konstanze had left out, and all the scores were bought by Hewitt from London: Paisiello, Cherubini, Spontini, all the men I knew back in Vienna or elsewhere, and I would not even admit to Hewitt that I never opened their scores, not because I thought they were bad. They undoubtedly were not. But I did, somehow, know what they were about, knew how they sounded. Remember, friends, I know things that others that do not. These compositions, unlike Ludwig's, were going to be predictable. I could tell what they were going to write before they wrote it, and they never disappointed me. But Ludwig could not be predicted. I stared at the final pages of the first movement of his D-major symphony, knowing that I had seen all of the specific musical gestures before, but never used so inventively. Ludwig seemed to never run out of ideas. The larghetto movement quickly became an obsession. It was absolutely the most beautiful music ever written. How was it possible that this vain and immature boy could produce such genius?

A score to *Fidelio* also arrived in the store, which was what Ludwig finally decided to retitle his *Leonore*. I was certain that Konstanze had attended this opera, probably with both Franzes young and old, but had neglected to write to me about it, the minx. I read through the work at the piano, astounded by some of the music but perplexed as to why Ludwig could not understand that opening the opera like a comedy focused on two minor characters would diminish the entire effect. As I read and sang the roles, I could not understand why he did not simply start the opera with Leonore's arrival. For all of Ludwig's genius, he was not a natural opera composer. This, I am ashamed to admit at this moment, gave me great comfort, for I knew he would never be able to compete with me in terms of opera. *Fidelio* had two exemplary moments that I could never surpass no matter how long I lived: "Euch werde Lohn," which may be the most beautiful melody of my lifetime, and the magnificent choral finale of the opera, which was unstoppably great. I read through it twelve times, crying each time, and I never wanted it to end.

Hewitt kept buying Ludwig's scores to sell in the shop, and each one gave me a little stab of pain. Jealousy is a terrible feeling. I wondered why Hewitt bought *Cantata on the Death of Emperor Joseph II*, as why would anyone in America care about the death of a man they never knew? I spent an hour in the shop poring over the cantata, having not thought of it since hearing it in Vienna many years before. I had never forgotten how glorious Ludwig's music could be, nor would I ever forget how heartbroken all musicians had been with the Kaiser's death. He had been the greatest of all friends to music, and his death left a great void in Vienna, indeed in the whole world. I had met no one to ever replace him until meeting Astor, and Astor was greater in a way, because Astor had no reason other than love of music to be so generous. It felt so odd to me to feel that, but it is an honest feeling, cherished reader of this, my private testament.

Staring at the score of Ludwig's cantata, I thought his music was screaming at God, when composers should let God speak through them. Ludwig's music was just too much of everything. Too much emotion. Too many contrasts. He asked things of voices that they could not do with any ease. There were certain passages with too many accented notes. In the cantata, Ludwig demanded the bass soloist hold the word *Stärke* longer than any human could achieve. Why ask singers for impossible things? All that accomplished was making singers feel inadequate, and drawing attention to the composer over the composition. And all of those heavy accents! So brutal for the players. Where did he get his intemperance?

I could only stare in wonder at the score. After all, it was the work of a teenager, but if he had learned anything, he would have written *Fidelio* differently, surely. There was beautiful music in his opera, but very little drama, thanks be to God.

CHAPTER 117

I wanted to have my own music in my mind when I finally was allowed to see Alice and Abraham together, but all I could think of was that glorious "Euch werde Lohn in besseren Welten" from *Fidelio*, and the sight of Alice in her bed, aglow with having the arduous birth behind her, brought the tune back to me so strongly that it refused to leave.

Alice burst with tears upon seeing me, as the weeks that had passed in my absence seemed to her like years. I held her as she cried. Abraham was asleep at our side.

"Ami, I missed you so much. I believe that I died for a time as Abraham was arriving," she said to me.

"But my darling, you are here so you cannot have died." I caressed her face and gorgeous hair.

"There is a place we go, Ami, I can tell you. It was beautiful and terrifying, like the bridge you have to cross," Alice said.

I thought of my bridge, and realized I had not had any visions of it in some time. The realization worried me until I remembered how unutterably terrifying the bridge could be.

"You are safe, my darling," I said.

"You do not understand, Ami. They are going to send our child to an orphanage. I can feel it. Abraham is an illegal child," Alice cried.

"Who told you that? No one is sending Mozart's son to an orphanage," I said, but my voice did not ease her fears.

"Everyone who works in the household has said that a child born of black and white is illegal. Aren't I proof of that?" She could not stop crying.

"Are you an orphan?" I asked, embarrassed that I had never asked her before.

"My skin is the color of rape, Ami." She said the words coldly, quietly.

"You skin is gorgeous, my darling," I said, trying to reassure her.

"I haven't thought of my parents in years, as I've had no cause to. But bringing Abraham into the world brought it all back to me," Alice said.

"Where are your parents?"

"My mother was a slave and my father was her master. That is all I know. I was brought to New York by the Astors before the time of memory. I have only ever known the Astors as those who raised me in their household."

I kept my voice as quiet as hers. "Who told you your mother was a slave?"

"My older sister came here with me, and she remembered quite a lot."

"Where is she?" I had never heard before about Alice having an older sister.

"She ran away, and I don't know where she is. I miss her so much. And now they are going to take away our son away, too." Alice started to cry again.

Abraham stirred, as if reacting to his mother's tears. Each time I had seen him he had been sleeping, but on that day I stared into the eyes of our son for the first time.

"Oh, my son!" I cried. "Look at his eyes! He looks like me. I have never had a child look so like me."

Alice looked tired, so I wanted to let her rest, vowing to return before the day ended.

I went to find Sarah, eager to learn if what Alice had said about Abraham was true. Now having looked into the child's eyes, I could not bear to part with him, even though he was only days old. I was relieved to find Sarah in the small dining room, the one the Astors normally used only for breakfast.

"Amadé! I'm glad you are here, as I've just returned from the Longacre farm and it has made wonderful progress. You and Alice will be able to move within a few weeks," Sarah said.

"Is it true that little Abraham has to go to an orphanage?" I asked.

"Heavens! Who told you that?"

"Alice told me just now that some members of the household staff have said it."

"It is true that in some states your child is illegal, but not in New York. Still, many people will think it scandalous. So moving up to the farm will be even more important."

"Will I have to keep my son a secret? Will no one be allowed to know he is a Mozart?"

"One must be willing, Amadé, to see what the years will bring. You will go to the farm and only come down alone to the store or the opera house. Out of the glare of the city, John and I feel all will be well." Sarah's voice was beginning to calm me.

"So Abraham will not have to be sent to an orphanage?" I asked again, needing a clear answer.

"Certainly not. John and I will not let Alice's heart be broken by such a thing, nor yours. Others might do that, but not us."

"Sarah, whatever I did in life to deserve such good fortune, I hope I can continue to earn it."

"You are earning it every day, my dear Amadé, by creating a musical culture in this land that has thus far been entirely free of civilization, from what I can tell. The more we can establish the opera house, and the more we can get people interested in music, the better this city and country will be, and the safer *you* will be."

"I've been thinking of abolishing repeat signs. I have always just accepted the repetitions as part of what we do, but I wonder if people really need them anymore?" I said, surprising Sarah.

"For what my amateur opinion may be worth, I would advise keeping all repeats in your symphonies and piano works. I think people need to hear all of your ideas once just to absorb them, and then really enjoy the second time. I know that is how I always enjoy them," Sarah said.

"But I have never written repeats in concertos; I am unsure why. I hate suddenly thinking about something that I've never thought about before. It makes me feel that everything up to that moment has been a lie," I admitted.

"I think repetition is important. Not everyone understands everything the first time," Sarah said.

"Yes, but we should be able to move beyond that. We should be able to say what we want to say without requiring repetition. Music should be understood at first hearing." I was surprised that I said it.

"Well, Amadé, I'm sure that is something for you to figure out."

"I think we need to think seriously about beginning a school," I said. "Musicians need schooling."

CHAPTER 118

My mind was such a jumble that it kept sleep away for many hours. Nancy, Nannerl, Lorenzo, Jefferson, Abraham, moving to the farm, and the letter from Konstanze—all in that one packed year of 1805! I knew that both Nancy and Nannerl could help me with teaching, and that I wanted to write two more operas with Lorenzo, if only to re-create the feeling of those years. *Figaro* had been one thrilling day after another, though I always feared that the work was too long. But every time we talked about removing something to shorten it, the extraction seemed unbearable. We had long ago discussed *School for Scandal* around the time we turned to *Così fan tutte,* but neither of us could find a way to make Sheridan's comedy redemptive, which was the only thing that interested either of us.

Almost slipping into sleep, I saw the bridge for the first time in months. I thought of an idea I had harbored for many years, which was to write an opera to complement *Così,* one in which the women play the trick and prove the inconstancy of the men. I thought it could be as funny as *Così,* probably more so, and the opera could be more realistic. I knew from my feelings about Konstanze's letter that I was the one who had been inconstant so many times throughout our marriage, and Konstanze had been so only when I had forced her into no other choice. I wrote down some sketches to discuss with Lorenzo.

I had worked hard all of my life but I had never seen anyone work like John Astor. He was the first one out of the house every morning and was often the last to return. I rarely saw him in the weeks following our return from Monticello, when everything in my life converged and changed so rapidly. And I needed to see John in those days, because the weight of my sister's arrival along with Nancy—followed by Lorenzo's sudden reappearance, which typical of him would not last—and our constant worries about little Abraham were all heavy things to carry when *Faust* needed my full attention. Little did I know then, in what turned to the early months of 1806, that the burdens placed upon my shoulders were to gain upon themselves.

Nancy and Nannerl had not known each other well before their voyage to America together. To my memory, they would have met on only one prior occasion, when we first did *Figaro* in Vienna, and even by then Nannerl was on the sidelines of my life, partly placed there by Papa but mostly by her own wishes. Nannerl was a tremendously happy child and indifferent in her maturity; as my symphonies and operas started to be noticed and talked about, she withdrew from me. I was the opposite: as I became more successful, I wanted to be closer to my sister, but she had no interest. Isn't it funny how separate a sister and brother can be from each other? Nancy approved of me marrying Konstanze but Nannerl and Papa did not, and my marriage, which should have been solely the concern of me and my wife, seemed constantly to divide the opinions of our friends.

Alice became another matter entirely, for Nannerl loved her immediately, while Nancy was indifferent. How divergent people are. In those first hours we were together in New York, I learned that Nannerl had written to me in London saying she wanted to visit, but she received no response because her letter arrived after my unexpected departure. How much of my life turned on letters I did not receive or, if received, I neglected to open in a timely way. Plaguing me always was the unopened letter from Ludwig, which had sat so long ignored that to open it felt a sacrilege. Had I survived long enough in London to have heard from my sister, perhaps we could have enjoyed a musical life together in London for the rest of our lives.

CHAPTER 119

I used to wonder who survived such terrible circumstances as being forced out of a country and onto a boat until it happened to me. Nannerl must have corresponded with Konstanze, because some impulse drew her to London to find me. Imagine my poor sister calling on me at St. James only to discover I was gone. She somehow found her way to Nancy, who had received my letter from New York by then, and they concocted their plan to find me across the ocean. When Nannerl's silly husband Berchtold had the good sense to die, she had a choice to either return to Salzburg alone or try to find her only way to an income, to me. Nannerl was always so obedient to Papa that it was difficult to know what she felt for herself. In those early days in New York, we spoke as we had not spoken since we were children.

Her arrival left me feeling she was lonely for her family, even that she missed her brother who loved her so much. Her Louis and Jeanette remained in Salzburg, already adults, and Maria Babette, just about the age of our little Franz, was suddenly to be an American child. Babette took to America faster than any of us, which was remarkable to see. As adept as we became in English, we retained our Salzburg accents, but not Babette. Within weeks she sounded like she belonged. I wanted to ask Nannerl why Louis and Jeanette had never much interested her, but this is not something a brother can ask of his sister. I believe I know the reason, though, which is that she did not love Berchtold enough to also love his children.

Nannerl is such a complicated creature. I love her, but she was not by her nature a mother. She did inquire about my little Franz in particular, knowing he was home in Vienna with Konstanze. Nannerl expressed to me her love and admiration for Alice, yet she was not particularly happy about being an American aunt, especially not to a child with dark skin and a mother who looked like Alice. I knew she would come around in time. When Abraham was old enough to talk, he called her Auntie Nanny. This made Nannerl bristle at first, but after a glass or two of sherry, she came to like it.

Nannerl's daughter, my glorious little niece Maria Babette von Berchtold zu Sonnenburg, whom we had called Babette for her whole life, immediately took to me. Children always seemed to be drawn to me, I think because I kept my spirit young even as my body grew older and more decrepit. The Astor children, especially Willie, was closer to me in his youth than even to his governess, and Abraham and I took to speaking a secret language, just as Nannerl and I did as children. One of Babette's first acts upon arrival was to sit at the fortepiano on Vesey Street and play not only one of my piano sonatas, the long B flat, but also one of her own that she had composed. This was a child who had not been near an instrument in months because of the arduous journey. I knew immediately that all of the collective musical talent of the Mozart family had accumulated in Babette.

Nannerl asked me to take over Babette's training, as she felt she had given her all she could. "Whatever I put in front of her she can do with no effort at all," Nannerl told me, and this proved to be true. I rigorously started training Babette's fingers, and her natural agility and force astounded me from the beginning. She was at first resistant to improvisation, as I could tell that her little mind was rather like Nannerl's: she wanted to plan and control her musical reactions to the world. Improvisation takes away some element of control, it is true, but I was longing to see what was beneath Babette's layers of protection from herself. She had a coldness about her at the keyboard, a seriousness that masked whatever caused fear in her. Papa had done this, as had Nannerl, but over time Nannerl let go her protections with me, and her complicated improvisations would make her laugh with joy.

I tried something with Babette I had never tried with another student. I asked her to begin an improvisation on the rondo of my simple C-major sonata, but I asked her to play it very slowly, much slower than normal. She did this with great ease. As she progressed, I got very close to her ear and began singing a counterpoint improvisation in her ear, which would have confused most students, but it freed Babette into incredible flights of melody and filigree, far beyond anything I could have dreamed. I kept singing, asking her to continue her meanderings around the keyboard. Eventually she found her way back to my rondo, but not after a fantastical journey. After this, Babette started bringing me her own compositions. Dear reader, I have no idea how or if I will be remembered, nor if any of my music will outlive me, but I can say with the certainty of a God that Babette is the finest composer the world has ever known.

Many a priest in New York City thought it unseemly that a young girl would have aspirations to compose music, and they made their displeasure known both to Nannerl and to me, but Babette combated every morsel of dogged dogma with a greater composition. There were many, for reasons I cannot deduce, who tried to say I was writing works for Babette and she was claiming them as hers. But these idiotic suppositions were themselves belied by the amount of music I was writing at the very time Babette began producing more works than I ever had in my life: symphonies, sonatas, concertos, string quartets…they flowed out of her, and they became more important works as she aged.

My own compositions from those years after Nannerl and Babette arrived remained incredible joys for me, but in hearing Babette's more mature music in 1806 and 1807, I came to a difficult realization that my music was approaching the peak of what I could achieve. *King Lear* and *Faust*, in particular, had drained some portion of my life force, as though they were lying in wait for someone like Babette. Her talent was beyond belief. I wanted to introduce her to Haydn as soon as possible, but had no way of doing so.

She was a serious child, not at all what Nannerl had been, and she seemed to carry some weight placed upon her shoulders by God, and the only thing that could relieve her weight was composition. I knew this feeling of having to get something out of the spirit like a protracted shit, but I had rarely encountered it in others. The composers I knew across my life were invariably craftsmen, exactly like cobblers or tailors, but their craft was music. Writing music was never like that for me, nor was it for Babette. It was something we did instead of going to church.

I wanted to unite with Nannerl to play together as we had as children on the violin and piano, with one of us on either instrument, and to fulfill again one of my favorite combinations: the two of us playing four hands on one piano. For a brief time long ago, we were the toast of the European courts and the aristocracy, and I knew we could also be this in New York and the other large American cities, if we chose to do so again. It was only on the surface that the New World was different from the Old World; underneath it was the same, with both an aristocratic and a servant class. But each time I mentioned playing again, she muttered something about not being able to play any longer, being out of practice, or times having changed too much. I knew this was false, as I had heard her amid lessons at the store and near the opera house, and she could still play bloody well. I conclude that she was worried about the talk and rumor spreading around New York about me and Alice. Despite all our efforts to keep our union quiet, as we were sequestered far north on the Longacre farm, rumors found their way around the city. I offer no testament, dear ones, to these endless rumors, because to comment on them would be to give them a matter they do not possess.

CHAPTER 120

Nancy and Nannerl were settled into a house near the Vesey Street property, and they dined with us often in the big house. I lost track of where everyone lived, really and truly, because every day I seemed to learn of another home or store or warehouse owned by the Astors. What would my life have possibly been without them? I owe the entirety of my American life to John Astor, but even that was all due to Lorenzo, the wily arse. Must all artists constantly owe their lives to the generosity of others? Lorenzo was forever getting me into difficult scrapes, but in the case of chasing after John Astor's ship, he nearly killed me, but the near-killing saved me. Still, I was happy to see him in New York, a friendly old face in a new city filled with strangers. He came to dinner many nights in a row in those early New York days, echoing our brief time in London, and John drew new delight from our Viennese remembrances. He was more interested in *Don Giovanni* than anything else and expressed great eagerness for it to be seen in New York.

Of my long-ago operas with Lorenzo, I wanted *Figaro* to be the first in America, so that I might have the opportunity to set Lorenzo's new poems based on the other Beaumarchais operas. This was a prospect that excited me enormously in those years! Of all of the people I should liked to have met, Beaumarchais remained forever at the top of the list. For all I knew, we were never in the same place, though I always asked after him in Paris, including the last trip there that I did not know at the time would be my last. Lorenzo most loved *Così*, but I was unsure that it would play well in New York and besides, the reminders of Konstanze within it were too painful to me. But with Konstanze gone from my life, those feelings changed. So much had happened. As I devoured Lorenzo's new poems for the other two plays, I was astounded that he again provided rhyming couplets for the entirety of each opera—who besides Lorenzo was gifted enough for such a task? And each ended with its own variant of "tutti contenti" and "questo giorno di tormenti," just like the end of *Figaro*, which absolutely delighted me. I could make references and jokes between them all, which no one had done in a series of operas before. Why waste a good idea on only one work? That wily arse was always so busy in New York, so difficult to find time for us to work, but yet the work always got done. I am confused to this day about Lorenzo and how I feel about him, and I have yet to fully know what happened to him during those times he would disappear.

Lorenzo made me promise to compose *The Barber of Seville* and *The Guilty Mother*, both of which were enthusiastically embraced by John and Sarah, and something in the way he made me promise told me he might abandon all of us again. Each day I would awake and wonder if that day was the last one I would see Lorenzo. But not only did he stay awhile, and though he did go away for a bit, I am astounded to say he is here still; he will no longer speak to me, but he is in the city.

Lorenzo was helpful to me as we began to produce larger and larger operas in the Astor Opera House, and he even quietly helped me to adapt *Faust* and *The Fairy of the Lake* and make them manageable on the stage. Lorenzo was so valuable to me in getting the operas produced, and he even managed to get some money for himself out of John Astor, which made me suspicious, because any time Lorenzo had money he disappeared. Only when his wife Nancy showed up in New York, having been long sequestered away in Susquehanna (or was she susquehanned away in Sequehanna? I can now joke in these bizarre American words!), did I finally realize that Lorenzo was likely in New York to stay. Lorenzo, for once, did not leave the city, though eventually he would leave our partnership, for reasons I still cannot deduce.

CHAPTER 121

The arrival of Nancy, Nannerl and little Babette, as well as Lorenzo, not to mention my wonderful Abraham and Alice, changed my working habits, in that I had to leave home to get anything done. I went from crushing loneliness and fear to always having too many people around. I found it curious that when my life was fuller and I should have less time, I was much more productive. I had never written so much music so quickly, far more than we could perform, which made no matter to me. I knew that time would get to my music even if I did not. Would anyone ever understand that the important thing for a composer is the writing, not the hearing?

Those early years in New York were like my big years in Vienna, before I was forgotten, the years of my best symphonies and piano concertos from my earlier life, the months of *Figaro*, *Don Giovanni*, and *Così*. Those were years that were so busy, and Konstanze and I were still capable of laughing together. I am not sure she would remember them in quite the same way, as I think they were difficult years for her, but that was before our memories were separated by will or circumstance. Then, here in my new life, those months that stretched into years after we returned from Monticello, I saw *Faust* pouring from my quill, and I could hear it all at once, no recitatives, and many great soaring ensembles, all of them longer than I had previously written, yet none seemed long.

But it was not only *Faust*, was it? It was *Baron Munchausen* as a gift for John. It was the three enormous operas of *King Lear*. It was *The Fairy of the Lake*.

CHAPTER 122

As it turned out, I did not have a fight about Alice as Pamina in *The Labyrinth* because she was unable to leave her bed following Abraham's birth, as bringing him to life took so much life from her. Sarah kept assuring us both that little Abraham would not be taken from us, yet there always seemed to be a threat of such an eventuality. Each day Alice seemed stronger, yet something always kept her from fully becoming herself again. She held little Abraham all day long, and fed him from her breasts. Sarah was kind enough to bring a nurse to Longacre to help her with our son.

In those days following our return from Monticello, each time I saw Nancy or Nannerl I would cry, and then my crying would make me bawl out in uncontrollable laughter. "Always some extreme," Nannerl would say, sounding exactly like Papa, but she was right. I could never say it to my dear sister, because I was sorry that she had endured the pain of loss, but I was happy she had been liberated from a husband whom I know she did not love. I'm sorry the poor sap had to die to free her, but that is one of the strangest puzzles of a long life: sometimes death is the best thing, though we are taught to fear it more than anything else. How strange that what we most fear is sometimes the thing we most need. I can say this now, as death approaches at its proper time.

More than anything, I wanted Nancy and Nannerl to get to work teaching. Nancy was most keen to help me with the singers for both the operas that she knew as well as anyone on Earth. Nannerl had virtually no English when she arrived, but she could teach in French, which for our wealthier students was actually of more use in the Astor store, as it had become the ultimate crossroads of musical New York. Within a few years, if you were a musician in New York, you came to the Astor store. We received so many bundles of music and instruments on each ship that Hewitt suggested to Sarah that we build a warehouse near the opera house, on land the Astors owned, and she agreed without even asking John, which amazed me—for the cost of erecting an entire building was not thought sufficient enough to be brought to his attention. As I would find out through Hewitt, to the north of the city, for as far as one could see, it would be impossible to find land that was *not* owned by John and Sarah.

This is how the Astors, bless them to Heaven forever, were able to build a home for us so far away: they owned everything between us and the new Longacre farm, and for all Hewitt knew they owned everything beyond that. Not so long ago, just before we moved here, Sarah said that city planners thought New York might someday cover the entire island of Mannahatta, which was thought impossible, yet within ten years of our move they had come within sight of Longacre, and we traveled through ever smaller routes of countryside to get to the Astor Music Store or to the opera house. I could not have imagined then how enormous the city would become, and now it feels larger than London. As I write, I know I will never see the grandeur of New York City again, but I also know it is now impossible that New York City could grow any larger, for the cultivation of every bit of land has been completed, even across both of the rivers that surround the island.

CHAPTER 123

A letter arrived from Konstanze, one which still stings my heart.

4 July, 1806

Darling,

We are moving through life so quickly, and time seems to have sped in Vienna. I can no longer remember what I have or have not told you, but I know I shall be the first to relay the dreadful news that your loyal assistant Süssie, yes, Franz Süssmayer, has passed to his Creator. Illness took him quickly. He was still loving the success of his *Il noce di Benevento* last year that brought him such fame in Vienna. I should send you a score, in case you would like to perform it in New York in his memory. You know that he loved you so. It was never his intention, nor mine, to hurt you in any way. I have not been able to bring myself to tell you that he is gone because writing the words brings so many tears. Little Franz has lost you and now with Süssie gone, too, he was in danger of having no musician from whom he could properly learn what God demands. He is such a talented boy, Amadé.

Little Franz is fifteen now, as you well know. For the last two years, long before I knew Süssie would be gone, I had Franz start lessons with another musician. I know how this will displease you, but now that Süssie is dead I have no choice but to tell you. Franz has been studying clavier and working on many compositions with Ludwig. If his papa was here to teach him, I would not have been forced to this. Franz adores Ludwig, which will give you no joy, I know. Franz has even started to sketch a symphony, at only fifteen! Ludwig has brought out qualities in him that I did not know were there.

Please understand that our little Franz loves his papa across the great ocean, and time moves so quickly. I hope to send you some of his compositions very soon.

When will I hear news from you? Your letters have become all questions.

Your Konstanze

I had to read the letter several times to fully understand. Indeed, the next morning I read it while using my chamber pot, because nothing could make me shit quicker than thinking of Ludwig teaching music to my own child. And Süssie dead. He had been a profound friend to me at one time, but hearing the news of his death was a mysterious experience, as I felt neither sadness nor joy. I felt absolutely nothing, perhaps because the news was so wrapped in finding out Franz was studying with Ludwig. I had then to await the letter from Haydn that would come weeks later revealing this same news to me again, as though I was not already in possession of it. Could Konstanze not have had our boy study with Michael Haydn? What about old Papa Haydn himself? He surely would have been happy to teach our son, the son of his once-favorite composer. No, she had to subject him to Ludwig. I wanted to write a furious letter back, but I did not. Silence is often the most perfect herald, as I read in one of the Bard's plays, a bit of wisdom I have learned far too late in life.

John returned home from his longest trip, and he was filled with excitement that the Louisiana Territory had finally been brought into the country's possession, just as he had discussed with Jefferson at Monticello. John reported that this would greatly increase his potential business, and he had made a deal with Jefferson, one I never understood and still do not, to be sure he was first in the fur trade in this new territory. What excited John, though, was that his success could be poured into the store and into the opera season and this, in turn, excited me. I could not understand money any more than John Astor could understand music, but he could appreciate it—and that was as far as I could go about money: appreciation.

Sarah Astor confided often in me that John's generosity to the cause of the opera house was surprising to her because John did not easily part with money, but she was always at pains to tell me that what they spent on the opera house and on me was but a pittance to them, and no kind of hardship. I believed her, because Sarah was a truthful woman, but I could never escape the feeling that if I committed one false move and found John's ire instead of his admiration, I would be out on the street. But John's generosity was so great that he prevented even this, because within a few years I was making my own salary from my own students and from schemes Hewitt made with the Astor company for how I was to be paid for my operas. Life was so different in New York, and we lived so differently from anything I had ever known, that I could never devise how much money I was making compared to what I had made in Vienna. I paid for no lodgings until we came to this new and quiet place from which I write, which I purchased with my very own American money, but I am getting ahead of myself.

Alice was an enormous worry to me in those early years of the Astor Opera House, as she worried about little Abraham so much, and not because he wasn't a healthy little guy. He was! And he was the most angelic and beautiful child. She lived in constant fear that he would be taken from us, not by death, but that he would be carried away if it was found out that she had delivered a baby out of wedlock, and to a white man, to a white *foreign* man. Alice was different after Abraham was born. She cried much more than he did, and in those times there was no consoling her. I tried all of our old ways of being with each other, and she was no longer happy to be touched by me in the same ways. Something had changed. She kept asking me to "give her time," a request I tried always to understand, especially now that our time has, of sorts, run out.

It will be difficult for anyone in the future, those not yet born, to fully realize what an earthquake was sent through the world when Napoleon declared himself Emperor of the French. Decent people had to wonder if the world had really grown to allow such a perfidy. Emperors were created by the heredity bestowed by God. Napoleon merely "declaring" himself as such was blasphemous beyond imagining, and what an affront to the memory of real emperors! I wondered what effect this would have on the spirit of Vienna, not to mention Paris, because Napoleon completely mesmerized New York. Dear Franz Mesmer. I put him in our opera, *Così*, and Lorenzo most wonderfully obliged, though I understand he did not like him at all. I loved old Franz, and I wonder if he is still alive. I met him through Haydn, just as I met many people. Not many get their name and their ideas passed into history, do they, Franz? No one will ever be mozartized but they will be mesmerized!

The mesmerizing of America by Napoleon was a surprise, as his name had barely even been heard before it became the only word spoken. With Napoleon came the realization that the great experiment of America could take a terrible turn. The American colonies were vulnerable to a Napoleon, someone who would tell them they were getting cheated by the government, that war was the answer to everything, that guns were superior to ideas. Jefferson was no Napoleon, but the broadsheets were filled with would-be emperors, and one could feel the constant unrest even within the safety of the island.

Napoleon's self-decrees made their way to our country. I can still scarcely believe it, but Hewitt showed me the broadsheet that announced it with great fanfare: the Italian Luigi Cherubini had been appointed "court composer" to the Emperor's Louisiana Territory, except by the time he made the journey all the way around Florida in some godforsaken ship, the Louisiana Territory suddenly belonged publicly to Thomas Jefferson and the United States and privately to my own patron John Astor.

What on earth was Cherubini going to do in New Orleans? I knew his music from my youth, and I always thought him one of the only Italians who could really compose. I had never met him, and I knew I would never make such a long journey as required to get to wherever New Orleans was. Many visited the southern city by taking a ship from New York, as that was the fastest way to arrive there, but I would never again set foot on a ship. By carriage, New Orleans was a month from New York at least, and that was too far for me. Had Cherubini stayed in France, I would have been happy to present one of his great operas in New York, but once he was on our shores I was not so sure. I wrote him a letter in care of Théâtre St. Philippe, where I was told he would be working, having no idea if it would reach him.

Christmas Day, 1806

Dear Luigi,

I loved your opera *Lodoïska*, which I saw in Vienna around the time we premiered *Das Labyrinth*. What operas are you planning for your new city of New Orleans?

The Astor Opera House has brought all kinds of new acclaim for our beloved art, and the city is growing each week. It all feels like a field of new flowers. Would you consider allowing me to perform one of your operas?

I hope we can meet each other now that we are neighbors, or at least closer than we have ever been before.

Mozart

I was lying. I had been in Paris many times when Cherubini had been there but had never taken the time to meet him. How precious is time! Luigi was younger than I, and in Parisian and Viennese circles much more acclaimed, especially by the time I was becoming known. Books had been written about him, but not me. This is the saddest part of a long life, my friends: when you have known the acclaim of the world as a child but then live too long, you watch everyone assume what was once yours. Their lamps burn brighter as you watch your own dimming away. It is incredible to me still, but I never once heard from the old shit Cherubini. Imagine being so awful!

He never wrote me directly, but he made his presence constantly known. I had not known him well enough to realize that he was so fond of intrigue and gossip. He was forever writing others in New York saying he was deciding to move away from New Orleans, so his arrival was a constant threat in those years. And the broadsheets were constantly declaring his immense achievements in New Orleans, leaving John and Sarah sometimes to feel that their work and investments in the cultural life of New York City were being ignored. Indeed, for many of the broadsheets most jealous of John's business, they were being downplayed.

And how did they imagine this left me feeling? I had established a major orchestra in New York City, largely by training them all myself, and was about to open an opera house in the New World, while the New York broadsheets went on each day about Cherubini's antics in a southern city that might as well have been in a different country! What was the use of it all? I would have thought all of the petty intrigues of Europe might have had the courtesy to stay in the Old World, but no!

CHAPTER 124

Sarah Astor sent me a dinner invitation for Vesey Street, and I was happy as always to oblige, though it became increasingly difficult for me to accept invitations that did not include Alice. I wanted to have a normal life with her, and we could only live normally within the distant safety of Longacre. At the opera house, where Alice should have reigned supreme, she had to hide, especially after showing herself to be among the greatest singers in the world. Musicians, you see, know a great voice instantly. They do not need to be trained beyond their own instrument to know what they are hearing. This was not true of anyone *else* who heard Alice, for they would judge her solely on the darkness of her eyes and everything that surrounded them. But musicians knew.

The dinner invitation was formal and official, as opposed to just a regular dinnertime, and in those years the Astors rarely entertained at Vesey Street, but rather in their newer house on the far eastern side of the island, far to the north—an incredibly beautiful place. This formality meant to me that the dinner was to honor a business associate of some import to John and Sarah. Dear reader, you are so patient to allow my testament to flit around like our very memories, for this dinner must have been 1806 or thereabouts. I was right about its import. The dinner was given in honor of two men whose names I had never heard before and not even since, though they were both remarkable. They were Meriwether Lewis and William Clark, who had mapped the perceived wholeness of the Louisiana Territory at the request of Thomas Jefferson and at the quiet direction of John Astor. They brought their wives, and the many guests were among New York's most wealthy and influential. They all gazed around the house as though they were in St. James's Palace. Indeed, the carved woods and oil lanterns illuminating beautiful works of art were a sight to behold. By that point I knew every bit of the house, so I was both surprised and proud to be able to explain to our guests what they were seeing. Alice, just as she had been on the night we met, was among those serving, and as always we stole many happy glances. I was surprised that President Thomas Jefferson was not there, as Meriwether and William seemed to be the most honored of their nation. A lowly composer for whom an opera house had been built was nothing compared to them.

John gave an impassioned speech about the land to the west of the country, the land purchased within the Louisiana Territory, places that did indeed sound boundlessly beautiful but which I was sure I would never see. He described vast rivers and mountain ranges larger than anything from my homeland. These were lands, he said, in which fortunes could be made by the adventurous; and he added, to my surprise, "And the more fortune I can make, the more Mozarts we can have," and the room applauded *me*. I had known many crowned heads of Europe, at least when I was a child, but only in my new country would I be allowed to meet such esteemed people, and meet them not as a servant but as their equal. Alice, though, remained as she had always been, and that gnawed at me.

Lewis stood up to speak, first thanking John and Sarah and then saying, "You cannot imagine the splendor of the west. We have seen wonders that almost no civilized men have ever seen. We were naturally limited in what we could see from the river."

"What about the uncivilized?" I asked, counting myself as just such a person.

"What do you mean, sir?" Lewis asked me.

"Are there people already on these lands, as there are right here on this island?"

"Savages, yes, but not landowners."

I said, "This great western land you describe is theirs, is it not?"

I do not know from where these words came, as I knew nothing at all about the interior of America, a land so vast as to remain unknown forever to the entire world. I now know I was speaking of the Indians, but I was speaking as though the Indians were a single people, yet they were many. Somehow I knew, yet I refused to believe that anything unfair would happen to them. They were even on our island, pushed ever northward by the Longacre farm on which I resided. I saw the Indians in the shadows each night, looking at us, wondering what kind of civilization we might be a part of. What would they have seen of me? A man hiding away on a farm with his black wife, a woman he loved beyond anyone or anything he had ever loved, but beyond our farm our love was forbidden, illegal, and scandalous. My music was heard all the time on the farm. I wonder what the Indians thought of it, but, in fairness, I never asked them. I never reached out to them. One day, for it happened in a single day, they were gone, chased away by the city's progress.

Lewis responded not to me but to the Astors. "I assure you, John and Sarah, that you can let Herr Mozart know that there is plenty of land in the west for everyone. We could move the population of the entire world to the west of the great river, the Mississippi, and they could each have a tract of their own land and never see one another. The world of the Louisiana Territory is boundless."

His words did not feel true to me, but my thoughts were of no consequence. Why would Lewis need to tell me the truth? And John's fortune was of huge consequence to my own life, but at what cost was he attaining it? These were questions I was never able to ask, and they plagued me as the years passed. John and Sarah both sensed my unease, and they always assured me that they were treating people well, but some mystery remained. John had seen parts of the American territories that I would never see, and I knew he harbored many secrets about what he saw there, even from Sarah. I knew these things.

The only other "official" dinner deserving of a testament was a very different affair from Lewis and Clark. I am ashamed to say that I ruined the famous pair for Sarah and John, though they never said a word to me about it. The other dinner was for one of the most remarkable men

I ever met, John James Audubon. He was so young on that night it was difficult to believe he had already accomplished so much. Though I was by then an old man, I had done practically nothing compared to him! We spoke only in French together through the whole evening. Though I knew him only for the few weeks of his stay with the Astors, our time together has remained with me for the rest of my long life. We shared a fascination with birds, he with their feathers and bodies, I with their voices and songs. He was fascinated that I could hear tones within their tones, which I tried to demonstrate to him, but with my limited voice it was difficult. I did show him several times on the keyboard what I meant, what I could actually hear within a bird's song. He asked how I might prove this was true, as if we can prove anything to be true. He, in turn, showed me some of the drawings of birds he had made, and they were remarkable likenesses.

Since Audubon stayed many weeks at the Astor home, I asked if he might draw Alice and little Abraham, as Sarah felt there was no way for Alice to do a normal sitting with our son, and I wanted a good likeness. To my complete delight he agreed, and not only to capture Alice with his paints but *me* with Alice and our son. I was able to take old frames brought to Longacre from the Vesey Street house and place Audubon's drawings within them. He captured the best likeness of me since Johann Edlinger, and I had not been captured at all in the New World. Audubon's likeness would become the only portrait I had of Alice, and I cherish it so deeply that I am looking at it right now as my quill passes over this parchment.

CHAPTER 125

John Astor seemed daunted by absolutely nothing. I had never met anyone like him, and even now at this end of my life it is still true. None of the obstacles of my Old World were obstacles to him in the New. He wanted *The Magic Flute* to be the first opera performed in New York City, and so it was, giving him more power over me than any king or emperor. *The Labyrinth* followed two nights later, and John's magnificent theater was probably remarked upon even more than my operas. It felt like the largest theater I had ever been within, larger even than the Burgtheater or the Kärtnertor. The audiences were delirious with happiness and wonder, and they were so proud to have this magnificent building where they could gather. Many of those in attendance were John and Sarah's good friends, so they were among the highest in the business and trading community. All, it must be said, were very wealthy themselves. But John and Sarah wanted to be sure that everyone who wanted to attend could do so, and they made an edict that all of the downstairs stalls would be sold for a penny, just like at some of the old London theaters that John loved so much.

I led the premieres of the two operas from the first violin desk, sitting next to John Moller, who was as fine a violinist as any I knew in Vienna, and after those first two performances I left the leading to either Hewitt or Moller, as I had to concentrate on preparations for *Faust*, which performance was approaching with a terrifying swiftness. I had to get all the copy books to the singers faster than I was actually composing. At the time of the opening of the opera house, I had so much music left to compose for *Faust*, but it was like one big cake already baked in my head. All of our singers had finally been found, especially with Nancy arriving with her voice completely intact, sounding just as she had when we did *Figaro* fifteen years before! Her voice had thickened and grown into the perfect instrument of beauty and warmth for the demanding role of Gretchen.

I had never written roles more grueling for the singers than Heinrich Faust, Gretchen, and Mephistopheles, as Goethe had provided an abundance of incredible poetry for this unique operas. I was able to write many ensembles and grand choruses, things I had not been able to compose so fully in an opera for many years. *Faust* poured out of me as no opera had since *Figaro* or *Richard III*. And *Faust* was a new kind of opera for the stages of the world, though New York was not a world stage in those years, as by the time *Faust* opened a few months later, they had only seen my two earlier operas. Within a half year, though, the Astor Opera House was in every broadsheet of London, Paris, and Vienna. Letters arrived from every ship. We were a part of the operatic world, and the Astor Opera House became the most important gathering place in New York.

The revelations of *The Magic Flute, The Labyrinth*, or *Faust* had little to do with my music, though, which was already known to the educated world. It was the stage settings of Tamu that had everyone talking. That was an amazing thrill for me, knowing how much it meant to Tamu to be working in this way. I do not know what kind of deal John and Sarah made with President Jefferson, but somehow they arranged it that Tamu was allowed to come to New York and paint our stage settings. This was a miracle for me at just the time I needed it the most. I explained each of the scenes to him, especially the all-important scene of the three doors of the temple in the first two operas, the scene with the speaker; and though he had never before seen an operatic performance, never even been in a theater, he was able not only to conceive of these grand settings but also design a mechanical serpent for the opening scene that was both whimsical and terrifying. The many men hired for the proper running of the stage could take Tamu's drawings and turn them into reality. For the scene in which the magical flute charmed the beasts of the forest,

Tamu designed perfect replicas of African animals, many of which none of us had ever seen before. For *Faust* he designed and painted huge vistas of the necessary libraries and cathedrals that he had obviously not seen before, either.

Somehow Tamu could hold vast visual ideas in his mind and paint the most intricate scenes. When I looked at them up close, they looked almost comical, but once they were placed on the stage and flown with gigantic ropes—for John had spared no expense for his opera house—they were of incredible beauty, often looking much like an actual vista outside. Tamu had so many gifts: he was a doctor, and he had cured my embarrassment with just a few plants, never asking me any questions or making any harsh judgments; and he had survived the terrible passage only to find himself at Monticello enslaved by a president who professed to honor freedom. But at least Jefferson appreciated Tamu's amazing artistic gifts, and somehow at Monticello it was discovered that Tamu had yet another extraordinary gift, for drawing and painting. His balloons were so realistic and beautiful that they filled me with a certain dread, as it felt they might be more real than they were.

Tamu was given a small cabin on the Longacre farm, not far from us and a bit closer to the river, and though my life was as complete as it could possibly be, especially being able to work with Tamu each day at the opera house, I worried constantly about Alice. And in truth, I worried about Tamu as well, because even though he was designing the settings and painting them himself, many people surrounding the opera house, those who worked for John, assumed that Tamu could not be given his proper due. No one would say this was because Tamu was an African, which for me made their decision even worse. If they had beautiful scenery for their operas, why would they care the color of the skin of who painted it? But they did, and for that first season we had to hide Tamu away, and the printed broadsheets said nothing at all about the theatrical scenery.

The areas backstage were small enough to keep Tamu from being well known, and his gifts kept everyone on their toes, but there had to be a foreman, white of course, who was credited with Tamu's work.

This was a difficult secret to keep, because Tamu's scenery was so striking, even to the point of bringing applause upon sight of it, something I had seen only rarely. It became a regular feature of our performances for the audience to clap for the scenery as much as any aria! I do not know from where Tamu received his gifts, but one can only say that God gave him so many more of them than he gave the rest of us. Tamu kept largely to himself at the farm, and I often saw him exchanging food with the local Indians when they still wandered into our part of town, none of whom I knew at all. It was Tamu who made the effort to know and reconcile with them; it was never the Mozarts or the Astors. I find that remarkable now.

Occasionally in those years, Tamu came and had dinner with us. As Alice recovered from Abraham's birth, she enjoyed Tamu's presence. Gradually his perfect French transformed into English, and he spoke often of his time at Monticello. Some of what he told us about Jefferson was unbelievable, even claiming that the President of the United States was carrying on full relations with one of his own slaves. How could he possibly risk it? Alice was not a slave, but that was only because she could not be so by accident of birth. She might be a slave in a different place.

Thinking back on our time at Monticello, I felt I knew the woman Jefferson was carrying on with, the one who played the violin with me. There was something special between them, and something unique about her, just like Alice.

CHAPTER 126

The success of the Astor Opera House overwhelmed all of us, and at just the moment that I was obliged to finish every detail of *Faust*. I was desperate for more time, so when Hewitt reported that among the arrivals to the music shop were the materials for performance of *La cifra* by Salieri, my ears pricked up like a dog hearing it is dinnertime.

Bless my arse, I thought. In addition to Gretchen, *La cifra* was the ideal role for Nancy, and I knew she had been royally ticked by losing the part to Adriana, whom she absolutely hated even though she always said she loved her. Adriana Ferrarese del Bene. Oh my, how much of my virtue had been lost in thoughts of *La Ferrarese,* whose voice used to make me swoon. I could never talk to Konstanze about her, nor Nancy, nor Aloysia…because even the mention of Adriana's name gave away any secrets I hoped to carry. Performing *La cifra* in our first season would allow me more time to finish *Faust*, and allow Tamu time for his imagination to run wild with the settings. Though it was an opera of convenience only, it also allowed me to write Salieri and tell him we were programming one of his operas in the New World, which would no doubt delight the old goat.

We needed all sort of settings for *Faust,* and as I said earlier, the only part of Europe Tamu had ever seen was Boulogne! I spent much time with him, with drawings from some of Lorenzo's books. Tamu had to rely on all of us telling him about the mountains and the cities he had never seen, the cathedrals and great libraries of Goethe's imagination, except Goethe had never had to imagine them; he *knew* them. It was similar with *La cifra*, which was set in Scotland, which none of us had ever seen! What Tamu could visualize from words was remarkable to everyone who saw his drawings, but then something even more remarkable happened: he asked to draw while I played music, claiming that my music brought more of his art to the surface than any number of words. Tamu's cabin at the Longacre farm quickly became like the great art studios I had seen in Vienna, those marvelous rooms that smelled of oily paint and charcoal. When Tamu was not at work on my operas, he would paint on paper or bark, anything he could find around Longacre. Anything he touched turned into art.

I made many new friends in New York. Henri Capon, a fine composer, became one of my closest new friends besides Tamu. Hewitt warned me that Henri would be "another Salieri," but he was speaking only of the ghosts and rumors about the old Italian. The last I heard, Salieri was still alive but had gone thoroughly beyond his mind and into a world of childish fantasy. Konstanze's sister Aloysia wrote me to say Salieri had confessed to poisoning me after hearing *The Magic Flute*! He could be a wily man, and he was always interested in the cabals around Vienna, but it was just gossipy interest. He had no reason to pay for a cabal against a composer, as he was so far ahead of all of us in renown and the good graces of our dear Kaiser.

Salieri was, I hate to admit it, a mighty composer of operas. Well, he was a mighty composer of *music* for operas, and he knew how to please the public and how to bring the most applause at the right moment. He was a master at pleasing. I learned a great deal from him about meeting an audience where they can be met. I knew I had the greater gift, and Salieri knew it, too. But he certainly could never have gone so far as to poison a person, and of all the people he might have poisoned, it certainly would not have been me. Of course, I was so sick that winter anyone who *wanted* to poison me would have found their most opportune moment, for it would not have taken much to carry me off. I know I had never been so close to death, and Salieri even came to visit, I believe. I can no longer remember what was in waking and what in sleeping of those awful feverish weeks.

I brought Nannerl and Nancy into the confidence of my life with Alice, as Abraham's life left no further way for me to hide her from them. Nannerl seemed angry at me for being unable to resist my desires, especially desires she considered so very base. Until she arrived I had not seen her in nearly ten years, and in that time she had changed from my shy and laughing sister into a version of Papa, with all of his judgments. I knew exactly what Papa would have thought of Alice, as I could hear his own words come from my sister. "How can you lie in bed with a black woman, a slave? How?" I also knew that no matter how shocking Nannerl might find Alice, it would not last. She would come around to loving whoever I loved because her love for me was always stronger than her fears—in this she was completely different from Papa.

Nancy immediately loved Alice, and she betrayed no judgments to me about her. This was the Nancy I had long known, and within days of Nancy arriving and Alice starting to recuperate from Abraham's birth, Alice asked Nancy to help her with singing. Nancy knew what it was like to sing after having a child, and she knew how to speak to Alice in a way that I could not, singer to singer, whatever it was they talked about.

And it worked. Nancy taught Alice only at the Astor home or at Longacre so that she could not be seen entering the shop. We took enormous care to protect Alice from appearing as anything that would arouse suspicion in strangers. Alice always entered the Astor home through the servant's entrance, and she and I never traveled together in a carriage.

I put both Nannerl and Nancy to immediate work at the music shop, which was becoming *the* place to study music in the city. We quickly developed problems of space. Hewitt, always enterprising, convinced Sarah and John to acquire yet another building just down the street from the shop, one formerly used as a school but which had grown too small for its purpose, where we could teach more pupils. This meant that Nannerl and I could teach the best pupils seeking instruction in clavier or the string instruments. Hewitt could teach very well on the clarinet, oboe, and bassoon, and Nancy took control of all the singers.

While I was consumed with getting *Faust* to the stage, Alice was becoming more of herself, recovering at last from the difficulty of bringing little Abraham into the world. Naturally, gentle reader, every father thinks their child is the most beautiful, but it was actually true of Abraham. He was the most divine-looking little boy I had ever seen, like the paintings one saw in Schönbrunn or St. James. His complexion was not entirely that of Monostatos, but he was certainly a darker boy than I. His skin alone, though, would not make him noticed. His hair is what worried both of us from his earliest days, for as he grew it was clear that though his skin was fairer than Alice's and darker than mine, his hair was completely that of Alice. When he was a baby, Alice kept his hair cut so short that no one would notice, not that anyone really saw the boy, but one cannot keep a child looking old and bald as he gets older. Thank the Lord on high that the boy did not get my hair, which can barely be seen even with a looking glass. But we had to be vigilant in keeping his hair short so as to betray no curl.

By the time we moved completely to the Longacre farm, Abraham was already more than two years old, and we could not have imagined raising him at the Vesey Street house. He was such a rambunctious boy! Alice was still in the employ of the Astors, but they moved her duties entirely to their new home on the East River, a short ride away, and Alice loved riding her own horse to the Astors'. Our home, a lovely brick residence, sat to the west of Longacre toward the Hudson River, surrounded by beautiful trees, and there was a small cluster of houses on the property where other servants lived, and I loved having Nannerl and Nancy in small homes nearby. We all went by coach to the store each day, far downtown, leaving Alice and Abraham on their own for many hours, and in this way we passed several happy years, or what felt like years, before the sword of Damocles was held over my head forever.

Babette was the only niece I would come to know well. I had met Nannerl's Leopold and Jeanette, both born in my busiest years, only once, when my sister visited Vienna about a year after Babette was born. Babette had a combination of Nannerl's gifts along with mine, and through her studies in the years from 1805 to 1810 we both kept throwing into her path what we thought would be obstacles, but she never found them difficult. Everything, indeed, was so easy for her that I had moments that approached jealousy. As my life passes into history, let it be known that Babette is the *real* Mozart, the one who will be long remembered, for she possesses every gift ever bestowed upon a musician, and she astounds us both.

Nannerl told me how the girl nearly had not lived at all, and we all heard tales of the priest coming to deliver extreme unction onto the baby when she was but a year old, when she became as close to death as I had been at the same time. I have always felt that whatever mysterious force saved me also saved her, and I know this because I know many things that others do not. As Babette grew to maturity, she wanted to be known as Babette Mozart, and my dearest cousin Maria Thekla, my beloved Bäsle, wrote constantly asking for news of Nannerl's little Babette. Now, as I write this long-demanded testament, the works of Babette are sweeping the opera houses in this country that were initially built for me. What a wonder life is. It pains me that I will never see cousin Bäsle again, and there is absolutely no chance for her to come here, but we write each other every week.

CHAPTER 127

Faust was my finest opera up to that time, though it is difficult for me now to reckon with a work that probes every depth of God and the Devil. How did I compose that as well as the lightness of *Tartuffe* or the wonderland of *The Fairy of the Lake* or the hilarity of *Baron Munchausen*? I don't know the answer, my patient friends, I only know that I was sometimes able to listen to the dictates of my heart. *Faust* secured the opening season of the Astor Opera House as an enormous triumph for John and Sarah. Even after I finished *Faust*, Goethe sent me countless packages continuing his story that I had already completed, and with each one I became more absorbed with his extraordinary tale, which seemed to sum up everything that could be said about life. I first wrote Goethe from America at the time of my journey on the *Gregson*, and told him we had entered an era that had no more need of devils.

In his very next letter, he quoted Shakespeare to me: "Hell is empty and all the devils are here." Isn't that magnificent? I was raised on the idea of Christ and the Antichrist, two opposing forces at constant war for power over us all, and each of us must choose which of the two forces to honor and obey. Papa made me memorize the passage from Revelation 12:12, never to be forgotten when I was faced with any choice in life: "Woe to the inhabitors of the earth and of the sea! for the devil is come down unto you, having great wrath, because he knoweth that he has but a short time." Those words used to chill my soul, but as my life has lengthened, I realized through Goethe that the devil we fight is not a person, not an enemy, but he resides within. What Goethe put forward in *Faust* was that each of us individually is both Christ and Antichrist, and this was an idea I had not considered. We are all imprisoned by our own opposites, and in the years in which I wrote *Faust* this was slowly revealed to me about my own nature. Every mysterious force of the world came into my view in those years, as though I had been living simply to write *Faust*. I am proud of all my musical children, and though *Oronooko* did the most for the world and *Munchausen* pleased John to no end, it was *Faust* that forever altered my soul.

What began to form itself within me was that I might be losing my need for the type of God to whom I had blindly prayed and given thanks throughout my life. These heretical thoughts brought me enormous distress at first, but as time passed, and as I saw the way Alice was treated by a world into which she had only poured forth beauty, I felt less remorse for thinking our man-made gods to be something other than what I'd been raised to believe. Unlike the terrible Voltaireans, and all the sickly sycophants who did not have their courage but retained their abhorrent blasphemies, I could never doubt the existence of God. But Goethe set before me a God infinitely greater and more expansive than the constant invigilation of my childhood deity. In my years at St. Stephens, I made God into an image of my own father, just as in my youth I had made my father into God. As the events of my life accelerated, and as I reached the age in which age made itself known to the body, my spirit altered. At Longacre I could stare into the firmament just as I had for my whole life, but I began not to see but to feel God in that presence. I felt God not in how small Alice and I were by comparison, but by my being, perhaps my soul, which seemed at moments to expand infinitely outward to touch the heavens themselves. I had brief glimpses of everything above the mountains and above the clouds, the stars we could see in the mysteries of the night sky—that they were all a part of one unity that I could not name except to call it God, a great D major master of my soul.

CHAPTER 128

In our first season at the Astor Opera House, *The Magic Flute* played sixteen performances, *The Labyrinth* fourteen, and *Faust* an incredible twenty-seven. These were performance numbers I had not experienced anywhere, and they defied all the lore of "new world." I went to each performance, and the public seemed genuinely happy to see me, as though instead of being just a man I was a creature from the *Terra Australis*, a place they had heard about but would never see. Of those three operas, only *Faust* had been created anew, but all operas are new when an audience has never experienced them. And how curious and welcoming were those early New York audiences—and much more vocal about their own feelings than I had imagined. I came away from each performance of my dear *Magic Flute* feeling that audiences were delirious in their happiness. I loved seeing and hearing their pleasure.

Lorenzo and I got to serious work, which successfully took my mind from the grief I am shortly to describe, so in our second season we were able to do our new *Barber of Seville*, along with the comforts of our dear old *Figaro*, and also, then, the infinite pleasures of our delightful new opera *The Guilty Mother*—three operas that told a continuous story—along with Salieri's *La cifra*, which brings me the shameful schadenfreude of testifying that his opera was not a success. I had seen *La cifra* many times in Vienna, of course, and I always enjoyed so much of its music, but as a totality it was not up to my operas. How I adored composing *The Guilty Mother*! Very few works brought me as much joy as those marvelous operas, mostly because each of their characters are as real to me as Alice or Franz or Abraham. *The Guilty Mother* was, of all my operas besides *The Labyrinth,* the one in which I wrote the most extended and complicated ensembles, and there is nothing to equal their magnificent energy, though they are very challenging for the singers to keep in time.

CHAPTER 129

I have put off this recollection as long as I could, dear reader. It was in late 1805 when I was at the Astor Opera House about to attend a later performance of *Faust* when the news came, the most terrible news of my life. Somehow Hewitt heard it before me. As I would later find out so terribly, the letters informing me of this catastrophe had gone to the Vesey Street house and eventually made their way to Longacre. I had to read the horror again and again, from Konstanze, Haydn, Puchberg, Goethe, and even old Johann Naumann wrote me about it. It was naturally also in every broadsheet for weeks, as mankind seemed unable to believe the news.

I was not altogether surprised that Ludwig van Beethoven shot himself, as it was within his nature to behave as a god. Hewitt told me that Ludwig was dead. Even as I write these words so many years later, I cannot bear the idea. It was not Ludwig's violence to himself that made the news so unbearable, it was knowing in my deepest heart that I was responsible for it. Yes, the fault of his death lay with my life.

One must be truthful to one's testament, and I must face some difficult truths about my little Franz in those years. In my heart, I knew he was my son, but it remained entirely possible that he was the son of Franz Süssmayer, my contemporary and onetime friend, now in purgatory. We have no way to know with certainty, so I must follow the dictates of my heart where both Franzes are concerned. I have not wanted to face this reality, but each time I looked at little Franz when he was a baby I saw the eyes of Franz Süssmayer, as the baby did not in those years resemble me or anyone on the Mozart side of the family. The truth is that Konstanze allowed both Süssie and me within her body in those months when little Franz could have been conceived. Where is God at these moments? And what has this to do with Ludwig? Please have patience, dear ones.

Ludwig took his life because of my Konstanze, making me responsible for his violence against himself. Ludwig killed not only himself, but also a part of all of us who loved or feared him. He undoubtedly killed Konstanze's spirit, already so broken by our separation. Süssie died far too young, as did Ludwig, so she was left with no one. Little Franz was Ludwig's prize pupil, and in those terrible months when the news of Ludwig's suicide raced around the world like cannon fire, I could not give my boy the comfort he needed. Why do the great geniuses die young?

Ludwig heard his first two symphonies before his death, his C major and D major, three utterly magnificent piano concertos, only six of his fine string quartets, four of the greatest piano trios imaginable, and seventeen piano sonatas that are some of the greatest music to be thought or felt, except the ones that are absolutely mad! His ridiculous *Rage Over a Lost Penny* should have been enough for anyone to realize he was simply too crazy and impetuous to live for a long time. But why, Ludwig, why do it in this way? Why force the entire world to wonder why you could not face your life? And Ludwig accomplished in death what he could not in life: he made me into the person who killed Beethoven.

CHAPTER 130

The scores kept arriving to the store as if to taunt me. Twenty-five fair copies of that terrifying "Ah! Perfido!" he wrote for Josepha Dussek, trying for all the world to copy what I wrote for her, "Non temer, amato bene." It was *such* music, the bastard. The central aria, I know, was written solely because he knew what it would mean to me. "Per pietá, non dirmi addio"—"Don't say good-bye to me"—was always sung directly from Ludwig to me, making it the most painful music I know. How could I say *addio* to you, Ludwig, when you took all chances away? Why did you not demand that Konstanze go off to London and away from Süssie, or why did you not go elsewhere yourself? You wanted her for yourself, that's why! Why did you not come to the New World, where you likely could have found happiness at least in continuing to torment me?

The letter. I am so ashamed, dear reader, that it was only at that moment that I recollected the long-distant letter he had delivered to me when we first left for Vienna. I had to work to find it, tucked into one of our trunks which, thank the good Lord, was moved to Longacre. In the lid of the trunk, there was Ludwig's letter, unopened, weathered almost beyond recognition from its own journey which had also been mine. My heart stopped to open it, terrified of what it might say. I placed it on my desk, but I could not yet tear it open even though the wax had almost entirely fallen away.

In more recent years, Anton Schindler wrote me asking about Ludwig, as he wants to write a biography of his short life. How can I say no to him, but how could I possibly ever talk freely about Ludwig?

I recall the horror I felt when reading Konstanze's correspondence about Ludwig's death that she included his final letter to her, in which he made clear that he removed the life from his own body because of her and, to my everlasting perfidy, my unknowing coldness to the pleas he made to me. She could not keep the letter so she sent it to me—how about that? How can I ever be forgiven this enormous injury to the world? Within my own fears of Ludwig, I made it possible for him to take his own life and leave me alive to watch his reputation grow and witness affection for his music gain in strength while I became like a comfortable old shoe. I have enjoyed success, it is undoubtedly true, and my final operas, *Oronooko* and *Idomeneo,* have given me the utmost joy and satisfaction. But it has come at what price to me?

My mind is flitting about, dear reader, for which I apologize. Shortly after Haydn died in 1809, I conducted a memorial concert in his memory in the Astor Opera House, a concert that was both enormously successful and immensely meaningful for me. With Haydn gone, not to mention Ludwig, my youth was well and truly finished. It long had been, of course, but not within my spirit, not after all I endured. I wrote a work in his memory, *Threnody for Franz Joseph Haydn,* for orchestra alone, and within it I tried to bring many memories of him, to capture his immense humor and depth of generosity. I played also, to finish the concert, my Masonic Funeral Music, as my greatest memories with Papa were in the Lodge. How blessed my long life has been that for every ten scoundrels there was a Haydn, or a Kaiser Joseph, or a John Astor? How many lives have been as blessed as mine to have had such figures of immense love and tenderness? Haydn's death, though, came as nature intended, with a fine man slipping away after a beautiful life. Ludwig ensured his fame by killing himself. God! Why?

CHAPTER 131

Konstanze's letter about Ludwig arrived along with two large trunks, an unexpected arrival at Longacre. I shuddered to see they had been routed through Liverpool, meaning those trunks had probably sat on that horrid dock near that more horrendous man who tricked me onto a ship. I was never able to ascertain why she sent and packed them at that moment, knowing their contents would cause me enormous pain, so I let them sit for nearly a year before claiming the courage to open them, by which time I was muddled. Ludwig had still been living when she packed the trunks; he had to be. They could not have arrived so soon after his death otherwise, as her trunks arrived in the same day as Haydn's letter.

They were filled with some pieces of my music, even a fair copy of all of the parts of *Lucio Silla* and *Mitridate*, operas of my youth that I had nearly forgotten. Looking through them again, I briefly became the age I was when I wrote them. But other contents of the trunk would allow for no youth. I found two letters to Konstanze from Ludwig, though their ink was not old, and I read them with horror:

July, Morning

My angel, my all, my own self—only a few words today, and that too with pencil (yours, or Amadé's!)—only till tomorrow is my lodging definitely fixed. What abominable waste of time in such things—why this deep grief, where necessity speaks?

Can our love persist otherwise than through sacrifices, by not demanding everything? Canst thou change it, that thou are not entirely mine, I not entirely thine? O God, look into beautiful nature and compose your mind to the inevitable. Love demands everything is quite right, so it is for me with you, for you with me—only you forget so easily, that I must live for you and for me—were we quite united, you would notice this painful feeling as little as I should…

We shall probably soon meet, even today I cannot communicate my remarks to you, which during these days I made about my life—were our hearts close together, I should probably not make any such remarks. My bosom is full, to tell you much—there are moments when I find that speech is nothing at all. Brighten up—remain my true and only treasure, my all, as I to you. The rest the gods must send, what must be for us and shall.

Your faithful, **Ludwig**

And the very next day he wrote her again, a letter she saw fit not only to save but likely to instruct someone to send to me. Even in her passage, which she could not then have known was nigh, she sought to hurt me further.

Good morning, on 7 July

Even in bed my ideas yearn toward you, my immortal beloved, here and there joyfully, then again sadly, awaiting from fate, whether it will listen to us. I can only live, either altogether with you or not at all. Yes, I have determined to wander about for so long far away, until I can fly into your arms and call myself quite at home with you, can send my soul enveloped by yours into the realm of spirits—yes, I regret, it must be. You will get over it all the more as you know my faithfulness to you; never another one can own my heart, never—never! O God, why must one go away from what one loves so, and yet my life in W. as it is now is a miserable life. Your love made me the happiest and unhappiest at the same time. At my actual age I should need some continuity, sameness of life—can that exist under our circumstances?

Angel, I just hear that the post goes out every day—and must close therefore, so that you get the L. at once. Be calm—love me—today—yesterday.

What longing in tears for you—You—my life—my all—farewell…Oh, go on loving me—never doubt the faithfulest heart of your beloved,

Ludwig
Ever thine.
Ever mine.
Ever ours.

Then, the harshest cut of all, and I must have read it a thousand times in the hours of opening it. I place his testament within my own, for absent it my life lacks all meaning. Here it is:

To my immortal beloved, Konstanze, how can I ever make you understand that depth of my love for you, the love you will not accept? You and others say that I am malevolent, stubborn, or misanthropic. How greatly do you wrong me, you do not know the secret causes of my seeming, from childhood my heart and mind were disposed to the gentle feelings of good will. Amadé displayed no understanding of this at all, nor that I was even ever eager to accomplish great deeds, but reflect now that for six years I have been a hopeless case, aggravated by senseless physicians, cheated year after year in the hope of improvement, finally compelled to face the prospect of a lasting malady (whose cure will take years or, perhaps, be impossible), born with an ardent and lively temperament, even susceptible to the diversions of society, I was compelled early to isolate myself, to live in loneliness, when I at times tried to forget all this. Oh, how harshly was I repulsed by the doubly sad experience of my bad hearing, and yet it was impossible for me to say to men, "Speak louder, shout, for I am deaf!" Ah, how could I possibly admit such an infirmity in the one sense which should have been more perfect in me than in others, a sense which I once possessed in highest perfection, a perfection such as few surely in my profession enjoy or have enjoyed. Amadé had the most perfect hearing of any person I ever knew, and he continued to enjoy all of the sounds of the world while mine were slowly and malevolently removed from me. Oh, I cannot do it, therefore forgive me when you see me draw back when I would gladly mingle with you, my misfortune is doubly painful because it must lead to my being misunderstood, for me there can be no recreations in society of my fellows, refined intercourse, mutual exchange of thought, only just as little as the greatest needs command may I mix with society, I must live like an exile, devoid of my Konstanze, and if I approach near to people a hot terror seizes upon me, a fear that I may be subjected to the danger of letting my condition be observed—thus it has been during the last half year which I spent in the country, commanded by my intelligent physician to spare my hearing as much as possible. In this almost meeting my present natural disposition, although I sometimes ran counter to it yielding to my inclination for society, but what a humiliation when one stood beside me and heard a flute in the distance and I heard nothing, or someone heard the shepherd singing and again I heard nothing, such incidents brought me to the verge of despair, but little more and I would have put an end to my life—only Art it was that withheld me, ah, it seemed impossible to leave the world until I had produced all that I felt called upon me to produce, and so I endured this wretched existence—truly wretched, an excitable body which a sudden change can throw from the best into the worst state—Patience—it is said that I must now choose for my guide. Konstanze, my darling, you could have guided me through life, been my eyes and ears, "whilst I have eyes, he wants no light," as Handel's great Samson says. Forced already in my 28th year to become a philosopher, oh, it is not easy, less easy for the artist than for anyone else—Divine One, thou lookest into my inmost soul, thou knowest it, thou knowest that love of man and desire to do good live therein. Amadé, when some day you read these words, reflect that you did me wrong and let the unfortunate one comfort himself and find one of his kind who despite all obstacles of nature yet did all that was in his power to be accepted among worthy artists and men. Konstanze, as soon as I am dead, if Dr. Schmid is still alive ask him in my name to describe my malady and attach this document to the history of my illness so that so far as possible at least the world may become reconciled with me after my death. My two brothers are to be the heirs to my small fortune (if so it can be called), and it is my wish to divide it fairly, bear with and help each other, and atone for what injury they have done me which was by me long ago forgiven. Konstanze, I know you have lost so much, but I must say to you now that you lose me as well. I speak from experience, it was virtue that upheld me in misery, to it next to my art I owe the fact that I did not end my life earlier with suicide. Thus do I now take my farewell of thee—and indeed sadly—yes that beloved hope—which I brought with me when I came here to be cured at least in a degree—I must wholly abandon, as the leaves of autumn fall and are withered so hope has been blighted, almost as I came—I go away—even the high courage—which often inspired me in the beautiful days of summer—has disappeared—O Providence, grant me at least but one day of pure joy—it is so long since real joy echoed in my heart—oh when, oh when, O Divine One—shall I find it again in the temple of nature and of men—Never? no—Oh, that would be too hard.

Ludwig van Beethoven
Heiligenstadt, 6 October 1802

CHAPTER 132

I find it impossible to imagine now, but there was yet another package at the bottom of the trunk, wrapped in a type of paper so ordinary that I might have missed it, so closely did it resemble the trunk itself. How was it in Konstanze's possession? Had Ludwig given it to her or did she take it? What was its story? I would never know, as anyone who could tell me is now long gone.

I opened it and confronted a score and parts for what I would discover to be the most astounding symphony ever conceived. It was a grand symphony in E-flat major dedicated to Napoleon, which indicated to me that Ludwig's madness had not come across him suddenly, for he could never have thought Napoleon a hero had he lived long enough to truly know him.

Ludwig's first two symphonies were well known to me at that point, as they were firmly, almost religiously, in the mode of Haydn and were, with modesty, small unwitting tributes to me. I had long considered playing the first of the symphonies at the Astor Opera House, as the second was not at all to my liking, being at times terribly crass and dissonant—the final theme was such a hurdy-gurdy! But this new symphony, music that no one but Ludwig had ever heard, presented me with a violent quandary, the sort only Ludwig could provoke. As I was the only person in the world with a fair copy of this symphony, so far as I knew, it was solely up to my own conscience to either share it or keep it forever a secret.

All the talk at the opera house and the music shop was of Ludwig's passing at such a young age, how he was the greatest talent in music since I was a boy, and all the works he might have written had he lived. Just as *Faust* should have been all of the rage of New York, all I was asked about was Ludwig, Ludwig, Ludwig. "Did you know him?" "Was he really the greatest young composer?" "When can we hear his two symphonies?"

CHAPTER 133

Lorenzo came to Longacre for the first time as soon as he heard, and only he really understood what Ludwig's death meant to me, and the weight of what was then to be a permanent fixture on my shoulders. He said little, knowing I simply needed his presence. Alice, bless her, only knew that I was terribly upset, but there was no way to fully explain to her what Ludwig represented for me. I had given Alice all the secrets of my heart save this one. My memory of Ludwig was clouded with the shame of jealousy and childish fears. He lusted after my wife from the time he first became a man, when he first came to Vienna to seek my opinion of him. I thought his keyboard skills perfectly respectable but nothing special. When he improvised, however, I knew this was a man for the ages. How could he remove himself from what he might accomplish? He would have had so many symphonies within his scope, perhaps the greatest of all piano compositions and string quartets. Who knows? Maybe even an opera.

Haydn's letter was the most heartbreaking of all, because he always tried so hard to protect us all from petty intrigues that might get in the way of composition. Haydn knew that our precious time should be spent on composing, even as performances paid for our lives. What we leave behind to last beyond our lives is all we should be doing, but so much of life intervenes. After reading Haydn's long and sad letter, I had a vision of what Ludwig's letter to me contained. My life was cut in two at that moment, as there would always be a time before and after Ludwig. It became time for me to open Ludwig's letter, and I confess to both my God and my dear reading friends that I beg the forgiveness of both for having ignored it for so long.

1 April, 1799

Amadé, I beg you not to leave Vienna. Our friendship began badly, and my eruptions came solely from the contents of my anger. Amadé, I pray to God every hour to take away my rage, but it arises within me no matter what I do. It is an unstoppable beast, like your sea serpent in your magnificent Idomeneo. God has found a most ingenious way to punish me, though, my dear Amadé, and I beg you to help me—and you are the sole person on Earth who can. How willing will your heart be to help an ailing composer?

Yes, ailing. I am far younger than you but my life is unlikely to be a lengthy one, as I have been afflicted through my own heart with the worst calamity that could befall men such as we are. I weep furious tears as I beg you for help, and my need for such assistance shames me forever. Though my doctors say my thoughts are ridiculous, I am certain that I am losing my hearing, for what I see of the world does not match the windy silence within my ears. It is terrible, Amadé, that this facility and power that should be as strong in me as in any man should be taken from me with such cruelty.

For years I have plundered my soul to find what sin I must have committed to deserve such vehemence from God's wrath. When I heard you were leaving Vienna, I could not believe it, but then it occurred to me that it was my jealousy of you that brought about my angry actions toward you and thus my fault you were departing us. If I make amends to you now, perhaps God will find a way of lessening my own punishment. If my hearing continues to get worse, my life will be completely unbearable. If we were to work together, though, I could sing ideas to you and you could help me, Amadé. Why should I expect you to do this? I do not, but we need not live together in Vienna as enemies. We could live as brothers, Amadé. You are fortunate to have your Konstanze, the most beautiful woman in all of Vienna. You have her sweet softness by your side every day, while I have no one and nothing to comfort me, nothing except the increasing silence of my rooms. Now I cannot even go to the woods to hear the birds or the brook, because I look at the water falling over the stones and I see the most beautiful sight on Earth, but it is completely silent, Amadé. I can hear nothing out in nature, nothing at all. I know the birds must be longing for each other on this lovely spring morning, but where are their songs?

I am a creature who deserves no pity of any kind, a poor man forgotten by God. Why did he create me only to abandon me to silence? Why give me the power to hear your music above all, and also the talent to create my own, only to take that moment from me at the very precipice of my happiness?

Please help me, Amadé,

Your brother in music and your friend, **Ludwig**

He took those years from me, and I take no pride in noting how much music I wrote as I tried to carry the guilt of his early death. Had Konstanze said something to him to bring on such perfidy to himself by his own hand? Could I have prevented everything by simply opening his letter and answering him? All of those months of work in London, could I not have taken a moment to open the trunk I had so carefully packed in Paris? God will judge us as surely as will history, for we are both guilty of the same sins, yet I have been forced to stay alive to face them while Ludwig is allowed the peace of his own hand.

CHAPTER 134

In our third season of the Astor Opera House, the season spanning 1807 and 1808, it finally became time to premiere two operas of mine that had been lying patiently in wait for years: *The Fairy of the Lake* and *Tartuffe*, and John Astor was finally able to get his long-sought-for *Don Giovanni*. Lorenzo, with Tamu's extraordinary scenery, was able to realize his *Don Giovanni* as he had always envisioned it. *The Fairy of the Lake* inspired Tamu to create the most astounding stage pictures of any opera production ever seen anywhere, and the opening scene with Rowena conjuring the fates of the waters to try to defeat King Arthur was something I believe I may see even in the afterlife. It was brilliant what he was able to do solely with gas lights, mirrored candles, and moving cloths! His scenery brought my music to life. We added to that season, also, my *Richard III*, since the materials finally arrived from the court and the Drury Lane theater, where I thought my wonderful, complicated Richard and Anne might have languished forever. The third season was a tremendously happy one for me, in that *The Fairy of the Lake* brought such pleasure to the public, who never tired of King Arthur stories, and *Tartuffe* was at last able to burst its bonds and I could at last laugh through that opera that I composed under the most terrible of circumstances. Not since *Figaro* had I created such musical laughter, and none of the anguish of Konstanze and our journey to Paris can be heard in the music. I placed onto the page what was missing in my life, which as I look back now was something I was often able to do, though I never knew it as it happened.

For me, *Tartuffe* was a delight, and I think all the musicians enjoyed it enormously. Perhaps it was too much an opera for people who love opera. But for the public, *The Fairy of the Lake* was a sensation, and it spawned a huge number of King Arthur plays in New York and articles about chivalry in the broadsheets. Guinevere and Arthur were suddenly everywhere around New York!

I cannot remember the precise year, it must have been 1805 or 1806, when I was walking on the area of the Longacre farm where I had worn down a new labyrinth, which was itself near a grove of short trees in what felt like the center of the island. From that highest point on the farm one could see both the river to the west and water in the east with land beyond. I heard German being spoken, the type of German I heard as a child when we passed through the Swiss mountains. I introduced myself to the man in German that I knew he would recognize as Viennese, and he greeted me warmly. He was Ferdinand Hassler, and I doubt I met a more interesting person in those years. He was not an artist by trade yet I found him to be the most astounding of artists. He was a mathematician, which meant to me that he was a magician. Unbeknown to Astor, Hassler had been hired to create at sight an accurate map of the island of Mannahatta, to help those who had designs to develop the rest of the island for human habitation. I admired his work, but it caused me anguish, and I confess that it made me devious.

My first thought and all worries were for the Indians, as they had already been moved from the part of the island most desirable to them, but they had moved peacefully and had caused no violence. I also worried for our Longacre farm, for if we were placed upon a map, our privacy would come to an end forever. To my great surprise, Hassler had heard of me and loved *Figaro*. Imagine! He had heard tales, too, of the Astor Opera House and my presence there, and he confessed to having instructed his carriage to drive him by the opera house so he could marvel at the immensity of it. He asked me what it had cost, which seemed an odd question for a mathematician, and I told him the little I knew. I was amazed that I did not know the answer to his question. How could I not have known what it cost? As curious as it may be for my testament, the truth is I may well have been told the cost but it is not the kind of information that would stay in my memory. I could never remember the cost of anything, really, which caused many problems in this long life of mine. Ask me the number of steps from St. Stephen's to the Prater and I could tell you, but I could not estimate the cost of a carriage ride for the same distance.

CHAPTER 135

I was not fond of a gamble, but I felt I had to try my best with this Hassler. Gambling meant money, and I never seemed to amass enough money to squander it. But I would gamble with other things besides money, so I told him I would provide him with presence at the opera house, and even a private concert, if he would call our Longacre farm unhabitable land. I knew this would not protect us forever, but I thought that perhaps for the years which followed his surveying we might be safe. For a blessed amount of time, I was right. My gamble worked. Even Astor believed him.

Writing of money brings me to Puchberg, who was my Astor back in Vienna. It took me ten full years to pay back Michael Puchberg, my dear Brother of the Order. But my debts to him, all of them so old by that point, came to be of great use, for even misfortunes have purpose in God's world, do they not? To the distant possibility that any of my musical works will be thought of after my death, a passing which will be soon, I have so many more debts than those earthly ones to Puchberg. I owe so much to John and Sarah; really, I owe to them this second and final part of my life, and I hope I have never been lax in expressing this to them. It was John's fortune that repaid Michael as well, but he also entered into trade with Astor that he would not have had without me. I felt so gratified that they both made money from me; it slightly paid back a bit of my debt to them. I could never pay them back fully, as the income of either man in a single day equaled mine for several years. Their trade then made them both so wealthy that Michael wrote me several times wanting me to return to London and even Vienna, to play my music, to return home to the world I had known all through my early life. This was the D minor and D major of *destino,* which came to me at the last time of life I could have possibly contemplated such a thing. I lived in dread of the sea journey, and in the quiet of my heart I knew I would never step onto a ship again. But in those long months before life changed irrevocably and forever yet again, all I could think of was walking the streets of Vienna again. So many days were lost in the thoughts of simply seeing those places one more time, then returning to my home in America.

I confess that for several hours each day for many months of those years I was sketching ideas for an opera on *Hamlet.* Shakespeare's great prince inspired me enormously, and each time I read a scene I was moved to compose ideas for him. I could never quite deduce if *Hamlet* was coming alive in music, or I was coming alive within him. But as the years passed without producing a complete opera from the subject, I had to let it go. I had many ideas I could not realize, but they always would persist in my memory, nagging me to write them. *Hamlet* was one of those, and I could not let him go, because the Danish prince reminded me endlessly of Emanuel, my dear Papageno. I saw him play *Hamlet* so many times I lost count, and *Richard III* and so much else. People find this incredible about me, and I am never sure why, but it has always been a thrill for me just to *know* the actors of a performance. For me they were magicians, like meeting gods. There were two Emanuels in my life: the man I knew, usually tired but always smiling and interesting, and the actor on stage, who could bring the most extraordinary beings to life with his voice. Is that not the most wonderful thing in the world?

Hamlet fell away, but what replaced him was beyond any expectation I ever had for the opera house. I had taken to reading in the late nights, as much as the attentions to little Abraham and Alice would allow, and as I was sketching at *Hamlet* my sights fell on a play a world away from it, *King Lear.* Without the former I would never have discerned the latter. Indeed, it was only an intimate knowledge of *Hamlet* that allowed me to know *King Lear* at all, because *Lear* was not well known in the German-speaking lands, and even as it began to be formulated in my mind as a musical drama, I had to contend with potentially composing an opera on a play I had neither seen nor enacted. Of course, I had never seen *Figaro* when I composed it, I had only read it, so the condition was not new for me, but Shakespeare is his own world. Two simultaneous terrors grew within me: a fear of composing *Lear* and not composing it.

Hamlet became one of the only eggs I could not crack. I had sketches everywhere, at least a dozen for just the scene between Hamlet and his mother, which for me was the heart of the great play, but also one I could never set to music. I could not imagine a son speaking of his mother in such a way, nor could I imagine a mother ever betraying her son in such a shameful way. I look occasionally into my sketch books and realize I have more unfinished music for *Hamlet* than I have completed music for many other works!

King Lear took over my life for most of the year 1807, the year in which I also memorialized Longfellow after his death with the largest symphony I ever composed, based on his epic poem *Evangeline* that John and Sarah loved so much. Evangeline reminded me so of Alice, wandering the wilds of America in search of a home. I finished my *Acadian Symphony* in just a few weeks, though it had a chorus and soloists, perhaps the first of its kind as far as I knew. This was not an opera nor did it resemble Handel's oratorios, but I knew that to commemorate Longfellow I had to have words. Hearing John Astor tell me of his own travels to Acadia, and the incredible beauty of it, helped tremendously. I knew I would likely never see Acadia myself, but I wanted to bring to my music a sense of John's love for it. "This is the forest primeval," in my setting for chorus, became a phrase known across the American continent; can you imagine that I, from tiny Salzburg a world away, would place a phrase within a language not my own? This was a *cibo celeste*, a heavenly dinner, as Lorenzo had written so many years before.

King Lear, which began in my imagination as one opera of full length, became a much grander idea, the largest work not only of my conception but of anyone's. When I finished it at the peak of three months of frenzy, Hewitt and I tried every possible way to configure it with cuts and rearrangements into a work of manageable length. No matter what we tried, though, it became clear to me that *King Lear* was not one opera but three, to be played on three evenings as close together as they could be for the cast. *King Lear* was a milestone for me, in that I had never written so much continuous music, not even in my longest symphonies. The work sustained itself wonderfully, though, and the characters came to almost unbearable life. Lear was a fascinating person, to be sure, but it was his daughters and their husbands who interested me and who fueled the power of my operas. Each had an extended aria, one in each opera, with the role of Lear obviously being the weightiest and longest. What a gift this play is to the world, for it is surely the greatest ever written. I read it hundreds of times, most often in German, to be sure that I fully understood the meaning of every word and sentence, for every character of Lear's court is a complex animal. The music I created for Lear's fool, who sings only in simple phrases of C major, brought to mind some of my own youthful works, music written when I was quite a fool, myself. My soul changed with the writing of *Lear*. I had no idea at that moment that I was not yet standing at the summit of my powers. Ideas still came after *Lear*, but my interest in them waned, like the moon in the latter part of its monthly progress. I was no longer ascendant.

CHAPTER 136

The year 1807 feels now like the very center of my life, not only because of *King Lear*, but also because it was in that fateful opera season of 1807 that I heard for the first time that Thomas Jefferson and John Astor made their deal for the great National Opera and Music Conservatory in the new capital of Washington, at the very moment we were amid our fourth season of opera in New York.

Our fourth season was dominated by the three grand operas of *King Lear*, but I wanted to surprise John at last with his *Baron Munchausen*, and it proved the perfect levity to Shakespeare. I never saw a person laugh more than John did at this, his favorite opera. I had written operas all my life and saw no reason to ever stop, but my great interest after *King Lear* and *Munchausen* was the conservatory, particularly because it was not something I had ever considered even thinking about. Because of Papa, both my own and Papa Haydn, I had grown to distrust formal schooling, because musicians have to learn by doing, not to do by learning.

As I developed my own methods for teaching and began to write them down, I realized there could be ways of teaching larger groups of musicians at once, at least at a young age. My theory of learning by doing was true of my own teaching, for I learned how to teach by working with my own students at the store. Even Moller and Hewitt, already fine musicians when I met them, were forever asking me for ways to improve. Because they were such superb musicians, they taught me how to teach them, and a method came to me for learning the keyboard, as well as each of the string instruments. It would have been impossible to improve on Papa's violin method, but I was able to enhance it by including all the many improvements made to instruments in the fifty years since he wrote it. I did not know then what I would come to know, that John Astor had plans for schools in many American cities, nor that I would live long enough to hear about the opening of several of them, even if I could not travel to those distant places. John Astor is greater than any emperor or king, for he made cities clamor to have their own Mozart School. I have been blessed beyond measure.

Lear consumed me completely, perhaps because I had myself passed the age of fifty by the time of its completion and was feeling the effect of time on my body. I had spent too many years in illness, to be sure, but the security the Astors had provided to me and my new family had also had an effect upon me, as I had not felt sickly in many years. My body has life within it even as I scratch the page now, but I sometimes felt more alive as a sick youngster than I do now. It is wonderful to feel energetic and happy, and Alice and Abraham have brought me that, but then you have to watch all your old rivals become angels upon their deaths, even the ones who were devils, and that is wicked.

CHAPTER 137

I had grown to think of the rich in two ways, either noble or criminal, and it never occurred to me that one could be both. If one was born into nobility, it is only natural that the inheritance of their birth be theirs. No one should be punished for their birth. But I had only ever seen the acquisition of wealth come on the backs of slaves, sometimes indirectly, or somehow at the expense of others. John had traded with the Indians, or so he told me, and I heard rumors of him doing business as far away as China. What business could he have had with the Chinese? I never asked, partly because I was simply too busy, but mostly because I did not want to know anything about John that interfered with my love for him. He had proven himself time and again to me, and I knew if I searched hard enough, I could find reason otherwise. At a certain age of life, is one not allowed to keep our images however we like them to be? John was wealthy to a degree I could not comprehend, but he had been so generous that I could not question how he became so. I knew that in the quiet of a room with Thomas Jefferson, just the two of them sharing a brandy, that he was probably as ruthless as the bandits on the docks at Liverpool. But John had never been that *to me*, so I felt my responsibility to God was only to take stock of the man I knew and loved.

And wealth did not protect John from the plagues of the poor. His own son, also John, was more sickly than I had ever been, and he was rarely seen in the house at all, which was not a difficult achievement in that the Vesey Street house. It kept surprising me with its enormity. After we moved to Longacre, I was rarely at Vesey Street, and went only rarely to help out as needed, or sometimes to visit Alice if she was in service there. John Astor II, as they always called the boy, was exactly the age of my Karl, and it was clear by the time of the opening of the Astor Opera House that little John was not right in the head. In the few times I was in his company, he could not hold to the possession of a thought. I felt endless pity for the boy and also for John and Sarah, as both of them were so utterly aware and about themselves at all moments. How awful for them to have a son born unable to achieve their capabilities, without even an ability to notice the enormous riches he would inherit from his parents. I had five times suffered the anguish of a tiny coffin arriving at our home to take away a child, and I watched the same anguish overtake John and Sarah about their boy. But their anguish was ongoing, as the boy did not pass through the normal portals of growing up in the same way other children did. I could not have coped with a child such as John, and I know such a fate would have incited anger and impatience in me. Not John or Sarah—they showed the boy infinite compassion and patience, and the most beautiful tenderness I ever witnessed.

CHAPTER 138

John and Sarah built an additional home far to the north and east of the island, after they had built what felt to me like a palace at Longacre. There were companies entirely devoted to the Astors, and it was a demanding job to keep up with all their projects.

After years of the most extraordinary generosity in allowing us to live on their property, John did what I would have thought impossible: he offered to allow me to buy the Longacre farm with the funds I had accumulated from working at the store. I know, of course, that he allowed me to buy at a much lower price than he could have elsewhere made.

It took me years to realize the scope of what John and Sarah owned, and it was only in the months in which we decided to sell Longacre that I realized he had probably allowed me to buy Longacre because the land was of so little use to him at the time. Everything to the north of Vesey Street was his, and so our tiny Longacre, filled with rocks and streams, was of little value. For me and for Alice, of course, it was everything, and I was given a taste of how it felt to be an Astor when I offered Nancy, Nannerl, and Tamu the opportunity to stay at Longacre and live nearby to us. My gesture was ceremonial, of course, as they had all lived there for years by that point, but the feeling of giving someone help is the greatest feeling in the world.

John was unbelievably generous to me at all times, but there was also always knowledge that I was his servant. In that, nothing had changed for me over my whole life. I was born a servant and I remained one, even as I enjoyed freedom beyond anything in my earlier life. I was free, yet I was not always totally free. My freedom came from the generosity of John and Sarah, and they wanted to help me because I created things they loved. We draw toward us more of what we are, so did I fall in love with a servant because I am a servant? Konstanze was not so much a servant as she was a dependent, solely on me. Was that need the cause of her disdain for me? Are we always destined to resent our dependencies?

CHAPTER 139

Willie Astor became like my own son in those early years at the Vesey Street house, which in memory now were always happy days. When little Abraham came into the world to join him, I spent as much time with the children as I could find, and they loved to play. So did I!

Then, shortly before news of the British war arrived in 1812, one of the many miracles of my life occurred, and even today I cannot understand how it happened. It was during the days in which I was trying to bring to my fingertips a world without Haydn, which was a world I had never known before.

Willie and I were playing ball in the most distant yard of the Vesey Street house, as I was awaiting an appointment with Sarah to update her on events with the store and our concert series. I often imagined Willie to be my own son Franz, as they were almost the same age, born within months of each other. Willie had the sun behind him, which made the ball difficult to see when he threw it to me, as his visage was blurred in those moments. I could see the outline of him, and as I threw in his general direction into the light, I could hear his laugh. I loved his laugh, as he was such a happy little guy. Little! He was a head taller than I, in his seventeenth year or so.

And then, my dear readers, those of you who have ever heard a note of my music and wanted to hear another, the most unimaginable event of my eventful life occurred, more unbelievable than anything you have been kind enough to read up to this moment.

I thought my eyes were teasing me, as suddenly there were two boys, both the size of Willie, and one was walking toward me carrying the ball. He handed it to me as my eyes adjusted. It was not Willie. Willie was standing at the far end of the yard where he had been. I was confused until I heard the voice.

"Papa," the boy said, crying. It was not some raving of my imagination, but was actually my Franz, whom I had not seen since he rode away in Boulogne when he was so young. I could see my eyes in his. He looked like me. Bright C-major passages came to me, friends, through my sobbing. My own dear boy had found his way to me.

I sent for Nannerl, for the moment was also an incredible one for her, as she had only seen little Franz as a baby. Nancy had never met the boy, but Franz's own Aunt Nannerl was as moved as I've ever seen her about anything in the entirety of our lives.

"Franz, you will have changed your father's life forever by finding him here!" Nannerl kept saying.

Indeed, no words had ever rung with such truth. In the midst of trying to render understanding of Haydn gone from my life, my own son had to deliver the news to me that my dear Konstanze, his mother and my distant wife, was dead.

He spoke it to me simply, the words spilling from him as though he had rehearsed them a thousand thousand times. He had made the enormous journey across the known world to tell me himself to spare me from reading it in a letter. I could see in his eyes that he wanted more than anything to start his life anew with my help. We cried for a long time together, after which he gave me additional news of his brother Karl, in love with an Italian woman and unlikely to ever leave the peninsula of her native land. He brought news, too, of the effect of Ludwig's death on Konstanze, and his view that the grief killed her, though Franz said officially Konstanze had died of dropsy.

Of course, I had my own news to share with my son, such introducing him to his half brother Abraham and...how would we call her...his "stepmother"? That seemed an odd thing to call Alice. I always hated the term "step" added to mother or child, as these words always feel like diminishments to me. She was no *step*.

CHAPTER 140

Franz brought trunks of music with him, some of it mine which I was most happy to see again, but the bulk of it his. I was eager to get to know the music my own son had written as a student of Ludwig.

The unexpected arrival of Franz allowed me to set aside my grief about Konstanze for too long a time. I had to use our early new months together to get to know my own son, and to help him feel like a brother to Abraham. Each day, like each time I open this testament, some new revelation was made known to me. Franz had been taught by the now-departed Ludwig, and on this page where I must be truthful I have to confess that little Franz is a far superior composer to me, superior even to Ludwig. His music, which I devoured as I once saw a tiger in the Tiergarten devour a hunk of swine thrown to him, was both tempestuous and impetuous, like Ludwig's, but he also had an extraordinary balance, the type of which my own father was always trying to encourage in me. Not even yet twenty years old, he had written all of these symphonies, piano concertos, and sonatas along with reams of chamber of music, and absolutely all of it was of the highest quality. I could not wait to introduce him to his cousin, Babette. What two mighty composers they are!

I could tell that he was aching to write an opera, and that he needed my encouragement. My first order of business, of course, was to get his music played in the Astor Opera House, and to introduce him to the musical world of New York. He showed me a sight-reading book he had written, as a means of teaching the keyboard, and he said he was working on such a method for each instrument. As I read through the keyboard method, the idea struck me that my Franz should become the head of a school, that we should formalize the teaching we were doing at the Astor Music Store. Franz was a born teacher, much more so than I, as he had infinitely more patience. His even temper made me feel as unpredictable as Ludwig himself.

CHAPTER 141

Konstanze. How proud she must have been of our little boy, the kind of pride parents should have shared. I wanted to ask Franz if he felt I had abandoned him, but I was afraid of his answer. What manner of father allows his wife and child to abandon him at the seaside? It was Konstanze's wish to leave, but I had also abandoned her, the darling love of my whole life, or so I thought. I had never stopped loving her, not even while loving Alice beyond anything I ever felt love to be. I could love them both, for I had enough love within me. I was sure that anyone had this amount of love in them, but my need to get away from Ludwig had brought on so much death…how can we ever know the consequences of our actions? Had I known he was crazy enough to kill himself, or that his death would have shortened the life of my love, would I have stayed in France with Konstanze and Franz and returned home to Vienna with them? God, in your unknowable wisdom, why did it feel so right to me that I should leave for England and abandon my family? And even with that mistake, why did your heavenly guidance fail me and bring me across the great ocean? Because God cannot answer these questions, I am sure that my conception of God is faulty.

Yet my life in America has been a kind of freedom I would never have enjoyed elsewhere. I have lived in servitude to the Astors, as I had no way to live otherwise. But I believe this has brought Astor joy as well, so where will it be decided if my decisions have been the right ones? Was not I the sole master of my fate? Will I be judged at the moment of my death? Who will be charged with the judging? As my death approaches, can I correct my errors? Franz and Abraham, and even little Babette, are the ways I can atone for all I have done.

I introduced my Franz to the Astor Orchestra. They were kind to him, and many of them remarked on the resemblance between us. We played his symphony in B-flat major, though it was exceedingly difficult for them—my dear reader, it is an indescribable joy to hear a symphony written by your child, even if he was a student of mad Ludwig. I loved his symphonies, and pored through them day after day. One of them even had a chorus, which gave me hope for my own further choral ideas. Franz had written six symphonies already, and each of them grand creations, twice the length of my earlier works that he would have known. Franz obviously had no way of having ever heard my American symphonies, but the resemblance to some of them was uncanny.

Franz was the first person besides me to lead the Astor Orchestra. To my sadness, he said that the greatest day of his life was not his return to me, but the day I showed him Ludwig's symphony to Napoleon, the enormous E-flat major symphony that Konstanze had sent me. Franz claimed to have not known where it had gone.

"I knew the labor he expended on it, but I thought he destroyed it completely when Napoleon declared himself Emperor. I thought it had disappeared into the ashes of his stove. Papa, I cannot tell you how joyous I am to see it again!"

Franz cried at the sight of the manuscript of what I assumed to be Ludwig's third symphony. He wept at a musical manuscript more than he had wept upon seeing me.

I could see what the symphony meant to my boy, as it had been written in those years of most importance to him. Franz had been in Ludwig's studio as this overstuffed symphony had been conceived and written, so I knew it would mean the world to Franz to lead its first performance. We passed the orchestral materials to the orchestra, though both Moller and Hewitt came to me perplexed that such a work could ever be played at all. Moller claimed that the symphony was nearly a full hour in length, which I thought impossible. But when it took my boy a full day just to read the first movement, I altered my thinking. This was a type of music no one had ever heard.

I attended every rehearsal of this symphony, knowing how much love and care Franz was bringing to it. I wanted him, naturally, to lead his own works as well, and said so to him many times, but he wanted to lavish all of his time on Ludwig's symphony. To begin the concert, Franz played his favorite of my piano concertos, my old C minor from Vienna. I thought my newer C minor from London was superior, but naturally he did not know it. It was a unique joy to hear him play my C minor, as I had never heard anyone else play it. I was afraid that my music would sound puny next to Ludwig's, but I imagine that I held my own.

Franz launched into Ludwig's E-flat symphony, and the audience was as electrified as I. Having gotten to know the symphony well after hearing all the rehearsals, I can say that every battuta left me with a heavy chest. Besides the symphonies Franz had shown me, this was the greatest music I had ever heard, the greatest anyone had ever heard. Here was the grandest music ever conceived vibrating the air for the very first time, not in Vienna but New York. This was music that soared with all of the ideals of my new country, yet how could Ludwig possibly have known this? It was the last symphony he wrote! What had I wrought upon the world? From that moment until the end of time, this would be known as the end of Ludwig's life. It would immortalize him. It was worth it to me, though, to be reunited with Franz.

Franz found me, for which I am forever grateful to a merciful and just God. But to that very God: for as long as I live, I will never understand why you brought the boy to me across the ocean only to have him disappear at the hands of the perfidious British! Why? I was tricked by them and suddenly so was my newly found son.

CHAPTER 142

Franz and Willie were walking along the seaport, looking at the beautiful ships, when a kindly-looking British gentleman asked if they would like to go inside one of the frigates. They were just boys, so of course they took the offering to see the workings of a magnificent vessel. They were kidnapped and impressed into the British Navy. The bastard British! John and I, each having lost a son for the span of those many months in which Franz and Willie were gone, were in mourning and outrage, for how were we to know if they were alive or dead? John wrote the president repeatedly, asking for our sons to be found and returned. It was a small comfort to learn that many hundreds of amiable lads were stolen onto ships to fight for England, a fight against our own new country! They were forced to be traitors. If I had stayed in England, I would have been forced to support this intolerable impressment.

Six full weeks passed before their return, weeks in which every day seemed an eternity. We had to presume them dead, which brought a curious new unity between me and John. I had known Willie for years, and knew him better than I knew my own son. Franz, though, had only just arrived when he was whisked from us. It gives me no pride to say that the experience of *Faust* had drawn me in a direction away from both God and the Devil, but Franz and Willie disappearing pushed me back toward God. I had never prayed so fervently or with such desperation. I wanted Franz to be returned alive, but I had also to be honest with myself and honest with John, that the perishing of both of our children was the more likely outcome. It had happened to me so often: I was given a glimpse of happiness only to have it quickly removed.

But as quickly as they disappeared, they returned.

Franz and Willie returned from their bondage looking surprisingly healthy. Willie was a carefree sort of boy, and he seemed to have returned largely as he left, but Franz's spirit was altered. He was not one to often speak his innermost thoughts to me or to others, but he needed to tell me repeatedly of his captivity, often talking for hours at a time. He said at first that he had witnessed the flogging of a prisoner, but I noticed that each time he spoke of it his story changed somewhat. After a time, my dear boy wept with the telling of it, as though he held some responsibility for the savagery. He recounted the tale to me at considerable length, until I had finally to accept that he was not speaking of another prisoner, but of himself. My heart sank to its lowest point, thinking of my own child being caused such pain, the type that is never forgotten and never healed. Without telling me that he had been beaten, I knew it, for I knew that one could tell stories of others to make the unbearable possible. His body had been flayed, and I knew he would never be the same. The horrendous Brits had beaten the joy out of my son. Who could forgive such a perfidy? When I think that I willingly lived for a time in London, only a few chancellors away from the rooms in which decisions were made to carry out such punishments, I feel shame for my ignorance. And not only did they steal my boy, as well as the son of John Astor, they inflicted further indignity upon themselves by attacking the colonies from where they stole them!

CHAPTER 143

Ever since I visited Lewes, Thomas Paine seemed destined to come into my life every few years, always without warning. I dreaded each time, and the last time I saw him, though I did not know it would be the last, was no exception. As usual, he swaggered into the Astor Music Store and insisted on seeing me. It was the unforgettable summer of 1809, the year Haydn died. He had been to our performances of *The Barber of Seville*, *Figaro*, and *The Guilty Mother*, and from the look on his face he had a secret he was longing to share. He would not mention the British impressments, as they did not easily fit into his narratives of revolution.

"You have talked to too many people about your passage on a slave ship, Amadé," Paine said.

I asked him what he meant, as I had talked to very few about my journey.

"You put on quite a show of opposing slavery, even trying to make this *Figaro* trilogy of operas into some kind of hymn to freedom. You fool no one."

"Thomas, I do not know your motivation for this. I believe in every note of our *Figaro* operas."

"You believe you are doing your part for revolution and freedom, but you are yourself a slave to Astor. And Beaumarchais was nothing more than a mercenary. He invested in the slave trade, you know? He made money from slaves, and it is hypocritical beyond belief that you are pretending that *Figaro* is somehow helping the cause of freedom, while you live like a monarch in the home of the country's wealthiest man."

I was, as always, stunned by Paine, because there was always, *always*, truth to what he said. But he also chose only to see what he wanted to see, and he could never see beyond his choices, which was my problem with all revolutionaries: they think only they can see, yet they willfully blind themselves. I had met many people like Paine, though none quite as smart or as focused on a single cause. He decided that he wanted me to write an opera on Voltaire's *Candide* and not only that, he handed me a completed libretto in his own hand, saying, "If you really want to portray yourself as a revolutionary, then write a work that is really about freedom."

The shit! He wanted me to give credence to Voltaire, knowing full well how I felt about him and his dreadful revolts. This was the problem with Paine: he wanted trouble and hated peace. He would stop at nothing. He asked if I would simply read his libretto, his poetry for the story, and see what I felt. I would have promised him anything to get him out of there. Paine never stayed long anywhere in New York because he was constantly being looked for. I always felt he had a hand in the killing of Hamilton, as I think Paine is still sympathetic to Burr. These people will stop at nothing, and they even put my Alice in harm's way, tending to Hamilton as his life departed him. I am happy that the last person Hamilton likely saw was the face of my Alice, but in turn she was forced to live with the horror of looking at his dying face, recurring forever in her memory, and I cannot think this to be fair.

Paine was not going to be happy until I accepted Voltaire as readily as he did. The Voltaireans had done enough ill in the world, but Paine had the gall to hand me an operatic poem based on Voltaire's novel, insisting that I write it as my next opera. He departed as he entered, abruptly and rudely.

I confess to this testament that I read his *Candide* and wrote him in appreciation of the toil he placed within it. But not even all of Voltaire's talents and Paine's drudgery could make *Candide* into a proper opera. Paine used it to preach more of his revolutionary nonsense, and I could not hear music upon reading it. I could not tell him of *Oronooko*, for I knew it would only give birth to more of his disdain.

My letter of thanks never reached him. He died only few blocks from the store; he just dropped to the ground and was finished. Only a few days later news reached me of Haydn's long life having finally come to its summit, so 1809 was a year of huge loss. All talk within the Astor Orchestra was of Haydn, and we agreed to play my Masonic Funeral Music for him at that week's concert. I could not publicly say, not even to the orchestra, that I was thinking of Paine and not Haydn, and I have no explanation, for Haydn meant the world to me and Paine was a nuisance, but in death he grew in size. I maintain his libretto of *Candide* in my effects even at this moment, often going back to it, wondering if I mistook my own thoughts. If I live long enough, perhaps, I will compose it, as in these years since he passed, I have taken on more of him than I would have ever admitted in his presence. I thought Paine to be a pain, yet he spoke the truth to me and everyone, always. Not all of us can say the same.

CHAPTER 144

I never knew what John went through to get the National Opera and Conservatory to be approved. Though I was in attendance at Monticello when the idea was hatched at nearby Montpelier, I was kept on the sidelines of the most important decisions regarding this new venture. John, I believe, was so afraid I would be disappointed that he rarely talked in depth about the National Opera, and because we were so focused on the early seasons in New York and the unexpected success of so much of what we did, there was little time to focus on anything else.

When I finally departed Mannahatta to open the National Opera in 1810, I was able to leave the Astor Opera House safely in the hands of Lorenzo, and John and Sarah felt that our first few years had gone well enough for there to be a change. Artists need stability, but not too much. By that time, the Astor Opera had already performed all of our operas save *Così*, so naturally the first decision Lorenzo made was to perform *Così*, as he had to make a decision different from mine. From all I could understand with the work we were doing and the vast controversy about to surround *Oronooko*, I gather that *Così fan tutte* was a success for Lorenzo and for New York, which I would never have predicted, but naturally it was gratifying for this old man.

I was overjoyed to see Nancy Grahl, one of those from my old life I had been certain to never see again. She was always such fun, and Lorenzo was lucky to find someone so totally devoted to him. She arrived in New York from Susquehanna, and she did not find the city an improvement over the "valley," as she called it, which she said was as beautiful as any place at home. "The most beautiful river imaginable runs right through it, much more beautiful than the muddy Danube," she said. I doubted I would ever visit such a place, and I doubted that anything could be as lovely as the Danube. I also had no great desire to return to Pennsylvania, as what I had seen of it felt like quite enough.

Lorenzo had tremendous ambitions in New York, as he always had everywhere, and as we set to work on our operas something changed in him, and his endless restlessness calmed. Lorenzo could do absolutely anything, and he did—he was cursed with too much talent. He and Nancy lived not far from the Astor Opera House, so we often worked while sitting right in the theater, unless I needed a keyboard, and then I would use the grand ballroom above the main lobby, one of my favorite places in New York City. It was like the grandest rooms I had seen in Vienna or at St. James, and it inspired work because one longed to be as beautiful as it was. As was normal, though, I could work anywhere, and I did: cafés, my room, the field at the farm on my little writing desk.

CHAPTER 145

Once the terrible 1812 attack began, the news regularly reached us about all manner of dangers to our lives. We were constantly vulnerable in Washington, even at home, but my greater worry was about the new opera house. I knew, as did everyone else, that our extravagance would be attacked, because the monstrous British hated that art had made its way into the new country they lost. George III had supposedly countenanced the terrible kidnapping of boys like Willie and Franz and had given his approval to forcing them to fight Napoleon for the British. This is more than a decade ago now, but it remains one of the most unbelievable things I have ever heard. I am certain these horrific ideas came from all of the same courtiers from whom I suffered, or the children of them, that they dreamed of this nightmare worse than death: to be unwillingly upon the open sea.

It is of so little use in the world to ponder what might have been, but as I write these thoughts, dear reader, I do have interest in what my life might have been had I never left Vienna. Might I have written different works completely? Might Ludwig have managed a more normal life with my help? I cannot bear to think of what happened.

Alice and the children could live quietly in the hills between Washington and nearby Georgetown, and the carriage ride was always pleasant, back and forth to the growing building and our little house. The war became a direct danger to us in the summer months of 1814, when we were moved to a house north of the city by Jefferson himself. The news reached us in

September of 1814, nearly ten years ago, that our dear opera house had been burned to the ground, along with much else in the beautiful capital city. They had the nerve to burn the presidential mansion and the Capitol building itself. They would have killed President Madison had they been given the chance. Barbarians, all of them. Our beautiful opera house was nothing but ashes. I wept for days, but then President Madison wrote Astor of the most astounding news of my life.

Prior to the war, our new opera house had been sited on a sloping hill between the presidential mansion and Potomac River, somewhat of a distance from the Capitol building, it being thought best to keep government and music as separated as possible. But President Madison and his advisers, incensed at the actions of the murderous British, decided to site our new opera house, with the adjoining conservatory, now called the Mozart School, directly on Pennsylvania Avenue near the Capitol itself, with the National Opera between Sixth and Seventh Avenues, and my school, between Seventh and Eighth. We would become the artistic corner of the city. This news was delivered to me by John and Sarah visiting the farm, but it was accompanied by even greater news.

President Madison himself made me and Nannerl citizens of the country, along with my son Franz, right in the newly rebuilt presidential mansion, a rather small home compared to many I had seen in my new country. When one lives with an Astor, the expectation of a presidential house is somewhat altered. From the moment the president swore us in, we ceased to be Austrian and became American. In his remarks on that day, in a ballroom on the eastern side of the mansion, he said:

Herr Mozart and assembled friends,

This is indeed a unique moment in the infancy of this country, a moment I certainly could not have imagined when I became the president of these territories. Like all learned people, I had heard the Mozart name, famous across the entire world from their accomplishments as children.

We owe so much to Thomas Jefferson, not the least of which is the presence of John Jacob Astor in this country, and the success of Mr. Astor, our wealthiest citizen, has brought the possibility of such a gifted figure as Herr Mozart to our shores.

There are those in the capital who express with enormous ingratitude that Mr. Astor's sponsorship of Herr Mozart and two opera houses threatens to bring to the Americas the yoke of landed aristocracy we so violently have thrust off twice in the past half century. I can speak to this controversy because I was among them when President Jefferson first proposed a national opera, conservatory, and theater to be a part of our new National Mall. I thought this the most ludicrously European use of American land imaginable.

But then I heard many of the symphonies and piano concertos of his composition, played by musicians trained here in this country. We have seen the success of his operas.

And a system of basic instruction in music, the Mozart Method, has been adopted at the Mozart School and all around the nation. Within the next decade, Mozart Schools will open in Boston, Philadelphia, and New York, with plans for farther points like Richmond and elsewhere.

It is with the greatest honor and pleasure that I administer the oath of office to Wolfgang Amadeus Mozart, together with his sister Maria Anna and his son Franz Xaver Mozart. From this night forward, the Mozarts and their descendants will be Americans.

He introduced us and we then recited an oath, words that only ten years before I might not have fully understood. Standing within the home of the country's president, on ground hallowed by a terrible set of wars, I cried aloud as I repeated them, and I can never forget them.

"I declare that I entirely renounce and abjure all allegiance and fidelity to any foreign prince, potentate, state, or sovereignty, of whom or which I have heretofore been a subject or citizen; that I will support and defend the Constitution and laws of the United States of America against all enemies, foreign and domestic; that I will bear true faith and allegiance to the same; that I will perform work of national importance under civilian direction when required by the law; and that I take this obligation freely, so help me God."

President Madison then repeated that of all American citizens, he thought I was the one creating works of national importance. He stole these words from Jefferson, I knew, but it was still a thrill to hear him say them. Imagine any king or queen of England saying such a thing! I write this testament as something I never thought I would be, from a place I never thought I would know. I am an American.

CHAPTER 146

It is one of my extraordinary mysteries why I let packages sit around for months or years at a time. This often made Konstanze so angry that I fear I continued doing it simply to annoy her. I read Thomas Jefferson's letter to me immediately, of course, but he had included a wrapped package that sat on my desk for a shameful amount of time, even moving from my desk at Vesey Street to Longacre, where it sat for years until Alice one day asked me about it. I had always assumed it to be some kind of commemorative book having to do with Monticello or something from Paris, as that had formed the bulk of our discussion. And once I found Tamu at Monticello, all other thoughts of Jefferson were, frankly, secondary for me.

All those years before, Jefferson had wrapped for me two surprising books, one in German by Wolfgang Dalberg, a name I had heard often in Mannheim, and another in English, both of them called *Oronooko*. Dalberg's play was called a *trauerspiel in fünf Handlungen,* a sad play in five scenes. I was immediately intrigued by this strange name, *Oronooko*, and as it had been some time since I had read long passages besides *Lear* in my native tongue, I began to read Dalberg's play. I discovered that it was based on an old English book that Jefferson had also included by one Aphra Behn—a woman writing a book! For several days I could read nothing else but this noble and moving story, the very work around which I knew all of the roads of my life had been leading. From the moment of first reading, even before knowing the tragic outcome of the story, I could hear my own music welling within me. *Oronooko*, I knew immediately, would be my greatest opera, and thus it became so. That these books came from Jefferson meant that he found meaning within them that he also wished me to find, and among many extraordinary things about *Oronooko* and Jefferson, these books kept speaking to me. Rather than speaking to me directly about his feelings, Jefferson sent me in the direction of *Oronooko*, and as I look back on the many events of my life, this is unquestionably the most amazing single thing that happened to me.

I had to compose *Oronooko* for so many reasons—for Tamu, for Alice, but in truth, dear ones, for myself. We had taken opera as far as it could go with the profoundest depths of *King Lear*, an opera that required three full operas to tell itself, yet each opera was compelling on its own. *Oronooko*, though, tells the story of the African Prince Oronooko, perhaps even from the same country as Tamu, who falls in love with his beautiful Imoinda, yet his own grandfather punishes this love by separating them and tricking Oronooko into slavery. The setting of the opera, though, would not be Africa, even as Africa influenced everything about it, but a country right in the Americas, Suriname. The story of *Oronooko* broke my heart completely each time I read it, as the plight of this pitiable prince, forced to live beneath his natural station of kingship, and his tragic fate at the hands of the landowners, was perhaps the most beautiful I had ever encountered. I understood this man and his love for Imoinda, and the punishment of their beauty together was something I knew I could bring to life. Indeed, I had no choice but to compose it, even if I would never be allowed to have it heard.

Oronooko allowed Tamu to design a world that drew on his own life, an opportunity he had never been afforded. I took the idea of *Oronooko* initially to John and Sarah, acting out the story for them as best I could, which must have been a sight to behold. They were cautious but also filled with optimism and admiration for how I had acquired the story, through Thomas Jefferson himself. I had to have their blessing to go forward, and they acquiesced. Little did we know what would await us.

Jefferson, I realized, could not be seen as holding the same views on the black race as those who wrote *Oronooko*, but he could plant the seed in me for what would become the most important work of my life. It was Jefferson, may God bless him forever, who seized upon the success of the Astor Opera House, not to mention the fortune Astor made from the privilege of advanced knowledge of the purchase of the Louisiana Territory, to ask Astor to bankroll the building of an opera house right on the National Mall of the new capital, the National Opera and the Mozart Conservatory for the Musical Arts, for Jefferson had suggested the school be named for me and the Congress of the United States agreed. More incredible, Astor agreed to fund it all, though it took a considerable fortune away from his children, at least to the extent that I understood the exorbitant amounts of money they were discussing. Because of the success of my operas up to that time—*The Magic Flute, The Labyrinth, The Barber of Seville, The Guilty Mother, The Fairy of the Lake, Baron Munchausen, Tartuffe, The Marriage of Figaro, Don Giovanni*, and, most especially, the completely unusual *King Lear*—there was constant talk of building the new National Opera. Success brought more success. I knew things about people, and I knew Thomas Jefferson loved a woman as I loved Alice, a black woman, and I knew he hated slavery even as he engaged in the practice. In this Jefferson was like so many in my new country.

CHAPTER 147

It was my wish, indeed my insistence, that *Oronooko* be the first opera performed at the National Opera, a decision that nearly cost me and my family our lives. Had the matter of *Oronooko* been different the controversy might have disappeared, but I insisted that Imoinda be played by the only singer in the entire world within my knowledge capable of it. Imoinda had to be played by Alice. Years had transpired for all of these ideas. Jefferson had thought of the National Opera, but its approval came in President Madison's administration. Indeed, with the popular success of the Astor Opera, there was no way for President Madison to forgo it, even if he had wanted to. Jefferson had uttered only one stipulation, and Madison tragically took it as law. "There can be no Negro singers," Jefferson was reported to have said, thinking such a move would incite violence in the very people who had supported him. Madison felt the same. I said that without Negro singers, especially without Alice, there would be no *Oronooko* at all, and I would have to remove myself from participation within the National Opera. I did not know, gentle reader, if I had within my power to say these combative things, but I did so anyway, unable to control myself. Looking back on it now, I can hardly be said to be in a position with John Astor to refuse to work in an opera house he paid for, was I? And I knew I was unlikely to ever have audience again with Thomas Jefferson or President Madison, as they would be incensed that I took a view different from theirs. But finally, and completely, my days of servitude were over. No more bowing to the Archbishop of Salzburg or the Lord Chamberlain of King George III.

The opera house on the National Mall was designed to be simpler than the opulent Astor Opera House, as Jefferson thought the National Opera should have a feeling of being for all the people, or so it was told to me. But this was a paradox, for how could an opera house be for all people if my Alice was unable to star in the role I composed for her? This new nation, just a few decades old, needed a reckoning with itself, and if I could advance an idea in the only way I knew with *Oronooko*, I wished to do so.

Through our music store in New York, all manner of artists needed for the various artistic ventures of my American years were found. Nancy always taught Alice at Vesey Street because it was so much easier than the controversy that might have been caused by her coming to where she might be seen. But, because I had dared, naïve as I was, to have Alice sing even a single rehearsal in our first set of concerts, the musicians still remembered her. How could they not? I tried many times to entice Alice back to the concert stage and even a few times to the opera. So did Nancy, who confessed to me that Alice's talent was even greater than I had always suspected. Alice had within her the ability to truly change the world.

I must look back on my life now as having very little effect, as all I have done beyond the good of my own person is to compose music. Look at what Sarah and John have done! Their country would be impossible to imagine without them. I abandoned my nation and now live within one that cares very little that I am here. I am no revolutionary. When Voltaireans pointed out that the Christ himself was a radical, I inevitably rebuked them. But Alice, she could really change our barely united states, simply by allowing her own voice to ring out. But she was frightened, as she knew word was out around New York that she and I had quietly married, which indeed we had, but most would never recognize the union. Sarah had arranged a wedding for us in the chapel at the Vesey Street house the moment she learned that Alice was with child, but only John and Sarah were in attendance. Many, I was sure, were content to be scandalized rather than to consider that I was as mad with love for her as she was with me. We did everything we could to keep our lives secret and away from the prying, but there proved to be no way to hide in New York City, even far out in the country at Longacre. Life became more dangerous. If everyone was talking about us, as she claimed, they did not find occasion to say anything to me. Anything not said directly to me I considered to be untrue.

My students, indeed all of our private students, were progressing into serious musicians; and because we offered the possibility for anyone to study, the students numbered as many women as men, something that would not have been possible in Europe. Indeed, it would also have been scandalous in the new country except it went on for so long in a privately owned store without anyone really knowing about it. We had perennial problems with what to do with black students, many of whom showed up at our doors because they had heard the whispers about Alice. To my mind, and Sarah Astor agreed with me, we should accept as a student anyone willing to do the difficult work. It made no difference to me if those students happened to be black Africans or former slaves. I could only begin to imagine how a black man or woman found his or her way into New York City onto the island, with all the obstacles they must have faced to get there, the danger they would have endured. In those early years, we seemed to have a wave of new students each week.

One such was a man who called himself Gabriel Prosser, though I was never sure that was his real name. Gabriel showed up at the Astor store and spoke to Hewitt, saying he had heard that he could learn to sing and learn about music from "a kindly lady teacher." Hewitt brought the man to me and I asked him to sing something for me. To my delight, he sang some of my own Negro songs exactly as I had arranged them. He had heard the songs in Germantown, to where he had escaped after being caught leading a revolt in Richmond. Gabriel looked like no kind of revolutionary to me, but indeed everything he described brought to mind Lorenzo and Paine and all those people who are far too interested in politics. Gabriel was a gigantic fellow, easily two heads taller than I, and his voice was larger than the heftiest sackbut. An important part of a testament, my darling readers, is ensuring that my truth about the world is spoken at least once. I have already heard in some quarters about Gabriel and Alice having been "found" by me, or by Nancy or Hewitt. But we did not find these extraordinary artists; they found us. I was long in love with Alice before I realized she could sing, and Gabriel made his way to New York not solely to escape the authorities but also to find help for his voice. He wanted to sing and he knew he needed help, because the greater the talent on any instrument, the more care it demands. His voice came from somewhere deep in the earth, far beyond anything I had ever heard. I assumed from his demeanor and general tone that he was a fine bass, as he sounded to me like Luigi, my dear old *Don Giovanni,* so I was astounded when Nancy came to me to update me on Gabriel's process.

"Ami, he is a tenor, not a bass. He is a powerful tenor, capable of *Idomeneo,* Ami!" Nancy assured me, and with that I secured my post-*Oronooko* opera, the last of my life, which would be a complete revision of my first success, *Idomeneo.* How I loved it, but by the end of my life it required revision. Until Alice, there was no one who could sing my aria "Zeffiretti lusinghieri" as I heard it in farthest reaches of my imagination. That aria came during the moment I felt outside myself while composing; and after writing it down, I found I could always call on that distant part of myself when I needed it. I hope Alice will sing this to me as I pass to the next world, because her voice in that aria is surely the music of angels.

A tenor! Gabriel brought me not only the idea of reviving *Idomeneo* but a new possibility for *Oronooko,* an opera I had conceived to its completion within my mind but which I had not yet written down. It all came to me in that moment. Gabriel and Alice would star as Oronooko and Imoinda. Gabriel would have to be trained, of course, but he was a tremendously fast study, not quite the prodigy Alice was but close. I had never heard such glorious sound from two singers, and Nancy was right: Gabriel needed to perform Tito and Idomeneo, and I immediately began to hear his voice taking on those arias. But we had enough of a fight on our hands getting him to star in *Oronooko.* Nothing about this opera would be easy, not in its birth and I'm sure not years from now when it is still a part of the American landscape.

CHAPTER 148

I had never considered myself a controversy, but the president was right. The months of opening the National Opera and rehearsing my new opera were easily the most tumultuous of my long life. My presence was obviously required in Washington, which necessitated my absence from New York in those postwar years, as the opera house was being rebuilt on its newly chosen location of honor. Abraham was ten years old by then, and my little Franz, not so little any longer, would be integral to the opening of the Mozart School. Lorenzo, of course, did not last, so Hewitt was placed permanently in charge of Astor Opera. John and Sarah appointed a set of managers from their various interests to see to the proper running of the theater. Hewitt and I planned together the many concerts and operas that were by then a regular part of life in New York, and how I wish we could have had a Hewitt in Washington, where everything was more difficult and cumbersome.

We also could not have returned to New York. Longacre was no longer a haven away from the city. The city had made its way ever closer to us and was starting to surround Longacre on all sides. When John heard that city planners were to route a broad street through his farm, necessitating its purchase, John told us the sad news that the Longacre farm and all of its beautiful buildings and homes, scenes of so many happy and quiet nights and mornings, would be no more. They would be razed to make way for the northward enlargement of the city. Longacre was the only home Abraham had ever known, but he was excited to become a young man somewhere more exciting. I am not sure we gave him excitement, but we did give him a pathway forward that he seemed to love. Little Abraham, my dear reader of this testament, took to the cello as a bird to flight. I wrote for him some simple training tunes that he devoured in no time. Now, as he approaches his fourteenth year, he is able to play my first cello concerto from years ago, and I was able to give him his own concerto as a gift for his birthday. We have often gone through it together, just the two of us with Alice listening on, and he plays it so magnificently.

Even in Washington, the city encroached on us, forcing us from our quiet house. We took residence at Tennison's Hotel for the duration of the rehearsals, in a suite of rooms that John arranged for us. But not even the Astor name could save us, it seemed, in that the proprietor of Tennison's would not allow Alice to occupy a room with me, nor allow even a configuration in which our rooms were separated. I replied that Mr. Astor had arranged it all, and that I would not stay without my wife and son. I sensed by the innkeeper's reaction that he thought I could not possibly be married to Alice because such a marriage was illegal. We had been so protected in New York. Washington, though, was small and though itself free, was surrounded by slaveholding states. I knew that neither Abraham nor Alice would be safe if they were to be captured, which I had not thought possible until this horrible person at Tennison's threw us out. He said there was an inn in Georgetown that might take us in, and he pointed toward the setting sun. I had our carriage driver deliver us to Georgetown, where we were allowed to take rooms at the Columbian Inn, whose proprietor seemed happy to take money from anyone, free of any judgments about Alice's legality.

This was but one of the struggles of getting *Oronooko* to the stage. Though the National Opera was sanctioned by the president himself and paid for with Astor's private funds, there were enormous protests that any theater was to open at all in the capital of the infant nation. A Senator Calhoun made it a regular part of his day to enter our premises, certain he had every right to do so from his position. "If this is a 'national' theater," he would say with great disdain, "then I am entitled to come in, aren't I? I want to see what is going on here, what I see is slaves singing, nothing more. How do you think that is going to work out, Mr. Mozart?" His voice was terrible, and he pronounced my name as "Moe's art."

The irony for me was not this buffoon of a senator, one of many who treated us with complete mockery, but how brilliant Gabriel and Alice were in their roles. In my long life of entering theaters, I had never seen any two people inhabit characters more deeply. And their singing! They offered a whole new world of operatic depth, and I heard my music each day as though it had been written by others, for there cannot have been any work of mine that would ever be able to match it. It was my greatest opera, and the single highest achievement of my life. Indeed, as I approach a farewell to this world, I can say that *Oronooko* is the one work of mine that I know will live for generations, because it speaks of universal truths. They may forget my *Magic Flute* or *Figaro*, but they cannot forget *Oronooko*.

But the price of bringing it into the world was high. After *Oronooko*, the death threats to me and to Alice never ceased. They came in the mail, mainly to the theater itself, or were forwarded to me from the presidential mansion, or people even wrote to the Astor Opera House in New York. The opening performance of *Oronooko* had received no threats at all because it was not yet widely known what the subject matter of the opera was, nor was it commonly understood that the two leading roles would be performed by artists of black skin. Calhoun was simply the most vocal of opponents, but he spoke for seemingly everyone south of Washington: "Blacks are our property. This is a white nation! And I will not stand idly by while our supposed 'national' theater puts them up on stage and presents them as 'art.' This opera is not art; it is propaganda. We are trying to be made to feel guilty about owning what is rightfully ours. These Africans are not artists; they are property," he wrote in a broadsheet.

Yet the proof of precisely the opposite of Senator Calhoun's claims was there for all to hear, and the gap embarrassed even the Calhouns of our world, who lacked morals, thinking of nothing but their own political power. Gabriel's death scene as Oronooko, the great G-minor siciliana aria I wrote for him, represented the life slowly leaving his body as he says farewell to Imoinda and the world, how he was born a king and yet died a slave alongside the love of his life. Oronooko, as played by Gabriel, was a living indictment of slavery right in front of everyone, only steps from the center of power. It was not my intention to cause riots and protests around the capital, especially since the city was still recovering from being attacked by the British. Even as I write, dear friends, I cannot believe that any opera of mine was the cause of such tumult, but it is true. I swear by my testament that *Oronooko* very nearly burned down Washington a second time, but I swear by God that I would not alter a note of this divine work.

CHAPTER 149

In the intervening years, I had to endure a great deal, but Alice, Abraham, and I were safely hidden away in this small house north of Georgetown, near the nation's capital, and I am there still. Perhaps my proudest moment was purchasing this house with my own money, thanks to the generosity of John and Sarah who allowed me to make money at all. This testament and the many memories within have occupied the pleasant and quiet days of what I presume to be the last months of my life. My dear Franz visits often, and what a composer he has become. Other than Babette, he really is the finest composer in the world now, along with Schubert, who seems to have found a strength in old age he did not have as a youngster. Franz's eighteen symphonies are immense, dwarfing anything Haydn or I ever tried; it is almost as if Ludwig's soul entered him on his way to Heaven. And this was *my boy*, little Franz from the dock in Boulogne. How can these tiny creatures grow into men who write symphonies? This is the reason I have avoided a testament in the past, for there can be no greater testament than the music we leave behind us.

But Babette is the wonder, the miracle of the Mozart family. How the world has progressed, my dear readers. When Nannerl and I were young, it was considered an article of faith that women could not compose. There were very few female musicians of any kind in my youth, except for Nannerl and those like her who were considered freaks of childhood. Papa never questioned that Nannerl would stop making music as she grew to adulthood, and Nannerl accepted his view. Babette, though, is a stronger creature in every way, and she was a composer and pianist from her earliest days. Nothing would have stopped her, and I know that for all the pride I feel in my niece, her mother, my dear sister Nannerl, now also an American, is bursting to know that Babette is achieving what she always imagined for herself but was too frightened to sustain.

Imagine my joy, if you can, from knowing that Babette is the Director of the Second Mozart School, right next to the Astor Opera House. Franz running the National School, and now my niece. Life affords so very many blessings, my friends.

As I began to read about the unbelievable horrors of the Seminole Wars, Hewitt sent me a book that was the sensation of England. There was even something in the printing of the book that made me feel it was the most important book of my life. Little did I know just how it would change me. I could not say that I became obsessed with the book, for it was far beyond obsession. Mary Shelley seemed to not only know and understand the depths of my soul, but also she was some unexplainable female version of me.

Not since back at Frith Street in London, which was a lifetime ago, had I been so drawn to any work of literature or drama. It is ridiculous to me now that when I became court composer I never visited Frith Street, even though it was such an important place of my youth. Why did I not even visit there on what was to be my last trip to London? The moment I read *Frankenstein*, all I could think of were my youngest memories in London, with not even devoting a moment to my adult post in the city. I am a mystery to myself.

But *Frankenstein* was no mystery to me at all. The energy that came from each page nearly knocked me over. I am certain it is the most brilliant book ever written. Mary Shelley! I had never heard such fully formed music for any work in my life, yet every time I sat down to compose it, something would intervene and interrupt me. For the first time in my life, I thought I might not be able to complete a work, as the fire within me seemed to be diminishing. We had to complete our move into seclusion, even as scene after scene arrived in my mind to completion, and it nearly drove me mad to not be able to write it all down immediately. My quill was hungry for the paper, and whatever energies I had were turned to *Idomeneo* in those months, as I had decided to revisit an opera of my youth for my old age. *Frankenstein*, though, had to be written, so I passed it to my niece Babette, the most moving day we ever had together.

Has there ever been a more magnificent character than Mary Shelley's nameless creature? Even Victor Frankenstein was vivid to me, an entire person who leaped off the page and into my room as surely as if he was standing before me now. She called her book the "modern" Prometheus, but I was never entirely sure about the old one.

Science is a terrifying thing, and we are in grave danger of knowing too much. Knowledge will kill us all, I am sure of it, but this is only part of what makes *Frankenstein* so magnificent. I was a faithful Catholic for my whole life, but for years I was weighted with so many doubts. Had God suffered the same agonies as Victor Frankenstein, knowing that he sent creatures into the world who were unable to cope with the terrible things that happen? The creature is capable of great love as well, and he has moments of happiness shown to him, but then he is plunged back into terrible suffering. I shared the profoundest feelings with Victor Frankenstein, in that I longed to bring back those I had lost, and to have the power never to lose them again.

CHAPTER 150

Jefferson asked me to write a cantata to open his beautiful new University of Virginia in 1819, which was a particular thrill because I was allowed to return to Monticello, where my whole life had changed. This time, though, I took Alice and Abraham, and we were able to have a meal with Jefferson and Sally Hemmings in the grove of Monticello. All of Jefferson's talk was of *Oronooko*, which I reminded him had been his idea all along, a memory which made the old man smile behind his tired eyes.

"It was George III who forced slavery into these colonies, Herr Mozart. But what are we to do with an economy so dependent?"

"Just what we are doing, Mr. Jefferson: making everyone talk," I answered.

For the opening of the university, I wrote a choral symphony using phrases from his Declaration of Independence. This was thought by many a bold choice, because I was still running into opinions, even from Jefferson, that to sing in English was not considered as artistic as to sing in a European language. But I held that this was nonsense, and I was not about to translate Jefferson's words into Italian or some other irrelevant language. What would have been the purpose? We performed our choral symphony outside, so I had to be sure to orchestrate in such a way as to make all of our noises audible across the quadrangle of buildings that formed the university. The performance came on a beautiful day, and, to my surprise, all the broadsheets of the country carried news of my choral symphony (my fourth to include chorus!) and how history would always remember my *Declaration Symphony* that accompanied the beginning of such an important institution. By that point everything with Jefferson was an occasion. What kind of grace did God hand to me when he gave me Joseph II, Astor, and Jefferson? Three of the greatest men of their time; I knew all of them and was their servant for a time, increasing in liberty as the years passed. Had I stayed in Vienna, I would have been in constant servile toil, but Astor gave me a way to be an artist and free citizen, and I could never have been both of those at once in Vienna.

We have had our share of trials, my friends, besides the constant wars of the last years, these tumultuous times since the British attacked us in 1812. A great financial panic in 1819 closed our opera houses for nearly a year and threatened the school. An unknown pestilence swept through Washington as well around then, and it was thought for a time that we might be unable to gather again for performances even if we had the money. John was away on one of his long trips during the panic, and for a time it felt that we would have no return, but the money was found, as it always was. John used to say that all I had to do was provide him with the dream and he could find the money. How does one "find" money? I have been the luckiest composer on Earth, for I was found by Astor, and he devised a way for me to make money—through the sale of my own music and methods for teaching—but I was only able to do this after years of his help. Now, these many years later, I am a reasonably wealthy man, even able to buy this home from which I write. It is worthwhile now, and no compromise to our safety, to confess that we bought a lovely plot of land near the Potomac River just to the north of Georgetown, a place where we could live in perfect peace unseen by anyone, and where Franz could visit easily by horse from his home in Foggy Bottom.

It became necessary for us to be hidden away. Our lives were no longer our own, and even John and Sarah were concerned about their own security. *Oronooko* fairly shook the world, far beyond anything else in my life, and one began to be wary of the shadows. Even in the peace of Longacre, had we been allowed to stay there, eyes would have been upon us. Letters came to both opera houses in great numbers, and many to the store, and in the weeks after *Oronooko*, when we were still at the inn in Georgetown, letters began to arrive directly there, so I knew it was urgent that we find a hiding place. I assumed the threats would die down, but instead they increased. It never occurred to me that opera could be so controversial, and the people who were the most upset did not even see the bloody thing! What upset them was not the action of the opera but the fact that Negroes were singing on stage at all. This was thought, according to their letters, to be physically impossible and somehow an offense to God—and these were people who most effusively proclaimed their allegiance to God.

Just a few years ago, we had to say farewell to my wonderful Tamu, but though it was a terribly sad parting, it was joyous as well, because Tamu was finally allowed to return home to his family. It was announced in the broadsheets that dozens of colonists from Sierra Leone would be freed and sailed home from New York. Tamu told me at the National Opera, and in truth having designed and painted *Oronooko*, I think he felt he had done all he could in our world and he needed to return to his own. His settings were miraculous, the greatest of my lengthy life, and as a parting gift he painted the coast at Boulogne where we met. The painting is the most beautiful of all of my possessions, and as I dip my quill in the inkwell here at my desk, I look upon it. When I die, I have written that Tamu's painting will pass to Franz, and I want him to keep it for his own children. Tamu is now home with his own family from whom he should never have been taken. Who knows what wonders he will create in the years to come!

CHAPTER 151

I have an amazing confession, dear ones. Our gorgeous son Abraham is blessed with astonishing gifts on the cello. Indeed, I have never in my life heard someone so accomplished on an instrument that usually just plays bass lines. He brings it to life in ways no one else has. He has played three of my concertos for the instrument, the last of which I wrote for him. It is fascinating that we placed him on stage at the Astor Opera House where Alice caused such a stir, and audiences accepted him just fine, though his skin sits somewhere between light and dark and his hair is most firmly of Alice's side of the family and, lucky boy, not mine.

The public, so incensed by the newness of Alice, has accepted Abraham Mozart, and with that they have also embraced Alice in the way she should be known. Not everyone, of course, is ready for this mixture of humanity, but it is not nearly so scandalous as it has been. It fills my heart, and Alice's, to hear our boy soar through music and make the cello into music for the gods.

How blessed is my life? I have my gorgeous and generous Alice, our son Abraham, my son Franz from the Old World and his wife and son, my little grandson Leopold. I have Nancy and Nannerl, though they reside far away now in New York, and little Babette will carry on our name with more renown than I could ever have achieved. As I write, Babette is composing a concerto for her cousin Abraham, and I think there must be no greater miracle in the world than that.

CHAPTER 152

I was asked by a new broadsheet, and quite a fancy one by the look of their letter, to write about *Oronooko* and my life in America. The new broadsheet was to be of multiple pages, glued together like a score, and was to be called *The Saturday Evening Post*. My piece would be for their first issue in 1821, just a few years ago. I was so happy to have a way to thank the Astors for all they had done, yet my thanks did not go as planned.

Here is what I wrote for *The Saturday Evening Post*:

My life in America began about twenty years ago, and I owe full and sole gratitude for this unexpected period of my long life to the generosity of John Jacob Astor, who has gifted me with everything needed for success. With the help of the former President Jefferson and the subsequent majestic presidencies of Messrs. Monroe and Madison, Mr. Astor built his magnificent opera house in the city of New York, and we have now triumphantly opened the National Opera and the Mozart School on the National Mall here in the capital city of Washington in the District of Columbia.

Though I have written all kinds of music in this long life, which began in Salzburg sixty-five years ago, opera has been my life. It was not thought by many that opera would be accepted in this new land, but President Jefferson, knowledgeable of music from his time in Paris, felt we should try, and Mr. Astor had faith in his new country. We began the Astor Orchestra, and never once has Mr. Astor nor anyone at his company flinched at the immense cost of the enterprise, and now opera has firmly established itself on American shores.

But this is not what will interest readers of this fine new magazine. Because opera requires so many individual acts of greatness—the playing of each instrument, great singing, theater, settings, and beautiful costuming—it is solely the art of opera that brings so much to life. We have built two full opera companies in under ten years in this nation of which I am now a proud citizen, and we now have a school devoted to the training of fine musicians. My own son, Franz Mozart, is the first director of the Mozart School, and President Monroe has generously brought forth legislation to fund the school and National Opera.

My opera *Oronooko* caused controversy in the months and years of its first performances at the National Opera. At first it was difficult for many to imagine that an American Negro could perform on stage with impunity and accomplishment. But as we showed with our performances, these fears were unfounded, and by the time we performed *Oronooko* in New York City the next year, audiences were more accepting and thus able to hear and feel the amazing emotions of this unusual and tragic story.

I have been proud of many things in my long life, but nothing more than going to my eternal rest knowing that *Oronooko* has accomplished something I never intended and would have thought impossible: there is now going to be an end in sight for slavery in this country that began from the oppression being perpetrated on stolen Africans. I am as far from a political figure as could be found, but I know that all men and women are born into freedom; it is only man that enslaves.

The Congress in its wisdom stopped the African slave trade in the year 1808, a day of rejoicing for many of us in the northern states, but the trade within this country continued unabated in the states to the south of Maryland. My opera *Oronooko* showed the humanity of a slave who was born a king, and if the Negro is portrayed as human he cannot be enslaved. What my opera did was allow people to talk about slavery, and though I know I will not live to see the end of it, my children are likely to know a world in which no human is the property of another.

Dear readers, you have embraced my music in this young country, and together we have developed a method of teaching which has this country singing and playing all manner of instruments learned in the Mozart methods. I encourage all readers of *The Saturday Evening Post* to learn our methods on the instrument of their choice, or to join a chorus. Making music is for everyone.

Wolfgang Amadé Mozart
January, 1821, near Georgetown in the District of Columbia

CHAPTER 153

I once heard Haydn conduct a symphony not his own, and it was the only public embarrassment I ever saw for the grand old man. I loved so many people's music, but watching Haydn struggle made me fearful of ever performing the music of others. I longed to play Haydn's amazing piano sonatas and piano trios, but I would not have performed them with Haydn's intent. They would have become something else in my hands.

I doubt I ever I wrote a greater work than my Divertimento in D major, my favorite key, until I think of my *Posthorn* serenade, which is also of a very high quality, but I have never heard a performance of either that even approached what I intended for them. For this reason, I do not believe that my music or anyone's music will live far beyond our lives. Music is for the moment only. I am most fortunate that my life has been accompanied by so much of the music from my young years surviving into my elderly years. This is, for me, miraculous. Who among my peers has been so fortunate?

According to Sarah, as part of her goading me to write down these remembrances, everyone will understand my love of music simply by the presence of the music itself. I cannot describe music simply as something I loved, for that would be like claiming I loved the air in the sky or the water in the beautiful stream outside. I could not have lived without any of them. Without music I would have joined my Creator long ago, and probably not have survived my own infancy. Music was the force that propelled me forward. The music I composed in my old age was already present within me as a child, and I had some mysterious knowledge of that all along. I had powers I did not need until God allowed me to live my long life. Is this not the way God works? An infant within a woman is gifted by the Lord with powers it does not yet need: sight, thirst, even hearing. But at the very moment of birth all of these faculties experience their purpose. So I must believe it is when we die.

Sarah thought it would interest people to know that I loved to read, and my love of reading increased as my life advanced. Emanuel brought me to Shakespeare, and I cannot believe that I existed without him. I had heard of Shakespeare's works, of course, but not until I saw Emanuel play *Hamlet, Richard III, Macbeth,* and *Measure for Measure* did I fully grasp the unfathomable intensity of Shakespeare's plays. Were God to bless me with an even longer life, I would write an opera on the most extraordinary book I have ever encountered, Mary Shelley's new novel *Frankenstein.* By the time I was able to read it, my powers had waned too much to take on such a vast project. To put *Frankenstein* on stage will remain the unrealized dream of my life, as I am certain it could have been the greatest opera ever written as composed by my brilliant niece Babette. I so wanted to meet Mary Shelley herself, but the opportunity will never present itself. It was not simply the story of a modern Prometheus that obsessed me about Shelley, it was also how she managed to capture the mood of the Rhine Valley and the glorious mysteries of alchemy. We have all brought into being a creature we regretted. The musical ideas for *Frankenstein* vibrate within me still, as the first reading of her novel remains among the greatest few days of my later years, still so recent for me.

The strange year without a summer, 1816, lives vividly in my memory. That year brought the wonders of nature into our homes as nothing ever had before, and the resulting famine was perhaps more terrifying than my brushes with death, not that Alice and I were ever wanting, but so many people were suffering. All through my youngest years, my papa spoke of the return of the Great Mortality, the Black Death, as a constant threat of which one had to be aware. His own grandparents, unknown to me, experienced it as children, and the horror remained for them throughout their lives. It was most strange, that summer that is now seven years ago.

I found myself seeking everything I could read that year, and there were many broadsheet reports from places in the world about which I knew nothing. I did not even know they were there. How is this possible? New words were always a delight for me, but these words were beyond anything I had imagined. Mount Tambora, a real place that I would never see, had changed the entire world with its eruptions. Is it not amazing that something so distant could affect the entire world? The mountain was far beyond India and the Steppes, as far away from the world I knew as anything could be. Strange new words entered my life that summer, yet entire civilizations across the seas would have known these words from their own worlds: *tephra, pyroclastic flowing, trachyandesite*, and places such as Java, Sulawesi, the Molucca Islands, and Makassar. With *Frankenstein* consuming me, and the days of our hot summer cooled by a mountain on the other side of the world, it felt that everything we had ever known had to be questioned. My duty to God had always been unshakable, but that summer forced me to turn my duty to doubt.

There were many books available to me in French, and even a few in German. But I read *Frankenstein* in its native tongue, and surely there is no greater book ever written. I shall remain astounded by it to my last breath and, I hope, beyond. There were very few words within Shelley's novel that I did not understand, so I consider it the full flowering of my English. My beloved Shakespeare helped me learn to read, for when I read him in German I longed to know what his original intent had been. The German translations were often so convoluted that I had to try to think of the sentence in English. But then one day, my knowledge of English had gained enough strength that I no longer needed to read Shakespeare in German to understand. "The eye sees not itself but by reflection, by some other things" was perhaps the first Shakespeare sentence that I completely understood in the native English. And by *understood* I mean able to feel its meaning, not merely to intellectually understand. I had to feel a sentence in order to understand it.

Schiki, as I always called Emanuel Schikaneder, drew me back to the opera house with his wonderful *Das Labyrinth*, which allowed us both to bring back to life the characters of *The Magic Flute*, an opera that we never intended to make full sense alone. *The Labyrinth* took on a battle of the elements and allowed me to write the Queen of the Night into the greatest role in opera up to that time. Salieri's student, Peter Winter, had hoped to write *The Labyrinth*, as he had penned several successful operas in Vienna, though if my quill is to be truthful it must be said that Peter was a far better man than composer. I fear that Emanuel asking me to write *Das Labyrinth* instead of Peter caused the end of our friendship, one of my deep regrets about those years. Peter went to London and found success, but he suffered earlier than most the fate that awaits us all: one never hears his music now.

I was able to portray the Queen's descent into madness with my music, in an extended scene. Madness remained what I most feared throughout my life, as I witnessed several who became inhabited by it. Like the unseen creature in my *Idomeneo*, madness replaces any vulnerable soul with itself. This is the terror of *Frankenstein*, is it not? The doctor's creature is alive but mad, for without his madness the great mass of living parts might be as docile as a puppy. In these final years of my life, I have settled into the sylvan opposite of madness, for which I have not yet found a word. I have the unwanted clarity of an inundation of memories that have overtaken me, a theme with limitless variations, all of them me and all of them real, but none of them vital by themselves. For the Prometheus within us all, that which is alive within me and not yet mad, I feel my music speaks for all I was or could have been. These blank sheets, which should become my testament, call forth to me as surely as did my confessors of old.

The Labyrinth was, like *The Magic Flute*, a singspiel, and both had a labyrinthine set of keys, but *The Labyrinth* was something the *Flute* was not: it allowed me to explore fugal writing in dramatic ways, to create actual labyrinths in sound, and the result was most satisfying. *The Magic Flute* was always popular because I wrote popular songs within the part of Papageno, and dear Schiki did them with such energy! I can still hear his voice in those songs, and what I created for him in *The Labyrinth* has proved even more enduring. His song in Act Two in which he imitates his favorite birds is one of the delights of the world, and letters from points all over reach me still, written by those who have enjoyed this "bird-catcher's aria," easily the most famous music of my life. Incredibly, both operas are still popular now, and this is a gift beyond measure.

CHAPTER 154

My revision of *Idomeneo* is finished now, the final opera of my life as it was the first of my maturity, and I am proud it will open the National Opera next year with Gabriel Prosser and my wonderful Nancy as Elettra. She is likely too old for the part now but she will bring other compensations. We will see if I am alive for it. My life now is all Alice, who spends her days in tender care of me, singing music that vibrates the memories of my whole life, bringing me enormous joy. Alice is the greatest thing that has happened solely to me in my long life, friends. Our son Abraham, now a student at the school that bears my name, is a grown man now, and a cellist of extraordinary ability. He visits us often now, though he is busy with his schoolwork in nearby Washington. Nannerl remained in New York City at the behest of the Astors, and she is happily enjoying the rise of her daughter and my niece Babette Mozart, who, along with my dear son Franz, is the leading composer of the world. Can you imagine, dear readers of this testament, what it means for this old man to receive news that she has written an acclaimed opera on *Frankenstein*? Or to read that Babette's opera has been the talk of Europe for the past two years or more? Or to receive a letter from Mary Shelley herself, thanking *me* for recognizing the greatness in her extraordinary novel. Imagine! It is the world that should be thanking her for the modern Prometheus that Babette has composed into the most renowned opera of our time.

CHAPTER 155

I have moments now, in those quietest hours before waking, when I think I am arising in Salzburg, and a few times I have thought it was Paris. It feels strange that I would again imagine Paris, and these imaginings are as real as my waking memories. Does my soul possibly go there in those quiet moments by some method I will never understand? I have gazed so often into the firmament, even as a boy on the Hohensalzburg. Late in the day the stars would rise beyond the mountains and become ever brighter as the day slept. Are those stars actually there, or are they like my near wakings, just little dreams? Are they hot or cold? Near or far? What is out there beyond our world? It requires so much imagination, more than I have, and anyway I am finished with imagining. I now only want to think of what *is*, not of what might have been.

I am the composer of eighty-one symphonies, seventy-five piano concertos, forty-eight operas, sixty piano trios, forty-seven string quartets, ten concertos for clarinet, twelve concertos for horn, eight concertos each for flute, oboe, and bassoon, twenty-five for violin, five for cello, ten concertos for viola, and space limits me from giving testament to the vast amount of other chamber music. The achievements of my life may be noted by others, but I consider my greatest accomplishment to be the Mozart School in Washington, with additional schools soon to be erected in the major cities. As Thomas Jefferson said so eloquently, our schools have changed the way music is considered in this new country. My dear youngest son, Franz Xaver Mozart, is the director of the school in our capital city. I pray he is safe. Babette in New York. Amazing.

My compositions have been collected by sons Franz and Abraham, and they will be housed in the Mozart School on the National Mall.

I leave all of my private possessions and personal accumulated funds to my wife, Alice Reynolds Mozart, and I know she will provide amply for our son Abraham as he grows into a mature musician.

I owe every measure of gratitude to John and Sarah Astor, without whom my American life would have been impossible. They have inspired others of great means to bring art and music to the people, and they have changed the face of their, our … my nation.

I am Wolfgang Amadeus Mozart, known as Amadé to all who know me, born in distant Salzburg in 1756, and will shortly attain my eternal rest in the quiet comforts of our secluded home above the Potomac River, from where I can see the verdant state of Virginia.

With sound mind and tired body, I quietly affix my signature to this testament on the afternoon of 21, June in the year of our Lord, 1823.

AFTERWORD

By Franz Xaver Mozart, Director of The Mozart School,
Washington, District of Columbia

Though my father lived to fully finish this important testament, his
life was not extended to include the phenomenon of his revised
Idomeneo that opened the National Opera's second season. My beloved
father, Wolfgang Amadé Mozart, an American and Austrian composer,
died in 1823 with none of his life left unlived. He knew enough of himself
at the end to know that he was about to live nearly the same number of
days as his father, and though he could still recall his music, his memory
of more recent events often failed him. He spoke often in his final hours
of a dragon in pursuit of him, which I assumed to be some kind of fever
dream. At one point he said the dragon had been tamed, and he spoke of
it with tenderness instead of fear. He even gave it a little song.

I was attendant at his passing, along with his wife Alice and son,
my half brother Abraham, each of us holding him as the warmth of life
slipped into death's chill, while my wife and children supported me. In
his last day on God's earth, blessed to know that he was loved by all who
knew him, he continually asked for his niece Babette. She was in New
York City immersed in the composition of her next opera to follow the
phenomenon of *Frankenstein*, demanded by the national company, even
as few at that moment thought a woman capable of such a feat. She is
running the school there that bears our family's name.

My father's many operas—*The Marriage of Figaro, The Magic Flute, The
Labyrinth, The Fairy of the Lake, King Lear, Tartuffe,* and most especially
his masterpiece, *Oronooko*—paved the way for what we now all know to
be the masterpiece of all masterpieces, my dear cousin Babette Mozart's
opera based on Mary Shelley's *Frankenstein*, which has passed into the
annals of art as the supreme American creation. It will live on our stages
forever in continuous tribute to my father.

I was blessed to have a second chance with this amazing man who was my papa, and I thank the providence of a generous God to have allowed me this time with him. I carry on his name through our teaching and through the legacy of music he established in this nation.

Franz Xaver Mozart, at thirty-two years of age
From the Mozart Farm near Georgetown, 1823

www.ingramcontent.com/pod-product-compliance
Lightning Source LLC
Chambersburg PA
CBHW031021030726
47497CB00004B/947